Love's Christmas Hope

Eagle Harbor Book 5

Naomi Rawlings

This is a work of fiction. Names, characters, places, and incidents are either a product of the author's imagination or used fictitiously. Any resemblance to actual persons, living or dead, actual events, or actual locations is purely coincidental.

Love's Christmas Hope: © Naomi Mason 2017

Cover Design: © Clarissa Yeo 2016

Cover Photographs: Shutterstock.com

Editors: Melissa Jagears; Roseanna M. White

Formatting: Polgarus Studio

To Brian, whose kindness and love is a reflection of God's own heart. May you grow in grace and in knowledge of God. I'm grateful to call you my husband.

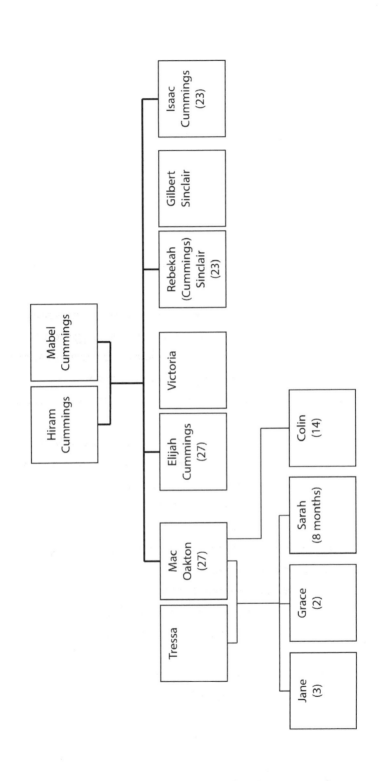

Chapter One

Eagle Harbor, Michigan; November 1883

"Look out!" Thomas Dowrick's shout echoed over the angry noise of the waves. He bent his head against the wind and staggered toward the gunwale, moving as quickly as he could over the water-slickened deck toward the young sailor caught against the railing.

"Help!" Young Ronnie clutched the railing half a ship length ahead.

Snow drove down from the heavens with the force of buckshot, stinging Thomas's face if he dared look up at the sky. And the frigid waters of Lake Superior sloshed across the deck, freezing the bottom of his trousers. He hurried past where the captain and sailors huddled by the gunwale, and toward the boy needing help.

One of the sailors looked up from securing a rope to the dinghy. "Do you need me to get Ronnie?"

"I can manage." Never mind that he was a miner by trade, not a sailor, and that it had been five years since he'd last been on a ship. The captain needed every spare hand to prepare the dinghy that would carry them away from the rocks that had wrecked their ketch.

The snow nearly blinded him as he approached the bow of the ship and Ronnie. "What's wrong?"

The brown-headed boy seemed far too young to have a job at all, let alone be a sailor. "I'm caught."

Indeed he was. The cabin boy was wedged between the gunwale and a crate that had broken lose from its chains when the ship hit the rocks.

"Let's see if we can move this." Thomas pulled at the wooden box trapping the boy, but pain ricocheted up his weak shoulder. The crate wasn't overly big, but whatever it held weighed a great deal.

"Watch out," Ronnie shouted. "There's another wave."

The warning came an instant too late. A vicious wave doused him from behind, splattering its icy spray against his back and causing the ship to sway. His foot slid out from beneath him, and the deck sloped so steeply he careened into the gunwale.

"Don't go overboard." Panic laced Ronnie's voice.

"Don't plan on it." Thomas clung to the top of the railing with both arms, his feet fighting for purchase against the slippery, slanting deck. Then he glanced down into the water below.

Mistake. Craggy gray rocks and white churning waves confronted him. He clung tighter to the railing, but the narrow strip of wood suddenly seemed too flimsy to hold a man his size.

Why hadn't he taken the train and rented a horse rather than boarding the mail ship this morning in Houghton? It might have meant an extra three days of traveling, but he would have at least been alive—even if his wife and daughters were still missing.

You can't let me die, God, not here, not now. I need to find them first, need to know they'll be safe without me.

"Can someone else help us?" Ronnie called to the sailors handling the dinghy.

"I'm all right. I just need to…" Thomas inched his foot all the way against the gunwale and put a bit of weight on it. Then he did the same with his second foot before standing and releasing the railing, never mind how he couldn't stop his jaw from chattering against the cold. "There. Now let's move this crate again. As soon as the weight shifts, you slide out from it, understand?"

The boy nodded, his face white.

"One, two, three." Thomas braced his feet against the gunwale and shoved. Pain shot up his arm like lightning. He gritted his teeth and put the full weight of his body into the crate. It moved about a half foot, just enough for Ronnie to scoot out from beneath the box.

A loud crack sounded above the roar of the storm—the unmistakable sound of splintering wood. Thomas clutched the railing and looked up. Were the waves breaking the ship apart already?

Shouts and curses from the group of sailors rang over the howling wind, then one of the sailors hastened toward them.

"The waves dashed the dinghy into the rocks." The sailor pointed to the frothing waves below. Sure enough, the bow of the little boat jutted up from a craggy rock, while splintered wood churned in the wild waves. "There's a lifesaving team at this port though. We'll just have to jump rather than take the dinghy to meet them."

A life-saving team? Thomas shivered against the cold wind quickly turning his damp clothes stiff with ice. "What in tarnation is that?"

"They've got a bigger boat, and they're coming to rescue us. See?" The sailor pointed toward the harbor.

Thomas blinked away a fleck of snow clinging to his lashes and turned to face the gray waves that were somewhat calmer inside the wide, shallow bay. Indeed, a boat headed in a straight line toward the ship, undeterred by the angry water that would keep any other boat off course.

"Let's go." The sailor motioned toward the opposite side of the deck. "They'll approach from the open lake."

"Can you walk?" Thomas clamped his hand on Ronnie's shoulder, half to get the boy's attention, and half to steady himself against the rocking ketch.

"I-I think so," the boy stammered. "My leg got stuck when the crate slid into it, but I don't think it's broke."

"I'll help you." The sailor swooped Ronnie up in his arms.

"I can help too." Another shiver swept through him, this one so fierce he reached for the railing. Curse his wet clothes. At this rate, he'd be lucky to make it across the deck without freezing solid.

The sailor frowned. "Save your landlubber legs for walking yourself across the deck."

Thomas took a step across the deck with the sailor, but the slope was so steep and the wood so slick he nearly slid back down to the gunwale.

"Come on." The sailor glanced over his shoulder. "We don't got all day. Least not if you want to be off this ship before it goes down."

"Coming." Thomas inched his way farther up the deck. White snow, gray sky, and violent, white-capped seas surrounded the boat. A little town sat shrouded in shadows across the harbor. It seemed so close, and yet so very far. Beside it, the Eagle Harbor lighthouse swathed a path of illumination across the storm, but the beam was weakened by the snow.

He reached the side of the ship and leaned over to glimpse a rowboat filled with people. It floated in a patch of water that wasn't churning as much as the rest of the lake. Something hit the deck beside him with a thud.

The sailor next to him picked it up and held out a ring that looked to be made of cork. "Put this on," he shouted over the storm. "It'll make you float."

"Don't you need it?"

The sailor shrugged, then pointed to one of the men that had just jumped into the water. Sure enough he was floating over the swelling waves, the cork ring keeping his shoulders and head above the water. "I'll find Johnson once I get in the water. We can share."

"What about Ronnie?"

The sailor who'd carried the cabin boy across the deck was already slipping another one of the cork rings over Ronnie's chest. "We'll share." The man looked at Ronnie. "You ready?"

The boy gave a nod, and the two of them tumbled over the side of the ketch together, leaving him completely alone on the wrecked ship. Thomas clutched the large ring and slipped it over his head, only to have it get stuck around his shoulders. He forced the ring down anyway, never mind how tightly it squeezed his chest.

A foaming wave slammed into the wood and rocks below, and he gripped the railing until his knuckles turned white. Give him a pickax, and he'd burrow into the dankest, darkest, narrowest tunnel and splinter rock until he found precious metals. But put him on the sea, and he was useless. He'd spent his childhood days in Cornwall hauling rocks out of mines, not fishing off the coast.

Ronnie and the sailor surfaced in the water and swam toward the small boat.

Maybe if he timed his jump to miss one of the large waves, he'd have a chance of reaching the rescue boat. He had to try jumping. Either that or give up all hope of finding his missing wife and daughters.

Just the thought of Jessalyn, of her long, blond hair and vibrant blue eyes and hopeful smile, caused guilt to rise in his chest, so thick and cloying it nearly choked him.

On the little vessel, a form stepped apart from the others huddled together. It almost looked like the man was preparing to…

"No!" Thomas shouted.

But the man jumped anyway, diving off the side of the boat and disappearing beneath the water. Was the swimmer coming to get him off the ship? He'd never forgive himself if the other man drowned.

Clutching the ring about him, Thomas balanced on the railing, drew in a breath of stinging, frigid air… and jumped.

Cold. The wind and snow up on the ship might have seemed cold, but it was nothing compared to the icy, watery fingers that worked beneath his woolen clothes until his breath nearly froze in his chest. Yet despite his weight and the sodden garments tugging him downward, the ring pulled him up to the surface.

The instant he broke through the waves, he sucked air into his starved lungs.

"There you are." A man bobbed in the water not five feet from him, then swam closer. "I lost sight of you when you jumped. You floating all right?" He tugged on the rope attached to Thomas's life ring.

"Fine." Or he was if he didn't think about how he couldn't feel any of his limbs. "You didn't need to come after me. I was going to jump."

"Didn't look like it."

There was a jerk on the rope, then it started moving, pulling him toward the lifeboat. The man gripped the rope right before it attached to the ring and half swam, half let himself be pulled toward the boat.

Who was this man? Even with snow driving into the water and wind stinging Thomas's eyes, the swimmer looked vaguely familiar. They crested the swell of a wave, then dropped into a trough, but the man didn't lose his grip on the rope for even a second.

Wasn't he cold? So numb he couldn't move? Shouldn't his lips be turning blue and his teeth chattering? "You're crazy," Thomas muttered.

Somehow the man heard him over the roar of the storm. "Saving lives isn't crazy."

Well, no. But risking his own life like this surely was.

They reached the boat, which was larger up close than it had looked from the ship, and the man let go of the rope and reached up, where he was pulled into the boat by the men huddled inside.

Then several sets of arms reached down to haul Thomas up. Pain tore through his shoulder, blinding and lightning hot despite the cold. A cry wrenched from him, only to be swallowed by the roar of the storm and the thud of his body landing on the bottom of the boat.

"Get that ring off, then sit." The man who'd rescued him gestured to the bench near where he stood. He'd already pulled on a woolen coat and settled a wide-brimmed hat atop his head. "You've some blankets there to wrap up in. It shouldn't take long to get to town."

"Places, men." The man's booming voice echoed louder than the wind, then he sat and took up his oar. A moment later the boat surged forward.

It provided Thomas the first chance to look at the man without water splashing into his face.

"You're one of the Cummings boys." He attempted to wriggle out of the ring around his chest, then gasped at the fresh pain in his shoulder. He could only imagine what Dr. Torrell would say if he'd seen the way his shoulder had wrenched a few moments ago. "Isaac, is it?"

His rescuer laughed, bitterness edging into his voice. "Not Isaac. Definitely not Isaac."

What was funny about his question? Surely he wasn't the first man to mix up two brothers' names. "Elijah then."

"That'd be me." He plunged his oar into the water, grim determination etched onto his jaw. The boat rose on a crest of wave and then dropped into a trough.

Finally wriggling out of the life ring, Thomas set it in the hull by

7

his feet and scooted closer to Elijah. "You might be able to help me."

Elijah stopped rowing and looked at Thomas. "Do I know…? Wait, you're Dowrick. Thomas Dowrick."

He offered the man who'd been half boy when he'd left town a wry smile. "Five years older and a little worse for wear, but yes, I'm Thomas Dowrick, and I'm here to look for my wife and daughters. They've gone missing, and this is the last place I saw them." He reached out and clutched Elijah's sleeve with his stiff, cold fingers. "Do you know anything about where she might have gone?"

"Missing? You mean Jessalyn Dowrick?"

Just hearing her name caused a pang to resonate through his heart. "She was supposed to go back to her family when I headed west, but she never arrived in Chicago."

"And you just now realized she was missing from Chicago?" The harsh look on his rescuer's face told him exactly what kind of man Elijah thought would abandon his family for half a decade.

Except he hadn't known they were abandoned. Didn't that count for something?

Guilt welled in his chest once more. But rather than look away from Elijah's stormy gray eyes, he held the other man's gaze. Because he needed help. Because he'd been wrong to leave Jessalyn and his girls in the first place, and if he had any hope of restoring their relationship after he found them—*if* he found them—then he needed to admit his failures. "I just learned she never arrived in Chicago, if that's what you mean."

Elijah turned his gaze back to the churning sea and took up rowing, his oar plunging into the water in perfect time with the other rowers. "I don't know what arrangements you and your wife made when you left, but she's still in Eagle Harbor."

Thomas sucked in a breath of sharp, crisp air. She was here? In town? "Will you take me?"

"Have to stop by the doc's first. It's my rule for everyone who rides in my lifeboat, but yes, after that I'll take you."

Thomas tilted his head up to the gray sky and pelting snow, while a warmth he couldn't explain spread through him. His Heavenly Father had seen fit to answer his prayer before his feet had even landed on solid ground.

Thank you, God. He was finally going to see his wife...

After five years of hearing nothing from her. The cold crept back in.

He knew why she'd refused to come west with him initially, but why had she been hiding from him for five years? And what would she say when she realized he found her?

Chapter Two

Jessalyn Dowrick bent her head over the sketch of the bridal dress and rubbed her bleary eyes. Should she use four-inch lace around the sleeves, or three? And what about adding lace to the collar? The sketch she'd been sent from Chicago didn't have any, but unless styles were changing, she—

"Ma." A slender hand settled itself atop the pattern. "Can we go to the doctor?"

Jessalyn drew her head up and blinked at her oldest daughter, who was tilting her head to the side and pressing a rag to her right ear.

"Oh, honey. Another one?" She set down her pencil and held out her arm.

"It hurts." Tears glistened in Olivia's eyes, and she leaned against Jessalyn's side. "I don't know why I keep getting them."

"Sometimes earaches just happen."

"Then how come they don't happen to Claire and Megan?" Olivia rested her sore ear on Jessalyn's shoulder. "Or you?"

Jessalyn sighed and stroked her hand up and down Olivia's arm. "I don't know."

And it was hardly fair to say they "just happened." They'd been "just happening" a lot over the past two years, almost to the point that her daughter had a constant ear infection.

Jessalyn glanced out the large display windows facing North Street to find the snow coming thicker and faster. The tiny pellets of white weren't obscuring the bar on the other side of the road yet. But it wouldn't be long given the dark gray clouds and whipping wind. It might only be November, but the first storm of the season was here. By tomorrow morning the dirt road and dry autumn grass would be covered in snow, and they'd stay buried for the next six months.

The hills surrounding Eagle Harbor might be rich with copper, but Michigan's Copper Country also sat on an unprotected peninsula that jutted into Lake Superior. The big lake to their north gave them at least twenty feet of snow every winter, and that was in a mild year. Some winters saw closer to thirty feet.

"Let me see if we have any willow bark tea in the kitchen. Perhaps that will suffice until the storm stops, and we can visit Dr. Harrington tomorrow." Provided the storm didn't keep up for two or three days.

"We're out. I already checked."

"Drat." Though she shouldn't be surprised. Olivia's last infection had only faded a week ago, and she'd not replenished the usual supplies and medicine yet.

Olivia bit her lip and glanced at the bridal sketch. "Will you be able to get your work done if we visit the doctor?"

"Of course." She'd just be up past midnight doing it. She patted Olivia's side. "Get your coat and boots on while I fetch Claire and Megan. Maybe we can make it back before the snow gets too deep."

Ten minutes later she pulled open the door to her shop, herded her three girls out into the storm, and stopped short at the sight of a hulking man approaching through the snow.

"Can I help you?" She pulled her youngest daughter, Megan, to her side to shield her from the wind.

"I need my coat back." The man's broad shoulders and towering form proclaimed him to be either a miner or logger.

She squinted at him. He looked vaguely familiar. "I just finished a pile of them this morning. What did you say your name was?"

But since he was already wearing a drab brown coat, the better question might be why he was asking for it back during a blizzard.

"Ebberhard. Frank Ebberhard."

The name was familiar as well. "Yes, I'm pretty sure I finished it this morning. Didn't you need buttons replaced?"

Something unsettling moved through the man's dark eyes, and he didn't bother to answer her, just glowered.

"Um, why don't you come inside? It might take a minute or two to find it."

"I'll wait here."

A frisson of fear shivered through her. She'd had strange requests before, yes, but nothing quite so odd as this.

"Go back inside, girls." At least they could wait in the warmth. She certainly wasn't going to leave them alone with a man like Frank Ebberhard. She followed her daughters inside and hurried toward the stack of mending she'd finished, waiting on the table at the back of her shop. His had been a mackinaw coat, hadn't it? The red and black plaid pattern was popular among loggers in Copper Country.

She rounded a final table and stepped over a pile of socks that needed darning before reaching the stack of coats. Spotting the mackinaw fabric in the middle of the pile, she set the top of the stack aside and grabbed the two plaid coats, then glanced at the scrap of paper she'd pinned to each of the collars. Emmett Tungston and Frank Ebberhard.

She moved to lay Mr. Tungston's coat back with the others, only to find a piece of paper had slipped from its pocket. She shook her head and retrieved the paper, then put it back into the closest pocket. Must the men who dropped off mending always leave their pockets full of papers and trinkets? It seemed she was always picking up something or other. If she actually kept all the change that ended up on her floor, her savings account at the bank would be double its current balance.

She draped Mr. Ebberhard's coat over her arm and rushed through her shop, weaving her way between tables and around stacks of scraps. Outside, the wind was so frigid it nearly sucked the breath from her lungs. "Here you are, that will be—"

"Keep the change." He shoved a dollar at her and turned, stalking away.

She blinked down at the bill. She only charged twenty-five cents to replace buttons, but the man's shadow had already faded into the storm.

Oh well, she'd use it to purchase an extra bag of willow bark tea. She pulled the door to her shop back open. "Come along girls. We can go now."

They filed back outside, and she gripped five-year-old Megan's hand in hers, then bent her head against the wind before starting down the road. "Stick close."

"The cold makes my ear hurt." Olivia pressed a hand to her ear, which was already covered with a scarf.

"I know, honey. I'm sorry."

"Jessalyn? Is that you?"

She looked up to find Isaac Cummings, the newly-elected town sheriff, crossing the street toward them.

"What are you doing out in this?" A scrap of auburn hair peeked out from beneath the wide-brimmed hat he wore, and his breath puffed cold little clouds into the air. He took the hand of her middle daughter, Claire, and started walking.

"I should ask you the same question." She closed her eyes against a particularly harsh gust of wind, then looked over her shoulder to make sure Olivia followed.

"Just came from The Rusty Wagon." Isaac jutted his chin toward the bar that sat across the street from her shop, his chiseled features implacable amidst the driving snow and wind. "Wanted to make sure things were staying calm inside."

She nodded. The sailors, loggers, and miners that filled Eagle Harbor never needed much excuse to visit the bar, or the brothel farther down the road, for that matter. Rainstorms and snowstorms actually gave them an excuse though. But she hadn't considered Isaac would have to work in storms such as this. Would the jail be full by the end of the night?

"You still haven't told me why you're out here," he called to her. "Or where we're going."

She trudged through a snowdrift that rose overtop her boots. "Olivia has another earache, and I was out of willow bark tea, so—"

He looked over his shoulder and scowled at her. "You should have waited a few more minutes. I was headed to your place to make sure you had enough firewood to get through the storm."

He was? Though she shouldn't be surprised. Isaac Cummings helped her whenever he could. And since he lived in the apartment above the telegraph office that sat next to her shop, those situations arose more often than a person might guess.

"I could have gotten Dr. Harrington, and then you wouldn't need to bring your girls out in this. The doc would have paid a house call." Isaac turned down Front Street and headed south along the harbor, his tall form cutting easily through the blizzard.

"We've survived worse, but thank you."

"Ma, you're going too fast."

She turned to find Olivia struggling through a drift the wind had blown across the road, a mitten-covered hand still pressed to her ear.

"Here. You take Claire." Isaac thrust Claire's hand into hers and tromped back toward Olivia, then swooped her into his arms.

The low sound of his voice rumbled through the storm as he spoke to her oldest daughter, and her heart lurched. What would it be like to…?

But no. She'd not let her thoughts wander in that direction. What would it be like if Thomas had never left? If he were the one carrying Olivia now and not a neighbor with an overly vigilant sense of duty?

That was the better question, but she'd stopped asking herself those things years ago. After five years of not hearing from him, Thomas was surely dead. Besides, there was no sense in letting her brain wander into the land of "what if," only in taking stock of the resources she had and making do. Which meant a trip to Dr. Harrington's at the moment, snowstorm or not.

Numbness was creeping into her nose and cheeks by the time they reached the doctor's sprawling log cabin. She guided her children up the steps, and Isaac pulled open the door to let them pass, all while keeping Olivia tucked against his chest.

Warmth enveloped her the instant she stepped inside the parlor… that was filled with people despite the storm?

"Take your things off and hang them on the pegs." She tugged at Megan's hat and surveyed the men. Most were strangers, with Ian Fletcher and Emmet Stone being the only familiar faces.

"Was there a shipwreck?" Isaac's voice was rough and dark behind her.

The bearded man nearest them nodded his head. "Afraid so."

"Is Elijah all right?" A flicker of fear laced the darkness in Isaac's voice that time.

"Elijah?" The man gave Isaac a blank stare.

"He's fine," Ian Fletcher, one of Elijah's lifesavers, called from across the room. "Took a little swim, but Doc Harrington has him warming up. He's in the sickroom while the doc looks at the passenger he rescued."

Isaac kept his jaw hard, his face resolute, but she caught the flash of relief in his hazel eyes. The entire town knew Elijah Cummings went out on volunteer rescues, just as assuredly as the entire town knew his brother Isaac opposed the idea. What must it feel like to be Isaac? Stuck waiting while a loved one risked his life to save others?

"Will Dr. Harrington be very long?" Olivia huddled against Isaac's chest.

Isaac looked down, seeming to realize he still held Olivia, then carried her to the sofa and set her down, never mind Olivia's boots getting snow on the couch.

"Something wrong, sweetheart?" A weathered sailor stopped at the edge of the couch, concern etched into the craggy lines of his face.

"My ear hurts." An icy little tear slipped down Olivia's cheek.

Jessalyn bent to undo Megan's buttons, then hung her daughter's things on the peg before scurrying over to Olivia.

"I'm sure it won't be much longer." She laid a hand on Olivia's brow. Though the girl had just spent a quarter hour outside, her skin was turning warm with the fever that often accompanied her earaches.

"I'll get the doc's wife. See if she can help with anything." The sailor turned for the kitchen.

"Thank you." Jessalyn bent to work at the laces on Olivia's boots. She couldn't complain about Isaac laying her daughter down, but surely Dr. Harrington and his wife Lindy didn't want snow ruining their sofa.

She'd just set the boots on the floor when Lindy swept into the room, her honey blond hair glistening in the lamplight. She headed straight for them and gave Olivia a side hug. "Don't tell me you have another earache, Olivia. I'm so sorry."

"Do you have some willow bark tea while we wait?" Jessalyn unbuttoned her own coat.

"Of course, but it shouldn't be much longer before Seth's done with his patient." Lindy gave Olivia another squeeze, then headed into the kitchen in a flurry of swishing petticoats.

"Here, let's unbutton your coat, even if you don't want to take it off." Jessalyn began at the bottom of the coat while Olivia started at the top. A quick sweep around the room told her Megan and Claire had headed straight for the toy box in the corner—bless Dr. Harrington for thinking of children and keeping toys in his parlor. Isaac paced by the door to the sickroom, his wide shoulders hunched and his face as dark and brooding as the storm clouds outside. The other men were milling about, some drinking coffee and eating cookies, some sitting in the chairs placed around the sizable parlor.

"I said I don't need any more treatment." A voice rose from behind the door of the large sickroom, loud enough to drown out the chatter in the parlor. "I'm perfectly fine, or I will be…" The door flung open and a large man stood in the frame. "As soon as I find my…"

The man stared at her.

Jessalyn sucked in a quick breath, but just as suddenly, her lungs forgot to work, trapping the air inside her.

"Jessalyn," he said.

Or maybe he didn't say it. Maybe he whispered it, or mouthed it, or thought it.

But she felt the impact of her name on his lips through every inch of her body.

"Thomas." He was back. The man who had once shared her life. Her husband. Her heart hammered against her chest. How many times had she dreamed of this day, ran it over and over in her mind until her body ached with the loss of not having him beside her? How many times had she imagined what she'd say when he finally returned, each and every word of it?

17

He took a step toward her, his body so large and familiar she nearly went to meet him, nearly wrapped her arms around his chest and settled her head on his shoulder. How long since she'd felt the strength of her husband's arms as they held her?

How long? She stiffened. Five years, five months, and eleven days. She'd thought him dead, but he was certainly alive and well.

Which meant he'd knowingly abandoned her and their daughters.

And if it had taken him that long to come back, then she could stand on the other side of the room for five minutes without going to him. She could force herself to forget about the way his arms would feel around her and his heart would sound beneath her ear. She'd already forced herself to forget a great many things about him. Two more shouldn't be any trouble.

Except her husband hadn't been anywhere close those other times. It was a lot harder to ignore a person when they stood ten feet away.

"What..." She forced her tongue to move, forced her dry mouth to form words. "What are you doing here?"

"Do you need to ask? I came for you, Jess." His gaze slid past her to Olivia on the couch. "For my daughters." He started toward her, his heavy footfalls causing the floor to tremble.

Whatever he'd been doing the past five years hadn't turned him soft or weak. She didn't need him to roll up his shirtsleeves to know that corded muscles still rested under the fabric. If anything, her miner husband seemed larger and stronger than she remembered.

He stopped a couple feet away from her. Close enough she couldn't take her eyes from him, yet far enough away she couldn't tell whether he still bore his once-familiar scent of sunshine and work and man. She swallowed, and the dryness in her throat made the simple action painful. If he wasn't dead or hurt or injured, then why

18

had he stayed away so long? And why had he decided to come back now, of all things? The time for that had been in the months after he'd left, when she hadn't known what to do with herself, when she would have starved if not for the generosity of folks like Elijah and Isaac Cummings.

"I'm sorry, Jessalyn." Elijah came up beside her, his cheeks ruddy and wind-chapped. "I was going to bring Thomas by your shop when we left, that way half the town wouldn't… well…" He scratched the back of his neck and glanced around. "…Know he was back before you did."

The entire town. She looked up to find every person in the room staring at them, save Claire and Megan, who were playing with a doll and swing in the corner. Even Lindy stood by the kitchen door with a steaming mug in her hand.

If only she could close her eyes and melt into the floor. There was a time when she would have thrown herself at him and wept at his return, no matter how callous he'd been when he'd left them. But those days had come and gone like a late spring snow.

"Mama, my ear." The small voice behind her shattered the stillness of the room.

Dr. Harrington stepped around a cluster of sailors and crouched down by the sofa. "Is it bothering you again? Why don't you come to the small sickroom with me, and I'll take a look? Maybe we can let your parents go into the big sickroom to talk."

"Parents?" Olivia asked. "I don't have a pa anymore, just a ma."

Thomas made a low, strangled sound in his throat.

Jessalyn wasn't sure what to call the look he'd given her when he'd first seen her earlier. Surprise, perhaps, or hope. But there was no hope in his face now, only hurt.

"Unless…?" The weight of Olivia's gaze bored into her before it shifted to Thomas. "Unless you're my pa?"

19

"No," Jessalyn whispered.

A storm gathered in his eyes, and the small muscle at the side of his jaw pulsed.

It only made her own jaw harden in response, her own muscles tense. "A real pa doesn't walk away from you for five years, especially not without sending letters."

Thomas crossed his arms over his impossibly broad chest. "I sent a letter every week."

She shook her head. "I only got two letters from you, both while you were traveling to California. The last letter was around the time I learned I was expecting Megan."

Thomas's gaze traveled across the room to the youngest of their three daughters. "Her name's Megan? And she's... and she's mine?"

"How dare you." She took a step forward, bringing her toe-to-toe with her vagrant of a husband, and raised her hand.

Before she could let it fly toward his face, someone caught her arm.

Not Thomas. He was looking at her with a calm sort of resignation, something he'd certainly never had during their arguments before he'd left. He'd been prepared for her to hit him and hadn't intended to stop it. A sickening sensation twined through her stomach.

"Jess." Isaac's voice was low, his mouth near enough her ear he wouldn't be overheard. "How about you move this conversation to the sickroom, like Dr. Harrington suggested?"

She drew in a shaky breath and looked at Isaac, his face sincere, his hazel gaze filled with concern. Tears burned her eyes. But when she looked back to Thomas, something else burned entirely.

"I don't want to talk to him." Her voice was sickeningly soft, perilously close to breaking. How was it that she could look at Thomas and banish all thought of tears, but the second she turned to Isaac, she wanted nothing more than to go home, crawl into her bed, curl up, and cry until morning?

Because Isaac chopped her firewood, escorted her through snow storms, and helped wrestle giant sewing machines through small shop doors. Because Isaac took her children to the beach in the summer so she could squeeze in a few hours of work, and invited her to Thanksgiving dinner with his family. Because though Isaac Cummings was only her neighbor, he gave her more support in half a day than Thomas had given her in the entire decade they'd been married.

"Well, I want to talk to you." Thomas's voice was calm and controlled, not shouting, not drenched with fury like hers would be if she spoke. "I thought you were in Chicago. I told you to go back there, remember? It was one of the last conversations we had."

She pressed her eyes shut as the memories filled her mind. Not one of the last, the absolute last. Though calling it a conversation was rather charitable on Thomas's part. They'd argued about money, of course, the same thing they always argued about. Thomas had lost most of their savings investing in a copper mine that played out early and didn't yield dividends. He wanted to take the last little bit they'd saved and use it to go to California where there was gold. She'd said no, that they needed to save more first, that they couldn't afford to take four people across the country, even if Thomas could find better work there.

She could still recall his hard jaw, the angry note in his voice as he told her he was taking the last of their savings and leaving in the morning, but if she didn't want to go with him, he wouldn't force her. She could go to Chicago and stay with her cousin while he got settled, and he'd send for her later.

She'd thought they'd been empty threats. The last thing she expected was to get up in the morning and find him already gone.

A lump rose in her throat. She couldn't deal with this, not now, not with a room full of people. Not when she'd been completely unprepared to face the man who had been all but dead to her for five years. She met Thomas's eyes and forced a calm to her voice despite the shaking that had taken over her hands. "I don't know what brought you back to Eagle Harbor, but I hope you conclude your business here quickly and leave me out of it. Now if you'll excuse me, my daughter needs to see the doctor."

She turned her back to Thomas and found Dr. Harrington looking into Olivia's ear with his otoscope. "Do you mind carrying her into the sickroom for me?"

"Certainly. Can you take this?" He handed her the cone-shaped instrument that allowed him to see deep inside her daughter's ears, then stood and hefted Olivia into his arms before heading across the parlor. She rushed behind him, head down to avoid the questioning gazes of everyone else, but Thomas's unmistakable footfalls resonated behind her.

When she reached the door, she paused and turned back. "I'm afraid you don't understand. You're not the one who's cared for Olivia for the past five years, so you're not welcome inside."

She swept into the room and closed the door, or would have—if his arm didn't catch the door before it latched. He pushed back on the wood, forcing it open in a match of strength she had no hope of winning. But rather than come inside and settle himself on one of the chairs, he stopped in the doorway, his burly form so tall he had to duck his head.

"You can go into the room, that's fine. I'll wait out here and visit with Megan and Claire. You can leave the doctor's office, that's fine too. I don't mind following you, or talking in a blizzard, or doing any other number of things to get you talk to me. But how quickly I finish my business in Eagle Harbor depends on you." His gaze swept quickly down her, but not in a romantic way. He may as well have been a clerk taking inventory: blond hair—check; teeth—check; four limbs—check. "Because you and our daughters are the reason I came back, and I'm not leaving town again without you."

He'd come back for her? This man who'd abandoned her and their daughters, leaving them with only the money she kept stashed in the jar in the kitchen?

Why?

"I'm happy here." That was the easier thing to say. The thing that didn't open up a conversation between them the way asking why would. The trouble was, her statement wasn't quite true since she was planning to relocate her dress shop to Chicago next summer. But she was happy enough in Eagle Harbor for the winter. "I wish you well with your life, wherever you live, and whatever it is you're doing."

She swung the door shut again, though she knew he'd stop it from latching a second time, but what else could she do? How else could she convince him that the door was shut on their past, even if he refused to let the physical door between them close?

Sure enough, the door bounced off the tips of his shoes and sprang open, leaving him to stand there and cross his arms. "It's been five years. You can't tell me you don't have questions, something you want to say to me." He dipped his head toward her, his voice turning softer. "That you haven't thought about what you would say to me a hundred different times and a hundred different ways."

"Possibly, Thomas. Right after you left. Maybe even a year after you were gone. But not anymore." It only proved how much she'd changed in his absence, proved how he didn't know her nearly as well now as he once had. "Now please leave me alone. My daughter's sick, and she needs me right now, whereas you haven't needed me for five years."

"I'm not leaving you alone until we talk." He gripped the top of the door with one hand and the trim lining the doorway with the other. "I don't care where, but there are things we need settled between us. Today."

He was still as demanding as always. Still insistent on getting his way. She may have changed while he was gone, but he hadn't seemed to change at all. Oh, sure, he'd ask politely for what he wanted at first, toss her a smile and wink and try charming her into it. And if she refused, well, then the demands would start.

"I said no."

"Ma," a small voice sounded from the bed.

She glanced over her shoulder at Olivia, who watched them with large, moist eyes and a trembling jaw. She was nearly oblivious to Dr. Harrington using a candle with his otoscope to see inside her ear.

Something hard and tight fisted in Jessalyn's chest. Claire was too young to remember Thomas, and Megan hadn't even been born when he'd left. But Olivia had been five. Was that old enough to have memories of her father?

Yes, if the way she watched Thomas was any indication.

She turned back to Thomas, and the determination in his eyes and stubborn set to his jaw only squeezed the vise around her heart. If she didn't listen to him now, he'd make good on his promise to follow her home. At least here they could talk behind closed doors, without Olivia hearing more than she already had.

She swept her gaze down him, the tall, muscular form that had once been so familiar to her, the blue eyes and blond hair that were so similar to her own. Did he have any idea how heartbroken she'd been when he left?

Hopefully her heart would survive a final conversation. "Fine, we can go into the other room."

Chapter Three

"Let's go." Jessalyn's eyes glittered with unshed tears, but she turned away from Thomas and stomped across the crowded parlor toward the room where the doctor had examined him earlier.

Thomas glanced at his daughter lying still while the doctor looked at her ear with an odd contraption that attached to a candle. He rubbed the back of his neck. Maybe he'd been too demanding by saying they needed to talk right away. Didn't Jessalyn want to wait until the doc had finished his examination?

But she'd already entered the sickroom and closed the door behind her all but a crack. He looked back at Olivia one more time, her angel blond hair spread against the pillows the doc had piled behind her. She was big now, much bigger than he'd imagined. Somehow in his mind she'd stayed five years old the entire time he'd been gone, and Claire had always been a baby.

He'd visit with Olivia after he talked with Jessalyn, maybe even pull the doctor aside and ask for a report. And then he'd visit with Claire and Megan, the daughter he'd never even spoken too. He'd already missed Claire's first steps and Megan's birth and Olivia's first day of school. So much of their lives gone without him being a part of it. How did he begin to catch up? An ache started in his chest, almost as painful as the one in his shoulder, except the one in his shoulder had a medical explanation.

Jessalyn poked her head out the door. "Are you coming?" The words were so full of prickles, she might have sent each one scurrying across the room on the back of a porcupine.

Because she doesn't know the full story. She thinks that I abandoned her and stopped writing after those first two letters.

He headed toward his wife, stopping to grab the soggy letter he'd left drying by the woodstove before he entered the room and closed the door.

In the time it had taken him to cross the parlor, she'd made her way to the window, where she stood peering into the storm that would soon be covered by the gathering dark.

How often had he seen her do that very thing before? Summer, autumn, winter, spring, the curtain drawn aside and her face peeking out the window to watch the weather. And she looked so very much the same while standing there. Her elegant green dress wasn't made of silk or satin or any other fine fabric, and yet she was as stylish and put together as one of the women living on Prairie Street in Chicago. A ribbon cinched tightly about her narrow waist, an extra splash of lace around her collar and sleeves, the row of double buttons that started at her neck and went clear down to the ribbon. She'd always been able to take a nickel and somehow make the coin go as far as ten dollars.

Her hair was done up in an elegant twist at the back of her head too, yet another thing that hadn't changed. No simple bun or sloppy knot for Jessalyn. Somehow, she'd learned to do her own hair as masterfully as any lady's maid in Chicago.

She turned from the window and startled when she saw him. "Sorry. I must not have heard you come in." She crossed the room, her gaze sweeping down him for what had to be the fifth or sixth time that afternoon, as though she couldn't quite believe he stood before her. "You have me alone now. What is it you need to say?"

That I want you back, that I want to be a husband to you, and a father to our daughters.

If only she were ready to hear it. "I want to know why you're not in Chicago. Why you made no effort to reach me after you decided to stay in Eagle Harbor."

"Why *I* made no effort to reach *you?*" Her eyes flashed. "What about you? You were the one who said you'd send for me, remember?"

"I did send for you, half a dozen times, giving you more than enough money to travel to me." Would she soften toward him now? After all, he'd just told her he'd not left her to rot while he'd been away.

She only blinked. "But how? You sent two letters."

"I sent more than two, but they were to Mathilda's address in Chicago. That's where I told you to go and wait for me, and since you were always talking about us moving back to Chicago and getting help from Henry and Mathilda, I assumed that's where you went." At least up until five months ago, when he'd been too injured to leave Deadwood and do anything about the wife he'd learned was missing.

Was she going to smile at least a little now? Tell him how sorry she was for the misunderstanding?

She only sighed. "I decided not to go to Chicago after all."

"I see that now, but you can't blame me for not knowing before."

She bent her head and rubbed her temple.

Because she had a headache? At one time he would have asked. No, at one time he wouldn't need to ask, because he'd been familiar enough with her mannerisms to know what they meant. But not anymore.

She pressed her eyes shut for a moment, then opened them and dropped her hand from her temple. "You didn't realize I was here, and I didn't realize you thought I was in Chicago. We were both wrong, and it's an even trade, but I'm not sure what you expect can be done about it now."

"Nothing." She had the right of it, neither of them could go back and change the past five years, but they certainly had the ability to alter their futures, to start living as husband and wife again. He reached for the letter he'd set on the bed. He'd taken it out of his coat and left it to dry as soon as he'd arrived, but the paper was still wet and crumpled from his swim in the lake. Surely once she saw the contents of the envelope, she'd want to share a life with him again.

She peeled the envelope back, gently tugged out the contents, and…

Nothing.

He frowned. Had she not seen the banknote lying atop the letter? Why wasn't she saying anything?

"I'm sorry, Thomas." She shook her head. "The ink is so smeared I can't make the words out, but thank you for writing. I didn't think… well, I didn't know what to think after you disappeared. What's this bank note for?" She held it up and squinted at it. "Ten dollars?"

He didn't need to glance at it to answer her question, but he stepped closer anyway. He'd forgotten how lovely she was, with her shiny blond hair and blue eyes, her petite, slender build and creamy skin. Deadwood had its share of beautiful women, all dressed in silks with their bosoms on display to the highest bidder, but not a single one of them drew him the way Jess did standing here now, her gaze latched onto the papers he'd given her, her simple yet stylish dress buttoned up to her neck. She smelled like oranges though, a scent far different than that of the rosewater she used to make and dab on her neck.

"Well?" She looked up at him. "Ten dollars?"

"A hundred." He swallowed and forced his gaze to the paper. "One of the zeros at the end smeared."

She dropped the paper, sending it to the floor with a soggy plop. "You sent this much?"

"Ah…" Wasn't she supposed to throw herself into his arms right about now? To fight back tears as she clung to him and thanked him for making her wealthy? "I own a hotel in Deadwood, South Dakota, and a half dozen boarding houses just outside Lead. I rent rooms cheaper than the Homestake Mine rents the company housing, and I've got another two boarding houses scheduled to be built come summer."

She stared at him, still no hint of emotion in her clear blue eyes.

What was wrong with her? Why wasn't she happy for him? For herself? Why wasn't she hugging him and covering his face with kisses? How much more did he need to explain before she understood? "I made money for you, Jess. You don't need to worry about running out of it or being forced to live in tenements again."

Silence filled the space between them, leaving no sound but the beating of the wind at the windows and dull roar of the lake outside. He nearly reached for her, nearly set his hand on her shoulder and pulled her into his chest. She'd feel the same as she always had cuddled against him, delicate, warm, soft.

But she bent to pick up the banknote instead, then straightened and handed it back to him.

"You're right, Thomas. I don't need to worry about living in tenements anymore." Her voice shook despite its quiet timbre. "But not because of anything you did. I made money on my own while you were gone, and strangely enough, since the money's mine rather than both of ours, I also don't need to worry about you taking it and abandoning us again."

She'd made money? Doing what? Though it made sense. If she hadn't gotten the money he sent, then she'd had to find some way to provide. The ache returned to his chest, and he rubbed at his breastbone. Caring for three girls without any support would have been hard on any woman, but it would have been doubly so for Jessalyn considering how she'd grown up.

He should have come here sooner, left Deadwood to escort his wife and daughters west himself after the letters had gone unanswered. But as he'd told her a few minutes ago, he couldn't change the past. The present—only the present. "Money or not, Jess, I'm here to take you and the girls back to Deadwood with me, where you should have been all along. How soon can you be packed?"

"Packed?" A hint of desperation crept into her voice. "You want me to pack?"

He gritted his teeth. None of this was happening like it should. She was supposed to be happy, grateful even. "You're the reason I left. You were mad we lost our savings and you wanted me to earn it back. You can't be that surprised I've finally come to collect you and the girls."

"I never asked for you to go in the first place. That was your choice alone." She gripped her hands in her skirt and took a step nearer him, her eyes filled with five years' worth of accusations. "And I certainly didn't ask for you to come back and collect me. But now that you have, winter is here. And after the shipwreck today, the harbor will be closed until May. If you don't intend to stay in Eagle Harbor for the next six months, I suggest you leave in the morning and walk to the train station in Calumet with the other sailors."

She huffed and spun toward the door, slamming it behind her a moment later.

His hand itched to grab the handle and yank it open, but what good would that do? He had no interest in exchanging another round of heated words.

Please forgive me for not coming after you sooner. That request should have come out of his mouth at some point during their conversation, but once he looked into her familiar blue eyes, old emotions and resentment had risen up.

God, how do I change it? He'd seen her for maybe a half hour, and they'd fallen right back into the same patterns that had plagued their marriage before he'd left. *How do I convince a wife I haven't seen for five years that I want to make things right with her?*

Jessalyn's voice sounded from the other side of the wall, calm and sweet as she spoke to the girls. He'd go out and visit with them in another moment, just as soon as he and Jess had a chance to calm down. Wouldn't do any good to argue in front of the children—or more townsfolk.

What more could he even say to her when she'd already decided all the money he'd made in Deadwood wasn't good enough for her?

He scrubbed a hand over his face. Of all the things he'd never expected to hear from his wife. But then, he really shouldn't be surprised. Seemed like he'd spent his entire life not quite good enough for any of the people around him.

"There's the Dowrick boy. Tell me, Thomas, did ya drag your pa out of the ditch last night? Good thing he has a son as big as you to get him home."

"Don't worry about giving him none of them extra crops. He's the son of the town drunk."

"Did you hear how much your brother lost at the card table last night? You'll end up a wastrel too. No use trying to be any different."

"You smell like stale whiskey and refuse. Did your pa retch on you? Didn't anybody tell you to take a bath after that happens?"

He could still recall the voices, still smell the rancid breaths of the coal miners and hear their wheezy coughs. It didn't matter that he never got drunk or gambled away his pay. His father and brother did, and he'd gotten lumped in with his family more often than not. He may have left Cornwall fifteen years ago, but those voices still followed him. As did Henry's.

You think you're good enough to marry my wife's cousin? I didn't feed her and clothe her for the past six years to watch her marry one of my foremen. She's marrying Walter Shunk, and we're going to purchase the cannery on the other side of the street from the warehouse. It's the least she can do for all I've given her. If I see you near Jessalyn again, you'll be looking for another job.

When he'd gone to Chicago before coming to Eagle Harbor, he'd learned Henry had died in a carriage crash six months ago, and yet the man's words still taunted him, as did the loss of the foreman position he'd worked his way up to.

He'd thought Jessalyn worth the sacrifice of his job at the time, but how quickly trouble had seeped into their marriage when he'd struggled to put a roof over their heads and food on the table, and all with Olivia on the way.

He shook his head and blew out a breath, long and deep. How could Jessalyn stand in front of him and say she didn't want his money when it had been so important to her before?

Later. He'd ask her about it later. At the moment, he had daughters to visit.

He turned the handle on the door and stepped into the parlor. It was empty save for Isaac Cummings standing near the stove with a cup of coffee. At least he thought it was Isaac, if his memory wasn't failing him again. Didn't the younger brother have auburn hair? Stand a little taller than Elijah, but have a narrower form than his brother? The man had to be a Cummings. There was no mistaking the chiseled jaw, high cheekbones, and broad forehead both the boys shared with their father, Hiram.

"Where did they go?" Thomas's brow furrowed as he scanned the room for his wife and daughters once more.

"Your family?" Isaac scowled at him over his coffee cup. "They went home."

He glanced out the large window that faced the harbor. Wind roared, blowing the pelting snow until it slanted sideways.

He grabbed his coat from where he'd left it by the woodstove. It wasn't entirely dry yet, nor were his boots, but he could endure a bit more wetness and cold to see that his family got home safely.

"And where do you plan on going in those sodden clothes?" Isaac asked.

"I'm walking my wife and daughters home." He pulled on his second boot and began to lace it, never mind the icy water that soaked into his dry sock the second his foot was inside.

"A little late for that, don't you think?" Sharpness bit into Isaac's words. "She's lived here what? Seven years? Eight? Reckon she can make her way around town in a snowstorm."

She hadn't wandered around town alone in snowstorms when he'd been here. The sour ball of guilt lodged in his gut once more, only to be followed by the ache in his shoulder. "Can't imagine they got that far ahead in this weather. I should be able to catch up."

"Elijah went with them."

"Elijah?" Why was a young, single man escorting his wife about town?

Isaac chuckled. "He's married, if that's what you're glowering about. Happily so. Got himself hitched this spring."

"And do you have yourself a wife too?" After all, Jess had listened to Isaac about not slapping him. Isaac had also been the one to go into the corner and play with the younger girls while Olivia was in the sickroom.

Isaac watched him over the rim of his coffee cup. "For a man who's been gone for five years, you seem awful concerned about your wife all of a sudden."

Thomas stood to his full six-foot, five-inch height and crossed his arms over his chest. "Answer the question."

"No, I don't have a wife. I've got myself a badge instead." Isaac jerked a thumb toward the shiny star on his chest. "You can call me sheriff."

"Sheriff? How old are you?" He bit the inside of his cheek. He shouldn't be mouthing off to the town sheriff, even if he could remember a time when the sheriff had been as gangly as a string bean and spoke with a voice as high as a woman's.

Isaac probably should have issued some kind of veiled threat to lock him up if he kept running his mouth, but the younger man only laughed. "I'm not still seventeen, if that's what you mean."

Thomas gripped the back of his neck, half because he needed something for his hands to do, and half because it was a good way to stretch his shoulder without making others aware of his injury. "Sorry, I guess in some ways, I thought everything in Eagle Harbor would be the same as when I left."

"Things change, and I imagine Jess is halfway home by now, so you may as well take off your wet boots and have some soup in the kitchen with everyone else."

Thomas looked around the empty room. Hot soup did sound good, and maybe some coffee to warm the parts inside that still felt frozen from his swim in the lake. But he had other business to attend. "I need to find a room to rent. Is the boardinghouse still on Center Street?"

"It is, but you won't find a room there. Mrs. Kainer's been all full up for a while now." Isaac took another sip of coffee.

Thomas tried not to notice the steam wafting from the mug, tried not to think of the rush of liquid sliding down the other man's throat to warm his belly. "Is there another boardinghouse?"

Isaac shook his head.

"A hotel?"

Another head shake.

"Where else can I try?"

"Somewhere in Central, maybe. Most people aren't exactly looking for rooms to let this time of year."

"Central?" The mining town was five miles away. "That's too far from Jess."

Isaac raised his eyebrows, and Thomas swallowed. Yes, he'd been much farther than five miles away for the past several years, but he was here to fix that now, and the rest wasn't the other man's business.

"There isn't anything closer." Isaac warmed his hands against the coffee mug. "Used to be rooms for let above the bakery, but an Irishwoman's renting those now."

That left him with only one place to go. So much for giving Jessalyn time. "Is my wife still living in the little blue house a block from North Street? Or Elijah mentioned something about a shop. Does she live there now?"

The coffee mug wobbled in Isaac's hand, sloshing a bit of dark liquid over the side. "You're just going to show up on her step and demand she take you in?"

"You have a better idea?"

Isaac took a long sip of coffee. So long, in fact, that he might well be using his drink to stall for time. "How long do you need this room for?"

That was a good question. Jess didn't truly mean to make him wait until spring, did she?

He'd been planning to return to Deadwood before Thanksgiving and had told his hotel manager to expect exactly that.

Which was even more frustrating. If he'd known she was here instead of in Chicago, he could have arrived a week ago, packed everything up, and sailed them to Duluth just ahead of the storm. From there they could have traveled to Deadwood by rail. But now they just might need to wait until the harbor opened—probably sometime in May—before they could leave.

Could they travel overland to the train station in Calumet before then? That would be a long, dangerous trip in the winter with three little girls.

"Don't know." Thomas scratched his chin and looked at Isaac. "At least long enough to pack up Jessalyn's things and arrange for them to be shipped in the spring."

Isaac set his mug on the table. "And you don't care what she has to say about leaving?"

He did, which was something of a problem. Five years ago, he likely wouldn't have listened to his wife, would have hauled her over his shoulder and carried her home and started throwing her things into trunks.

He didn't want to force her now. He wanted her to... to... want him. To want to be his wife and come to Deadwood and live in the lavish suite he'd furnished on the top floor of his hotel.

Maybe she didn't understand exactly how much money he had. Maybe if he sat her down and explained how well he could provide for her, she'd agree to come with him without any more fuss. "I'd like to say I'll be here a week, but the truth is, however long it takes to win Jessalyn over."

"Why did you come back?" Five simple words, but there was weight behind them, a certain heaviness that burdened the air between him and the sheriff.

"My wife and daughters are here."

Isaac rubbed his chin. "Then why leave in the first place?"

That answer got a heap more complicated. "I don't see how it's any of your business."

"You forget you're talking to the sheriff. Anyone who comes into this town with the potential of causing trouble is my business."

"I'm not here to cause trouble."

Isaac hitched a thumb through his belt loop, which wasn't all that far away from his holstered sidearm. "Not sure your wife sees it that way."

He hung his head. "Maybe you're asking me the wrong question.

Maybe it's not a matter of why I left, maybe it's a matter of why she refused to come with me." His voice grew hoarse, the last few words clinging to the inside of his mouth before he forced them out.

But it was the truth. He'd invited her to come with him, even if the cost of four people traveling west would eliminate their small savings. Then when she'd refused, he'd told her he'd send for her—and he had.

If only she would have gotten his letters.

"I wanted her with me the whole time." He cleared his throat and met Isaac's gaze. "Now about that room?"

"I have a spare bedroom in my apartment above the telegraph office."

Thomas laughed. "Does the sheriff position pay so poorly you need to rent rooms too?" It was the only reason Isaac might be willing to let one, because the man seemed more disposed to protect Jessalyn from her ogre of a husband than to help him get her back.

"The telegraph office is next door to where your wife lives. If you stay with me, you can be the one to rush down the stairs and help her haul in firewood, or carry bolts of fabric from the mercantile back to her shop, or do any other number of things you should have been doing for the past five years."

And that right there he couldn't argue with, because he'd carry all manner of things for his wife—no matter how much it pained his shoulder—provided she would let him. "All right."

But would carrying things convince her to go to Deadwood? If the hard gleam in her eyes earlier were any indication, he'd be hauling a lot of firewood before she agreed.

Chapter Four

Jessalyn sniffled as her legs worked the treadle of her sewing machine. Beneath her hands, the emerald green satin shimmered in the lamplight while she sewed lace along the cuffs of the elegant bridesmaid's dress.

It was the first of ten she needed to make before spring, followed by the wedding gown she couldn't seem to get right in her sketches. And since exchanging letters with her client in Chicago would take months now that the harbor was closed, she had to finalize a design quickly lest she run out of time to sew the final dress.

Her feet stilled on the treadle, and she clamped her jaw as she stared at the uneven seam she'd stitched into the sleeve.

Finalizing a pattern for the bridal dress hardly mattered if she couldn't do something as simple as sew lace onto a sleeve. She'd have to tear it out and start anew, and more carefully this time. The expensive satin wouldn't tolerate three attempts at stitching like cotton or muslin would.

She rubbed her forehead and glanced away from the sewing machine to the window. Icy pellets of snow pinged against the glass in the darkness and wind gusted against the building. This was her usual time to sew, the girls having gone to bed over an hour ago. But tonight she might as well curl up into a ball beside little Megan and try sleeping for all that she was accomplishing.

Except sleep wouldn't come, not when the sight of Thomas's face haunted her each and every time her eyes closed.

Seven months. That's how long she'd cried herself to sleep after he'd left. It had been clear the day he'd disappeared exactly what had happened. It wasn't as though she'd had no notion why he'd left and taken all but the money she kept stashed in a jar in the kitchen. Even though she'd tried to stem the tears, tried to smile when she walked down the road, tried to sing her best at church and carry on for her two young daughters and the one growing inside her, she still hadn't been able to stop missing him.

Or loving him.

How foolish. She shouldn't love someone who'd abandoned her.

But at least Thomas hadn't abandoned her in the tenements where she'd grown up in Chicago. Even now, she could still smell the stench of garbage and rotting rodents, the sourness of chamber pots being emptied into the streets. She could still feel the wind as it tore through the tiny apartment with thin walls and a leaky roof that she'd shared with her mother. She could still taste the runny gruel they'd eaten and the brackish water they'd gotten from the pump down the street. Just as she could still see her mother's sickly form lying on the straw pallet.

She swallowed. Look at her, sitting here and getting distracted with buried memories when there were problems to be solved at present—like what Thomas was doing back in Eagle Harbor.

She took her scissors and bent back over the green satin fabric to snip her first wayward stitch, then another. Thomas couldn't truly expect her to upend her life in Michigan and move to South Dakota, could he?

Of course he could. He was still her husband. She set her scissors on the small table beneath her sewing machine and hung her head in her hands.

Her *husband.*

The word made her stomach twist.

Why couldn't he have stayed away longer? Claire and Megan were still so young, so vulnerable. Olivia had asked over the years why her pa had left. Why he never wrote. Why he'd never come back when all her friends had pas. But Claire and Megan were too young to notice how different their family was from any of their friends'.

Or rather, they had been. Except Claire understood some of what happened today at the doctor's and had peppered her with questions as soon as they got home.

Jessalyn stood and turned down the wick on the lamp above her sewing machine, then picked up the lamp on the nearby shelf. She may as well head upstairs to bed, even if getting sleep proved as fruitless as sewing.

She swept her gaze over her shop, filled with tables and piles of clothing, bolts of fabric, scraps, buttons, lace, and ribbons. One day she'd clean it out and organize it. Surely she didn't need to save every last bit of extra fabric, or the buttons she'd never be able to match with others. But as haphazard as her shop might be, it was hers. She'd built her business from the ground up, all without a smidgeon of help from her husband. If she and the girls hadn't needed him for the past five years, then why let him back into their lives now?

Especially when he was so very likely to hurt them again.

~ ~ ~ ~ ~

Thump. Thump. Thump.

Thomas opened his eyes and glanced around the small white room, then muffled a groan with his pillow. Light shone through the window to his right, but a quick glance told him that though the storm had stopped, the day was cloudy and windy—just like every other winter day he remembered from when he'd lived in Copper Country.

Thump. Thump. Thump. The knocking sounded again, but not on his door, from somewhere else in the apartment.

"Morning, Isaac." A masculine voice carried from the other side of the wall.

"Hi, Uncle Isaac." A small child's voice followed.

Thomas groaned and rolled out of bed, the movement causing his shoulder to protest. Had he slept late? That's what happened when a man stayed up half the night thinking about his estranged wife next door. He glanced out the window at the building where his wife evidently ran her seamstress shop, but no flicker of movement shown in the windows.

"How long until they get here, Pa? I want to build a snowman." A child's voice again, followed by the muted sound of her father's response.

Thomas rubbed the sleep from his eyes and stretched his still-aching shoulder. Then he opened the door and headed into the living area that served as both kitchen and parlor. "Morning."

A clunk sounded from the table, and he looked over to find a hulking man bunched into one of the chairs. His coffee sloshed from his mug onto the table as though he'd set the cup down too suddenly.

"Didn't tell me you had company," the burly man muttered.

Isaac shrugged as he poured a cup of coffee. "Seemed like the thing to do, Mac."

Mac? As in Mac Oakton? Isaac and Elijah's adopted brother? Thomas narrowed his eyes. The man had filled out since he'd left, from tall, gangly youth into a man with muscles thick enough to rival his own. And if the two brown-headed girls dancing around the man's chair were any indication, he'd also gotten himself a wife.

"That still doesn't explain why you allowed a man that walked out on his wife and children into your home." Bitterness dripped from Mac's words.

Thomas winced. Mac's pa had walked out on him a decade or so back, resulting in the Cummings family taking the boy in. But did Mac really think him no better than Clive Oakton, the swindler who had skipped town with half the townsfolk's savings? "It's not what it seems with me and Jessalyn, but it's good to see you again, Oakton."

"The way I figure it, maybe Thomas here left his wife and girls when he shouldn't have. But he seems ready to make things right now, and that's a good thing." Isaac handed him a cup of coffee. "With Mrs. Kainer's boardinghouse filled up and Jessalyn needing some wooing, I figured it might help if he was living next door to her."

"Appreciate it." Thomas took a sip of the strong, dark brew and scanned the two bright-faced girls with their wavy dark hair and syrup-colored eyes. "Looks like you found yourself a Mrs. Oakton while I was gone, Mac."

"I did." Mac's eyes, the same shade as his daughters', pinned onto him. "She happens to be best friends with your wife—not that you would know."

Thomas winced again. No, he wouldn't know, and he had no one to blame but himself.

"Tressa was a mite bit concerned when Elijah stopped by the lighthouse last night, saying you'd sailed into town with the snowstorm, then insisted Jessalyn pack up for South Dakota." More accusation seeped from Mac's voice.

Thomas hid his next wince behind a sip of coffee. "I didn't insist she move, I... asked." *Rather insistently.*

"Go easy on him, Mac. You don't know what the man's been through, or why he left Jessalyn in the first place."

Mac turned to Isaac, eyebrows raised, which was probably about how Thomas looked at the moment. Had Isaac Cummings just defended him?

Mac settled into his chair and took a gulp of coffee. "I got time to hear the story."

"But Pa!" The larger of the two girls pulled on her father's arm, never mind she was causing more coffee to slosh onto the table. "You said we could build a snowman when our friends get here."

"And we will." Mac patted the small hand still gripping his shirt sleeve. "But they're not here yet, and Pa needs to visit."

"Actually, I don't intend to stay long, I want to visit your father this morning." If everyone in town was going to be this nosy about him and Jessalyn, he needed advice about what to say—along with advice about convincing Jessalyn to come to Deadwood. If anyone in town had wisdom to offer, it was Hiram Cummings. "Will he be at his cabin?"

Silence fell, as cold and bitter as the wind whipping at the window.

Had he said something wrong? The Hiram Cummings he remembered wouldn't mind—

"My father's dead." The muscles in Isaac's jaw pulsed, then he turned and yanked open a kitchen drawer, only to slam it a moment later.

Mac studied Isaac for a moment, his look dark, before he turned back to Thomas. "His boat capsized during a storm three years ago. Hiram didn't make it."

Hiram had drowned? The man had been a skilled sailor who could man a boat through the wildest winds. He could swim like a fish too. It seemed nearly impossible Hiram would drown.

But then, it had seemed nearly impossible a large man like himself with experience working underground would almost die in a rock fall. His shoulder throbbed with the memory, and he pressed his hand to the injury. What was that Bible verse about the length of a person's life? Something about how it was a vapor that appeared for a little while and then vanished.

Which was all the more reason he needed to convince Jessalyn to come to South Dakota. Life was too short for a man to turn his back on the gifts God gave him, like a wife and daughters.

But as for Hiram Cummings's death... He turned to Isaac, slamming about the kitchen with tight, jerky movements as he poured oatmeal into a pot. "Elijah couldn't rescue your pa? He sure seems like he knows what he's doing out there in those storms."

"Elijah wasn't here." Isaac's words were sharp and caustic, filled with a sharpness he'd never thought to hear from one of Hiram Cummings's boys.

"Elijah left town to sail the Atlantic shortly after you," Mac answered. "He started his lifesaving team after Hiram died. Doesn't want anyone else losing a pa if he can help it."

Thomas could almost feel the cold spray of Lake Superior as he clung to the mast of the ship yesterday while waves washed over the deck. Yet another time his life had been spared. Except Hiram's life had probably been more worthy of sparing than his own. He had so very much to be thankful for.

Thudding sounded from the bottom of the stairway, then girlish voices and giggles floated up the stairs. A moment later three girls with silver-blond hair and bright blue eyes appeared. His daughters looked so much like Jessalyn a person would never be able to guess who fathered them. The ache that had welled in his chest when he'd first seen them yesterday returned.

"Claire!" The oldest of Mac's two girls rushed up. "Do you want to build a snowman with us?"

The children erupted into a fit of shrieks and giggles while Mac stood and donned his winter coat. "Jane, best put your coat and mittens on."

His daughters were the girls Mac's children wanted to play with? He'd not had a clue. What other friends did his girls have? Ruby

Spritzer was sure to have children Olivia and Claire's age, if the family was still in town. Did they play together?

He scratched the back of his head. There was so very much he didn't know about his children. He'd wanted to play with them yesterday, but as he stood in this strange apartment, watching their smiling faces and listening to their young voices, he may as well be trapped in a cage of glass. Able to watch, but not able to speak or play.

Could he offer to build a snowman with them? Would they want his help?

Did they even remember him?

Olivia stepped away from the others and came toward him, a scarf tied around her head to cover her sore ear. "You were at Dr. Harrington's yesterday. Are you... are you really my pa?"

The younger children quieted and turned their direction. Isaac's gaze bored into his back from behind, and Mac made no pretense of looking elsewhere as he helped his younger daughter push her arms through her coat.

"I really am, yes." Thomas swallowed. "Though I'm sorry I've been gone so long."

She tilted her head to the side. Did she always do such a thing when she was thinking? Or only when she had an earache? Jessalyn would know, and possibly even Mac and Isaac. Yet another thing he needed to learn about his family.

"You used to sing." Her voice was soft as she spoke. "In thunderstorms. You sang a song about the thunder, and it would help me sleep."

I see the stars, I hear the rolling thunder, Thy power throughout the universe displayed. The words and melody came back to him, as did the feel of his oldest daughter's slender body curled against him while she trembled during a summer storm.

"'How Great Thou Art.' You probably sing it in church sometimes." If they went to church.

"Claire doesn't remember you." She watched him with blue eyes that seemed far too old for her ten years. "And Ma says you ran off right after you put Megan in her belly."

"I didn't..." *Run off.* But that was a conversation he needed to have with his wife, not his daughter. "I'm glad you remember. I liked singing to you."

She pressed a hand to her ear, her brows furrowed with pain she must have been hiding when she'd come inside. "Now that you're back, will you sing again?"

"If you want me to." He glanced out the window at the snow coating the roof of Jessalyn's building. "It might be a while before there's another thunderstorm though."

Olivia laughed, not the childish giggle of her younger sisters, but the older, more mature sound of a girl not that many years away from becoming a woman. "It doesn't need to be for that. Do you know any songs to sing when you're sick?"

He cleared his throat and looked into those clear blue eyes that were so like her mother's.

"Jesus, lover of my soul, let me to Thy bosom fly,
While the nearer waters roll, while the tempest still is high.
Hide me, O my Savior, hide, till the storm of life is past;
Safe into the haven guide; O receive my soul at last."

The sweet notes and words were almost like breathing to him, but silence greeted him after he sang the final note, and once again the heaviness of everyone's gaze weighed him down. He had sung the entire hymn over and over to himself in the weeks following his accident, when the doctor had thought he might lose his arm. He could hardly help that he loved singing it, or that the words and melody brought him peace.

"Is there more?" Olivia finally asked, her hand still pressed to her ear.

"Three more verses." Though his throat felt thick and scratchy after singing only the one. "Perhaps I can teach them to you after we build that snowman?"

Her face lit with a smile. "All right. You won't forget or be too busy, will you?"

Too busy? For his daughters? *Never.*

Except that wasn't quite true, because he'd been too busy to leave South Dakota and get them ever since he'd built his hotel.

"No, I don't have anything planned for today." Besides convincing Jessalyn she needed to come to South Dakota.

His smallest daughter, a girl he hadn't even known existed until yesterday, bounded forward to stand beside Olivia. Her coat was buttoned all the way up to her neck, and her knit cap was pulled tight over her blond ringlets. "I want a snow doggy. Mama won't let us have a real doggy. Will you help me build a snow doggy?"

He hunkered down and ran a finger along the side of the girl's cheek, a smile creeping onto his face. "I'd love to help you make a snow doggy."

If Jessalyn was as easy to please as his daughters, he'd have the lot of them headed to Deadwood in no time.

Chapter Five

"You told him you wouldn't go with him? Jessalyn!"

Jessalyn cringed at the rebuke in her best friend's voice and stirred her tea, never mind her cup was nearly empty.

Across the table, Tressa Oakton closed her eyes and groaned, her wavy auburn hair piled messily atop her head while she held a tiny bundle against her shoulder. "He's your husband. What were you thinking?"

"Not about him being my husband, that's for certain." Jessalyn took a sip of bitter tea and refused to let the tears pricking the backs of her eyes drop. She'd shed enough tears over him five years ago. Becoming a watering pot now wouldn't do her or the girls any good.

"Oh, Jess." Tressa reached across the table and took her hand. The baby in Tressa's arms squirmed in protest at the movement, then settled right back into slumber. "I'm so sorry about all this. Well, not the part about Thomas finally returning, but about him wanting you to move. We'll miss you."

Jessalyn shot up from the table, the legs of her chair screeching across the floor. "Who says anything about me going with him? I told him to leave Eagle Harbor this morning with the sailors."

Tressa made a strangled sound, then sat back in her chair. "That doesn't mean he'll do it."

"He didn't have any trouble leaving me and the girls before." Oh, curse her wretched voice. Must it always tremble when she spoke of Thomas? "I don't know why he'd have trouble leaving us again."

"Elijah said something about him sending letters, but they went to Chicago instead of here." Her best friend's words softer this time, laced with a hint of something Jessalyn had no desire to ponder.

"Yes, he sent letters. And money."

"And that doesn't change anything?"

Jessalyn paced to the stove and lifted the kettle only to find it empty. Of course. Because there was still more tea in the pot on the table. She shook her head. What was happening to her? Thomas hadn't been back a day, and he was muddling every last thought she had. "I don't know what the letters mean. I suppose they mean he tried. But if he really wanted me and the girls back, why not leave his hotel for a few months and come get us? Why just send letters and money?"

"He did come get you, Jessalyn. That's why he's here now."

"And it only took him five years. Not five months or one year. Five whole years." She sank back into her chair and picked up the teapot, but her hand quivered so badly the lid rattled against the pot. "He might say he wants me to go to South Dakota with him, but how can I trust him? How can I know he won't abandon us if we have money trouble again? I don't have just myself to think of this time around. All of the girls are old enough to remember him."

Tressa stared down into her own cup of tea. "All right, I can understand why you're hesitating, even though I'm not sure I agree with it."

"Thank you." But was her hesitation only prolonging the inevitable? She was still married to Thomas, even if they'd spent half a decade living two separate lives, and that gave him legal rights to everything she possessed—no matter that she'd earned it without him.

"'Except the Lord build the house, they labour in vain that build it.'" Tressa's quiet words echoed through the kitchen.

"What was that?" She reached for the teapot again, managing to pour the liquid with nary a tremble in her hand.

"Psalm 127:1." Tressa patted Sarah's back. "Sometimes when I find myself struggling with Mac, or struggling with memories from my first marriage, I remind myself of that verse. God's the one who's in charge of building my life with Mac, not me, and certainly not my past with Otis. But I have a habit of getting in the way, of messing things up."

Except the Lord build the house… But no, it didn't apply to her and Thomas. "There's no point in discussing this. I bet he's already left town with the sailors like I told him to."

The tiny babe squawked, and Tressa rose from the table, swaying in that age-old motherly way while she patted Sarah's back again. "It seems awful improbable that a man who came all the way from South Dakota will leave after only talking to you once."

She'd had the same thought as she'd tossed and turned in her bed last night. What if Thomas didn't leave but found someplace to stay in town? What if he declared he'd wait all winter for her and the girls? She stared at the plain white wall of her kitchen that she'd always been too busy to paint. If Thomas had truly changed, if he was willing to stick by her rather than abandon her, then she'd have to give him another chance, wouldn't she?

She took a sip of tea and closed her eyes. A rush of memories flooded her mind. Good memories, the kind that warmed her heart the way the tea did her throat. Thomas mistaking her for the warehouse secretary the first time they'd met, and his rambling apology when he'd realized she was Henry's cousin-in-law instead. The spark of delight in his eyes the first time he'd called on her at Henry and Mathilda's house. The deep, happy laughter that had rumbled from his chest on their snowy walk back from the Chicago Academy of Science one winter day.

The way he'd smoothed hair back from her face in the falling snow and told her he'd make sure she never ended up back in the tenements. Then he was standing before her on their wedding day, his dark blond hair combed meticulously to the side and his cologne wafting toward her as he promised to love, honor, and cherish her until death parted them.

Crack! She looked down to find her tea cup lying on its side while tea quickly covered the table.

She jumped back lest it stain her dress.

"Oh dear. Here's a rag." Tressa rushed toward her with a damp cloth.

"Thank you." She took it and began sopping up the tea. "I'm sorry. I don't know what happened."

"I do. You were lost in thought and dropped your cup."

Her hand stilled on the tea-soaked rag, and she looked up and met her friend's eyes. "I don't know if my heart will survive if he stays, Tressa." How did she forgive a man who'd promised to cherish her until death, but had abandoned her instead? "I barely survived the last time around."

Tressa drew in a deep breath, then let it out. "I wish—"

"Jessalyn? Hello?" A familiar female voice called from downstairs.

Ruby. How could she have forgotten? The mother of eight was supposed to stop by for more mending this morning. "I'll be down in a minute!"

"Take your time," another familiar voice called, probably Lindy Harrington, the doctor's wife. The group of women who sewed for her must have all come together this morning. "We'll just look at the dress you've started."

"You go downstairs with the women." Tressa moved to the table and took the rag. "I'll clean up here."

"Thank you. I appreciate it." She spun away from the table and darted down the stairs to find Ruby Spritzer, Lindy Harrington, and Aileen Brogan in her shop. "Ladies, I'm so sorry I forgot."

"It's not any trouble." Lindy spoke from where she and the other women stood near the sewing machine, her blond hair glistening in the faint light from the shop windows. "I'm sure you've had other things on your mind."

That was one way to put it. Jessalyn glanced at Ruby and Aileen, neither of which had been at Dr. Harrington's last night. Had the other women heard of Thomas's return too?

"Is this for that fancy wedding in Chicago next summer?" Ruby fingered the emerald silk with her thin hands. "I don't think I've ever seen anything quite so lovely."

"Can ye imagine being able to afford dresses like this for yer weddin'?" Aileen brushed her hand against the fabric. "Aye, I bet those ladies will only wear this once and then be done with it."

Ruby dropped the fabric back to where it had been draped over the sewing machine. "A bolt of that fabric could feed my young'uns for a year."

More like a bolt of that fabric could buy Ruby a house strong enough to withstand the winter winds, unlike the hovel she currently lived in with her eight children.

Jessalyn scanned the shop, her eyes sweeping over the various stacks of clothing. Where had she put the extra mending? Ah, yes, there on the back table.

"Do ye have a sketch?" Aileen asked. The Irishwoman had come up from Chicago with Lindy and Isaac's twin sister Rebekah over the summer and didn't seem to mind that she was the sole Irish person in a town full of English and Cornish. "I always like looking at yer dresses."

"Yes, yes. It should be on the table there with the sewing

machine." She stepped around a basket of shoelaces on the floor, making her way to the back of the shop.

"This one?" Aileen held up a piece of paper, then scrunched her nose at it. "It's for a shawl, not a dress, and I think ye showed it to us last time."

Jessalyn looked back over her shoulder and blinked. The sketch of the new shawl was on the table? She could have sworn she'd filed that in her cabinet yesterday before she'd taken Olivia to the doctor's.

"I'll come look in a minute. Just let me get the clothes I set out for you first." She scooted past another basket on the floor and a heap of the quilting scraps she saved for Mrs. Kainer, before reaching the piles she'd put little paper tags on. Who said she couldn't be organized?

"Is this it?"

Jessalyn looked up to find Lindy holding up a sketch. "No that's the bridal dress. Well, not really, because I can't quite figure out what to do with the collar and sleeves." But hadn't she left that sketch beside the bridesmaids' one and not next to the shawl one? "Are you sure there's not another dress pattern by the sewing machine?"

Lindy shook her head. "Just these two."

"Maybe the bridesmaid's pattern is in the cabinet somewhere." Though she didn't remember filing it away. And while she might have a host of sketches stashed in her shop, she usually didn't have trouble keeping track of the ones she was currently using.

"We'll let ye get it out, iffin ye don't mind." Aileen cast a wary eye at the cabinet.

Lindy waved her hand in the direction of her stash of sketches. "Last time you told me to open that, I ended up buried in a mound of papers."

Jessalyn winced. That hadn't been pretty, and it had taken her over an hour to reorganize the papers. "Just a minute."

She shoved a pile of socks that needed darning under the table with her foot and moved another basket of lace.

"Can I get my things first? Ellie's at the bakery, and I just have Leroy and Martin watching the little ones." Ruby stepped around the pile of quilting scraps, carrying her basket. The woman's graying hair, worn face, and shadowed eyes contrasted with an unmistakable lump in her belly.

Could she be pregnant again? Ruby could barely afford to feed the children she had now, and she seemed too old to bear another.

It's not your business. Jessalyn drew in a breath. She'd started giving work to Ruby as soon as she'd had extra, had even taught the woman a little sewing so she'd have a way to provide for her family. With eight children and a husband who disappeared for months at a time, Ruby didn't have an easy life.

But despite how much she tried to help, Ruby had never once shared a confidence with her.

"Here's your pile." Jessalyn lifted it in her arms and plopped it into Ruby's basket.

"I was wondering, Mrs. Dowrick." Ruby ducked her head and lowered her voice so it didn't carry across the shop. "Do you have a few extra pieces I can take? Don't give me none from Aileen's pile, you hear? That woman, she needs work too. But maybe if someone dropped off something extra you don't have time for?"

"Yes, of course." She had piles and piles of extra work, which went part and parcel with being the sole seamstress in a town full of men who didn't have an inkling how to sew a button onto a shirt.

She spun around and found four pairs of trousers with the hems already marked. "Will these do?"

"Appreciate it. I was trying to save up, you see." She rested a hand on her belly, which looked almost painfully distended given how thin the rest of her frame was. "But then with Leroy and Martin and Christopher all getting the diphtheria, well, I owe the doctor something, and—"

"I'm sure Dr. Harrington will work something out about the bill." Jessalyn rested a hand on the woman's reedy shoulder. "He's always been good that way."

"It's not that." Ruby sniffled, and a tear plopped onto the brown trousers on the top of her basket. "Dr. Harrington says I don't owe him nothing, but that just don't feel right. I know that medicine he gave my boys cost money, even if I can't afford to pay for all the time he spent tending them."

"I understand."

"Thank you." Ruby rested her feather-light hand atop Jessalyn's. "Your help means a lot to me." Then she turned and headed to the door, her threadbare skirt swishing behind her.

Jessalyn pressed a hand to her throat. The hardest thing about moving to Chicago was going to be leaving Ruby Spritzer behind. If anyone needed the work she provided, Ruby did.

Yet how many more women like Ruby would she be able to help if her dreams for Chicago came true? Eagle Harbor had a handful of women in need of money, sure, but the Chicago tenements were teeming with them.

Aileen and Lindy had both moved up from Chicago this summer, and though she might not know all of what they endured, it had been clear neither woman had a penny to their names when they'd arrived in town. What if they'd been able to find work at a dress factory in the city? Would that have helped them?

Well, maybe not Lindy. She'd been glowing ever since her marriage to the town doctor, but something haunted Aileen. The Irishwoman hadn't fallen into life in Eagle Harbor as easily as Lindy. Would Aileen be happier in Chicago if she had a job there? Jessalyn tilted her head and studied the redheaded woman who'd decided to try opening her cabinet. Maybe she should invite Aileen to come along when she moved. She could certainly use the extra help getting started on her plans.

"You're mending is over here," Jessalyn called.

Lindy held up a sketch. "Is this the bridesmaid's dress?"

"No, it's—"

"What did you say you would do if Thomas stayed in town?" Tressa plodded down the stairs with little Sarah awake against her shoulder.

Jessalyn turned and narrowed her eyes at her friend. "Why?"

Tressa gestured out the window that overlooked the small yard behind them. "Because he's outside building a snowman with the girls. At least I'm guessing that's Thomas."

Jessalyn made a beeline for the window, or as much of a beeline as she could considering all the things she stepped around to get there. Outside, five girls and three men rolled snowballs until they grew as big as boulders. Thomas and Mac were nearly the same size, their broad shoulders and tall bodies unmissable, but her gaze travelled instantly to her husband. He moved with a quiet sturdiness, bending to chuck Megan beneath the chin and speaking to Olivia when she pressed a hand to her ear.

He'd been like that when they'd first met in Chicago. Steady, stalwart, always finding time to stop and talk to someone who might be injured or ill or just plain having a bad day.

Which made it all the more unbelievable that he'd left her and the girls for so long.

Jessalyn reached for her cranberry-colored coat hanging on the peg beside the door and slipped it on. "I'll be back in a moment."

"Take yer time," Aileen called behind her. "We found some other sketches to look at."

She hurried into the cold before her coat was fully buttoned. "What's going on here?"

"Mama, come help." Megan ran over and tugged on her sleeve. "We've already built a snow doggy. Now we're gonna build the biggest snowman in Eagle Harbor."

Thomas straightened from where he'd been rolling a snowball that now stood taller than his waist and headed toward her.

"Jessalyn." A smile curled his lips as he said her name, soft and tender and full of more memories she couldn't afford to dwell on.

"What are you still doing here?" she choked.

"Didn't you know, Ma? He's our pa!" Megan clapped her hands.

"You told them you're their father?" Of course he would. It was the truth, after all, even if it horribly complicated things for their daughters.

"I didn't, no." Thomas's breath puffed a cloud of white as he came up beside her. "But Olivia mentioned it upstairs."

"Upstairs where?"

He pointed to the second story windows above the telegraph office. "There's no room for me at the boarding—"

"I know." The entire town knew. It was one of the reasons she'd been so sure he already left. There wasn't anywhere for him to stay.

"So I'm staying with Isaac Cummings."

"You're staying with…?" She felt it then, the careful world she'd built cracking like glass around her. And she couldn't lose it. It was the only thing she could count on. Her shop, her business, her way of providing for her children. None of it included the husband who'd abandoned her. None of it included moving to South Dakota. None of it included letting her heart get broken all over again, or opening her daughters up to the pain of their father leaving a second time.

"Megan, dear." She reached down and patted her daughter's shoulder. "Why don't you help Mr. Oakton and Jane with their snowball?"

Her daughter turned and darted off, the snow scattering around her boots as she tromped through it.

"Jess?" Thomas's forehead drew down. "Is everything all right?"

All right? How could he ask such a thing? "You're supposed to be on your way back to South Dakota. Didn't the sailors leave this morning?"

He leaned an arm against the shop, half trapping her between a wall made of wood and another of big, towering man.

That wouldn't do at all. He was entirely too close and entirely too big and entirely too impossible to ignore. How was she supposed to keep her wits when his scent twined around her and his breath heated her cheeks?

He even had a bit of scruffy whiskers on his chin. Had he been too busy to shave, or had he remembered how she'd once liked to brush her fingers over the stubble on his face? To raise up and plant a kiss against the short bristles?

"I don't know what the sailors are doing this morning, seeing how I'm not going with them." His words sent another puff of warm, clean breath across her face.

"W-why not?" She could barely force her tongue to move. Could he not take a step back? Give her some room to think? "I told you to leave yesterday, remember?"

He bent his neck, lowering his head until she had no choice but to press fully back against her building or bump foreheads with him. "I'm staying, Jess."

"For how long?" She wet her dry lips. It was just as Tressa had asked upstairs, just as she'd worried herself. Did this mean she owed him another chance at their marriage?

"However long it takes."

"However long *what* takes?" Couldn't he see he was messing everything up? Or maybe he knew exactly how much of her life he was messing up, and he simply didn't care. He'd never seemed to care what she wanted before either, otherwise they'd not have wasted their savings on that ridiculous mining investment he'd claimed would make them money.

"Getting you to come with me."

Tears smarted her eyes, but she wouldn't shed them, not in front of the man who'd once promised her the world and then left her with nothing but ashes. "I told you yesterday. I can't go with you."

~ ~ ~ ~ ~

Thomas shifted away from his wife, giving her a bit of space. Staying was supposed to make her happy. After all, wasn't she glad he'd returned? Glad he'd decided to stick things out in Eagle Harbor for a few weeks rather than dart back to South Dakota?

Instead, she looked ready to dissolve into tears.

He rubbed the back of his neck, stretching his sore shoulder at the same time. He was going about things all wrong again, but what was he supposed to do differently? "Look, Jess. I'm not trying to fight with you or rile you. I promise. I'm just trying to make the best of things."

"Make the best?" Her voice stung, the low tone as piercing as the wind off the harbor. "Did it ever occur to you that the best was not to abandon your family?"

"I wanted you with me." His own voice shook this time, and he wasn't quite sure why. From anger? From frustration? From the sensation of standing close to the woman he'd pledged his life to and yet feeling as though a hundred miles separated them? "You're the one who refused to come."

"Because we couldn't afford to take four people across the country while you chased dreams of wealth! I wanted you with me too, but not in California or South Dakota or any of the other places you went. I wanted you here in Eagle Harbor. It's hardly my fault you refused to listen." She shoved her hands into her pockets, which had to be nigh frozen since she wasn't wearing mittens.

"I didn't know what else to do. Staying here longer... it wouldn't have been good, not after we lost our savings." He'd exhausted himself trying to make enough money for them to live on here. "I needed to leave, and part of you should be glad I did. I own a hotel now. My ideas for wealth weren't just dreams."

Besides, lots of families that settled the frontier sent the husband first and then followed later. He hadn't done anything unordinary.

But waiting five years to collect his family himself when they'd failed to come via letter?

He shifted closer again, but not so near she pressed up against the building. "That day I left, I never thought we'd be apart so long, and I never once imagined you weren't getting the money I sent. It was enough for you to live on. That should count for something. It's not as though I left you expecting you to fend for yourself. I left you so I could better provide."

"And yet I ended up fending for myself anyway." Her words weren't angry but soft, resigned, a mere whisper of the truth both of them already knew.

"Yes." He barely rasped the word over his aching throat.

"You weren't the only one who made mistakes, Thomas." The wind whipped at her hair, tugging a handful of flaxen blond tresses out of the pristine twist at the back of her head and blowing them across her face, yet still she met his eyes. "I was wrong too. I realized it after you left, but I never had the chance to tell you. I was too focused on money, too apt to believe that having more of it would solve our arguments and problems."

"You spent ten years living in one of the filthiest, poorest tenements in Chicago." Before her mother had died and she'd gone to live with her second cousin. What a shock it must have been to leave behind the squalor of that one room apartment and move in with a warehouse owner who could afford to host dinners and clothe himself and his family in fine suits and dresses. "I don't blame you for wanting to make sure you never ended up back in those tenements, even if it caused arguments between us."

"Thank you for understanding, but I still shouldn't have let money—what little of it we had—come between us. I'm sorry."

A smile crept across his mouth. Here she was offering him an apology when he hadn't even been in town twenty-four hours. Maybe if she was willing to admit she was wrong about before, she'd be willing to forgive him and come to South Dakota now. "I... I agree, we both made mistakes. I'm sorry too."

"I didn't expect money from you right away, no. But eventually, as more and more time passed without hearing from you..." She slipped a pale hand out of her pocket and wiped the hair away from her face, only to have the wind blow several of the strands out from behind her ear again. "At some point I started assuming you were dead."

Dead. Did she realize her guess was only off by a hair? That if he'd been standing five feet to his left when the mile tunnel collapsed, she never would have laid eyes on him again? "As I said before, I had no idea you weren't getting my letters. I thought you had them but were too upset to write me back."

She pressed her lips together, her blue eyes and blond hair and dark red coat a startling contrast of color against the white snow. "It doesn't matter now."

"It matters at least a little. Those letters prove I never meant to leave you entirely on your own."

"The past is past. Neither of us can go back in time and change things." Her gaze slipped around him to their daughters, whose happy voices carried across the snow. "I know you want to make up for the time we spent apart, but your version of that involves moving to South Dakota, and I can't because I'm moving to Chicago in the spring. I've got clients, well-paying ones, who want me to make them

61

dresses, and it's too good of a chance to pass up. So you really should consider going back to Deadwood now, before we get more snow and travel becomes more difficult."

Chicago? No. No. No. This was all wrong. He raked a hand through his hair. She'd just apologized to him, now she was supposed to forgive him and agree to leave for South Dakota.

Jessalyn dipped her head toward their daughters, where her gaze had been fastened this entire time. "And in that regard, I saw you were playing with the girls earlier."

His body, which had been warm from romping in the snow beneath his heavy coat, turned suddenly cold. She wasn't going down this path, she absolutely wasn't.

Except she was Jessalyn Dowrick née Hessleman. The woman didn't leave a pebble unturned or blade of grass unplucked if either stood in the way of something she wanted.

"They're everything to me, Thomas. The shop I own, all my hard work, it's for them, so they can have a better childhood than I had. I understand they're your daughters too, but you've been gone for most of their lives. I won't say you can't spend time with them, but please be careful. You'll have to say goodbye eventually, and I don't want them hurt when that happens. Olivia cried herself to sleep every night for a month last time, and that's not something I want to repeat with Megan or Claire."

Olivia had cried herself to sleep? Something twisted in his stomach. What other things had happened after he'd left?

"Since you've had them to yourself, maybe they should come live with me in Deadwood for the next five years. It would only be fair." He blurted the words before he could think better of them. He didn't intend to take his daughters from their mother, but he didn't want to never see them either. Surely it wasn't asking too much for Jess to move to Deadwood. If she could sew for clients in Chicago from

Eagle Harbor, why not from Deadwood?

"You wouldn't take them from their mother." Jessalyn's face had gone as white as the snow blanketing the ground.

"I want a chance to be their father. Ideally that involves you being by my side. But if you dig in your heels..." He tilted his head up to the sky, but the dark clouds didn't offer any insight. "I'm praying it won't come to that."

"You'd truly try taking them from me?" Her voice carried a panicked, squeaky edge.

"Jess." He nearly groaned her name. "Why are you looking for a fight when there doesn't need to be one? Just give me a chance."

"A chance to what?" She swiped more hair away from her eyes, this time keeping her hand behind her ear to pin the wayward tresses. "I know I was wrong for letting money get between us before, but that doesn't mean I can trust you now. And I certainly don't intend to give you another chance to abandon us. Especially with the girls old enough to remember you."

"I won't abandon you, not ever again, no matter whether you tell me to or not." He reached for her hand, which was probably half frozen, and rubbed her pale fingers between the mittens Isaac had lent him. "I was wrong when I took the last of our savings and left five years ago. I was wrong every time I sent a letter to Chicago rather than coming to collect you myself, each day I threw myself into work in Deadwood instead of leaving. I'm sorry, and I need you to forgive me. And then I need you to try building a life with me."

"I forgive you, Thomas. But as for building a life with you all over again, I don't see..." Tears gathered in her eyes, and she shook her head. "I can't..."

He sucked in a breath of sharp, frigid air. How could he convince her to try again? Or was everything lost to him? It was almost as though she'd turned into the miners in Cornwall, the people who took one look at him and decided he'd never amount to more than a drunkard like his father.

What would she say if she knew about his shoulder? Knew that if his hotel failed for some reason, he'd never again be able to earn a living by swinging a pickax, or pushing a tram filled with mine rock, or hauling crates around a warehouse? Would that make him only more worthless in her eyes?

Surely not. She'd never thought him worthless before. Maybe he was rushing into things, not giving her enough time to adjust to the idea of moving to Deadwood. He blew out a breath and met her eyes. "I still want a life with you, Jess. Are you sure you can't give me a second chance?"

Tears filled her eyes. "How am I supposed to build a life with you when I can't trust you?"

"So let's start with the trust part." He was a different man than the one who'd walked away from her five years ago. Surely she'd see that if they spent some time together. "What if we go to the bakery tomorrow after the girls are at school? We can sit and talk, catch up. You can tell me some of the things I've missed over the past five years, and I can tell you about Deadwood."

Her eyes flicked to the girls, and she bit the side of her lip. "I don't know, Thomas. I need time to think about it."

"Time to think about eating pastries with me?" Were they really that distant from each other? Yes, he'd been gone for too long, but in his mind, she'd still always been his wife.

While you'd been dead to her.

She shook her head again, her eyes still moist with tears. "We both know it's not just eating pastries."

"No, but I'd like to try it anyway." *And have a chance to prove myself to you. A chance to show you I've changed.*

She gave her head a small shake. "This is all coming so fast. At this time yesterday, I thought myself a widow. But I'll let you know, about the bakery, that is. Will you send the girls in if they start to get cold?"

She didn't really wait for an answer, just turned and disappeared into her shop, closing the door on him.

But the door to a life with her wouldn't stay shut to him forever, would it?

He couldn't afford to let it, not with three beautiful daughters and a lovely, if hurting, wife at stake.

Chapter Six

Elijah Cummings lifted the cup of piping hot coffee to his mouth, then held it there for a moment, inhaling the steam and letting the warmth brush his face and seep into his hands. It had been over twelve hours since he'd taken his swim in Lake Superior, yet his insides still felt cold.

His wife's voice drifted across the room, the rich, steady cadence of it as soothing as the warmth from the coffee.

He took a small sip, then another, before setting his mug on the kitchen table and looking toward the open parlor where Victoria sat reading on the sofa. Three-year-old Toby snuggled on her lap and five-year-old Alice pressed against her side. Jack, who was entering that painful stage where a boy becomes a man, sat on the other side of the room, head bent over his whittling as though he was too mature to listen. But when the riverboat in the story almost collided with a fishing vessel, the boy's hands stilled on his wooden figure and he looked up at Victoria.

Elijah sighed and stared down into the murky brown of his coffee. She was going to have trouble saying goodbye when it came time to give the children back.

He leaned back in his chair and reached for the top drawer on the hutch, the one filled with papers and pencils. He pulled out the first sheet of paper and read the words he'd nearly memorized by now.

O'Byrne—Information wanted about Norman O'Byrne, who left his family near the Central Mine in May, 1883. His late wife's name was Beverly, and he had four children in his charge, Jenny, Jack, Alice, and Toby. Any information will be thankfully received by the sheriff of Eagle Harbor.

The ad had been printed in the paper over in Central and circulated up in Copper Harbor, over at Lac LaBelle, clear down into Eagle River, and probably even in Calumet. He hadn't gotten a single response when he'd been acting as sheriff, and as far as he knew, Isaac hadn't gotten any word either.

Was it because the man's name wasn't truly Norman O'Byrne? Jack had said they'd gone by a different surname in the town where they'd lived before. But still, O'Byrne was the only name he had to go on.

Elijah sighed. It'd be one thing if they knew the children's pa was dead, knew the O'Byrne young'uns needed a home. But what were they supposed to do with three children whose older sister had died while waiting for their father to return?

Besides keep them.

And fall in love with them.

Elijah stiffened. No, seeing to the children's needs was one thing, but getting too attached wouldn't lead to any good, specifically where his wife was concerned.

A thumping sounded from outside, the telltale sound of someone coming into the entryway. Elijah turned toward the kitchen door that led to the room where they hung their coats and dried their boots— a necessity for any house in Copper Country at this time of year.

Another day, he'd have gotten up and opened the door. But his muscles still ached from rowing the surfboat through the storm yesterday. It was probably just Mac, who didn't bother knocking anyway.

But Isaac stepped inside, his boots and coat gone and his stockinged feet treading across the kitchen floor. Elijah hid his grimace behind another sip of coffee.

Maybe Isaac was here for Ma. She was in the bedroom catching up on some correspondence—and probably hiding from the noise that had been filling the house with young'uns around.

"You look like the lake chewed you up and spit you out." Isaac plunked himself across the table, empty mug in hand.

"Morning." Elijah set his coffee down and braced for the lecture that was sure to follow. When would he stop going out on rescues? Stop risking his life? Didn't he know he was going to end up buried on the top of the hill, his body lost at the bottom of the lake, like Pa?

Isaac reached for the kettle filled with coffee, then snagged a biscuit off the platter in the center of the table. "I've been thinking about Mrs. Ranulfson and her stolen jewelry. I don't know where else to look for the necklace and earrings."

Elijah narrowed his eyes. Isaac had come to discuss sheriff business and not lecture him about yesterday's rescue?

"Well?" Isaac polished off a biscuit in three bites. "Don't you have any ideas?"

Elijah shifted. He should. He'd been the temporary sheriff before Isaac had been elected, and even for a week after the election, when Isaac had still been in quarantine from his own case of diphtheria.

"Have you asked their neighbors? Maybe somebody saw something suspicious." He'd been so busy handling the diphtheria epidemic and making sure people abided by their quarantines that he hadn't had time for much investigating.

"Already did that. Are you sure there wasn't anything unusual when you checked the Ranulfson's bedroom? I'm thinking if there was some kind of clue, it would have shown up right away, not a month after the fact."

Elijah shook his head. "Not that I know of, but it's not like I had all that much experience sheriffing."

"And I have so much more." Isaac ran a hand over his auburn-colored hair, then slumped over his coffee. "You have to help. I'm out of ideas, and Mrs. Ranulfson has taken to calling on me daily to see if there's any news about her necklace and earbobs. If she can't find me at the sheriff's office, she comes to the apartment."

Elijah winced. He could well imagine Betty Ranulfson clomping up the stairs to Isaac's apartment, muttering about how the steps were too steep or too narrow or too something, ostrich feathers swaying on her overly large hat, and all so she could demand news from Isaac.

"Oh." Isaac grabbed yet another biscuit off the platter. "I invited Thomas Dowrick to stay with me for a bit. Figured I should tell you before you hear it from somewhere else."

"The wastrel that left his wife and daughters?" He eyed his brother.

"He's not a wastrel, and he seems awful intent on winning his wife back and spending time with his daughters."

"How long is 'a bit?'"

Isaac shrugged. "I think he's resigned himself to staying through winter. Though if the way he and Jessalyn were arguing earlier means anything, I doubt he'll convince her to move to South Dakota by then."

Elijah opened his mouth, then snapped it shut.

Isaac wasn't fighting with him about yesterday's rescue, but had opened his apartment to a man that abandoned his family?

That bout with diphtheria must have addled Isaac's brain, because though the man sitting across from him looked like Isaac with his tall frame, unruly auburn hair, wide shoulders, and narrow waist, he certainly wasn't acting like the brother he'd known for the past twenty-two years.

"I made this for you last night," a sweet little voice said. Then a sheet of paper slid across the table in front of him. Elijah looked down to find Alice standing at his side, her dark eyes sleepy but full of hope. "Do you like it?"

The paper had a line running down the middle. One side had stick figures praying at a sofa, and the other had a stormy sea and a little boat, which was also manned by stick figures.

"It's you rescuing the sailors." Alice climbed onto his lap and curled her small body against his. "And this one is of me and Jack and Toby and Miss Victoria praying. Did you know we prayed for you last night?" A yawn cut off her words, and she rested her head on his chest.

Elijah swallowed. He'd known the young'uns would tug at Victoria's heart, but he'd not reckoned on them yanking on his. "It's a lovely picture, sweetheart."

She snuggled her head against his chest and let her eyes drift shut. "I'm sleepy."

"I can see that." He stroked his hand up and down her arm as she curled even tighter against him.

"Can you take him while I make some tea?" Victoria approached Isaac, a sleeping Toby in her arms.

"Looks like your reading put both of them to sleep." Isaac took the boy from Victoria and held him against his chest.

Elijah grunted. That was a picture he hadn't thought to see anytime soon, his brooding baby brother holding a small child.

"Reading is the easiest way to get them down for their naps. Though Toby in particular seems to crave my touch. I wonder how much Jenny or his pa bothered to cuddle him." Victoria filled a kettle with water and set it on the stove to boil, then turned back to them and crossed her arms loosely over her chest.

Elijah let his eyes skim down her, the dark hair that seemed to grow richer with each passing day, the pink lips that quirked up into a smile whenever her eyes rested on him, the lithe form that nearly stood as tall as he. If he got closer, he'd smell that expensive flowery scent she insisted was better than the rosewater and lavender water most of the other women in town used. Jasmine, was it?

"I want to keep the children past Christmas." At his wife's words, the comfortable warmth invading the kitchen left.

"What? No." Elijah set his mug down with a thump. It didn't matter that he'd seen this conversation coming since the first afternoon they'd brought the children home, this discussion wasn't going to be pleasant.

"They need to go back to the Harrington's. I'm sure Lindy misses them." The O'Byrnes were only supposed to be here for six weeks or so while the doc and his new wife Lindy settled into life as a married couple. There'd be nothing left of Victoria's heart if the children stayed on longer.

"Lindy won't mind if they stay."

Something about the way Victoria said it, the certainty and sadness that laced her tone, made him look up. "How do you know?"

She pressed her lips together, her face turning white.

He guessed the answer before the words left her mouth.

"Because Lindy's pregnant, or at least she thinks she is. She says it'll be another week or so before she knows for certain."

He drew in a breath, long and deep, then let it out. "I'm sorry, love." He opened an arm for her, the one that wasn't busy holding Alice, but she stayed beside the sink.

"I'm not sorry. Of course I'm not. What's to be sorry about? I'm happy for Lindy. I'm sure she wanted children. And she's been through so much. She deserves to have a happy family and a happy…" She pressed a hand to her mouth and blinked furiously.

"Come here." He held out his hand, and this time she came, clasping her palm tightly around his.

Isaac looked between them, his face almost as white as Victoria's, then he scooted back his chair. "I, ah, need to head out. Should I lay Toby on the couch?"

"Probably on our bed." Elijah stood. "I'll lay Alice down too."

"Don't leave on my account." Victoria sniffled and wiped at her damp eyes. "I'll be fine in a moment."

But Isaac was already halfway down the hall.

"Give me a minute, sweetling." Elijah patted her arm, then followed Isaac into the bedroom.

His brother had already pulled back the covers and positioned Toby in the bed. Elijah laid Alice beside her brother before pulling up the quilt.

"Speaking of pregnant women." Isaac spoke low as he slipped a hand into his pocket. A moment later he pulled out a letter. "I guess this came in the day before the storm, but Mr. Foley forgot to give it to Victoria when she was in the mercantile yesterday."

Elijah recognized the prim, elegant handwriting on the sealed envelope, and his heart plummeted. "Beatrice had her baby, didn't she?"

"Don't know, I didn't open it."

Victoria's sister had been due at the beginning of November, and his wife had been watching the mail for weeks. Elijah took the envelope, a lump rising in his throat. Did he tell her today and let her get all her crying over at once? Or did he wait until she'd calmed down and hope she might take the news better?

"Thanks for not giving it to me in front of her."

"Truth is, I would have forgotten if she hadn't mentioned that bit about Lindy being pregnant." Isaac glanced toward the door, as though expecting Victoria to appear and snatch the letter. "I'm sorry, Elijah. Really. Victoria is a fine woman, and I know how much having a babe means to her."

Elijah fiddled with the corner of the envelope. Maybe he shouldn't be working quite so hard to find the O'Byrne children's father. If the man never showed up, then what would prevent him and Victoria from raising the children as their own? And what was he thinking? He had to find their father, if for no other reason than they couldn't keep going like this. The longer they had the children, the worse it would be when their father returned. And the last thing his wife needed was more heartbreak.

~ ~ ~ ~ ~

"Sure I can't offer you a drink, Sheriff?"

Isaac stiffened at the sound of the smooth, cultured voice, then turned to face the speaker. Though he sat at the back of the room with a clear view of the tables and door, he hadn't noticed Reed Herod approach from the side. Had that been intentional on Herod's part? Or was he showing signs of being a poor sheriff after only two weeks?

"About that drink?" The owner of Eagle Harbor's one and only brothel sat down, then slid a glass of foul smelling amber liquid across the table to him before taking a sip of his own. "You look like a whiskey man."

"I'm here to work, not drink."

Herod chuckled. "I don't think anyone in the place doubts that with the way you're sitting here glowering."

"I'm not glowering. I'm watching."

Raunchy piano music echoed from the other side of the bar. And smiling lumberjacks and miners filled the tables and talked with too loud voices, all while leering at the waitresses with low-cut dresses and heaving bosoms who would go upstairs with them for the right price.

Would he get used to it? The rowdiness and lechery that crowded this place? An itching sensation crept over his skin. He'd come from a home where they quoted Bible verses after dinner every night, not where they sang lewd songs. He could only imagine what his pa would have done if they'd gone to dinner and he'd stared down their waitresses' dress—and it wasn't laugh and jeer and elbow him.

"You didn't even smile when Star approached earlier." Herod set his whiskey glass on the table with a thunk.

Was it bad of him to hope a fight broke out so he had a reason to end this conversation? "Yeah, well, I probably don't get the same amount of enjoyment from ogling your women as the rest of your patrons."

The brothel owner chuckled. "That tells me you need to take one upstairs. Work out some of the tension you're always carrying around."

Isaac's stomach churned, never mind he hadn't had a drop of the swill in front of him. "I'm not going upstairs with any of your women."

"It's on the house."

"No."

Herod's lips curved into a smile. "Didn't think so. But a man has to try."

"Or a man could leave another man alone so he can do his job."

Herod reached over and snagged the untouched whiskey, then leaned back in his chair and sipped. "I voted for you in the election."

Isaac kept his eye on the group of men tromping through the door. "The other sheriff was dead, and I was the only name on the ballot. Everybody voted for me."

"No, even if you'd been running against Jenkins, I would have…"

The commotion near the door grew louder. The lumberjacks dressed in red and black plaid mackinaw coats were being crowded by the two burly guards that patrolled the brothel.

Herod jutted his head in a shanty boys' direction, then turned to him. "Have you run into much trouble with the new loggers?"

"Broke up two fights at the Wagon last week." Isaac crossed his arms. "They said you wouldn't let them into the Penny anymore."

"I can't figure out where they're staying or what logging camp they're working. If it's close enough for them to come to town every night, you'd think someone would know about it."

"Probably a haywire camp they don't want you to find." Though most haywire camps didn't bother hiding. There wasn't anything illegal about felling trees without proper equipment. Men who valued their lives knew not to work at such places, and those who didn't, well, they were also the type to come into town and make trouble in their time off.

"Probably." Herod fiddled with his whiskey glass, but didn't sip. "While everyone was sick with diphtheria, they gave me enough trouble that I kicked them out."

Which explained why they'd taken up at The Rusty Wagon. Since that bar was across the street from his apartment, it was easy enough to keep an eye on things there. But it didn't look like he'd be getting a lot of calm, peaceful nights this winter either.

"Do you want me to remind them they're not allowed in?" Maybe they'd listen to a man with a star on his chest better than the brutes that worked here. Isaac scooted his chair back, but Herod's hand on his shoulder stopped him from rising.

"I've got it handled. Though I can't promise you won't have trouble with them when they leave."

One of the guards approached their table and stopped near Herod. "The leader wants to know if a couple of them can come in and use the women."

The sickening sensation twined through Isaac's stomach again. What would Herod think if the town sheriff grabbed the empty whiskey glass and emptied his stomach into it?

"Two at a time, and no service at the bar." Herod leaned back in his chair, surveying the shanty boys. "If they prove they can behave with those rules, then we'll discuss opening the bar to them. They need to understand I run a tight establishment. I don't want trouble here, and neither does the sheriff."

"I don't want trouble anywhere, Herod, including a brawl on the street right outside your door."

The other man shrugged, evidently not concerned as long as none of his glassware or tables would be ruined in a fight.

"All right." The guard turned and headed back for the door, his slow plod causing the other patrons to quiet and watch as he passed.

A few moments later, whoops and hollers sounded from the loggers. Then one of them made a big production of stepping forward and heading toward a waitress. He tipped her head back and kissed her on the lips, causing more hollers to follow. Then he grabbed the woman's hand and tugged her toward the staircase. She didn't seem to mind in the least, even turned back to the room, winked, and blew everyone a kiss before she disappeared up the stairs.

Isaac nearly reached for the empty whiskey glass.

"Daisy was a good choice." Herod drained the last of his swill. Did the man sense that he might need to empty the contents of his stomach into two of the cups? "Men always leave her bed happy. If you change your mind about my offer, I'd recommend Star for you. She's the quieter type. Won't mind your brooding."

Star and Daisy. What kind of names were those? And what kind of man found enjoyment in letting an entire brothel know he was taking a woman to bed? Isaac pushed back from the table and stood. "There doesn't seem to be much trouble in here tonight. I'll be either at the Wagon or my office if you need me."

Herod's loud, bawdy laugh followed him across the room.

If he had a choice, this would be the last time he ever darkened the door of The Pretty Penny. But Eagle Harbor had two bars, one of which had a brothel upstairs, and most of the trouble in town broke out where the drinking took place. If he wasn't seen a couple times a week in those two places, then he was going to have a hard time maintaining order.

He grabbed his coat from one of the guards at the door, who'd taken it off its peg when the man had seen him coming. He shoved his arms through the sleeves before stepping out into the November night. The cold blade of wind off the lake sucked the air from his lungs. He stood in the road for a moment, looking east toward where the drive to his family's cabin lay a quarter mile down the road. Elijah would be there, alive and well despite the dangerous rescue he'd made yesterday. The lout was probably sitting by the woodstove with Victoria this very second, and Victoria just might have one of the O'Byrne children snuggled in her lap.

But instead of turning toward the warmth of his childhood home, he headed down North Street toward The Rusty Wagon. He supposed this was what a man got when he decided to run for town sheriff on his death bed. Did it matter his mind had only been half working when he'd agreed to such a thing, and that the working part had been convinced he was going to die?

Now that he'd been out of quarantine and wearing a star on his chest for two weeks, it was becoming more and more apparent that he didn't have the first clue what he was doing.

Isaac dug into his pockets for his gloves, then slipped them on. Ahead, the lights from The Rusty Wagon poured out the bar's windows. And across the street, a dimmer light filtered through the downstairs window of Jessalyn's seamstress shop, just like it always did this time of night. It seemed the woman never slept, always staying up until the wee hours of the morning to finish her mending after her girls had gone to bed.

Would that change with Thomas here? Maybe yes and maybe no, but one thing had already changed concerning Jessalyn—his help was no longer needed.

Was he crazy for enjoying carrying Olivia to the doctor or aiding Jessalyn with her firewood? Probably. But now Jessalyn and Thomas needed to get back together, which meant he should stay as far away from them as possible.

Especially with his habit of failing people when they needed him most.

Chapter Seven

Jessalyn bent her head over her sewing, ignoring the delighted squeals coming from behind the building—or at least trying to. This was the second day in a row Thomas had walked the girls home from school, and the third day in a row he'd played with them in the yard before sending them inside. Yesterday, they'd built a snowwoman to go with the giant snowman they'd made after the storm, but today they were having a snowball fight, one Thomas seemed determined to lose.

She sighed, leaving the emerald fabric on the machine and resting her head in her hands. If he was so interested in getting to know them, then why hadn't he asked her to go to the bakery again? She still wasn't sure she'd say yes, but if talking was so all-fired important to him, the man could ask her more than once.

Unless he was trying to make her stew over it.

She scrubbed a hand over her face. None of this should be happening. He was supposed to change his mind about waiting and leave. Any day now. He might have promised he wasn't leaving again, but he'd promised to cherish her on their wedding day too. It wasn't as though she could believe him straight off.

Except he hadn't left yet, and he was spending time with the girls. He'd written her letters and sent money the entire time he was gone, and he'd even apologized for not leaving Deadwood sooner to come get them in person.

She propped her elbows on the sewing machine and leaned her forehead against her hands. What was she going to do if he kept wedging himself into their family instead of deciding to leave?

The door to her shop opened, and the little bell above the door jingled wildly.

"Good afternoon." She stood and stepped out from behind the sewing machine, catching the expensive fabric before it slipped to the floor.

"Good afternoon." At the sound of the lazy Southern drawl, she looked up to find Dr. Harrington closing the door and hanging his coat on the peg beside it.

"Doctor." She stepped over a basket of leather thongs and around a heap of dark-colored coats that needed to be washed before they were mended. "Did Lindy send you for more work? I have plenty. Let's see. Where did I put the—"

"Not work, Jessalyn, at least not for Lindy." The somber tone in the doctor's voice caused her to still, though he weaved his way toward her through the piles of clothes and numerous tables scattered throughout her shop. "I need to talk to you about Olivia's ear. Is there someplace private we can go?"

She glanced out the windows facing North Street and the bar across the road. No one appeared to be paying her shop much attention, though several men loitered about The Rusty Wagon's porch. "Here's fine. The girls are outside playing, and I don't want to go too far in case they need something."

"How is Olivia's earache?"

"The same as usual. The pain is the worst of it. She cried herself to sleep last night, even after I gave her extra willow bark tea. But her fever wasn't bad this morning, and she said she wanted to go to school, so I let her. You said she can't get other children sick, right?"

"Right." But his voice held a somber note. "It might be best if you sit, Jessalyn."

Sit. Of course. She spun around, looking for a chair or two that wasn't piled with clothing. Unfortunately all she had was the stool by her sewing machine. She moved a heap of children's clothing off one of her other chairs before offering it to the doctor. "Sorry about the mess. I keep telling myself I'll get this place cleaned up, but the second I get a table cleared, more mending comes in."

"It's quite all right." The doctor sat, then simply looked at her, his green eyes weighted with sadness.

Her heartbeat quickened as she slid onto her stool. "There's not something wrong with Olivia, is there? I mean, I know she gets earaches, but lots of children get earaches. They'll go away eventually, won't they? And Olivia will get back to normal?"

"Usually yes, but Olivia is a special case." The doctor blew out a breath, his eyes meeting hers directly. "She needs surgery, Jessalyn."

Surgery. The word rattled around inside her head, not staying quite still enough for her to latch on to it. "Like the surgery you did on Tressa to save her and the baby?"

A little over a month ago, Dr. Harrington had done a fancy surgery to cut Sarah out of Tressa's stomach when the baby had gotten stuck during labor. Though the doctor claimed the surgery was dangerous, a person couldn't tell it from looking at Tressa now. She'd been about town after only a few weeks of recovering.

Maybe surgery for Olivia wouldn't be so bad, especially not if it took care of her ear infections once and for all.

"No." Dr. Harrington leaned forward and rested his arms on his legs. "I'm afraid the only similarities between Tressa's surgery and the one Olivia needs are that they both require scalpels and chloroform. Everything else will be different, including the doctor who does Olivia's and the place where it's performed."

"The doctor? The place?" Her voice squeaked, and her hands dampened with sweat. "What are you saying?"

"Please understand I'm not an otologist. Nevertheless, I'm concerned Olivia's ear infection has spread to the bone behind her ear, which is why it keeps coming back. I can treat the infection in her ear by poking her eardrum and draining the fluid, then keeping the area clean. But I can't treat the one in her mastoid bone. Her ear keeps getting repeated infections because the bacteria from her bone leeches into her ear.

"The surgery is called a Mastoidectomy." He shifted, causing his chair to creak in the otherwise silent shop. "And it's not something I can perform. I've sent out several letters regarding Olivia's case, and it turns out one of my colleagues from medical school is now an otologist practicing in Chicago. I wrote to him about Olivia's situation, and he thinks she likely needs a Mastoidectomy, though he can't make a decision without examining her himself."

Ear surgery. In Chicago. She bit the inside of her cheek and drew in a long breath through her nose. *Think.* She needed a moment to think everything through. She should be able to manage the surgery for her daughter, especially since they were moving to Chicago. "What does this surgery entail?"

"He'll make an incision behind Olivia's ear and remove the diseased bone before sewing the incision back up." Dr. Harrington turned his head to the side and used his finger to draw a line behind his ear.

"And this will get rid of her ear infections?"

"It should, provided the doctor removes all the diseased bone. I want to warn you, though, if the infection is extensive, she might lose some of her hearing."

"But she's so young." Jessalyn twisted her hands in her skirt, never mind the wrinkles it would leave in the sapphire blue fabric. "Are you sure these infections won't clear up by themselves?"

"She's been suffering from this off and on for two years." Dr. Harrington's voice took on a clinical tone, one that made him sound as though he'd spent half a century in medical school, even though he wasn't yet a half century old. "It's gone well beyond the pale of a usual childhood ear infection. I started writing letters this summer, when Olivia had her sixth ear infection of the year. She's had three more since. Furthermore, if her mastoid bone is infected, and we don't remove the infection, it will only spread."

"To more of the bone around her ear?" She worried her bottom lip with her teeth.

"To her skull, and possibly even her brain."

The air she inhaled burned its way down her throat until it felt as though her lungs were aflame.

Dr. Harrington reached out and took her hand, his skin startlingly warm against her cold fingers. "Infections in the head are nothing to be trifled with, Jessalyn. Even if Olivia loses every last bit of hearing in that ear, the surgery will still be necessary to prevent the infection from traveling further."

"That could happen?"

At the sound of the warm masculine voice behind her, Jessalyn turned to find Thomas standing by the backdoor that led to her small yard.

"She could lose all her hearing?" Thomas stepped farther into the room.

Jessalyn jerked her hand away from Dr. Harrington's. "What are you doing in here?" *And how long had he been there?*

"I wanted to take the girls to the bakery for cookies, if that's all right with you."

"Yes, sure." Anything so that she'd have a few minutes to herself to think about everything the doctor was saying.

A look of surprise lit his eyes. "Thank you. I thought you'd say no."

He had? Of course he had. The last time they'd talked she told him she didn't want her daughters getting overly attached to him. But he'd been so kind and attentive to the girls that she'd be a shrew to say no.

Or maybe she was being too soft by saying yes. She pressed a hand to her head. Or maybe she didn't have the first clue what to think at all these days.

"I'd still like to know more about the surgery, Doc." Thomas's gaze moved past her to the doctor, and he took another step inside. "Can Olivia really lose all her hearing?"

She bristled. "I can take care of this, Thomas."

"Olivia's my daughter too." Thomas came up beside her. "No matter how much you try to forget."

Heat rose in her cheeks, and she swallowed, unable to meet the doctor's eyes. What must a man like Dr. Seth Harrington think of them? A Southern gentleman through and through, he couldn't be used to people airing personal affairs in front of him, and today was the second spectacle she and Thomas had provided him inside a week.

"Just in one ear." The doctor's calm voice seemed to drain tension from the room. "And that's an extreme situation. Though the sooner you get to Chicago, the better."

"But it's winter. I can't take the girls to Calumet in the winter." It would be too cold and too long of a trip to the train station, especially for little Megan, who was barely five.

"I'll write Dr. Seaward and tell him to expect you in the spring. I never envisioned the surgery happening before then."

"But in the meantime, the infection will grow worse?" Thomas kept his gaze pinned to the doctor.

"It's possible." Dr. Harrington's chair creaked beneath his weight. "Though remember it's taken two years to get to this point. You don't want to leave a mastoid infection untreated for years, but a few months will likely mean more ear infections and little else. If you're insistent on going to Chicago now, I won't stop you, but I don't think the situation warrants—"

"As soon as the harbor opens, we'll take a boat to Houghton and travel the rest of the way by rail." Thomas hung his hands on his hips and gave a brisk nod. "Then we don't need to worry about early spring storms like we would if we went entirely by ship."

We? "I figured you'd be headed back to Deadwood right about then." Or maybe even a couple months before then.

"Suppose I can take a detour…" Thomas's voice was calm and even when he spoke, no hint of the anger simmering beneath her own words. "…Since it involves the health of my daughter."

"Well…" The doctor shifted uncomfortably, then rose. "If you've no more questions, I'll take my leave."

"Yes, yes." Jessalyn stood as well. "I'm sure you're anxious to get back to Lindy."

The doctor gave her a goofy smile that said his new wife was indeed the reason he didn't tarry longer.

"Can I ask one more question first?" She followed him to the front door.

"Certainly." The doctor slipped on his coat in a gentle, unhurried manner and gave her another smile.

But the fire returned to her lungs nonetheless, licking its way up her throat as she asked the thing that could ruin so many of her plans. "How much do you expect this surgery will cost?"

"I can pay for it, however much it is." Thomas's footsteps thudded behind her.

"No. I'll pay." At least she hoped she could. But she should have had the sense to stop herself from asking in front of Thomas.

"I'd not thought to ask the fee." Dr. Harrington settled his hat atop his head. "I was more focused on finding a remedy for Olivia than the money involved. I'll write the doctor, but as you know, mail is slow with the harbor closed."

If only he'd give her an estimate. Would a hundred dollars be enough? Considering her sewing job for the Hanover wedding, she should be able to manage a hundred dollars, but probably no more than that without cutting into the money she needed to move to Chicago and set up a shop there.

"Thank you for your time." She wetted her dry lips.

The doctor pulled open the door, letting in a gust of frigid winter air. "I'm sorry it wasn't better news."

"It's all right. I'd rather know and deal with the infection than let it go untended."

"Good day, then."

She closed the door behind the doctor and turned, only to find her husband's thunderous gaze riveted to her.

"There's no sense in you paupering yourself because you're too stubborn to take my money."

"I'm not paupering myself." She'd not argue the part about being too stubborn to take his money though. Except it wasn't being stubborn as much as being smart. Nothing good would come of making herself and her daughters dependent on the man who'd walked out on them.

Yet, he'd just offered to accept responsibility for their oldest daughter and her surgery. If he was waiting until things looked less than perfect to abandon them again, this was his opportunity.

She bit the side of her lip. What if she was wrong about him? What if he really had changed?

"You own a seamstress shop." Thomas lifted his hands to encompass the cluttered room. "Maybe you've got enough saved to pay for the surgery, but you can't have much beyond that."

A torrent of rage rushed through her, boiling her blood as assuredly as the woodstove in the corner boiled the soup simmering on it. If he cared so much about what she had, then where had he been during the two hard years she and the girls endured after he left? Where had he been when she and Tressa boiled the same chicken carcass three days in a row and shared the meager soup between both of their families? Or when their only bread had been loaves from the bakery that were so old Tressa couldn't sell them any longer?

Sending letters and money to the wrong address, too busy to come see her and the girls, was where he'd been.

"What would have happened if you hadn't arrived four days ago? Or if you'd been delayed another week on your way here? Who would be paying for the surgery then?" She straightened her spine and took a step closer to him, bringing them toe to toe. "That's why I don't want money from you for the surgery."

He raked a hand through his hair. "I told you, Jess, I thought you were getting those letters but were too angry to write me back."

"But I wasn't getting them, and you never once bothered to come check on us—for five whole years. You think you can come in here and throw about banknotes and news that you own a hotel and it will solve everyone's problems, but it won't." She crossed her arms over her chest, half to ward off the chill from standing near the open door with the doctor, and half because her hands itched to reach out and throttle Thomas. "The only thing that's changed is instead of figuring out a way to manage everything without you, I now wonder how I'll manage everything when you leave us again."

~ ~ ~ ~ ~

Not *if*, but *when* he left again. Their daughter needed surgery, and Jessalyn was more interested in fighting than letting him help Olivia.

Had she always been so hard? So certain everyone would hurt her? So callous toward other people's generosity?

He shook his head. He remembered her eyes lighting up when he brought flowers home for her. Remembered the smile on her face when he'd taken her dancing in Chicago. They might not have had the best marriage when he'd left, but she'd not been this hard either.

Was he to blame for the change?

Whether he was or not, he still needed to break down the barriers she kept throwing up if he had any chance of convincing her to go to Deadwood. He'd seen her peek out the window earlier, had half expected her to tromp outside and demand the girls come in without playing. At least she'd given him a half hour or so with his daughters, even if she still hadn't given him an answer about sitting down and talking at the bakery.

But how to make her accept money for Olivia's surgery? "I'm only trying to help, even if you don't see it that way."

She sighed, long and deep. "There's a part of me that appreciates that, Thomas. Truly. But simply put, I don't need your help."

"Ever again." He may as well finish her thought. Because she wasn't just refusing help with Olivia's surgery. She was bound and determined to never need help from him in the future, and her silence now only confirmed it.

She'd told him she wanted more money, that things would be better once they had some funds set aside, a bit of a nest egg so they'd never have to end up in the tenements. So he'd gone and done exactly that, and now she decided his money wasn't good enough? She used to look at him and see potential, see what he could become, even if he was only an immigrant living from one banknote to the next. She'd never been like her cousin-in-law, Henry, who treated the immigrants working for him like dung clinging to the soles of his boots. Nor had she been like the townsfolk in his Cornish village who'd decided he was fated to be a gambling drunkard while his mother yet carried him in her womb.

But now? He huffed and turned for the back door. He didn't know what she'd become now.

And she still doesn't know about my shoulder.

But telling her that meant confessing he was no longer the able-bodied man she'd once loved. Plus it would mean telling her how he'd injured his shoulder, which would lead to why he'd returned— and why he'd truly left in the first place.

She wasn't ready to hear any of it. He stepped around a table heaped with clothes and over a pile of socks. Did she always keep her shop this cluttered? A person couldn't walk from one side to the other without stepping around half a dozen piles of things and skirting two or three tables.

"You seem to get a lot of business," he gritted through the frustration that still clung to his voice.

She gave him a bitter laugh. "Too much. As though you can't tell by the state of this place."

Yet another thing that had changed about her. When he'd left, she'd wanted everything to be neat as a pin.

"I should check on the girls. I'm surprised they haven't come in yet and asked about the bakery." He'd leave the discussion about paying for Olivia's surgery for another day, when it had a chance of actually being a discussion rather than an argument or shouting match.

But the toe of his boot snagged on a basket of something or other on the floor, and he went careening toward a table piled with shimmering green fabric and papers.

"Be careful," Jessalyn called. "That's my satin."

He attempted to catch himself, but the table wobbled beneath his weight.

Crack!

He landed with a thud on the floor, the wooden table splintering around him while the papers went flying.

"Oh!" Jessalyn raced toward him. "I knew it was too messy in here. I'm so sorry." She gathered the shiny material in her arms and moved it to another table, then turned to survey the rest of the damage. "Are you all right?"

"Fine." Or he would be if not for jarring his shoulder.

"Just look at my sketches." She scratched her head, a frazzled type of panic on her face. "I should have put them away last night, but I meant to organize them first."

"Guess now they need to be extra organized." He grabbed one of the papers that had landed by his hand.

The dress was beautiful. The sketch alone caught his breath, almost making him ask what color it would be when it was finished. But he didn't bother to open his mouth, because he was already imagining the dress on his wife in a pale blue shade that matched her eyes. With her silky blond hair curled and piled atop her head, she'd be the loveliest woman in Copper Country.

Not that she needed a fancy dress to be beautiful, but—

"That goes here." She took the paper from his hand and set it on the sewing machine, which was covered with more of the shiny, deep green fabric.

"It would be prettier in blue," he muttered. "Like your eyes."

"What was that?" She bent and started piling papers into her arms.

"Never mind. Is that your design?" He gestured toward where the paper now sat on the sewing machine.

"Yes. I'm making bridesmaids' dresses for a wedding next summer."

"In Chicago." No one in Copper Country would have dresses so fancy for bridesmaids. This must be one of the wealthy clients she'd spoken of, one of the reasons she planned to move.

The back door opened without so much as a knock, and Isaac Cummings poked his head inside. "You're girls are asking about… Oh. Looks like you had a bit of a mishap."

"You could say that," Thomas drawled.

Jessalyn shook her head. "It's my fault. If I didn't keep things so messy, this wouldn't have happened."

Isaac looked between him and Jessalyn. Could he tell he'd interrupted something, even if it had been a terse conversation? "Want me to take your girls to the bakery for you? Give you a chance to clean it up?"

"That'd be great. Thanks," Thomas quipped before his wife could respond.

Jessalyn glared at him but didn't offer another answer.

"See you after a bit." The door shut behind Isaac with a soft click.

"That was unnecessary." She plopped herself on the floor, where she piled her stack of papers in her lap before picking up more. "I was going to suggest you take the girls while I cleaned."

"I'd rather talk to you."

"About women's couture? I doubt it."

"About what's important to you, what you've spent your time doing while I've been gone." He jutted his chin toward where the sketch of the bridesmaid's dress sat on her sewing machine.

She looked at the floor, completely engrossed in the papers she picked up and not seeming to mind the silence filling the air between them.

"I asked if you were making that dress for a wedding in Chicago." He gestured to the sewing machine draped with green fabric.

"Yes." She continued to pick up papers without so much as a glance in his direction.

"Are you making the wedding dress too?"

She frowned. "I'm supposed to, but I can't get the design right. I just had the sketch, now where'd I put it?" She rummaged through the papers in her arm, mumbling under her breath.

Thomas stretched his sore shoulder, then leaned over and picked up several of the papers near him.

"Is this for another bridal party?" He held up a drawing of a dress with buttons sewn down the line of the bodice. "I like it, even if it's not as fancy as the other."

She glanced absently in his direction. "No, that's for the factory."

"The factory?" He picked up another paper, found another dress that he couldn't quite call highfalutin', but that had a polished look to it, like most of the clothes his wife wore. "Is this for the factory too?"

She didn't look his way as she stretched to collect more of her papers.

"And this?" He picked up half a dozen sketches that his wife stayed silent about before he came to a printed picture of a large machine. Definitely the type of thing that would go in a factory. "You can't try telling me this is for a seamstress shop."

She looked up, then waved him off once more. "That's textile machinery. I told Gilbert I had no need of it, but he suggested I keep a file on textile production since any changes there will affect the fabric I get."

He picked up the paper that had been lying beneath the one with the textile machine and found himself staring at a drawing with two long rows of sewing machines inside a narrow building.

"This one is of the factory." He spoke more to himself than her. If she refused to talk to him, then he'd let the sketches and prints tell the story.

But she snatched the paper away. "If J.D. Designs gets that large, yes. I'll be starting with a smaller shop this summer."

"But employing more than just yourself, and mass producing dresses." He hadn't even begun to guess. And why would he? How many women with an absent husband planned to start factories?

"Gilbert says I won't be mass producing dresses at that point. Still, I can have my workers make numerous versions of the same dress and put them into Chicago stores, while I'm personally creating individual dresses for high paying-customers." The words tumbled from her mouth in a rush. "I should be able to purchase a factory like the one in the sketch in five years' time, possibly four, if things go as well as I hope. Then I can employ as many as thirty women."

She stopped to suck in a breath of air, then swiped a strand of hair away from her face. "Gilbert knows of several who've had husbands injured on the docks and are in need of work. And he says we can go to shelters and see about hiring women from there too. I'll look for women with children to care for. If I can give them jobs, then they can provide for their families and possibly even purchase a home like I've done here. Or start their own businesses. The possibilities are endless."

He rubbed his head, which was starting to pound with the new information swimming inside it. "Who's Gilbert?"

"Gilbert Sinclair." Jessalyn tucked another strand of golden blond hair behind her ear and picked up another paper. "I suppose he was away at school for most of the time you lived here, but surely you remember Byron Sinclair's second son."

"A Sinclair has been helping you?" He sat back. "Be careful, Jessalyn, that family isn't the type to do things out of the generosity of their hearts."

She picked up the final paper, reached for his pile, and then straightened them all into a neat, if unorganized, stack. "Perhaps not Byron or Warren, but Gilbert is as fine as they come. Did you know he married Isaac's sister, Rebekah?"

"Well if that doesn't beat all." Thomas rubbed the back of his neck. There'd been no love lost between the Cummingses and Sinclairs when he'd lived in town. "A Sinclair-Cummings wedding. Who would have imagined?"

The corner of Jessalyn's mouth tipped up in a smile, and she rolled her eyes. "I'm not sure how well the news went over with Elijah and Isaac at first, but they came around. It was a lovely wedding at the church in town. Then they had a cookout on the beach across the street, but the best part was when Gilbert gave Rebekah his yacht for a wedding present. He had it renamed after her."

Jessalyn's eyes held a certain wistfulness, and a slight smile curled the edges of her lips. Thomas swallowed. He'd used to make her smile like that, be the cause of the tender look that crept across her face.

Now she looked that way when she spoke of other people's lives, not her own.

What would she do if he pulled her to him, kissed her jaw, and nuzzled her neck? Tried to get that smile to reappear?

But even if she let him hold her, what then? He could promise to buy her a boat and rename it after her if she'd take him back, but that wasn't going to fix things between them, not with her planning to move to Chicago.

"I have more than just the dresses you saw." She gestured to the cabinet against the wall near the sewing machine. "It's filled with designs that can be made easily and quickly, but look fancy and elegant. The manufactured dresses sold at most mercantiles are so boxy and shapeless the buyer may as well wear a potato sack."

"Sure," he croaked, his voice rough and gritty. He looked at the papers piled in her lap, papers that explained why she was adamant about not going to South Dakota. She hadn't been lying when she'd said she'd made plans without him. And she certainly hadn't been lying when she said she didn't need his help.

So where did that leave him?

Besides without a wife for another five years or better.

Chapter Eight

Thomas stood at one of the windows in his room, staring at the bar across the street, only half seeing the men that loitered on the porch beneath the lantern light. His wife had plans to start a dress factory in Chicago, pages and pages of business ideas, and a whole cabinet full of dress sketches.

And she intended to hire women in need. Thomas rubbed the back of his neck. Somehow that hurt almost as much as knowing his wife concocted the whole thing without even a thought in regard to him.

Because there'd been a time when Jessalyn was a woman in need—and he'd been the reason for it.

He pressed his eyes shut and leaned his forehead against the cold glass of the window. Could Jessalyn open a dress factory in Deadwood instead of Chicago? Mining was hardly a safe occupation, as the pain in his shoulder attested. Oftentimes the women whose husbands died left Deadwood as mail order brides, since there was little else for them in the mining town unless they turned to the brothels.

Thomas tucked a thumb beneath the waist of the too-tight trousers he'd bought at the mercantile that afternoon. *How do I win her back, God?*

He still remembered the way her face used to light with smiles, the tinkling sound of her laugh and brightness in her eyes when he'd teased her. Or taken her for a walk in the snow. Surprised her with flowers.

Had he ruined any hope of a good marriage by leaving five years ago?

Somehow, everything had seemed ruined before that, and he hadn't a clue how to fix it then.

Just like he didn't have a clue now.

But he did know how to fix his trousers. Or rather, how to get his trousers fixed. He looked down at where the hem of the pant legs rode two inches higher than it should on his boots. He'd purchased the longest size the mercantile carried, but just like the mercantiles in Chicago and Deadwood, nobody ever stocked clothes quite large enough for him. Or if the trousers were big enough in the waist— like one of the pairs he'd found today—they were five inches too short at his ankles instead of two.

He'd gone for the longer choice. Jessalyn should be able to loosen the waist and let the hem down a bit, shouldn't she? His shirt pulled at his shoulders too. But with his luggage lost on the ship, he'd had little choice but to buy new clothes. He'd meant to ask Jessalyn to make him some earlier, but once the doctor had brought up Olivia's ear, everything else slipped his mind.

Big mistake. He could hardly breathe in these trousers.

Whoops and hollers sounded outside his window, and Thomas looked across the street to find more people had crowded onto the porch of the bar. Two of the men held another back by his arms, trapping him while a third man stepped forward, fists at the ready.

Where was Isaac? Thomas glanced down the street one direction, then the other, but the darkness hid any movement save what was going on beneath the bar's lanterns.

No man deserved to be held down and beaten. But there was something overly familiar about the man being restrained. Something about the way he stood. Something that…

Isaac. Was he not intervening because he was the man being held? Something shiny glinted off the man's shirt in the lantern light. A tin badge, perhaps? And he was the right height and build, tall and thin without quite being reedy. Turning, Thomas raced out the door and down the stairs, bursting into the cold night air without his coat. There were maybe a half dozen men against the one they held. His presence would make it two against six.

Thomas clenched his jaw, his nerves tensing. Isaac or not, hopefully the other man knew how to swing his fists.

"What's going on?" Thomas's boots crunched against the packed snow as he hurried across the street.

The man with his hands curled into fists turned his direction. "Ain't none of your business."

"Probably not. But I can promise it's the sheriff's business."

"In more ways than one." Isaac's voice was unmistakable against the quiet night.

So he'd been right about Isaac being held. Thomas quickened his pace to a dead run.

Most of the men on the porch were still looking at him, and Isaac used the distraction to jerk away from one of his captors, spin, and slam his free fist into his other captor's temple.

A sickening crack split the night, only to be swallowed by shouts and jeers.

The man that had been ready to throw the first punch swung at Isaac, but Isaac ducked just as Thomas bounded onto the porch. Thomas jerked the would-be assailant back by the shoulder, then hooked an arm around his neck, trapping the brute.

Another man swung at Isaac.

"To your left," Thomas shouted.

The warning was a moment too late. The man's fist connected with Isaac's jaw in another sickening crack.

Isaac returned the punch, felling his assailant with the blow, then drew his gun from his holster. "This stops here and now."

"I got me a gun too." One of the men behind them slurred.

"Quiet, Finney. You ain't sober enough to use it."

"Here now, Sheriff." The first man Isaac had punched raised himself up on his elbows. "We didn't mean nothing bad ta happen ta ya. We's just having some fun."

"Didn't look very fun to me." Thomas gave the man's neck he was holding another jerk back, just to make sure the man didn't get any fancy ideas about trying to swing Thomas off his back.

"The lot of you are under arrest." Keeping his gun trained on the men sitting down, Isaac stepped forward and handed Thomas a set of handcuffs. Then he moved to the drunkard with the gun, who was leaning against one of the porch posts, and locked the handcuffs on him.

The bar door creaked open, and a bearded man stepped into the night. "Need any help out here?"

Isaac snorted. "You're a little late, Neville. Don't suppose you got some rope behind the bar."

The bartender mumbled something and disappeared inside, then returned a moment later with a length of rope long enough to tie up only one of the four left.

"Thank you for making them come outside, Sheriff." Neville scratched the back of his head while Thomas secured one of the men with rope. "Didn't want my place messed up."

Isaac sighed, his shoulders hunched. "You're welcome."

"Better get back inside now." And with that the man left the two of them on the porch with the ruffians.

Isaac gestured to the two men on the floor, one of which was unconscious. "Check them to see if they have any weapons."

Check them? He was the son of a town drunk. He could break up a fight or ten— he'd certainly stepped into the middle of enough fights to defend his drunken father while growing up. And the mining towns he'd lived in over the years had no shortage of fights to break up. But he wasn't exactly a lawman.

He eyed the conscious man who'd claimed they'd just been having fun. How hard could checking him for weapons be?

"I don't got no gun." He scooted back until he pressed against the wall of the bar.

"Then you won't mind letting me look. Stand up."

The man didn't move. "I said I don't got no gun."

"Good, this'll be quick and easy. Now I told you to stand."

The man still didn't move.

Thomas sighed. The ruffian wasn't much bigger than Jessalyn. Did he really think sitting on the frozen porch was going to get him out of being searched? He bent and grabbed the man's arms.

Rip!

The unmistakable sound of tearing fabric filled the porch, and a cool burst of air flooded his backside.

Heat rushed his face despite the cold in his nether regions.

A laugh broke out behind him. Then someone hooted.

"Well, well," one of the ruffians drawled. "Maybe your helper there'd be better served down at the brothel instead of working with you, Sheriff."

A fresh round of laughter started, the guffaws and hoots so loud Thomas half expected everyone at the Penny to rush down the road and see what the commotion was about.

The skin of his face burned against the winter night. He reached behind him to feel a tear right down the seam of his backside, exposing his union suit to the world. That's what he got for purchasing trousers at the mercantile. But did this have to happen now? When he was trying to help Isaac?

He clenched his teeth together. The story about his trousers would be all over town the second Isaac let these hooligans out of jail.

Even the man he was about to search was laughing, his rancid, wheezy breaths souring the air between their faces. Lovely. Just lovely He'd spent his whole childhood in Cornwall being laughed at and mocked, and he couldn't even get away from it by crossing an ocean.

He hauled the man up by his arms, then thrust him against the wall.

"Pants a little small?" Someone choked out behind him.

Thomas removed the gun holstered at the man's waist. "They were the biggest the mercantile had."

The ruffian he searched was still chortling, all notion of resistance gone from his limp, laughter-ridden body. He didn't seem to be carrying any other weapons at his waist. Thomas scratched the back of his neck. Should he check somewhere else? He dropped to his knees and reached for the man's ankle.

Rip! More air flooded his backside, and another wave of laughter swept the porch.

He clenched his teeth as he lifted the man's pant leg and removed the pistol and knife strapped there. No sense trying to cover the tear with his hands. That would only make him look more ridiculous, and Isaac still needed help, rip or not.

"Might want to find yourself a new pair of pants come tomorrow," Isaac choked through his own fit of laughter.

Or maybe he didn't need to help Isaac. Could the man even keep his gun trained on the untied ruffians with the way he was laughing?

Then again, he might not need to. The rest of them were laughing too hard to make an escape.

"You can stop now," he gritted. "It's not like you've never seen a man with a rip in his pants before."

"Ain't never seen a man rip his pants quite that-a-way though," one of the men jeered.

"And he was helpin' the sheriff when he did it!"

Would their laughter never end? It wasn't that funny. Really, it wasn't.

He moved to the man lying on the porch, only beginning to come around after Isaac's punch to his temple. He didn't have an ankle holster or a gun at his waist, just a knife strapped to his belt. Thomas took the weapon and stood.

"I suggest you pay a visit to the seamstress first thing in the morning." Isaac's laughter settled, but he still wore a grin the size of Lake Superior on his face. "She might be able to save those."

"She's a looker, that seamstress is." One of the men standing against the porch railing elbowed his friend. "I got me three shirts at her place right now. Might stop by tomorrow to see if they're finished yet."

"Careful." Thomas's voice was low and deep. "That's my wife you're talking about."

"She ain't married." The big man he'd put in a stranglehold earlier smirked. "Everyone in town knows that."

Thomas took a step toward him. "You're wrong. She is married. To me."

The laughter slowly died until silence filled the porch. A few of the ruffians traded glances with each other, but Thomas kept his eyes riveted on the biggest of the group and clenched his hands into fists. One wrong word about Jessalyn, and he'd knock the man cold.

"Then how come we've never seen you around the place?" This from the person against the post that Isaac searched for weapons.

"If you ask me, a woman don't need to be single to have some fun. Sometimes them married one's the best."

Fists still clenched, Thomas spun to face the short man who'd just fought being searched and knocked the lewd smile off his face.

~ ~ ~ ~ ~

"Did you see what he done, Sheriff? I think Griggs will want to press charges."

Isaac slapped a pair of handcuffs on the man he recognized as the one who'd made a show of taking a prostitute at the Penny upstairs several nights ago. Then he turned the womanizer toward the stairs and led him onto the road where Thomas waited with the other three troublemakers. He'd already made one trip to the jail with the first two hellions, since he and Thomas alone couldn't haul six men down the road in a single trip.

"Griggs didn't do nothing to get punched for." The womanizer seemed intent on running his mouth. "'Specially not standin' there unarmed an' all."

"What a shame my handcuffs are already being used," Isaac muttered. All of them. He'd had to get his two extra pair when he went to the jail. The town of Eagle Harbor, with its one lawman and four sets of handcuffs, wasn't exactly set up to handle six men being hauled to jail at once. "Come on, now. Down the stairs. You've got a nice little cell waiting for you."

"Virgil there's got a point." The short, slender man who'd insulted Jessalyn looked over his shoulder at Thomas. "He ain't the law. I want to press charges."

"He's the law as soon as I deputize him." Still holding Virgil by the handcuffs, Isaac took the slender man by the shoulder and started them down North Street. A quick glance behind him revealed Thomas followed with the last two men.

"You can't just up and make anyone a lawman on a whim."

Did Virgil think all this talking was going to accomplish something?

"Sure I can." He might not be able to pay Thomas, but he had the authority to swear a man in as a deputy and give him a badge. He glanced behind him at Thomas once more, the man's shadow looming large in the night. He was handling his two ruffians as easily as though they were his youngest daughter's age. Sure wouldn't hurt to have a man as stocky as him around to help.

Sure wouldn't hurt to have anyone at all to help. In fact, after tonight, he didn't have a choice about scrounging help from somewhere. These loggers might say they were just having fun, but there'd been nothing fun intended when they'd dragged him out of the bar after he'd broken up a fight between two of them.

A chill slithered down his back. It had almost been as though the loggers waited for him to come into the bar before they started fighting. Had they set a trap for him? Something that would allow a group of men to stop fighting amongst themselves and turn instantly on him?

Why?

The only crime committed of late had been the theft of Mrs. Ranulfson's jewelry. And while the town banker's wife was determined to get her missing baubles back, that hardly seemed like reason enough for a group of lumberjacks to pummel him. Even if one of them had taken the jewelry, why draw more attention to himself with an unnecessary brawl?

That scenario simply didn't make sense. Were these loggers planning something big, and this fight was supposed to distract him? Or at least make him fearful enough that he ignored their illegal activities?

Isaac shook his head. He'd probably never know for certain what the men had been attempting to accomplish tonight, but one thing he did know—he'd be bloody and unconscious had Thomas not rushed across the road to help him.

"Want to be a deputy for the Eagle Harbor Sheriff's Office?" He called back to the towering man.

Thomas's wide shoulders rose and fell in a shrug. "Why not? Don't have much else to do."

"I still think Griggs should press charges," Virgil mumbled.

"Try it. See how far you get." Isaac pushed him and the other man up the steps into the brightly lit, if small, sheriff's office. "You're headed straight toward the back there."

He steered Virgil and the other lout toward the massive iron door at the back of the room. He could lock them in a cell for tonight, but without more evidence of wrongdoing, he'd have to let the lot of them go on the morrow.

Which felt about the same as giving a pack of wolves license to prowl Eagle Harbor during the annual Thimbleberry Festival.

He led them into the corridor that housed the jail and past the first tiny cell, already full with the two ruffians he'd dragged in earlier. The drunkard lay sleeping on the cell's single cot, and hunched in the corner, the large man who'd approached him with his fists drawn earlier now sat glowering, his gaze so dark and menacing a chill travelled down Isaac's spine. Thank God Thomas had come to help, because the man in the cell wouldn't have gone easy with the beating.

"This one here." Isaac gave Griggs a little push into the second cell, then stepped aside while Virgil followed. He locked the door behind them, then handed the keys to Thomas to lock his own two prisoners inside the final jail cell.

"Just a minute there." Virgil clasped the iron bars and peered at him.

"No." Isaac barely stopped himself from rolling his eyes. "Griggs can't press charges against Thomas. I'm deputizing him first thing tomorrow."

"Maybe second thing." One of the men near Thomas slurred. "Man needs to get himself a new pair of trousers first."

Red flamed onto Thomas's face, and another round of laughter followed, from everyone but Virgil, that was. The man stood suddenly somber inside his cell.

"This ain't about Griggs. I'm looking for my young'uns. Maybe you seen 'em? Left their older sister to care for them, but I found me a note saying she died when I got to the cabin."

Isaac stilled. Not the O'Byrne children. This man couldn't be their father.

But who else in town had a father away and a sister who died after she'd been left to care for them? Eagle Harbor was hardly teeming with young'uns, and the O'Byrnes were the only ones that came halfway close to fitting that description.

"You've been sitting around at the Wagon for two weeks, and this is the first you thought to ask after your children?"

The man shrugged, his round belly protruding over his britches. "Wanted to look around a bit. See if I spotted them on my own."

"Because so many children frequent bars after midnight," he muttered.

The man didn't even try to look abashed. "You're the law in this town, figured if anyone knew about some young'uns runnin' about without a ma or pa, it'd be you."

Isaac's tongue felt as heavy as a copper ingot. He knew about children without a pa, all right, had just held two of them on his lap when he'd visited his family for Sunday dinner.

The man narrowed his gaze. "You know somethin', don't ya? Now listen here, Sheriff. Thems be my young'uns. If you know where they are, you've got a legal obi… obo… oblagotation ta tell me."

Isaac scrubbed a hand over his face, his stomach curdling. He could already picture the silent grief on his brother's face when Elijah got his first look at Virgil. The unshed tears glimmering in Victoria's eyes at the thought of turning the children over to a ruffian. How was he going to tell them?

"Wait." He ran his gaze down the womanizer. "What did you say your name was?"

Elijah had been looking for a man named Norman, not Virgil.

"Norman Virgil O'Byrne." The man hooked a thumb beneath his suspenders and puffed out his chest as though the name were something to be proud of. "My friends here call me Virgil, but Norman's my official soundin' name."

"Where did you say you left the children? That you found the note?" But he didn't need to hear an answer, not really. He could look into the man's dark eyes and see they were the same deep brown as Jack's, his hair the same walnut color.

A fist tightened around his heart. Why had he ever agreed to run for sheriff? As if nearly being beaten tonight wasn't enough, he now had to tell his brother about the O'Byrnes' father, would probably even need to arrange an introduction.

Elijah had told him he'd make a good sheriff, but his brother didn't know the half of it.

Chapter Nine

Jessalyn set the red and black plaid mackinaw coat atop the stack of completed ones, then reached for the next one that needed mending and held it up. A jumble of coins fell to the floor and scattered. She rolled her eyes and bent to collect them. What was so difficult about cleaning out pockets before men dropped off their coats with her? Some days it felt as though she spent as much time stuffing things back into pockets as she did mending.

She set the pile of coins on the table, lest they fall again while she was mending the garment, then studied the coat. It was missing all but one of its buttons, two of which had left holes in the wool where they'd been torn off. It almost looked as though someone had yanked the coat open.

She had some buttons that should fit. She bustled around a table and stepped over a pile of trousers on the floor before reaching the buttons stacked on the shelf against the back wall. But where was the basket of men's buttons? And the children's buttons, for that matter? She kept five baskets back here, but somehow there were only three. And how had her basket of extra lace bits gotten on the shelf?

The girls must have been playing in the shop again. She pursed her lips together. Even Megan at five years old knew better than to move materials around. She grabbed the basket of lace and shuffled toward the next shelf, setting it right where it belonged—in the spot currently occupied by the basket of children's buttons? She'd have to talk to her girls when they got home from school today. But she needed the men's buttons now, not in six more hours.

She pushed onto her tiptoes and surveyed the shop. Where had the girls...?

The bell above her door jingled, and a gust of cold swept inside.

"Good morn—" She stopped when Thomas entered. She didn't need another interrogation about her dress factory, not when she had a stack of coats to mend and a second bridesmaid dress to start. "Sorry, I don't really have time to talk today. I'm in the middle of something at the moment. The girls just left for school, and I have to make use of my time."

Maybe she needed to hire a fourth woman to work for her, because at the moment, she was barely keeping up with her Eagle Harbor clients, and that didn't count the Chicago wedding job.

"I can wait." Thomas shrugged. "Olivia said you were busy on the way to school."

He'd walked them to school? She'd known he was walking them home, but she hadn't seen him around when she'd sent her daughters out the door in the mornings. Had he listened even a little when she'd asked him not to get too attached to the girls? Evidently not, which left her no choice but to...

What?

He was their father, after all. This was Megan's first chance to know him, and he was so good with their daughters, always carrying one of them around or making snowmen with them.

He cleared his throat. "Uh, aren't you going to finish whatever it is you're doing?"

"Oh, right."

She turned her back to him and forced her eyes to scan the nearest table for the basket of buttons. Not there. Maybe they were on the floor?

She glanced around for the rather large basket with its brown handle, or tried to, but her gaze kept drifting back to Thomas. He was making such a mess of things. Her plans had been so simple before. Go to Chicago, start a dress shop, help other people, start a factory, help even more people. But she'd made every one of those plans with the assumption her husband was dead. What was she supposed to do now that he—

Thunk!

She looked down, where her foot had just discovered the basket of buttons—and knocked them over.

Served her right for letting Thomas distract her.

"Here, let me help." Thomas made his way through the cluttered shop with a large sack in his hands. Had he been carrying it when he walked inside? "After we get this cleaned up, maybe I can order some trousers from you?"

Trousers. "I didn't realize you had work for me. I thought you were here to…" *Argue. Debate. Demand.* She looked back down at the spilled buttons rather than finish the sentence.

He squatted beside her, his large hands scooping up buttons at twice the rate of her small ones. "I don't mind waiting. Your windows are so large I can see half of North Street."

"Um, all right. That's… nice?" Why would he want to watch North Street through her window?

They both reached for the last two buttons. Her hand got there first, but Thomas's large palm clasped overtop of hers an instant later. Warmth rushed up her arm. She dropped the buttons and yanked her arm away, only to feel a different kind of warmth flood her face. That had been a simple bump of hands. Nothing more and nothing less. Why was she letting herself get so flustered over it?

Thomas picked up the last two buttons, dropped them in the basket, then stood and set the basket on a table. A moment later his hand appeared in front of her face, still as large and rough and familiar as when he'd worked in the mine, though he claimed he'd owned and ran a hotel for four years. "Can I help you up?"

She could get up just fine on her own.

But she wouldn't, because a man helping a lady off the ground was a completely innocent thing—just like a man and woman accidentally bumping hands.

He helped her to her feet and released her hand immediately after, his every action painfully proper, which drenched the room in even more awkwardness. She'd made three children with the man. How could such simple contact between them be so stilted?

"My trunk was lost in the storm. I've been to the mercantile to purchase clothes, but, well…" He dug into his sack and pulled out a pair of trousers.

Trousers. Yes, best think about the trousers and not her husband's large, calloused hands.

She ran her gaze down him. He'd never been able to purchase manufactured trousers, and she'd been making his clothes for as long as she could remember, right up until the day he'd left. The ones he held out now looked to be two or three inches too short. "What kind of fabric?"

He shrugged. "You pick. Just as long as it'll match the shirts I bought yesterday."

"Do those fit?" Manufactured ones had always been too tight across his shoulders.

A flush spread up his neck. "Ah, better than the trousers."

She glanced at the strip of plain cream shirt peeking out from beneath his open coat. "Is that one of your new shirts? Take off your coat and let me see."

He shrugged out of the plaid mackinaw that looked just like the others in her pile of mending. The taut movement across the fabric on his shoulders already told her the shirt was too tight.

"Turn." She twirled her finger in the air. "Stretch your arms in front of you."

He did so, and she sighed. He'd already strained the material along the back of the two shoulder seams to the point the fabric would fray. "That needs to be mended too. I'll have to look at the stitching to see whether it can be saved, but it could be I need to make you an entirely new shirt."

"Do you think you can alter the trousers to fit? They were the longest the mercantile had."

She looked at the pair of gray trousers hanging limply from his hand. She could make some minor alterations, yes, but she doubted she could find enough extra material to let out. "If you haven't worn them yet, you're better off returning them and getting your money back. Your shirts too. I imagine you have a tailor make your clothes in Deadwood."

"Nothing in the stores there will fit either." He shrugged, then reached behind him for another pair of pants. "I suppose if I'm returning everything I haven't worn, there's little hope of you repairing these."

She clapped a hand to her mouth and surveyed the seam split and fraying down the seat of his pants. She couldn't help the laugh that rumbled from her chest. "Oh, Thomas. Tell me you did that in your apartment and not somewhere in town."

The tips of his ears turned red. "Ah, not exactly at home, no."

"I don't think they can be saved," she managed over her laughter, all while shaking her head. "I mean, I can mend the seam, but you'd probably just split it again the next time you…"

"Bend over. I know, I know." He looked away, his cheeks now

pink with embarrassment along with his ears. "How long will it take you to make a new…?"

His words trailed off as he turned toward the window again, then frowned.

She peered around him. Was something going on across the street? He seemed to be watching the bar rather closely, but nothing looked out of place.

"Has anyone been bothering you lately?" His voice turned low and dark. "I know some of the loggers and miners who drop off clothes are rowdy. I want to make sure no one's giving you trouble."

There was, in fact, someone giving her trouble, but he was standing beside her, not loitering around The Rusty Wagon.

"No one's been bothering me, unless you count the girls moving my buttons on me, or me somehow sticking my bridesmaid's dress sketch in my collection of shawl sketches." She still hadn't figured out how she'd mixed up those two sketches, but at least Lindy had found the bridesmaid's sketch for her. "But thank you for asking."

He reached out and touched her chin, prodding it up until his eyes met hers. So many emotions lingered there. Tenderness, anxiousness… love?

Could he still love her after all this time?

He cleared his throat and let his hand drop back to his side, where he stretched his fingers and then relaxed them. "You'll tell me if they do?"

She blinked. "What?"

"If someone bothers you. You'll tell me." He spoke it as a statement this time, not a question.

"Of course." She wasn't so hard toward him that she'd turn away his offer of protection.

Just hard enough to turn down his money for Olivia's surgery.

She winced, even though the surgery was different. Ever since he left, she'd worked to build something she could be proud of, something that could support not just her family, but other women and their families. How much could she expect to help other women if she was incapable of paying for her own daughter's surgery? She shouldn't turn to another person for help when she was perfectly capable of providing for her daughters on her own.

"How many pair of trousers did you need?" She lifted the basket of buttons, then headed around Thomas and back toward the table with the mackinaw coats. Better think about buttons than ear surgeries.

"Three should do it. I still have the pair I'm wearing now, the one from when I was rescued."

"Stop by the shop tomorrow morning." She set the buttons by the coats, then sifted through them, looking for five large black ones.

"You're open on Thanksgiving?"

Was Thanksgiving truly tomorrow? How could she have forgotten? The days were slipping by faster and faster, each one ending before she got half her work finished. She glanced up at the first bridesmaid dress she'd completed last night, the emerald green fabric catching the light and shimmering in her otherwise dim shop.

"You're in need of pants that won't tear. I'll get at least one pair done, but there's no need to stop by. I'll have one of the girls run them over to Isaac's as soon as they're ready. If things go well today, they might even be done by tonight." She pulled two matching black buttons out of the basket, then searched for three more.

"Don't you want to measure me first? The tailor in Deadwood always does."

She dug deeper into the basket. His body hadn't seemed to change since she'd last measured him five years ago. He was still tall, thick, and muscular. Still straining the seams of any shirt he bought. His chest still so wide she wouldn't be able to touch her hands together if she wrapped her arms around him. But if she lowered her arms and wrapped them around his waist, then her fingertips would brush. His legs would still be long and powerful too, his trousers encasing well-muscled thighs the size of tree trunks.

"Jessalyn?"

She dropped a smattering of unmatching buttons back into the basket and reached for one of her measuring tapes that happened to be sitting on the table atop a stack of socks that needed darning.

Because taking his measurements somehow seemed easier than explaining she'd once memorized his body and hadn't been able to forget it. "Step over here, where there's some room."

He glanced around the cluttered shop, then raised his eyebrows.

Well, there would be room just as soon as she moved the stack of shirts. She bent and gathered them in her arms, then placed them on the table between the socks and mackinaw coats, which of course sent half the pile of socks plopping to the floor, but at least they took up less space than the shirts.

She measured his arms first, from wrist to wrist, never mind that his reach spread wider than the table where she'd just stacked the clothes. Then she did the length of his torso, from his shoulder seam down to his waist, ignoring the hard muscles beneath his shirt as she stretched the tape down him—or at least trying to. But when she wrapped the tape around his chest, much as she did when measuring one of their daughters, her breath hitched, and she stilled. Of course her left hand didn't reach the tape she'd stretched behind him with her right. She'd known her hands couldn't touch. So why had she measured him this way? Habit?

He looked down at her, not moving, barely even breathing. His face loomed over her own, her head tilted back to see the blue of his eyes. She needed to step back, put distance between her and this big, burly man who owned too many of her memories.

If only that big, burly man didn't have the power to trap her beneath his gaze until she forgot how to move.

"Do you do this with the other men that order shirts from you?" he rasped.

She dropped her arms from around him, then stepped back and pressed the tip of the measuring tape to his chest. "I ask them to bring me their measurements rather than measure them myself. Hold this here."

"Jess." His voice still held that raspy quality to it as he took the end of the tape from her.

He swallowed, his gaze darting about the shop before he spoke again. "You should make that dress in blue." He nodded toward the completed bridesmaid dress hanging near the sewing machine. "To match your eyes."

The ridiculousness of that. As though she had any need for a satin dress. And yet she could see it, the shimmering dress in a pale blue. A woman—not necessarily her, but someone with similar coloring, like Lindy Harrington—standing with golden hair piled atop her head and a necklace glittering at her throat.

She ducked her head and walked clear around him to get his chest measurement. A much safer way of doing things, even if she felt a bit absurd. "You'd better go now. I need to finish these coats before I can start on your clothes."

"You don't need to take measurements for my trousers?"

She nearly choked. Heavens, no. There was no possibility she could take his inseam. Not with the way he was looking at her, his eyes hot with something she didn't want to think about while he spoke of her wearing a blue satin dress. "I recall your old measurements well enough. You haven't changed clothing sizes, have you?"

He shook his head.

"Then good day, Thomas."

"Good day… and thank you." He left the shop on another gust of cold, November wind. But his presence seemed to linger there. His towering form, his woodsy scent, his earnest gaze.

She raised a hand to her forehead and blew out a long, shaky breath. She wouldn't have trouble keeping a man who argued and made demands of her at arm's length, but one who quietly watched her? Who asked if any of her customers had been giving her trouble, and talked about her wearing a dress fit for a princess?

If he made good on his promise and stayed until spring, how was she going to keep her distance?

Chapter Ten

"What do you mean you haven't asked anyone about my jewelry?" Mrs. Ranulfson leaned over the desk in Isaac's office, her hand splayed across the top of her ample bosom as though she were about to faint.

Isaac pressed two fingers to his temple, which was pounding like a miner with a pickax perched inside. Probably due to a night spent tossing and turning while he played out the conversation he needed to have with his brother in his mind. He'd finally concluded that there was no good way to tell Elijah and Victoria that the O'Byrne children's wastrel of a father had returned for them, but even that revelation failed to bring him sleep.

Then again, the pounding in his head at the moment probably had as much to do with the shrill ring in Mrs. Ranulfson's voice as his lack of sleep.

"I never said I hadn't asked anyone. I said I hadn't asked anyone since you were here yesterday, which was..." He looked at the clock hanging on the wall inside his office. "All of sixteen hours ago. You came in just before dinner, if you recall."

The woman huffed, sending the large ostrich feathers atop her hat swaying. "If you weren't looking for my stolen jewelry, then what were you doing? My husband's the chairman of the town council.

I'm sure he'd like to know how you're spending your time as sheriff too. And don't forget my tax dollars go to pay your salary."

More like her husband's tax dollars, since he didn't think Betty Ranulfson had ever earned a wage in her life.

She raised her eyebrows, her feet planted firmly on the wooden planks of his office's floor, and he sighed. Might as well list everything, then maybe she'd leave his office complaining that he was overworked and the town needed to actually pay the deputy he was going to swear in today.

"First, I patrolled at the Penny." He held up a hand to stop the question that was sure to follow. "I don't imbibe ever, Mrs. Ranulfson, let alone on the job." Yet another thing his father had ingrained into him.

"Things were quiet there, so I headed to the Wagon, where things weren't so quiet. I dragged six men in to spend the night behind bars on account of either public intoxication, disorderly conduct, or both." He'd leave out the part about attempted assault on a lawman. He didn't want every ruffian who passed through Eagle Harbor to know a group of shanty boys had almost beaten the tar out of the town sheriff.

"No sooner had I released them this morning than Mr. Fletcher came in asking if I could take a look at his warehouse." That had been after he'd headed out to Elijah's to talk to him and Victoria about Virgil O'Byrne. However, Elijah had already left to check one of his small trap lines, and he couldn't quite force himself to tell Victoria about Virgil without Elijah there. "Someone stole a couple crates of spirits along with a collection of baubles and…"

Betty Ranulfson's eyes rounded and her tongue slipped out to wet her lips. "Things were stolen from the warehouse?"

Isaac sighed. "Now just a minute, Mrs. Ranulfson. Mr. Fletcher lost a decent amount of merchandise with this burglary. You might want to be sensitive about that, considering you recently lost something valuable yourself."

"Yes." She leaned forward over his desk. "But certainly everyone needs to know about the robbery, right? This is the first I've heard of it, and I've already been to the bakery this morning."

Yes, the town needed to know, but did she have to seem so happy about telling the story? "Like I said, the Fletchers are pretty upset by this, so maybe you could use a little tact?"

"Tact, certainly." The woman's eyes gleamed. "Well, I best be on my way. Have to stop by the mercantile yet, you know. If anyone there saw something suspicious last night, I'll come straight back here and let you know."

"Um… Thank you?" He could just imagine Mrs. Ranulfson interrogating poor Mr. Foley's customers. "And so that you're aware, I sent a note about your missing jewelry to the sheriff up in Central." It had been the only other thing he could think to do. "They're on the lookout for anything that matches your necklace and earbobs."

He'd done that last night before he'd learned about the burglary at the warehouse, but now they had two robberies nearly a month apart. What were the chances they were unrelated?

Though jewelry from an unoccupied house would be much easier to steal than entire crates from a warehouse.

"Well…" She eyed the papers cluttering the top of his desk. "It does seem as though you've got work to do, so I'll leave you to it." She gave a curt nod, which once again sent the feathers atop her hat swaying, then swept out the door.

Isaac sank back into his chair and rested his head in his hands. He should probably have lunch, then see if his brother had returned. He glanced out the window. What were the chances a snowstorm would blow in while he was eating, and he wouldn't be able to get out to Elijah's for a day? Or maybe two days? A month, even?

He reached beside his desk for the sack containing his bread and ham, but the door opened. Thomas Dowrick stepped inside and hung his coat on a peg.

Isaac eyed the back of his trousers, unable to stop the grin that spread across his face. At least the red flannel of Thomas's union suit wasn't hanging out. "Been to visit your wife, I see."

The back of Thomas's neck turned red, and he stalked toward the chair across from the desk. "As a matter of fact, I have."

"Good. Can't have Eagle Harbor's newest deputy showing his union suit to the world." Isaac rummaged in his bottom desk drawer for one of the little tin stars he'd inherited when he'd taken over as sheriff, then slid it across the desk to Thomas.

"I think the story will do enough damage on its own," Thomas spoke through a tight voice.

"Already around town, is it?" Looked like Betty Ranulfson wouldn't be the only one telling stories at the mercantile today.

Thomas glowered and grabbed the star. "I remember being asked to stop by so you could deputize me, not so you could laugh at me."

Isaac muffled another round of laughter and stood to grab the Bible from the shelf behind his desk. "Stand up and place your hand on the Bible."

Thomas did as instructed.

"Thomas Dowrick, do you promise to uphold the law?"

"I do."

"Then I hereby deputize you as an officer of the Eagle Harbor Sheriff's Office." He nodded toward the pin in Thomas's hand. "Go ahead and put that on."

Thomas sat back down and worked the pin through the fabric of his shirt. "Been thinking about what happened last night. Those men didn't want to kill you. Otherwise they'd have used your gun on you."

Isaac scratched the back of his neck. Looked like his new deputy had a good head on his shoulders, and here he'd just been happy to find a man as big as Thomas who'd work for nothing. "No, they'd have used one of their own. Several of them were armed."

"Why, then? Surely they didn't think beating up the sheriff was a good idea."

Isaac put the Bible back on the shelf, then sat. "Trying to teach me a lesson, as near as I can gather."

"And this lesson is…?"

"Probably to leave them alone and let them do whatever they want. Like Jenkins."

Thomas frowned. "Who's Jenkins?"

"Don't you remember the former sheriff? Big." Isaac extended his arms out in front of him to resemble the size of Jenkins's stomach. "Always drunk. Always willing to look the other way during a crime if there was some sort of benefit to him."

It was how he'd gotten roped into running for sheriff when he didn't have a lick of lawman experience. Though anyone had to be better than Jenkins.

Thomas squinted. "I suppose. Never had much cause to run into him before."

Isaac fiddled with a pencil on his desk again. "Well, either those loggers think they can intimidate me, or they're trying to distract me from something else."

"Like what?"

"Like Betty Ranulfson missing her ruby necklace and earbobs. Or Mr. Fletcher reporting three crates of goods stolen from his warehouse."

"Did that happen last night? When the men were locked up?"

"The jewelry's been gone for over a month, but as for the warehouse burglary, I don't know. It happened within the past several days, but Fletcher only noticed this morning."

Thomas shifted, then leaned forward in his chair. "What about that man who claimed to be looking for his young'uns? Do you believe him?"

Isaac swallowed. If he thought hard enough, he could still recall the feel of little Toby sitting on his lap during Sunday dinner. The toddler had eaten all but two bites of Isaac's pie. "Since there's three children staying with my brother with a story that matches the one O'Byrne gave last night, I've got no choice but to believe him. Besides, the oldest boy is twelve, he'll be able to tell us if the man is lying or not."

Thomas shook his head. "But why try roughing you up instead of asking for your help?"

Isaac shrugged, his heart lodged in his throat. Why, indeed?

But no matter how many questions he and Thomas could conjure up, none of them changed the plain fact that he needed to find Elijah before the day was over.

～ ～ ～ ～ ～

"Do it again, Mr. Elijah. Do it again!" Toby squealed and threw a handful of snow Elijah's direction before turning and running as fast as his stubby little legs would carry him.

"Don't forget me," another young voice called.

Elijah swung toward Claire, Thomas and Jessalyn's middle daughter, his chest heaving with exertion. From the top of the hill, Jack and Colin, Mac's stepson, let out a whoop before jumping into their sleds and racing each other to the bottom.

"Yes, Elijah," Mac hollered from where he stood several feet away surveying the chaos. "Don't forget Claire."

"No, get me instead!" This from Mac's oldest daughter, Jane, who sprinted after Toby.

Elijah drew another breath into his burning lungs and took off after Jane. The womenfolk were at the lighthouse visiting this afternoon while the men took everyone sledding after school. But after walking up the hill twice, the littlest children had been exhausted and begged to be carried. Playing snow monster had seemed easier than dragging young'uns and sleds up the hill.

Or so he'd thought. Suddenly trudging up the snowy slope with Toby on his shoulders didn't seem nearly as difficult as chasing children.

He had to credit Thomas Dowrick, though. The man was faithfully slogging up the hill with Megan and Olivia for what was probably the thirtieth time that afternoon, and he didn't even seem winded. During the week he'd been in town, the man had certainly gotten to know his daughters. They'd lavished their father with squeals and hugs and kisses when Thomas arrived in the schoolyard, then argued over whose sled he would ride on first.

Elijah ran a few more steps, then lunged for both Jane and Claire, who were standing together waiting for him to catch up. His fingers found Claire first, and he hoisted her up into the air, then caught her amidst a fit of giggles and dropped her into the snow.

"Me snow monster. Me hungry. Um num num num num." He made a chomping sound as he pretended to eat Claire's arm. She curled against the snow and laughed so hard tears leaked from her eyes.

"My turn, Mr. Elijah," Toby called from halfway up the hill. "Come get me!"

Halfway up the hill? That wasn't going to happen.

"No, me!" Jane shouted.

His chest still heaving, he headed toward the closer child.

"Elijah."

At the sound of Isaac's voice, he slowed.

His brother headed over the snowy field toward them, a slumped set to his shoulders. "Do you have a few minutes?"

As long as it didn't involve chasing children. "Sure." He slung a hand on his hip and waited for his brother to come to him, his chest still laboring for breath. "Want to play snow monster?"

Isaac muttered something about another kind of monster, then blew out a breath. "Last night, there was an... incident, and afterward one of the men involved—"

"Sheriff! Sheriff, I need to speak with you."

Elijah looked up to find a squat, balding man that was nearly as round as he was tall hurrying over the snow toward them.

Isaac's gaze darted to the man, and his face went pale. "I'm so sorry, Elijah. I didn't realize he was following me."

"Who is he?"

A small hand wrapped around Elijah's leg, and he looked down to find Toby pressed against him. "Something wrong?"

The boy only clung tighter to his legs.

Elijah settled a hand on Toby's head. "Why don't you go play with the others while I talk to the grownups?" He raised his voice loud enough for Mac and the children to hear. "I bet Uncle Mac will be the snow monster for a while."

Mac sent him a glare, but Toby stayed by his side while the balding man took the last few steps to them.

"Well looky here. Ya led me straight to my young'uns." The man slapped Isaac on the back. "Thanks, Sheriff."

His young'uns? The hairs on the back of Elijah's neck prickled. He'd seen the squat man around town maybe once or twice in the past few weeks, but not often enough to know his name or what he did for a living.

"Didn't realize you were following me, O'Byrne." Isaac's shoulders slumped even more.

"Followin' ya? Naw, I wasn't followin' ya. Just saw ya walking is all. Decided to see if you'd learned anything about my young'uns yet, but I didn't expect you'd lead me straight to them." The man's eyes narrowed in on the children the way a trapper's would when counting his precious furs at the end of a season.

Isaac muttered something again, then cleared his throat and stuck a finger beneath the collar of his blue wool coat. "Elijah... I'd, ah, like to introduce you to Norman O'Byrne. He's been living near town for a few weeks, but going by his second name, Virgil, which is why it's taken... ah, so long to find him."

A dull buzz started in Elijah's ears as he stared at the rotund man with shifty eyes. The man who'd caused Toby to stop playing and burrow into the side of his leg.

It wasn't supposed to be like this. Their father was supposed to be... different, better, the kind of man that would give Jack, Alice, and Toby all the same chances in life his own pa had given him.

How could he let a three-year-old boy go into the care of a man he was frightened of? And why was Toby frightened in the first place?

"Hello, there. Good to meet ya. Thank ya for looking after my young'uns after what happened to Jenny. Sure was surprised to hear about that. She was just like a ma to the kids, ya see. So I didn't know there'd been any trouble till I got to the cabin and saw the note ya left." Norman—or was it Virgil?—extended his hand.

Did he have to shake it? He'd rather grab the three children, rush home, and lock himself and the O'Byrnes in the cabin for the next six years until Jack was legally old enough to look after Alice and Toby.

"Um, you're welcome." He reached out and gave the man's hand a shake anyway.

How was he going to explain this to Victoria? Victoria, who had held back her tears, forced a smile, and told him how happy she was

126

that her sister just had a second child when he'd given her Beatrice's letter. Never mind her heart was breaking over her own lack of children. She'd cry the whole night through when she heard about O'Byrne returning.

"Who did you say this was?" Mac came up beside Elijah, settling a big, bear-like hand on his shoulder. "I don't think we've been introduced yet."

Elijah swallowed the thickness in his throat and half listened while Isaac stumbled through another introduction.

"Pleased to meet you." Mac's gritty voice sounded anything but pleased, but he shook O'Byrne's hand anyway.

"Like I told Mr. Cummings here, thanks for looking after my young'uns while I was away. Though I've got another request to make, if it isn't too much trouble, ya see." O'Byrne turned back to Elijah. "I'm working at a logging camp just outside of town for the winter, so I don't got a place for the children to stay just yet. Maybe you could keep them for a few more days while I get some things together?"

Elijah rested his hand back on Toby's head. "We're happy to keep them as long as you need."

Longer, even. Dare he hope the man wouldn't be able to find somewhere to live until spring? That they could keep the children several more months?

Except the children would have to go back to their pa eventually.

Even so, maybe a little more heartache on their part would be worth giving the children a good, loving home for as long as they could.

Feet pounded the snow behind him, and a second later Jack and Colin appeared by his side.

Jack froze, his gaze glued to his father. "You're back."

"That I am, son." O'Byrne gave a stout nod. "Now come on and give your pa a hug."

But rather than go into his father's arms, Jack took a step back, then turned to Elijah. "Do we have to live with him?"

"You complaining about the kind of home I provide for you?" O'Byrne's voice came out as a threatening growl, and Toby burrowed himself harder against Elijah's leg.

Jack's jaw moved from side to side, but whatever angry thoughts flitted through his head, he kept them to himself and turned to Elijah. "I don't want to go with him."

"He doesn't have anywhere for you to stay at the moment." Elijah looked to O'Byrne. "Right?"

"I'm looking for a job in town but haven't been able to find one. Might not be able to until logging season's over and the harbor opens. I can work the docks then."

"Sure you will," Jack mocked, but an angry look from his pa cut off any further words.

Elijah shifted, the week-old snow crunching beneath his boots. "Ah, we're having some folks over to our place for Thanksgiving dinner. You should come and spend some time with your children." He nearly had to drag the words from his mouth, but really, it was the least he could offer considering half the town was coming. It was also the right thing to do considering this man was blood kin to the O'Byrne children.

Jack sent him a look that could shoot daggers, but O'Byrne's lips curved into a sly smile. "Just might take you up on that. Now I'd like a word with my son, if you don't mind."

"No!" Toby clung so tightly to his leg the child might leave nail marks despite the trousers and gloves.

O'Byrne didn't even glance at Toby. "Not the little one..."

Little one? Did O'Byrne even know Toby's name? And he seemed to have completely forgotten about Alice, who was off playing with Jane and Claire.

"Jack, here." The man motioned for Jack to follow, then walked far enough away that whispering wouldn't be overheard.

Jack looked to him, eyes questioning.

Elijah gave a swift nod. "Go on with your pa. See what he has to say."

But as Jack trudged through the snow to his father, a copper mass formed in Elijah's stomach, hard and heavy. Maybe Victoria had been right, maybe they'd all be better off if Norman Virgil O'Byrne had stayed lost forever.

Chapter Eleven

"So what took you away from Eagle Harbor?"

The bite of turkey on Jessalyn's tongue turned dry as sawdust. She looked at Dr. Harrington, seated across from her and Thomas, his eyebrows raised as he waited for an answer. When her husband's gaze flicked to hers, she nearly sank beneath the table—not that there'd be room for her given the horde of people's legs crowded beneath it.

The Cummingses' rambling log cabin was packed for Thanksgiving dinner. The children had their own table by the sofa, and the adults were all scrunched around Elijah's kitchen table plus an extra table that had been moved inside.

If she had been seated at the far side of the table where Victoria and Mabel Cummings were, she'd not have even heard the question Dr. Harrington asked Thomas. But somehow she'd ended up right next to her husband, and across from Lindy and Dr. Harrington.

Would Thomas blame his leaving on her so that he didn't need to admit guilt in front of half the town? Tell everyone about the argument they'd had after their savings were lost?

"We lost some money in a poor investment shortly before I left." Thomas's voice was calm and even, as though he discussed the weather and not the reason they'd been separated. "So I decided to head west, see if I could stake a claim on my own rather than working for a big outfit like Central. I grew up in the mines of Cornwall, so making a claim didn't seem all that unreasonable. Jess here didn't want to leave until things were more settled though, so I went ahead without her."

For five years. She dropped her fork, causing it to clink against her plate with enough force to draw attention from Aileen seated next to her.

Oh, why had she come tonight? It hardly mattered that she'd shared Thanksgiving with the Cummingses every year since Thomas left. She should have sent her regrets the second she learned Thomas would be here.

But there he sat, in the middle of the table, surrounded by the Cummingses, Oaktons, Harringtons, and O'Byrnes as though he belonged with them.

Not the actions of a man who was planning to leave town tomorrow or even next week.

Each day he stayed, each day he settled a bit more into Eagle Harbor life, he came closer and closer to making good on his promise not to leave again.

She fiddled with her fork. Maybe she owed him that visit to the bakery after all.

"I didn't realize you were a miner." Dr. Harrington's brow drew down as though trying to solve a puzzle. "Somehow I thought you were a hotelier. I must have heard wrong."

Jessalyn let out a little breath. At least he wasn't asking why Thomas had stayed away so long.

"No, you heard right." Thomas paused for a moment to take a drink. "I headed to California first, but the gold strike there was already playing out, so I ended up in Deadwood a year or so after the mining there started. Figured since I'd been mining copper at Central, I'd do a good job of sniffing out a new vein somewhere else.

I took turns mining for the Homestake and searching for my own claim. The claim didn't happen, but the Deadwood fire did."

"Deadwood fire?" This from the scruffy round man who was seated near the end of the table. Elijah had introduced him as the O'Byrne children's father when she'd arrived that evening, but something about the man's shifty eyes caused her to scoot a little closer to Thomas.

"Yep." Thomas wiped his face with his napkin. "I'd been in Deadwood about a year when the town burned. It left a bunch of miners without lodging. I scraped every last cent together to purchase property and put up three boarding houses. Turned out renting rooms paid better than mining. I got a bank loan to start building a hotel two months later. Paid it off just before coming here to find Jess."

"How come you didn't write Ma any letters while you were gone?"

Jessalyn turned to find Olivia standing behind them, her empty plate in her hands. Had she come to the table for more food, or to listen to her father's story? Either way, her question did precisely what Dr. Harrington's questions hadn't—focused everyone's attention on the fact her husband had been gone for half a decade without sending word.

She pressed her eyes shut and drew in a breath. Yes, she definitely should have stayed home. She probably could have finished the bodice on the second bridesmaid's dress if she'd begged off.

"I did write her letters." Thomas reached out and bonked Olivia on the nose with his finger. "Your ma just never got them, and I'm very sorry she didn't."

What if things had been different? What if instead of simply assuming she was in Chicago after a few months, he wrote one last letter to her in Eagle Harbor? A letter with a return address so she could have answered him. Would the past five years have turned out differently for them?

Oh, it hardly mattered. It wasn't as though either of them could go back and redo the past. Besides, Thomas must have eventually realized she wasn't getting his letters. "Why didn't you figure out I wasn't with my cousin when she sent the letters back?"

His brow knit with a pained look. "Jess…"

"You said before that you thought I was in Chicago and had been sending letters all this time. But wouldn't you have realized I wasn't with Mathilda when she returned your letters?"

Thomas leaned back in his chair and ducked his head near hers. Only then did she realize the entire table had fallen silent, all eyes looking their direction.

"Jess, we need to talk more, but not here."

"You make any of that pumpkin pie, Ma?" Isaac's loud voice sounded from the far end of the table. He stacked his empty plate atop Mr. O'Byrne's and patted his stomach. "I've been hankering for it all day."

"I'll get the coffee." Victoria shot up from the table and wedged herself between the back of Aileen's chair and the stove to boil water.

"Did Miss Victoria say she was getting pie?" Alice appeared at the table beside Olivia, her declaration loud enough the rest of the little ones climbed off their seats and headed over to the adult table.

Jessalyn leaned closer to Thomas while commotion continued around them. "I don't understand why we need to wait. I only want to know why you never realized something was amiss when Mathilda sent your letters back."

Thomas ducked his head so near his breath ruffled the flyaway hairs that had escaped the twist at the back of her head. "Most of the letters were never returned. I assumed you were getting them and keeping the money all this time, even if you were too angry to write me back. It wasn't until six months ago, when I suddenly started getting the letters back, that I realized something was wrong."

"The letters weren't..." Her mouth filled with sawdust, but this time she hadn't even taken a bite of food. "What do you mean they weren't returned? That doesn't make any sense."

"Jess, like I said, this really isn't the time to talk. How about I come by your shop tomorrow?"

She glanced around to find Mrs. Cummings and Aileen dishing out pie while Victoria and Lindy poured coffee. The men at the far end of the table had started a conversation about trapping and the price animal pelts were expected to bring.

If everyone had gone back to ignoring them, surely Thomas could explain more now. "I don't want to wait until tomorrow."

His jaw tightened. "It's as I said. The letters weren't returned for most of the time I was gone, so I assumed you got them."

"What about the money?"

"What about it?"

"You said you were sending it for five years, right? Or nearly five years? If the letters weren't returned to you, then what happened to the money you sent?"

He looked down at the table, where someone had taken his dinner plate and replaced it with a piece of pie. "The banknotes were cashed, which is why I assumed you were getting my money, even if you were too angry at me to write. And that's part of why I didn't come looking for you sooner. I figured if you were too mad to write, then you wouldn't welcome a visit in person either."

"But..." If the banknotes had been sent to Henry and Mathilda's home and had been turned into cash money, that could only mean one thing. She pressed a hand to her belly, her stomach churning though she'd barely touched her dinner.

"If you'll excuse me, I need to use the necessary." She pushed back from the table and stumbled toward the door.

~ ~ ~ ~ ~

"Jess." Thomas called after his wife, but she didn't stop to look at him, just rushed through the door that led to the entryway where the Cummingses stored their coats and boots. A moment later the outside door slammed.

He should have followed his hunch and kept quiet until tomorrow. He rose from the table, only to realize everyone was watching him again, including Olivia and Claire at the children's table.

He squeezed between Aileen's seat and the stove, then shuffled around the back of Victoria's chair before leaving the kitchen.

A quick glance at the coats hanging on the wall told him Jessalyn's was still there, the deep red color sticking out from the drab brown, blue, and mackinaw coats everyone else wore like a single beam of sunlight through storm clouds. Of course his wife would have the most stylish coat of the lot. And knowing her, she'd bargained with Mr. Foley at the mercantile until he'd sold her the entire bolt of fabric for a dollar, then made the coat herself. He shoved his arms into his own mackinaw coat before snagging hers and heading out the door.

She hadn't gone to the outhouse but stood on the porch, leaning against the log wall of the house, her arms clasped tightly about her.

"I'm sorry, Jess. I shouldn't have answered Olivia's question about the letters, at least not in front of all those people." He held out her coat.

She extended her arms, letting him hold it while she slipped it on. "Don't apologize. I bullied you into telling me. Just like I bullied you about things when we were married."

Were married? "Are married, Jess. We *are* married." And if one of them claimed the title of bully, it should be him. Jessalyn could be stubborn about certain things, but not nearly as stubborn as him.

She wrapped her arms around herself again and looked over the porch railing into the quiet, windless night. "Six months ago would have been when Henry died."

He shoved his hands into his pockets. What was there to say? He'd never cared much for Jessalyn's cousin-in-law, not even when he'd been a new immigrant just off the boat from Cornwall and Henry had offered him a job at his warehouse—a job where Thomas had quickly worked his way into a foreman position.

"That's when you started getting my letters back, isn't it? After he died."

"Yes." He and Mathilda had figured out that much when he'd finally made it to Chicago. "Mathilda never knew about the letters or the money. When she started getting the mail after Henry's carriage accident, she promptly returned the letters to me. Before he died, it appears as though Henry was forging your signature on the bank notes and keeping the money for himself."

Jessalyn leaned her arms on the porch rail and hung her head. "Can you get the stolen money back?"

He shrugged. "Don't know. Mathilda seemed like she was in a rough place when I saw her. Evidently I wasn't the only one Henry had less then honorable dealings with. The authorities in Chicago are looking into it, and the bank notes are traceable."

"I had no idea, and I can't believe Henry would have..." She shook her head, her shoulders still slumped over the railing. "No, that's not true. I had an idea of what he was capable of, but I'd never realized he'd turn his ill intentions on you."

Something about the hard edge in her voice caused him to take a step nearer. "What he was capable of? What do you mean?"

She stared out over the yard, still and quiet even though Lake

Superior lay on the other side of the cabin. "I tried to go back there after you left. Not right away, but there was a time, maybe a year later, when the money was gone and Megan was a babe and I had barely any work and no way to eat. I sent Mathilda a letter asking if we could come."

"I was already sending money by then, though not as much as I was able to send after I built those boardinghouses." Thomas's hands curled into fists. "The thief. He was stealing money out of your hands, and then he wrote and said you weren't welcome in Chicago? If he wasn't already six feet under, I'd—"

"He didn't write."

"What?"

She kept her gaze on the snowy yard, the full moon illuminating the ground and casting its pale glow over her delicate face. "He didn't write. He came to Eagle Harbor in person, demanding to know what was going on."

"As though he couldn't figure it out from the letters he was stealing?" Thomas huffed a breath into the cold.

"Henry said he'd take me back, but not the children. Said he knew of a nice orphanage in Chicago where the girls could be placed with good families and be better taken care of than I could care for them on my own."

Henry had done *what?*

"Jess…" *I'm so sorry.* The words didn't seem like enough. He gripped her elbows and turned her to face him. "Had I any way of knowing, I would have left Deadwood and come to collect you and the girls, regardless of how much money I did or didn't have, regardless of the kind of life I could have given you. At least we'd have all been together."

And maybe he'd have had a better chance at restoring his relationship with his wife.

Jessalyn dropped her gaze to the snowy porch, though she didn't pull away from him. "Henry told me he'd decided who I should marry next. Someone more advantageous, even better than Walter Shunk."

"Someone you should marry?" Thomas's thunderous voice echoed across the snow, only to be swallowed by the silence of the pristine night. "You were married to *me*."

"He wanted me to get a divorce. Had some idea about getting one on grounds of abandonment. By that point, I was already wondering if you were dead. Even with our argument before you left, I knew you weren't the type to turn your back on us for good."

He sucked in a breath, sharp and cold. Did she realize what she'd just admitted? She might have put up a fight about him disappearing for five years, but deep down she'd known he'd never meant to do such a thing.

"I couldn't give up the girls like Henry wanted though, which left me here alone. But it also gave me a certain determination. Without anyone else to turn to, I had to provide for the girls, so I started taking in sewing. One thing led to another, and here I am today." She opened her hands and let them fall, drawing attention to the trim cut of her winter coat and the flawless way the thick fabric drifted over her. "I'm giving work to needy women in Eagle Harbor. I have dresses commissioned for a bridal party in Chicago next summer and a solid client base there that I can call on when I move my shop. And I plan to open a factory where I can help even more women who find themselves in situations similar to what mine once was."

He took a step back and let his gaze skim down her, the reflection of the moon on the snow so bright they might well be standing beneath the gas chandelier in his Deadwood hotel lobby. Her deep coat provided a perfect splash of color against a night bathed in white. Her silky blond hair was starting to fall from her updo. She'd curled her hair tonight too, similar to how she'd worn it the first time he'd met her, in the office of Henry's warehouse, waiting for a suitor who'd gotten drawn into a conversation with Henry.

He tried to swallow, but his throat muscles were so tight the task was nearly impossible. "You did well for yourself. I never had any doubt that you could. But now that I'm here, you don't have to do everything alone."

"Maybe I'm so used to doing things myself, I don't know how to stop." She bit the side of her lip, her eyes searching his, so open and trustful beneath the moonlight that he almost couldn't hold her gaze. "We should go to the bakery together sometime, like you said."

Yes. Tomorrow. First thing in the morning. He opened his mouth to agree, yet he couldn't quite form the words, not with her looking at him like that.

"There's something I have to tell you." He couldn't stand here and listen to her open up about Henry without being fully honest with her in return. "I'm not sure whether I should have explained when I first arrived or now. I prayed for guidance, but I still don't know the best way to go about it."

Probably because there was no good way for a man to tell his wife he'd deceived her.

"Were you unfaithful to me?" she whispered into the night. "I know what kind of women live in mining towns, and…"

He reached out and clasped her hand in his. "Not in the way you mean, but I was unfaithful in another way. With our savings. Before I left."

Furrows rifted her delicate brow. "I don't understand."

"I gambled it, Jess. I never invested it in that copper mine. I was going to invest it like we talked about, and I took that trip down to Calumet to do just that, but once I was there…" He still remembered walking into the gambling hall, the scent of spirits and tobacco, the rowdy laughter, the dim lighting, the scantily dressed waitresses, the hope in his belly that he could take the money they'd been setting aside and double it in a single night.

"No matter how hard I worked, how hard I tried saving, nothing seemed to be enough for you." He gave her hand a gentle squeeze. "I'd go home, exhausted and tired after a day on the docks, only to find you disappointed that a final ship hadn't come into the harbor so I could earn extra money. You insisted we save money every week, but that left us eating naught but porridge and beans and bread. Doubling our savings and bringing it back to you sure seemed like a good way to keep you happy. I figured maybe if you were happy, I could be happy again, and we'd remember how to be happy together, and..."

He was rambling now, but she'd made no effort to stop him, just stood there with a devastated look on her face, the moonlight that had been so kind to her a few moments ago now illuminating her hurt and disappointment.

He shoved his hand into his pocket, and it clenched around an errant scrap of paper it found. "Yeah, foolish, I know. Like you said last week, money wouldn't have solved our problems, not when there were so many other things wrong between the two of us. The sad thing is, for a long time part of me still thought about what might have happened if gambling had worked."

Maybe her silence was good. At least she hadn't started shouting. And she hadn't thrown up her hands and run off the porch either, or told him she'd never talk to him again. All she did was take her hand from his grasp—and he couldn't blame her.

"But this past spring, I realized I was glad I lost that money straight off. If gambling would have worked, well, I'd have tried again. And again. And again. I'd have never kept a dime in our pockets. There are enough gambling dens in Deadwood for me to see the pattern." He'd have turned into his brother in Cornwall.

"Still, I'm sorry I took the money and gambled with it. I always imagined you suspected something. There were only two weeks between when I took it with the intention of investing and when I told you it was gone. No mine plays out that quick." He finally clamped his mouth shut and looked at her, waiting for her to say something, anything that would end her silence.

She swiped a strand of hair from her face and tucked it behind her ear, then looked at the porch floorboards. "I didn't think about it that much, I suppose." Her voice held a slight tremble. "Only about how the money was gone and we had next to nothing. We had two daughters, and I didn't want to end up back in the tenements."

"I wrote the story to you in a letter. In some ways I feel like I've already told you once." What Henry must have thought when he'd read that. The do-nothing immigrant from Cornwall had failed and couldn't provide for Jessalyn.

But then, that wasn't so different from spending his childhood as the do-nothing son of the town drunk. Seemed the lot he'd been given at birth was sticking to him no matter how hard he tried to run from it. And now he didn't even have the strength to work as a miner or toss crates around Henry's warehouse or haul his father home after a brawl.

"I also figured that was part of the reason you wouldn't write me back. I didn't…" His throat closed, and he cleared it before trying again. "I didn't even put together that you didn't know about the gambling until I got here and saw for myself how much Henry stole from us. It went far beyond money, angel."

Her head shot up, her eyes glassy in the darkness. "Don't call me that."

He didn't need to ask why, not with the way he'd once used the name for her. Did it matter that it was the only thing he wanted to call her? She still looked like an angel to him, even if she was a fierce, injured one rather than a sweet, loving one.

"This was why you wanted to meet with me at the bakery, wasn't it? Not to build a relationship as much as to tell me this. Except it wouldn't have…" She pressed a hand over her mouth, but that didn't stop the tears from streaking down her cheeks to plop onto her coat.

"Both, Jess. I wanted to tell you, yes, and start rebuilding our relationship."

She shook her head. "It's impossible. I don't know how I can trust you again. Ever."

She didn't mean it. She couldn't. She'd just offered to meet him at the bakery a quarter hour ago. Surely if she could trust him enough to overcome how he'd never set aside his work to come collect her and the girls himself, then they could work through something that took place half a decade back. He took a step forward, his hands clenching in his pockets. "I've changed since then. That's part of the reason I came back for you. Part of the reason I'm staying here all winter, even though there's a hotel in Deadwood I need to get back to."

"Don't stay here on account of us." She sniffled and wiped her tears with her hands. "Please. You won't get what you want in the end. Come spring, the girls and I are going to Chicago regardless of what you decide to do. You should just leave now, before we get more snow. There's not even enough on the ground for snowshoes yet. You should be able to walk to Calumet without incident. Besides, I wouldn't want your hotel to suffer because you're not there."

"I already told you, if I go, you're going with me." His voice shook with frustration. He wasn't going to give up on his wife and daughters because of a mistake he'd made five years ago.

"No, Thomas, I'm not. And staying here all winter isn't going to change that."

The way she said his name, so clinical and methodical, without any hint of emotion, caused him to take a step back. He was losing her, he could feel it in the way her eyes took on that detached glint, see it in the way her face had transformed from that of a lovely angel to a hurt one to a stone one. "Jess, can't you—"

"You have a hotel in South Dakota, yes?"

He nodded.

"I assume you left it in the care of a manager of some sort, someone trustworthy and capable."

"Of course."

"Imagine if Henry were still alive and he asked to manage your hotel while you were gone. He promised you could trust him despite the money he stole from you in the past. He promised he'd be responsible and report back to you. Would you let him?"

He closed his eyes, felt the brush of winter air on his cheeks, and drew in a breath. "No."

"And that's precisely why I can't go to South Dakota with you. You're asking me to give up everything I've worked for and offering promises I can't trust in exchange."

The air he'd just drawn into his lungs turned to shards of glass, tearing through his insides until it hurt to breathe. He looked out over the moonlit yard, toward the winding path that would lead him back to town.

"Tell the girls I'll be by to visit them in the morning. If that's still allowed?"

She shrugged before turning her face away.

Fine then, he'd keep visiting his daughters. But as for their mother? Seemed he had as much chance at winning her back by staying in Eagle Harbor as he did by returning to Deadwood and writing another five years' worth of letters to the wrong address.

Chapter Twelve

A lone wolf's howl echoed through the night as Isaac stomped across the yard, the snow crunching beneath his boots. Behind him the lights from the cabin glowed brightly, spilling their warmth through the windows. He couldn't stay there any longer, not with all the cheerful faces. Not with all the well-intentioned questions about how Tressa's baby was doing, whether Lindy was excited to be expecting her own child, and what projects his mother and others on the beautification society were planning for next summer. An endless circle of happy thoughts and cheerfulness.

A circle where no one talked of Pa.

Surely Elijah had to miss him tonight, and Ma had to think of her lost husband at least a little. Pa had always loved Thanksgiving, had made everyone who shared their meal—and there had always been plenty of people—go around the table and say what they were thankful for as well as quote a favorite Bible verse.

He'd sat in Pa's spot tonight at the end of the table. Had Elijah noticed? Had Elijah cared? How could his brother laugh and eat pie and play games with Pa gone? Isaac huffed, holding out his lantern though he hardly needed it with the reflection of moonlight on the snow. Or was he batty for not being able to enjoy Thanksgiving three and a half years after their father died?

No, he wasn't batty, not when he'd been the reason for his father's death.

He trudged toward the workshop on the far side of the yard. People in town might say a sudden storm had killed Pa three summers ago. But no one who said that had been in the lighthouse tower watching their father's little mackinaw fishing boat flounder. None of them had stood rooted to the iron platform when the boat capsized and Pa started swimming toward shore. A wave had washed over Pa, and he'd been so sure Pa wouldn't come back up, but Pa had. Isaac had counted all the waves, one, two, three, four. And then… no Pa.

His twin sister Rebekah had stood there with him, along with Mac, who'd been the assistant lighthouse keeper then. She'd tugged on his arm, begging him and Mac to take the dinghy down by the beach and row out and rescue Pa after his boat capsized.

They'd told Rebekah they'd only get themselves killed by attempting such a thing.

But when Elijah had come home from sailing the Atlantic, he'd proved everyone wrong, starting a lifesaving team and showing just how easily Pa could have been rescued—if Isaac had only been willing to try.

Isaac pushed open the door to the workshop, the calming scent of sawdust and pine filling his nostrils. Just what he needed. A few hours of—

Crash!

His free hand immediately slid between the buttons of his coat to grip his gun. "Who's there?"

"I-I'm s-sorry," a familiar, lilting voice stammered.

He picked up the lantern again and peered deeper inside the building, leaving the door open behind him.

"I wasn't expecting anyone, and ye frightened me." Aileen Brogan righted the wooden chair she must have knocked over when he'd come into the building. If her Irish accent hadn't given her away, her fiery red hair glittering in the lantern light would have. Had he ever seen hair such a shade of deep, rich red before?

He slid his hand off his gun and pulled the door shut behind him, then headed toward where she stood by the potbelly stove at the back of the shop. "Are you by yourself?"

She gave him a look he didn't quite understand. "I was until ye arrived, but I'll leave now, so as not to be in yer way."

She grabbed her coat from the end of one of the tables filled with wooden toys he'd made over the summer. He'd meant to get them shipped to Chicago at the end of the season, but hadn't reckoned on getting diphtheria and then being elected sheriff.

"Wait." He reached out to put a hand on her arm, to stop the anxious flutter of movements and keep her from running out so quickly. But the instant he moved his hand toward her, she jumped back, bumping into the chair once more and sending both it and herself to the floor with another crash.

"Are you all right?" He bent to where she lay sprawled on the wooden planks and extended a hand to help her up. "I'm sorry. I didn't mean to frighten you again."

Instead of reaching for him, she scrambled to her feet on her own and took a step back, her hands trembling.

Isaac bent to pick up the chair with slow, measured movements. Perhaps he'd startled her when he'd first entered the shop, but there was no reason for her to act so scared of him now. Had she been attacked like Victoria and Lindy had this fall? The town council had removed the former sheriff from his position for good reason. Maybe something happened to Miss Brogan during that time as well. "You know I'm the new sheriff?"

"I'd heard, aye." She watched him through large eyes the color of a glass-green sea.

They'd be pretty, if not for the terror swirling in them. "Miss Brogan, if someone in town hurt you, I need to know so I can deal with the situation and prevent it from happening to someone else."

"No… no one in town… did anything to me."

Something about the manner in which she spoke, the halting pattern of speech, the way she'd carefully chosen her words, caused the hair on the back of his neck to bristle. She'd been skittish ever since moving up from Chicago this past summer. She'd lived with Elijah and Victoria for several months, and even then she'd barely said two words to him. Had something happened to her before? In Chicago, maybe? Or in Ireland?

"I was just coming out here for some quiet," she spoke in her lilting voice, and a bit of the fear leaving her eyes. "'Tis busy in there. All the voices. All the people. No place to move. No quiet to think."

"I know. It's the reason I came out here too."

"For quiet?"

"For quiet." And for a peace that always seemed to elude him, though Mac, Elijah, Rebekah, and even Ma had all somehow found it since Pa's death. Would Miss Brogan understand if he told her as much? Maybe so, she already had the same sense of disquiet in her spirit that plagued him.

She glanced around the sawdust-filled workspace. "If it's quiet ye be after, I won't disturb ye any longer."

"I don't know about you, but I can tolerate being around one person a little better than twenty." He grinned at her, but she didn't smile in return.

Instead, she drew back a step and glanced at the door.

"Miss Brogan?"

"'Tisn't proper, the two of us alone out here. I best be going." She whirled and fled outside without even a look backward.

He grabbed her coat and headed for the door after her, but by the time he pushed it open, she was already halfway to the cabin. So he settled for watching her run beneath the light of the moon until the slap of the cabin's door closing behind her echoed through the night.

Was she upset over something he'd said or done? He'd only tried to calm her, yet she'd run from him as though he was the cause of every problem in the world.

He turned back toward the workshop and his bevy of toys that sold for a premium price in Chicago, then reached for a nearly finished wagon and the sandpaper lying beside it. It was, after all, the reason he'd come out here. The wood and saws and sandpaper, the mindless work of putting a toy together with his own hands, sanding it smooth, knowing it would find its way into a smiling child's home someday.

But peace escaped him tonight, the repetitive motions of sandpaper against wood refusing to calm his mind. Besides, he needed to get Miss Brogan's coat back to her before she headed home.

He pushed his arms into his own coat and picked up Miss Brogan's. Holding the lantern high, he shut the door to the workshop behind him and trudged across the snow. He'd go inside and give her back her coat, then head into town. Holiday or not, he still needed to stop by The Pretty Penny and The Rusty Wagon.

But Miss Brogan wasn't with everyone else like he'd expected. She sat on the bench in the entryway, her back against the wall with her head tilted up toward the ceiling.

"Miss Brogan."

She glanced at him to reveal a face streaked with tears.

"You might need this for the walk home." He laid the coat across her knees, then took a step back, giving her space aplenty if she wanted to flee from him again. "Did something happen today? Last night? What has you so upset? Are you sure no one hurt you?"

What a dolt he was. Yes, someone had hurt her, otherwise she wouldn't shrink from his touch or panic when they accidently bumped each other.

But she just tilted her head back toward the ceiling and shook her head.

Maybe he should go get Victoria or his mother. They'd be better at dealing with a woman this out of sorts. He turned for the door that led to the kitchen.

"I… I don't like the way he looks at me."

Isaac paused, his back still to Miss Brogan lest turning to face her stopped her from talking.

"The way he talks to me. It isn't… it isn't good."

"He… who?" Isaac asked, though there was only one man inside that made him uneasy.

"The stranger."

"Did he say anything untoward?" He turned around then. "Did he do something he ought not have?"

She wiped another tear from her cheek. "He asked me to marry him."

"He did *what?*"

"I was doing dishes, and he came up and said he needed a mother for his young'uns, then said I was pretty enough to look at. I tried to move away, but he had me cornered by the sink. And he touched my hair. And I just… couldn't…" She shook her head and let the words fade.

There was no crime in talking to a woman, no crime in proposing to her either. O'Byrne oughtn't have touched her hair without permission, but here Isaac was contemplating doing the same thing. How could a man resist feeling one of those fiery tresses?

Yet Isaac found soothing words leaving his mouth anyway. "If you're not interested in his suit, I'll have a talk with him about leaving you alone. A man needs to listen when a woman tells him no."

"Th-thank you." Her voice trembled, but she looked up at him without her gaze darting away. "I'm sorry to be such a mess tonight."

He shook his head. "There's nothing to apologize for."

And there wasn't. Not when he was a constant mess on the inside himself, even if it only showed on holidays or when his brother went on a shipwreck rescue.

~ ~ ~ ~ ~

"They deserve a better pa."

Elijah glanced at his wife's reflection in the small mirror above the dresser, where Victoria stood pulling pins out of her hair. The house had long since quieted, all of their family and friends going home, while the O'Byrne children were tucked into bed in the loft.

"Don't you agree?" Her eyes met his in the mirror, a sharp hazel despite the dim lantern light.

His mind flashed with images from dinner. O'Byrne's raucous laugh, the dark manner in which he watched Aileen Brogan, the way he'd sent Alice to get help from Jack when she'd asked her pa for a second piece of pie. If O'Byrne couldn't be bothered to get pie for one of his children now, would he bother to feed them when they were his responsibility alone?

But the worst part was the children's silence. It was as though they became mute ragdolls in the presence of their father. The only time he remembered any of them talking to their pa was when Alice asked for pie. Jack had avoided him altogether, walking around with tight shoulders and a clenched jaw all night, while Alice and Toby had mainly hid, finding corners to play in and ways to get lost in the group of other children.

Elijah unfastened the top two buttons of his shirt before yanking it over his head. "I agree."

"Do we have to give them back?" Victoria pulled another pin

from her hair, releasing a wave of dark brown hair to hang by her ear.

"Not this second, no. O'Byrne has to find somewhere to stay first, and he also needs to find a job he can work in town."

"He won't try to take the children to the logging camp?" She released more hair from her pins, then met his gaze in the mirror.

"A logging camp is too dangerous for children." He'd put his foot down on that one. No pa with a lick of sense would want his young'uns in a place where trees could fall on them.

Victoria looked away. "When the time comes, I just don't know if I'll be able to give them back."

He could give a hundred responses to that.

I told you not to get too attached.

I warned you we'd only have them for a short time.

You knew I was looking for their father.

I wondered if this was a bad idea from the start.

Instead, he came up behind his wife and wrapped his arms around her. "I know, sweetling. I don't know if I'll be able to give them back either."

She laid a hand on the union suit covering his forearm. "Did you hear what he said when Jack asked him if he'd heard about Jenny passing?"

"I wasn't aware Jack talked to his father at all."

"Only the once that I saw." She sniffled and shook her head. "It's probably best you didn't hear though."

"Ah, Vic." He tightened his grip around her. "I'm sorry."

"For what? You didn't do anything."

For the pain, for the sadness, for the way I wanted to help three children in need, but only ended up hurting you. He reached down and spread his hand over the flat of her belly. *For not giving you a baby.*

She covered his hand on her belly with her own. "How do you think Beatrice is faring with little Meredith?"

"Just fine." He used his free hand to stroke a strand of hair back from her face, then let his hand drift the rest of the way down her silky locks.

"I wish I could go see my niece. Hold her."

Was he allowed to be thankful she couldn't visit? That the harbor had already closed? The last thing she needed was to hold a wee babe in her arms. Giving Jack, Alice, and Toby back to their father would already be difficult enough.

Maybe by the time the harbor opened, Victoria would have a little one of her own on the way, and handing tiny Meredith back to her mother wouldn't be so hard.

"Do you think she has blond hair like Beatrice's? Or will it be dark like her father's? And what about the eyes? Beatrice didn't write anything about how Meredith looked, just mentioned she was healthy and seven pounds."

"Victoria…"

"I know Beatrice will be a great mother. She'll rock her to sleep, sing to her, dress her in the finest clothes, and… and… and…" Her voice broke, and she turned into him. "If God's going to take away the O'Byrnes, why won't he give me a baby of my own? Does God think I'll make a poor mother?"

Elijah opened his mouth to respond, then closed it again. Though he couldn't answer for God, he certainly doubted that was the reason. His wife would make one of the finest mothers in the whole of Copper Country. "I don't know what God's thinking. But Proverbs three promises that if we trust in God with all our hearts, He'll direct our paths."

A tear crested and trailed down her cheek. "But what if God's path never includes a baby?"

He swallowed and pressed his lips to the top of his wife's head. He could think of half a dozen Bible verses to answer that question.

But at the moment, he didn't want to recite a single one. As Victoria had said, he simply didn't understand. He knew what he was supposed to do—trust God's plan, even when it made no sense. But he wasn't sure he could find the patience to do it this time around.

Not when he wanted to give his wife a child of their own.

Not when he wanted to keep Jack, Alice, and Toby just as much as his wife did.

Chapter Thirteen

Jessalyn blinked at the sketch of the bridal dress before her and focused on the neckline that still wasn't laying quite right. Should she add some lace? Or maybe change it from a square cut to a scoop neck? The drawing blurred, and she rubbed her eyes.

She'd been right not to trust Thomas. What he'd confessed tonight may have taken place five years ago, but his deceit still hurt, even now.

But should she blame him for trying to solve their money problems? If gambling would have worked and he'd have come home with twice their money, she wouldn't have cared how he'd gotten it, only that there'd be more money to help with the constant stream of bills. In fact, they might have used the money to all go west with him.

She curled her hand into a fist. And why was she sitting in her shop in the dead of night wondering about things that might have happened years ago instead of working?

Because she still remembered how he looked three hours ago, standing in the moonlight, the dark porch casting most of him in shadow, but not quite enough to mask the lines of regret etched onto his face.

He should have never deceived her about their savings, but his apology tonight was sincere. She'd no doubt that he'd go back in time and change things if he could.

But that still didn't mean she could trust him.

Paper crinkled under her hand, and she looked down to realize she'd crumpled the edge of the sketch in her fist.

She set the paper down and glanced out the dark windows of her store. It had probably been time for bed two hours ago. She reached for her lamp and started toward the stairs, stepping around a pile of shirts that had spilled from one of the tables onto the floor. When she reached the second floor, she peeked in Megan and Claire's room, then Olivia's, before finally entering her own.

Of all the things she'd learned tonight, perhaps the worst was that Henry had known about Thomas. When Henry had come to Eagle Harbor because she'd asked to move back to Chicago, he'd known where Thomas was and that he was sending money. And still, Henry tried convincing her to give the girls up for adoption and make a marriage that would prove advantageous for him. The union wouldn't have been legal since Thomas was alive, but Henry hadn't cared.

She slipped into her nightgown and slid beneath the covers. Why hadn't Henry simply told her where Thomas was, that he was sending money? He wouldn't have even needed to give any of Thomas's money to her. She'd have written Thomas and gone to him in South Dakota at that point. She'd had nothing to keep her in Eagle Harbor then, not even work, and she'd still been half in love with her husband.

She turned out her lamp and burrowed her head in the pillow. Would things have turned out differently if she'd have gone west to find Thomas when Megan was a babe? Or would South Dakota have only held more arguments and anger for both of them?

But life hadn't always held arguments. She still remembered the first time he'd called on her. Henry had been working, but Thomas had somehow wrangled a day off. He'd taken her to the Chicago

Academy of Science, where they'd looked at all manner of specimens. The butterfly collection had been remarkable, displaying a host of brightly colored butterflies from various regions of the world.

It snowed that day—as it had always seemed to do that first winter when they met. On the way home, Thomas stopped and bought her an angel, one with blond hair and blue eyes. "Just like you," he'd said.

She could recall the day as though it were yesterday, with snow falling around them and the light from the streetlamps illuminating the rich blonds and browns in Thomas's hair. The noise from passersby and horses and streetcars, and the smoke from...

Smoke?

She coughed. There hadn't been smoke. The night had been cold and crisp. She didn't remember any smoke then, but there was certainly smoke tonight.

She coughed again, then her eyes sprang open.

More smoke. Even in the darkness, she could see the dirty gray cloud of ash surrounding her.

She dragged in a breath of thick, foul air, only to cough again.

"Mama!"

"Meg—" Her daughter's name caught in her throat, the smoke so thick she couldn't speak through it. She scrambled from bed and made her way toward the door, ducking her head against the burning in her eyes and throat while she groped for the handle in the dark.

"Mama!" Megan called again.

"Ma!" The second cry came from Olivia.

"I'm coming." She felt her way down the hallway in the thick, black cloud.

Olivia met her at the door to the bedroom. "I think there's a fire downstairs."

Yes. The heat of it rose through the floor, her bare feet absorbing the unusual amount of warmth for this time of year. But even worse than the heat was the sound, a dull roar, like the lake on a day when the wind didn't let up. A snap sounded from downstairs, followed by a popping sound.

She glanced toward the stairway, filled with smoke, but the thick gray cloud couldn't quite hide the eerie red glow from the first floor.

"Ma, where are you?" Claire's voice rose over the din.

"I'm here," she choked, her throat growing grittier. She made her way across the hall to the room opposite Olivia's.

Olivia clutched the sleeve of her nightgown and followed behind. "What are we going to do?"

"Mama, I'm scared." Megan rushed to her legs the second she stepped into the room.

"We have to get out!" Claire's shadowed form started for the door.

"No, we can't go downstairs. The fire's too bad to get to the door." She wasn't quite sure how she knew. Maybe it was the rumble she felt underfoot, the way the floor almost seemed too hot to stand on, or her memory of the piles of fabric and clothes that would be engulfed with flames in a mere second's time.

They'd have to go out a window.

A second story window. She swallowed. Was it too high to jump, even with a fire at their backs? If only they had more snow, then the mounds if white could cushion their fall.

She headed to the window along the opposite wall, thrust it open, and looked down. Too far to jump, yes. But a window in Thomas and Isaac's apartment sat directly opposite the girls'.

"Megan, find me a shoe. You too, Claire."

Did the window lead to Isaac's room, or Thomas's? *Please, God, let someone be in that room, let them sleep softly enough to hear.*

"Help!" She tried to call, but her throat was so raw she could barely speak above a whisper.

Olivia rushed to her side and shouted into the night, her voice stronger.

"Good." She patted her oldest daughter's back. "Keep shouting while I close the door." She rushed to the back of the room, where the smoke grew thicker. She didn't dare peek down the stairway lest she see flames climbing them already.

Latching the door, she hurried back to the window. All three of her daughters stood there shouting for help, their voices all carrying farther than hers could.

She took a shoe from Claire's hand and lobbed it against the window. It hit with a clank before falling to the ground below.

She picked up the shoe Megan had dropped on the floor, but the window opened before she could throw it, and Thomas stuck his head out.

The girls started speaking at once, words about a fire and smoke and Ma not being able to talk anymore.

She felt a tear slip down her face. Even if her throat wasn't aching and raw, she'd still not have been able to speak for the giant lump lodged inside it. She needed help, and Thomas was there.

Just a few hours ago, she'd told him she'd never be able to trust him again. Yet she had every confidence he'd get them out of this building unharmed.

~ ~ ~ ~ ~

Thomas barely took time to pull on his boots before he raced down the stairs and into the night. The red glow of the fire from the first floor windows of Jessalyn's shop sent eerie shadows over the melting snow.

"I need to get a ladder," he shouted up at his daughters, then darted across the street. He'd seen an old ladder lying along the side of The Rusty Wagon. Hopefully the thing wasn't broken or rotted through. But first he raced up onto the porch, thrust open the door to the bar, and shouted, "Fire at the seamstress shop. We need help."

By the time he'd raced around the building to the ladder, the handful of men who'd been inside were already trickling out, Isaac leading the charge. He appeared at Thomas's side and hefted the far end of the ladder. "Jessalyn and the girls, are they still inside?"

"Why do you think I need the ladder? They're at the window that faces your apartment. I think it's one of the girl's rooms."

Isaac gave a quick nod. "I sent Leo Crivits for the fire wagon and Neville and Virgil are heading down to the Penny to see if they can scrounge up help there."

"Sounds good." Thomas hefted the long ladder. Pain stabbed his shoulder and flashed up his arm, and he groaned. Of all the times for his shoulder to get temperamental. He gritted his teeth against the ache and turned back toward his wife's shop, then stilled. Through the windows that lined the street, orange flames covered the first floor of her shop. "Oh dear God, please let us get them out before that floor collapses."

"What was that?" Isaac called.

Thomas shook his head. "I didn't realize the fire was so bad. Now let's go."

He started across the street, not caring if he had to drag the ladder the entire way himself despite his screaming shoulder. But Isaac kept pace, following him to the side of the building and helping him place the long ladder beside the window.

Olivia reached for it instantly.

"Wait for me to come up." He checked to make sure the ladder stood sturdy, then climbed the rungs while Isaac held the bottom.

"Take Megan first." Jessalyn spoke in a low, gritty voice he barely recognized, then handed their youngest daughter out the window. Megan wrapped her arms around his neck and clung tightly. It was a

159

semblance of her usual hug, but this time panic and fear tightened her arm muscles.

"I'll be back for Claire in a minute." He met his wife's eyes, and nearly found himself reaching for her when he saw the dampness reflected in them. "Sit down, Jess. There's less smoke on the floor than there is up high."

He didn't watch to see if she obeyed, but headed down the ladder as quickly as possible with Megan's small body wrapped around him.

By the time he handed her to Isaac, others had arrived to help put out the fire, many with buckets they filled with snow rather than water.

He turned and raced back up the ladder for Claire, who came willingly and obediently, clinging to him just as Megan had while he made his way back down again despite his worsening shoulder. By the time he returned for Olivia, both she and Jessalyn were standing at the window while flames licked up the door on the opposite wall of the bedroom.

"Can I follow...?" Jessalyn's voice gave out before she finished.

It'd be better if she waited. Even if she still climbed down by herself, at least he could help her if she started to slip. But he wanted to leave her in a burning room even less. "Yes, follow me, but be careful."

Not until he climbed down several rungs and she stepped onto the ladder above him did he realize she was in her bare feet and nightgown. His daughters had all been dressed the same. But did half the men in town need to see his wife in her nightclothes?

He climbed to the base of the ladder, where he handed Olivia off to Isaac. Isaac didn't let her bare feet touch the snowy ground, just hefted her into his arms like a doll and carried her across the snow to the stairway entrance to his apartment.

Thomas glanced up the ladder to find Jessalyn making her way swiftly down. When her feet reached the final wrung, he swept her into his arms much as Isaac had just done with Olivia.

"Can't have your feet getting frostbit," he whispered, which explained why he was holding her, but not quite why he was hugging her so tightly, or why his heart thudded in his chest, or why she wound her own arms tightly about his neck.

"Thank you," she croaked, followed by a harsh coughing sound.

"Let's get you inside and find Dr. Harrington. You need to be examined."

She didn't argue as he turned toward his building, but at the sight of the fire wagon on the street, he paused.

Rather than pumping water at Jessalyn's building, the workers were dousing the telegraph office and apartment instead. The men with buckets of snow were doing much the same, slathering the side of the building that stood closest to Jessalyn's blazing shop.

He didn't need anyone to tell him why. His family might be safe, but Jessalyn was going to lose her shop and everything in it.

Chapter Fourteen

The rubble still smoldered. Even in the middle of the night, faint red embers glowed beneath the pile of blackened ash, while wisps of smoke rose into the calm, moonlit night. A night that seemed far too serene for such destruction.

Jessalyn stifled a cough and looked away from the window of Isaac's apartment, which wasn't really Isaac's at the moment, since he'd packed a bag and left the rooms to her and Thomas until she had someplace else to take the girls.

A shiver traveled up her spine despite the warmth from the woodstove Thomas had stoked. Because she still stood in her soot-blackened nightgown, of course. Not because she was worried about what would happen now that the past five years of her life had been reduced to a pile of ashes.

Rebuild? It would take four years to earn back what she'd lost in a single night.

And if she did find some way to rebuild, should she do so here or in Chicago? Chicago made the most sense, but could she afford that after losing her building, sewing machine, fabric, and everything else? She couldn't possibly finish the bridal party dresses now, not without more fabric, and there would be no more shipped to Eagle Harbor until spring. But without getting paid for that job alone…

She swallowed against her raw throat, wrapping her arms even tighter about herself as she looked back out the window to the rubble heap.

The drawings were gone too, every last idea she'd had.

A cough wracked her body with deep, harsh convulsions that shook the insides of her lungs. She'd hardly coughed at all when she'd been trapped during the fire, but the coughing was growing worse now, along with the nauseous sensation churning in her stomach. Dr. Harrington had said the smoke she'd inhaled needed to work its way out of her body, but did doing so have to make her sick?

"Jessalyn." Thomas's voice sounded from behind her, but she kept her gaze out the window, as if staring at the remnants of her building long enough might resurrect it.

"Angel." A hand landed on her shoulder, and the scent of soap mixed with smoke twined around her. "Your bath's waiting. Were you going to take one?"

She stifled another cough and looked down at her blackened nightdress and the dark soot smeared onto her hands and feet. It wasn't as though she had much choice.

"In a..." She swallowed against her painful throat. "...minute."

"Is your throat sore? Do you want me to make you some of Dr. Harrington's tea?"

She shook her head and leaned her forehead against the cool window. She didn't want tea. She didn't want a bath. She didn't want anything but her building back—and everything inside it.

She drew in a breath, but her lungs refused to cooperate, forcing the air she'd just inhaled back up with another harsh cough.

"Jess." Thomas's arm wrapped around her shoulders. "Come on."

He turned her to face him, and she found herself staring up into a face scrubbed clean from ash and soot, even if a bit of gray still streaked Thomas's wet hair.

She didn't need to wonder if her own face was dark with ash. She'd shed enough tears for at least her cheeks to be clean, and she'd shed more as soon as she curled up in her bed and tried to sleep.

Except she didn't have a bed anymore.

"We need to wash this filth off you." He turned her toward the kitchen, but she shrugged his hands away.

"I don't need..." Another cough claimed her, her stomach heaving along with the convulsions. She went down on her knees and wrapped her arms around her middle, but not quite quickly enough.

A bucket appeared in front of her a second before the blackened contents of her stomach erupted from inside her. Another wave of nausea swept her, then another.

At some point Thomas knelt beside her and held the hair back from her face, waiting until she quieted before asking, "How much smoke did you swallow tonight?"

She curled into a ball on the floor, which seemed easier than standing, given the way her stomach wasn't done churning. "I didn't know about not standing up, that there was better air on the floor."

He rubbed her arm with long, soothing strokes. "I hope you'll never need to use the information again, but in case you do, stay low to the ground during a fire. The smoke rises, which forces the cleaner air to the ground."

"All right." Her eyes drifted shut.

A moment later Thomas stood and lifted the bucket, his bare feet padding down the stairs to the door that led outside.

She rolled onto her other side. If she lay here long enough, maybe her stomach would settle.

Thomas's bare feet reappeared by her side far too quickly. "A bath, Jess, you still need a bath, and then a bed."

She pressed her eyes shut again. "I don't want a bath. I want my shop back."

"I understand." His words were soft against the stillness of the apartment, soft and sincere and entirely too compassionate coming from a man who'd once gambled away their savings and kept it secret from her.

"Don't tell me you understand. You're not the one who's lost everything." Her words came out on a sob, but she shoved the tears away. Crying wouldn't do any good, especially not in front of Thomas.

She expected him to get mad and huff away. After all, that's what she was trying to do, wasn't it? If she was mean enough, he'd leave her alone.

But why did she want to send him away? He may have made a mistake with their money five years ago, but there'd been no question about his loyalty to her and the girls tonight. He'd saved them, plain and simple. And somehow, despite all the hurt and misdeeds that lay between them, she'd hadn't once doubted Thomas would come to their rescue when the flames had been consuming her building.

Instead of stomping into the kitchen like he probably should, Thomas crouched beside her and ran a hand down her filthy hair. "No, Jess, I understand exactly how you feel. Because I lost the most important thing I've ever had, and I'm still trying to get her back."

The breath whooshed from her lungs. He couldn't be talking about her. He simply couldn't. If he'd wanted to get her back, then why hadn't he left Deadwood to find them sooner?

Because of Henry. My family ruined things, not his family or anything he did. Which was probably why she'd turned to him for help during the fire.

"Let's start with first things first." He picked her up in his arms, never mind that her filthy nightdress soiled his clean clothes or that the stench of smoke clinging to her smothered the fresh scent of soap on his neck. And just like when he'd saved her from tromping barefoot through the snow earlier that night, she couldn't quite tell him to put her down. In fact, a part of her might not complain if he never set her down.

But he set her down anyway, beside a large wooden tub filled with water.

"Lindy lent you a nightgown and dress." He nodded toward one of the chairs where he'd draped a white nightdress similar to her own before the fire. "You can put it on when you're finished."

His big hands dropped to the collar of her nightgown, and he fumbled with the dainty buttons.

She stilled, the air around her growing as heavy as the smoke during the fire. His thick fingers worked just beneath her chin, finally undoing the first button and then moving on to the second. How many did he plan to undo? Should she pull away, tell him she was perfectly capable of getting into the bath herself?

He unfastened the second button, then stepped back and set his hands on his hips, his eyes running quickly down her. "Do you need help with, ah… the rest?"

"I can manage."

He opened his mouth as though about to say more, then shut it and gave a quick nod. "Right then. I'll make that tea."

"I told you I don't want—"

"Tea. I know. Or a bath. Or anything besides your building back." He headed toward the stove and kettle, his gait calm and unassuming, even if the tone told her he was done with her excuses. "But you still need tea and a bath, even if you don't want them."

She sighed. She was being petty. If the girls had fought her about taking a bath after the fire, she'd have told them they were being ridiculous and dumped them into the tub, fully clothed if need be.

She undid another button on her nightdress. "Are you going to… that is, can I have some… privacy?"

"You need tea, but I won't turn around, if that's what you're asking."

She stood there for another moment, staring at her husband's broad, muscular back while he filled the kettle with water and set it to boil. Dare she get in the bath while he was in the room? What if he turned and looked? Unless he planned to stand there the entire time she was in the bath, he'd have to turn around when he left the kitchen.

And how ridiculous was she being? He'd made three children with her, had lived as her husband for five years before he'd headed west. He already knew every part of her.

But what if he turned and looked, and looking made him want… *More?*

More than she wanted to give.

More than she had to give.

Or what if he already recalled her body the way she remembered every last detail of his—down to the eighth of an inch measurement around his waist?

"On the other hand…" He spooned tea leaves into a small teapot, his voice still carrying a hard note. "If I don't hear you getting into that water soon, I just might turn around and wash you myself."

She turned her back to him so that if he looked over his shoulder, he'd not get a full view of her, then yanked the filthy nightgown over her head and set her toes in the water.

And sighed. It was the perfect temperature. Filled to the perfect level so the water would cover all but the tops of her shoulders once she sank down. Even after so many years apart, he still knew precisely how she liked her baths.

She couldn't stop the flutter of warmth that climbed into her chest while she slid into the water.

~ ~ ~ ~

It started as a soft sniffle. Then another followed, and another. Thomas shifted his position on the sofa. Probably best to ignore them. He could get up and ask Jess if she was all right, but she'd been adamant about having privacy as she bathed.

Besides, it was an inane question to ask. He wouldn't be all right if his hotel burned to the ground, so why would she be all right after losing her dress shop?

But when the sniffles turned to a sob, he stood and headed for the kitchen, keeping his face averted. "Jess… are you… can I… help?"

"Give me back my shop." She choked the words out between sobs.

He looked at her then. She'd tucked her knees against her chest and locked her arms around them, resting her forehead against her legs while her long blond hair fell in tangled waves down her back. The water was nearly as black as the crumpled nightgown laying on the floor, just as it had been after he'd bathed the girls and himself.

He approached, his bare feet thudding against the floorboards. But she didn't look up. If anything, she wrapped her arms tighter about her legs while her shoulders trembled with silent sobs.

He headed to the basket on the floor near the stove, where he'd set towels to warm, much like he did at his hotel in Deadwood. "Come on, angel." He picked up a towel. "Let's get you out of there and into bed."

"What bed?" She kept her head bent over her knees. "It burned to the ground, along with everything else."

"Jess…" He whispered her name on a sigh.

She looked up at him then. "Oh, I'm sorry. I don't know why I'm being so difficult. You saved our lives tonight. I should be thanking you, and instead I'm trying to start a fight." She took the towel from his hand. "Will you turn, please?"

He did, though it was the last thing he wanted. He'd much rather have folded her into the towel himself and then drawn her against his chest. "I know it feels like you lost everything tonight, things will look better in the morning. Once your fire insurance pays out, you'll be able to rebuild either here or in Chicago."

Was there any point in hoping she'd want to move to Deadwood?

"I didn't have fire insurance."

He spun around to find his wife standing in her borrowed gown, a hand pressed to her mouth while tears streaked her cheeks. How could she not have fire insurance? Surely she understood that a shop like hers, with all the material and clothing piled inside, would go up in flames in a second. Plus she heated with wood. Who didn't have fire insurance if they used wood heat? He had fire insurance on everything he owned. Anyone who didn't want to end up a pauper had fire insurance.

"I know. I know." She held up a hand, almost as though she could read his thoughts and wanted to stop them from spilling out of his mouth. "It was foolish of me. I should have had it. I meant to have it. But at the beginning I could barely afford to feed the girls, and insurance was so expensive. Then when things got busier… well, I always meant to get some, but I never had time to look into it."

"Just like you always meant to tidy your shop but never seemed to find the time."

"Yes."

"Or get the pile of trousers needing to be hemmed for the miners finished."

"Exactly."

"Or build a snowman with the girls."

She blinked. "They told you about that?"

He slung a hand on his hip. "You've been promising for over a week. Do you know how many snowmen I've built with them after school? They don't want any more snowmen from me. They want one from you."

169

"Yes, I meant to do that too," she mumbled.

He headed for the lantern on the table and snuffed it. He wasn't about to think her shop burning a good thing, especially if she didn't have insurance to help replace what she'd lost. But without the piles of mending and endless dress orders surrounding her, maybe she'd have time for some of the things she talked about doing yet never got around to. Time for some of the things she'd used to do before he'd left.

Like play with their daughters or make her famous sugar cookies. "Let's go to bed."

Jessalyn's jaw trembled. "I keep telling you, I don't have a bed anymore."

"Sure you do." She didn't fight him as he rested an arm across the back of her shoulders and led her into Isaac's small room with its double bed tucked against the wall. "Isaac said he'd stay with Elijah and Victoria until we have someplace else to go."

"We?" She looked at him, her eyes dull with fatigue.

"Yes, we."

Her shoulders slumped, but she didn't argue, perhaps because she didn't have the energy. Instead, she climbed into bed and met his eyes with her red-rimmed ones. "I never told you thank you."

"For kicking Isaac out of his apartment? You're welcome." He shucked off his shirt, leaving his union suit on underneath, then sat on the bed to remove his trousers.

"No, for saving us." Her finger traced the pattern on the quilt, and she looked down, swallowing. "After how I sent you away at the Cummingses' I hardly deserved to have you turn around and save me and the girls."

"I wish you hadn't needed saving, but you don't need to thank me for it. I'd do anything to keep you and our daughters safe." He rested his hand atop hers on the quilt, stilling her movements.

She drew her head up, her teary blue eyes meeting his. "I know. And yet I don't understand it."

"You don't understand why I want to protect you?"

"No. I don't understand why I knew that you would." Her voice was soft inside the small room, and yet he heard every word she spoke, every gentle breath that puffed from her lips. "I don't feel like I can trust you in so many areas, and yet when our lives were at stake, you were the first place I turned, and I never once doubted that you'd save us."

"I'd save you all over again if I could." His eyes felt gritty, as though he were still standing in the smoke from the fire.

"I know. Thank you." She glanced at him uncertainly, then tucked her bottom lip between her teeth. "Will you... can you... hold me? Just for a bit. Just until I fall asleep."

He needed no further invitation. He bent to unlace his boots, then tugged off his trousers, crawling into bed with his wife wearing only his union suit.

He nestled under the covers and pulled her to his side. She didn't even hesitate as she snuggled against him and rested her head on his chest.

I love you, Jess. But speaking those words would unleash a whole other conversation between them, one they were both too exhausted to deal with tonight. So he stroked a hand absently up and down her arm instead, once, then twice. Somewhere between his seventh and eighth strokes, her breathing evened with sleep.

He shifted against the mattress and pulled her closer, then stared up at the ceiling. This had been what he'd dreamed in Deadwood, when he thought of returning to Jessalyn and telling her about his hotel, about all the money he had, all the things he could give her. He'd expected her to jump and cry and smile, to throw herself into his arms and rain kisses on his face. To snuggle up beside him in bed and ask to hear the entire story about how he'd come to own a hotel.

He'd never imagined her own dreams would need to burn to the ground before he finally got to hold her.

Chapter Fifteen

"I can't afford Olivia's surgery."

Thomas blinked his eyes open, only to be greeted with a face full of silky blond hair. "Huh?"

The soft, warm lump nestled against his left side shifted, and he winced at the throb in his shoulder. Carrying the ladder during the fire last night must have strained it. Or carrying his daughters. Or probably even looking at it wrong. Sometimes the pain seemed to be growing worse rather than better.

"Olivia's surgery. I wanted to pay for it, and now I can't."

"I'll pay for it." He rolled onto his side and hooked an arm over Jessalyn's waist. The extra ache in his shoulder from lying on it just might be worth snuggling with his wife for another minute or two.

But rather than relax against him, she wriggled out from under his arm and sat up in bed, her jaw trembling when her vibrant blue eyes met his. "What if I'm too scared to let you?"

He huffed out a breath. He was waking up next to his wife for the first time in five years, and she wanted to talk about money and surgeries. This wasn't exactly how he'd envisioned the morning going.

"What are you scared of?" he mumbled, his eyelids drifting closed. Did she realize how late they'd gotten to bed last night? Even if she didn't want to sleep anymore, couldn't she wait a few more hours before she started talking about what would happen six months from now?

"I'm scared of trusting you… and then getting hurt all over again."

Trusting him and getting hurt? His eyelids sprang open. Hadn't she said that she'd never once doubted he'd save them from the fire last night?

Yes, right after she'd told him she couldn't trust him in any other area of her life.

He threw his head back against his pillow and groaned. There was so much he could say. That Olivia was his daughter too, and Jess really had no grounds, legal or otherwise, to stop him from paying for the surgery. That Jess had nothing to be scared of. That they were husband and wife and there shouldn't be some type of tally system that caused one of them to feel beholden to the other. There should just be love. A whole unconditional heap of it. A heap big enough to cover all the wrongs they'd done to each other over the years.

Trouble was, his wife didn't seem to want even a smidgeon of love from him, let alone a heap of it.

He shoved the covers away and reached for his shirt. *How do I win her back, God? Why does it seem like each time we should be growing closer, we only get more distant?*

"It's wrong, isn't it?" Her voice emerged small and weak, though the room was so tiny it could barely hold a double bed and dresser. "You're my husband. I shouldn't feel so strongly about letting you back into our lives, letting you pay for Olivia's surgery."

There were a lot of things they shouldn't feel toward each other, a lot of old resentment that kept coming back to choke both of them. "What do you think I'll do? Settle into a life with you and our daughters, and then up and run off again one day? Because I won't."

She fiddled with the edging on the quilt. "How can I believe that?"

Because I changed the day I got the scars on my shoulder. But that was another issue entirely. Something he hoped to tell her one day, if she was willing to listen... and care.

"Is there anything I can say that will convince you?" He shoved his arms through his shirtsleeves, then started buttoning his shirt, never mind that his thick, bumbling fingers struggled to slip the small buttons through their tiny holes. "Anything I can do to change your mind? To prove that I never intend to leave you again? You've discounted everything I've said and done thus far—everything besides rescuing you last night, that is."

"And why not?" She crossed her arms over the thin fabric of her nightgown. "You say you never intend to leave us again, but you still want to take us to Deadwood in the spring. This time around you've replaced leaving us with dragging us somewhere against our will. Being determined to take me to Deadwood doesn't make me want to trust you any more than confessing you gambled away our savings before you left."

And he was right back to the beginning. It was almost as though the argument was a circle with no end. He tilted his head back toward the ceiling and drew a breath. What was he doing wrong? Once she saw he was serious about staying in Eagle Harbor for the winter, she was supposed to soften toward him and agree to leave for Deadwood on her own. But if anything, she'd turned harder.

Jessalyn climbed off the bed and headed to the purple dress hanging on the peg by the window. It would be too long for her, and possibly a little tight in the chest. But if he knew his wife, she'd have it altered and fitting her to perfection before lunch. Her hair would be pulled up in that elegant twist she pinned at the back of her head every day too.

But she didn't look perfect now, standing by the window barefoot and rumpled, her long hair hanging down to touch the small of her back. No glimpse of the pristine, professional town seamstress. She might even be a miner's wife with nothing more than a fourth-grade education for how simple she looked.

Would she be more content then? More at peace? Maybe the problem wasn't that they'd never had enough, but that they'd had too much and never been thankful for it.

But how could they work on being thankful, restoring their relationship, or anything else when all they did was argue over what would happen once the harbor opened?

"I want a truce," he said roughly.

"A truce?" She turned from her place by the window, her eyes blinking in question. "Yes, all right. Let's call a truce. No more fighting this morning."

He shook his head as he got off the bed and snatched his trousers off the peg beside her dress. "That's not the kind of truce I'm proposing."

"What then?"

"I want to leave Deadwood out of things for a while. Chicago too. No more talk about spring and what will happen or where we'll move."

"We?" She raised an eyebrow at him. "Are you planning on coming to Chicago with us now?"

No. But he wasn't planning on spending another five years separated from his wife and daughters either. "I just think we'd do well not to talk about spring for a while. We can try living like a normal married couple until the harbor opens, with you letting me provide for you. While something tells me you might have enough money saved up to live in Eagle Harbor until spring, I've got income from my hotel coming into my bank account every week. You won't need to watch your savings dwindle, and we'll leave what happens four or five months from now out of everything."

She shook her head. "That won't work. April will get here eventually, and we'll need to decide what to do. Why not prepare now?"

"Because you're getting—or rather, we're both getting—so caught up in what might happen one day that we're cutting off any chance to enjoy what we have right now. Today I woke up next to my wife for the first time in five years. And do you know what? I liked it. Don't get me wrong, I wish your dress shop never would have burned, but I can't go back and change that. I can, however, change today. How I act toward you, how I smile at you, how I show my love for you."

"Your love for me?" She searched his face. "You still...? After all these years...?"

He rubbed a hand over his face. Hadn't he just told himself not to bring this up last night? They had enough other issues to deal with besides him declaring feelings for his wife that she might well reject.

And yet, she didn't seem ready to reject them, at least not entirely given the way her throat was working, the way she couldn't quite meet his gaze. If she wanted nothing to do with his feelings, then her chin would be up, her eyes would be flashing, and she'd be barreling through a whole list of reasons why he had no business loving her anymore.

"Of course I still love you," he whispered into the room. But did she still love him? That was the bigger question. He tried to swallow, but couldn't quite manage it, given the sudden lump in his throat. After the last five years, he hardly deserved her love.

"Look, Jess. I'm not God, and I can't predict the future, but I can see the clues sitting in front of me, the little steps we can take to get back what we once had." He paused, waiting for her to say something about not wanting their old relationship back, but the words never came. Instead, she watched him intently, as though her ability to draw breath hinged on the next words he spoke.

So he'd better make them good. He drew a breath of his own, shaky with nerves, and pressed forward. "I woke up next to you today, and I want to wake up next to you tomorrow. We've been through more than most married couples. Your cousin-in-law took my job the day we got married, then made it hard for me to find more work in Chicago. As if that wasn't enough, he stole several thousand dollars from me, kept my whereabouts from you, tried getting you to give our girls up for adoption, and forced you to live without income. While both of us are wrong for separating in the first place, we're not at fault for the rest of it."

"Yes, I'll agree with you on that." She dropped her gaze and stared down at where her bare toes peeked out from beneath her hem. "I never should have told you to go west without me."

"You see, this is exactly what I mean. Between the past and the future, we're so bogged down that we're having trouble looking at what we have in front of us. Yes, we want different things for the future. But we won't have any chance whatsoever at a future together if we can't find a way to stop fighting over it right now. So why not set the future aside and work on living as husband and wife today, maybe seeing if we can straighten out some of the past?"

Her forehead knit, and she opened her mouth only to close it again before shaking her head. "I don't know."

"We don't even have to try it for four months. Let's shoot for three. December is almost here, we'll go until the beginning of March. Just you and me focusing on our relationship. If there's hurt from the past or forgiving that needs to happen, then we'll talk about it, pray over it, and try our best to work through it. At the beginning of March, we'll stop and reassess, see how far we've come, and then talk about where we want to move."

He was allowed to pray every day that she'd come to Deadwood, right? She might want to go to Chicago, but she wasn't making dresses for that wedding anymore, and she was the entire reason he'd ended up in Deadwood in the first place. Didn't she at least owe him a trip to Deadwood to see if she could be happy there?

Surely that was what God intended for them. "Maybe by March, we'll both be in agreement about where we want to go anyway."

"Am I allowed to think about it?"

Think about it? She was so close to saying yes, he could almost hear her voice filling the room with the word. He reached out and took her hand, then used it to pull her toward him. "Do you really need time, angel?"

She bit her lip. "There's so much I don't know at the moment, like where we'll live until the harbor opens or—"

"Right here with me." She had to say yes. It wasn't that difficult. He was only asking her to try being something she already was—his wife.

"But this is Isaac's apartment. You can't just kick him out and move me and the girls in."

Or maybe she wasn't about to say yes at all, not since she was coming up with excuse after excuse not to agree.

He dropped her hand. Was he really that intolerable to her?

Probably. He was, after all, the maimed, good for-nothing son of a town drunk, the brother of a consummate gambler.

"I bet Isaac would be happy to move out for a few months if he knows it will help us." If she was actually interested in getting help, that was. "Even if I wasn't here, I bet he'd still move out and offer to let you use the apartment for as long as you needed."

She shook her head. "Everything's happening too fast. I need time to think your offer through."

"I understand." In more ways than one. Because while she might say she needed to think, she'd only use the time to do what she'd done ever since he'd arrived—pull farther away from him.

He sat back down on the bed and yanked on his trousers in one swift jerk, then stood and headed for the door. "I'll make us some breakfast while you dress."

"Thomas."

He paused halfway through the door.

"Whatever we decide about this truce, I still…" She cleared her throat and looked down. "I still need you to pay for Olivia's ear surgery."

"You need me to pay for it, but you don't actually want me to pay for it, do you? You'd much rather pay for it yourself, if you were able."

She swallowed but met his gaze again. "Olivia's more important than our squabbles."

That she needed to voice such a thing told him what she'd decide about the truce, even if she'd yet to figure it out for herself. He pulled the door shut behind him. Or maybe she did know what she wanted to tell him, and she thought she was being kind by not giving him her decision right away, but in truth—

"Um, hello Thomas."

"Tressa." He stilled at the sight of Jessalyn's best friend standing in the apartment holding her babe. Then he looked around the apartment to find the girls at the table busily eating muffins. They'd been so quiet that he'd assumed they were sleeping.

"I'm sorry. I meant to be gone by now. The girls let me in a few minutes ago to drop off food, but they didn't say you and Jessalyn were, ah…" Tressa ran her gaze down him once, then bit the side of her lip. "…busy."

A flush stole up the back of his neck. They hadn't been busy in the way she meant, but how to explain without looking like a fool?

"Will you tell Jessalyn to call on me at the lighthouse today? I'd like to see her. Or if it'll be easier, I can come back later."

"Tressa?" The door opened behind him, and his wife peeked her head out, her hair still long and free and tangled about her shoulders, though she'd put the purple dress on.

"Jessalyn." Tressa rushed toward her so quickly Thomas had to step out of the way lest he be trampled by a woman half his size. "I'm so sorry about your building. But how are you feeling? The girls said you were coughing up smoke last night."

The door clicked shut behind him, muffling their words.

Thomas scratched his head, then glanced at his daughters finishing up their breakfast. "I'm going outside with the girls for a bit," he called through the door.

He doubted the women would stop chatting long enough to hear him, but after the fire last night, he wasn't going to complain about his wife having companionship. She needed it from somewhere—since she was so all-fired determined not to get any from him.

~ ~ ~ ~ ~

"I think it was my lamp." Jessalyn looked through the window at the pile of rubble that had been her shop not even a day ago. Her children played with the Oaktons while Thomas, Isaac, and Mac shoveled debris into a wagon with its wheels removed and sleigh tracks added to the bottom for winter.

"Your lamp?" Tressa patted Sarah's small back, though the babe slept soundly in her arms. "What do you mean by that?"

Jessalyn rubbed her forehead. "Last night Isaac and Thomas were talking about how the fire probably started with the woodstove. I know my shop is cluttered, but I always kept clothing away from the stove, and the wall behind it is stone. There was nothing near enough to catch fire. But my lamp…"

181

She didn't remember turning the wick down. She'd carried one upstairs to bed with her, but what about the one she kept on the shelf above her sewing machine? Had she left it burning?

She stepped away from the window and sank onto the sofa. "It probably serves me right. Here I am telling Thomas I don't need his money or his help. But the truth is, I'm exhausted. I'm too busy to know which way is up or down, my pile of work only seems to grow despite how many hours I work of a day, and I never have time to spend with the girls while Thomas…" She thrust her hand toward the window that neither she nor Tressa could see out of. "Thomas is always with the girls."

Tressa sat on the couch beside her. "Do you have a problem with him spending time with them?"

Yes. No. She didn't know. All she knew was that her life had been going along smoothly until he arrived.

Or had it? Because whether Thomas was in Eagle Harbor or South Dakota, she still didn't have time for the girls—or hadn't until last night's fire destroyed the piles of work waiting. And not just piles of work waiting for her, but piles waiting for Ruby Spritzer and Aileen Brogan too.

Before, she'd always been able to blame Thomas for her lack. He'd been the one to leave her, and she hadn't gotten any money from him, which meant she needed to provide for the girls and herself.

She'd provided for them ten times over.

But as for being a mother to them? Olivia cooked dinner most nights and got her younger sisters up and ready for school. True, Jessalyn scrambled out of bed and made oatmeal for everyone before they left, but she was always too tired to remember most of it.

"I want…" Jessalyn bit the side of her lip. "I don't know what I want anymore, besides to not go to South Dakota. But I need to tell him about the lamp. He wants to blame the woodstove, but the truth is, I was so tired after that big dinner and… other things…" Like learning about Henry stealing her letters and money. Learning about Thomas gambling away their savings. "But I had work to do, so I tried staying up, and then I forgot about the lamp, and it probably caught my papers on fire, which would have caused the clothes stacked near them to catch fire. And once that happened, there'd be no hope of putting it out."

She swiped a tear from her eyes, then held up her handkerchief and coughed up more of the black phlegm that seemed to have settled in her lungs for good. "And here I was telling Thomas I could do everything by myself and I didn't need his help, not because I didn't need it, but because I didn't want it. And then I burn down my shop."

"No one deserves to lose all that work. And everyone forgets a lantern now and again, even people who go to bed at a decent hour." Tressa laid a hand on her shoulder, but it did little to calm her.

"I'll admit, I didn't know what to think of Thomas when he first came, but the more I see him…" Tressa rose to look out the window, where she could likely see the men working. "He seems sincere. Committed. I saw the two of you together at dinner last night. Honestly, if you don't go to Deadwood with him in the spring, I think he'll sell whatever he owns there and follow you to Chicago."

She swallowed and looked at Tressa, her dark hair awash in light from the window. "You really think he'd do that?"

"I do. He knows he made a mistake, and he seems like he'll stop at nothing to make it right."

I'll never leave you, Jessalyn. She could still picture his face in the lamplight so many years ago, the snow drifting around them in silent, gentle waves as he asked her to be his wife. *I might not have a house as fine as Henry's or a carriage as elaborate as Walter Shunk's, but I promise I can do better than the tenements you grew up in. I promise I'll love you and cherish you as long as I'm alive.*

She could still taste the crisp winter air and feel the brush of snowflakes against her face. But his promise had only lasted for the first five years of their marriage, and even during that time, the cherishing bit had faded rather quickly.

Tressa left the window and headed toward the sofa. "I know he hurt you before. And I know it's hard for you to open yourself up to others, even other women. For some reason, you always think everyone will hurt or betray you."

"You wouldn't. Mac wouldn't. Isaac wouldn't."

"If Isaac, Mac, and I are the only loyal people you can think up in this entire town, then that just proves my point."

She drew a breath into her raw, swollen lungs, but managed to hold back the cough that tried following. "He wants us to have a truce and both stop thinking about the future. He wants to see if Isaac will let us stay here, and we'll live as husband and wife until the beginning of March so we can just focus on, well, us. The girls. All the normal things married people think about, and not on what will happen once the harbor opens."

"Married people can think about some really wonderful things." Tressa smiled brightly, then slanted her gaze toward the bedroom door. "They get to do some of those wonderful things too, you know."

Heat climbed into her cheeks, and she cleared her throat. "Those aren't the kind of things we'd be focusing on. More like forgiveness. And just... getting reacquainted with each other. Letting him provide for me. Letting me have more time with the girls."

"That still sounds wonderful, even if you won't be tending to other aspects of marriage." Tressa's eyes sparkled with too much hope.

Jessalyn twisted her skirt in her hands. What made Tressa so sure good would come out of this truce and not more hurt? "I didn't tell him yes."

"Oh, honey. Whyever not?" Tressa glanced briefly around the apartment. "You don't have anywhere else to go until spring, do you? And even if you found somewhere to stay, you'd be living off your savings. I don't see how you can get a new sewing machine to town before the harbor melts, and all the mending you had waiting is gone. What do you have to lose?"

Everything. She pressed her eyes shut against the scalding tears. "I'm a mess, aren't I? Here I just lost everything..." She shoved a hand toward the window. "Or rather, most of everything, and yet somehow it's harder for me to tell Thomas yes than to face the loss of my shop. What's wrong with me? I see that you and Mac have a good marriage. He loves you, you love him, you both make sacrifices for each other. And somewhere deep inside, I want the same thing."

She didn't even try to stem her tears, just let them stream down her face and plop into her lap. "So if I know I want a relationship like yours and Mac's, and my husband has returned and wants another chance to be a family, why can't I summon up the desire to try?"

Tressa sat beside her, her hand rubbing little circles on Sarah's back while the babe slept blissfully unaware. "Because it's not the same thing. You forget that Mac isn't my first husband—he's not the one who did me wrong. Did I have a hard time trusting Mac would be good to me after I spent ten years with Otis? Yes. But it's still not the same as me looking Otis in the eyes and telling him I forgive him for all the lies, all the gambling, all the other women."

Tressa pressed a hand to her throat, her gaze lost in her own memories. "I don't know that I could have done it. Rebuilding a life with Otis would have been much harder than learning to trust Mac. Because Mac never hurt me the way Otis did, or the way Thomas hurt you."

Jessalyn sucked in a deep, shaky breath. "So you don't think I should try trusting him again?"

"I didn't say that." Tressa looked toward the window, though neither of them could see their children or husbands while sitting. "I just said it would be harder than what I did with Mac. But worth it, if you can find a way. Are there times, even now, when my relationship with Mac is hard? When I struggle with trust or when he does something I don't care for, and I see Otis's deceitful actions instead of Mac's oblivious ones? Yes. But my marriage is still worth the effort of working through those hardships. Very, very worth the effort. Plus you have the girls to consider."

"They love him." Jessalyn coughed another bit of phlegm into her handkerchief. "He's only been here two weeks, and I already can't imagine separating them come spring."

Tressa sat back. "Then you have to try that truce. And you have to let God do the work. Have you thought of that verse I shared with you? 'Except the Lord build the house, they labour in vain that build it.'"

"Not overmuch, no," Jessalyn muttered.

"I think Thomas is right about setting aside the future for a few months so you can focus on healing, on seeing if you can build a relationship on the rubble from your past. Could be the foundation is still good, you just need to clear away the ashes first."

Clear away the ashes. Jessalyn stifled another cough. That didn't sound too hard. Now if only she could be guaranteed her heart wouldn't break in the process.

Chapter Sixteen

Jessalyn huddled deeper inside her borrowed coat to ward away the wind whipping off the lake. Clearing away the ashes of her marriage and rebuilding on its foundation had seemed possible earlier, just like rebuilding her shop didn't seem hopeless when she had been looking down at the rubble heap from Isaac's apartment window. But now that she stood beside it?

There wasn't anything of value left. Not half a sketch of one of her dresses, not a single remaining shirtwaist. It was all ruined.

There certainly wasn't a foundation left beneath all the burned wood. What if Tressa was wrong about her marriage too, what if there was nothing valuable worth salvaging between her and Thomas?

"I don't think it was your lamp, Jessalyn." Isaac called from where he stood with Thomas on the other side of the rubble heap. He pointed to a black, sooty spot at the back of her building. "It looks like the fire started there, by the back door. Unless you left your lamp there?"

"No, here by my sewing machine, where I always leave it."

Isaac came around the destroyed building toward her, looking at the westward wall where her sewing machine had once sat. Or rather, where it still did sit. Not all of it had burned. Evidently the fire hadn't gotten hot enough to melt all the metal, despite the mounds of clothes that had gone up in flames.

Another gust of wind from the lake lashed at her, tearing bits of hair from her updo and plastering them across her face. Above, the sky was a dark gray, almost the color of the smoke that had risen from the fire last night. At least it hadn't been this windy yesterday, or half the town would have burned.

"Well, wherever it started, we were wrong to assume it was by the stove." Thomas still stood by the opposite wall of the rubble heap. "This is the only section of the building that didn't burn."

She left Isaac and headed around the remnants of her building to her husband, his dark coat nearly causing him to blend into the rubble and soot-blackened snow.

He'd not said anything when she told him she was responsible for the fire. Not a single word about how she should have let him help with her shop or how she was doing too much. Nothing about how she should have gone to bed at a decent hour. He hadn't even suggested that if she'd forgiven him for gambling their money, she might not have gone to bed angry and lost her common sense. He'd only said Isaac wanted her to come down and look at the building before they cleared away too much of it.

It was somehow worse than shouting or lecturing her. He'd never had trouble pointing out her mistakes before. But today his forehead had scrunched down into a pained look, and then he held out one of Isaac's coats for her to put on.

So here she was, clad in Isaac's overlarge mackinaw coat, the red and black plaid clashing horribly with her purple dress.

"Almost all of the woodstove, wall, and chimney are still standing." Thomas pointed to the blackened stone. "If the fire would have started here, there would be more damage. It's almost as though the flames left the stone section alone since there was so much fabric and wood to devour."

She swept her gaze over the woodstove, still standing though coated with a layer of grime, then surveyed the chimney and stone wall behind the stove.

She had to agree to his truce. How else would she be able to tell whether their marriage was like the logs turned to ashes or the standing chimney?

"Jess?"

She bit the side of her lip and ran her gaze over the charred stone once more. "So if the fire didn't start by the stove, then it must have begun by my lamp. There was no flame near the back door."

Thomas looked to the sooty mess where her back door had once stood and rubbed his chin. "Did you see anything suspicious last night?" he called to Isaac.

Ash crunched beneath Isaac's boots as he picked his way over the charred logs toward them. "No. If anything, the town was calmer than usual. I assumed it was because of the holiday. You?"

Thomas shook his head. "I stopped at the Penny and the Wagon before you got into town, but—"

"You went to The Pretty Penny last night?" Her face turned cold, and she sucked in a breath of stinging winter air.

"Wait a minute, Jess." Thomas held up his hands, as though that would somehow absolve him from visiting a brothel after their fight. "I didn't—"

"And not only did you go to a brothel, but you turned straight around this morning and asked me to live with you as a wife and give our marriage another chance. Are you insane?" She shouted the last words louder than intended. So loud, in fact, that a couple of passersby stopped and looked their way.

She didn't care. The entire town could look if they wanted to, but they wouldn't find her standing here any longer. She turned and stalked toward the apartment above the telegraph office, where she certainly wouldn't be staying with her husband tonight.

"Jess, stop." Thomas snagged her arm before she reached the entrance. "It's not what you think. I was working."

"Working. At the Penny. Sure you were." She tried to shrug off his hold. "Let me go."

"No, I work for Isaac now. As his deputy. I was making sure things were under control."

"You're Isaac's…" She turned to find Isaac, who had also followed her to the door and was standing just behind Thomas. "Is that true?"

Isaac gave a brief nod. "I swore him in the day before Thanksgiving."

The rage simmering in her chest cooled faster than a tub of hot water tossed out the window into the snow, and she looked down before meeting her husband's eyes once more. "I didn't know."

Thomas dropped his hand from her arm. "Maybe not, but as soon as you heard I was at the Penny, you assumed the worst."

Her cheeks heated. "It's a brothel. Everyone in town would assume the worst unless they knew you were a lawman."

He scratched the back of his neck and blew out a breath. "Suppose I forgot to mention my new job, what with Thanksgiving and the fire and all."

"Yes, I suppose you did." She swiped a strand of hair behind her ear. "I'm sorry for assuming the worst. If I would have stopped and thought before I spoke, then I probably would have realized your visit wasn't what it first seemed."

"I forgive you."

He did? That simply? She fiddled with the lining inside her coat pocket. Was this what he'd been talking about when he'd mentioned they needed to focus on their relationship, on healing from the past and forgiving each other? Maybe this was one of the areas they could work on—not spouting the first accusation that came to mind but stopping and thinking before speaking. Being quicker to forgive when one of them was offended.

Or rather, *she* might need to work on these things, because Thomas hadn't done anything wrong.

"I'm going to head over to my office." Isaac took a step back from them. "See if there's any business that needs tending there."

"I'll go with you." Thomas turned to follow Isaac. "Then maybe come back and clean up more of this mess."

"Wait."

Both men paused and looked back at her, and she moved her gaze between them before settling it on Thomas. "What if I don't want you working for Isaac? If we're going to try being a family, why would you choose a dangerous job?"

"Does that mean you agree to the truce?" His voice was quiet, perhaps even timid.

Did it? She dug the toe of her boot into the snow and sighed. This seemed like such a simple decision for him, so cut and dry. Maybe it would be for her too—if she could forget that he'd once promised to cherish her but ended up leaving instead. "I said I wanted time to decide. An hour is hardly enough. Go ahead with Isaac."

His eyes grew distant and he took a step back. "I see."

"Thomas..." She swallowed the lump in her throat, then shook her head. "Never mind."

He turned and left with Isaac, his broad back rounding the corner of the telegraph office.

The ache in her chest only grew as he disappeared from sight. She'd have to give him an answer about the truce soon.

If only she knew which choice would lead to less heartache in the end.

~ ~ ~ ~ ~

"It was arson."

Thomas could barely make out Isaac's words above the wind

whipping over the lake. "I was thinking the same thing."

"There's no other explanation for why the back door is burnt to a crisp, especially not when the stove is mostly intact." Isaac shook his head, which was already bent low to ward off the wind as they headed down North Street toward the sheriff's office. "If the fire would have started where she says she left her lamp, then her sewing machine would be in worse shape, but that's still mostly standing, just covered in soot."

Thomas glanced over his shoulder at the charred remains of his Jessalyn's building. "Why would someone want to burn my wife's shop down?"

"You tell me." Isaac's jaw was rigid as he spoke.

Thomas lifted his shoulders, then let them fall. "Ah, she overheard something she shouldn't have when some ruffians dropped mending off?"

"If that's the case, then your wife was the target, not her building, which means she might still be in danger."

A chill slithered up his spine, and he glanced over his shoulder a second time. Was that Jess's form watching them from the window above the telegraph office? "Don't suppose you have any other theories about why someone would burn down her place. Preferably one that doesn't want my wife dead."

"Only the same theory I had about why those shanty boys tried to bloody me."

"A distraction from something bigger going on?"

"Got any other thoughts?" Isaac climbed the steps to the porch.

"No, but the fire was the only trouble last night, right?"

"So it seems."

Which left someone attacking Jessalyn the bigger possibility. "We'll need to watch the town carefully tonight."

"Already planning on it." Isaac's gaze traveled down the road to the telegraph office. "Is she going to be all right? She seems pretty shaken up. But I reckon I'd be the same way if my home and shop burned."

Thomas rubbed the back of his neck, stretching his shoulder at the same time. His wife hadn't seemed all right since he'd returned. She might say she was well and claim she could do everything on her own, but she was always so overworked and frazzled.

"I suppose we're both a bit of a mess, and not just because of the fire." Thomas glanced at Isaac, still standing in front of the door to his office, his gaze riveted on the apartment.

Thomas let the next words drop from his mouth straight and direct. "Is there anything between you and Jessalyn that I should know about?"

There hadn't been an affair, surely that would have come out by now, but maybe a kiss or two? Intimate talks shared over coffee in the morning or while watching the girls play? They seemed too close, Jessalyn too willing to share things with Isaac that she struggled to share with him.

"Not in the way you mean." Isaac unlocked the door to his office. "She's always been married in my mind, even when half the town thought you were dead. She never spoke of having you declared dead, nor did she speak of getting a divorce for abandonment—so she left no hope for anyone that might have interest."

"The divorce would have been null the second I returned and proved I hadn't, in fact, abandoned her." He followed Isaac into the warmth of his office. Jessalyn pursuing a divorce had never crossed his mind in South Dakota, not when he assumed she was getting his letters and cashing his banknotes.

"The two of you seem to be doing better than that first night." Isaac hung his coat on one of the pegs by the door.

"Better?" Thomas blinked. "Us? Didn't you just see us fight?"

"Maybe, but she cares about what happens to you, even if she doesn't want to admit it. And I saw you two at Thanksgiving last night."

"Where we fought."

Isaac plopped into the chair behind his desk and reached for a stack of papers. "Where she couldn't keep her eyes off you before your argument. I also happened to notice you went after her when she stormed off."

Imagine Henry were still alive and he asked to manage your hotel while you were gone. Would you let him? ...And that's precisely why I can't go to South Dakota with you.

Yeah, following Jess last night hadn't ended so well for him.

Thomas sighed and hung his coat on the peg beside Isaac's. "Any chance I can take over the lease on your apartment for the next three months?"

Isaac's gaze lifted from the paper in front of him. "Did she agree to stay there with you? That seems like a sure sign the two of you are doing better."

"She's thinking about it, or at least about staying there with me and trying to be married." Given her concern about him working for Isaac, she might truly be considering his offer and not trying to let him down gently.

"You're going to *try* being married?" A grin covered Isaac's face. "I thought you already *were* married."

Thomas rolled his shoulder, still aching from carrying the ladder and his family last night. "Turns out the legal definition of marriage is a bit different than the practical one. We spent five years living like we weren't married, and now that I'm back in Eagle Harbor, we're both so involved in the lives we built separately that we can't figure out how to have a life together anymore."

Isaac stood from his desk and moved one of the chairs along the side wall, clearing a path to a door that had been partially covered. "You can have the apartment for as long as you need it. I'll let Mr. Ranulfson know the lease is switching hands for a few months, but I doubt he'll care as long as he gets paid."

Thomas held up his hands. "Better wait a day or two on that. She hasn't said yes yet." And he should know better than to get his hopes up with her.

"Sounds fine. I can wait a few days." Isaac unlocked the door and disappeared inside, but rather than emerge a moment later with a broom or some other object from storage in hand, clomping sounded.

"Isaac?" Thomas stood and headed to the door. "Where are you going?"

Isaac paused halfway up a cold, dusty staircase. "Jenkins's apartment. Might need a place to stay for the next few months."

"There's an apartment up here?"

"If you can call it that."

It made sense. The building was clearly two stories, but he'd never given much thought to what sat above the sheriff's office and jail. Thomas's boots left prints in the dust as he headed to the top and followed Isaac inside the apartment.

Or rather, he tried to follow Isaac inside. But there was barely room for one person to stand in the dusty, cramped space, let alone two.

"Don't tell me the former sheriff lived here?" He looked around the small room with crates and sacks scattered haphazardly over the floor. There was probably a bed underneath all the clutter... somewhere. If they spent a weekend shoveling this place out, they might even find it.

Isaac grimaced. "Rumor has it he saved every sheriff's report he ever filled out."

"I thought you said he was remiss in his duties."

"At the end, but he was sheriff here for over thirty years, and he wasn't always a drunkard."

Thirty years of papers crammed into a one-room apartment. Great. Thomas grabbed a sack of papers, opened the top, and glanced at an arrest record dated 1868. "Looks like there's going to be another fire soon, but one we'll set."

Isaac reached into one of the crates and pulled out a glass bottle. "Want a bottle or twelve of whiskey?"

"No, thank you."

Isaac put the whiskey back and pulled the lid off another crate. "Jenkins didn't have any family to collect this stuff when he died. Technically the apartment comes with the job, but I didn't want to live above the jail—it'd feel like I'm always working. Plus I still don't have the first inkling what to do with Jenkins's stuff."

"Wait. When I first arrived in town, you could have given me this apartment to rent and told me to clean it out, but you offered to let me stay with you?" Thomas dug deeper into the sack. Were any of the reports recent, or were they all fifteen years old?

"Because you'd be right next to Jessalyn. And I figured… well, that you'd need to be close." Isaac's eyes met his, serious and sober. "Because there was no way she'd be inviting you into her shop on her own. There was a heap of hurt lying between you."

"I feel like all that hurt's still there, like it gets worse the longer I stay, not better." He pulled out a couple more papers, but held Isaac's gaze rather than read the dates. "Thank you. Being next door helped."

Isaac swallowed, then muttered a few words about doing something right for once, before opening another sack. "Glad I could help."

Thomas grabbed two sacks of papers by their necks. "So do you want to start cleaning this out or wait until Jessalyn decides what she's doing?"

"May as well clean it out. It has to get done at some point." Isaac surveyed the piles of papers and crates. "Virgil O'Byrne needs a place to stay with his children too. Thought about letting this to him, but I don't like the notion of him being above the jail. With you above the telegraph office, that'd leave me nowhere to stay but with my brother. It wouldn't be difficult for someone to find me while I walked home in the middle of the night."

"And attack you," Thomas growled. "And maybe not just one person, but a group of someones."

Isaac tugged at his collar. "Yes, that."

"Sheriff? Sheriff Cummings?" A man's voice echoed up the stairs. "Where are you?"

"Coming." Isaac grabbed a crate and clomped down the stairs. Thomas followed, both sacks of papers slung over his shoulders.

A handsome blond man in a suit paced the office. Thomas set the sacks down and narrowed his eyes at the familiar-looking businessman.

"Herod." Isaac gave the man a nod. "What's happened?"

"It's gone. All of it. Last night. Someone must have stolen it."

"Stolen what?" Isaac found a spot on the floor for his crate and set it down with a thud.

"My safe. It was blown open. The gold's gone too, candlesticks and chandeliers." The man spread his arms wide before dropping them back to his sides. "All of it except the few pieces I keep in the girls' rooms for show."

Thomas's stomach soured. That's why the man looked familiar. He'd been stalking around the saloon part of The Pretty Penny giving out orders when Thomas had stopped by with Isaac his first night on duty.

197

Isaac took a notepad off his desk and began scrawling details. "What time do you think the theft occurred?"

"When we heard about the fire. I closed down the brothel and sent everyone to help... well, besides the girls." The man paced from one side of the office and back again, fiddling with a gold pocket watch while he walked. "I locked them in their rooms and left Rufus to keep watch."

Isaac paused in his writing. "And Rufus didn't spot anything suspicious?"

"Rufus was knocked out and tied up. Didn't find him until I opened the place up this morning."

Thomas moved his gaze to Isaac, and he could see the sheriff thinking the same thing as him. Jessalyn's fire had been arson, all right. But if the target had truly been The Pretty Penny, did that mean his wife was safe?

Chapter Seventeen

"No, you spin it like this." Jessalyn turned away from the pot of simmering soup and plopped herself onto the floor. Then she took the top in her hands, threading the string around it, and letting it loose on the wood boards.

"Ma, where'd you learn to do that?" Olivia picked up her own top and tried spinning it. "You're better than Ivy, and she's the best in the whole school."

"Can you teach me?" Megan peered over her shoulder.

"Of course. All it takes is a bit of practice." She picked up the top again, then paused. Three sets of blue eyes blinked expectantly back at her. Her lips tilted up in a slow smile as she wound the string around the top once more.

The door to the apartment opened just as she released the toy.

"Aw, Pa, couldn't you have waited?" Claire stuck out her bottom lip, but pushed herself off the floor and went to her father rather than watching the top. "Ma was teaching us to spin tops."

"She's good at spinning tops, isn't she?" Thomas hefted Claire into his arms, then winced.

Winced? Why would Thomas wince when picking up their daughter? Had he already injured himself working as a deputy?

"What's that I smell?" He sniffed the air. "Cookies?"

"We helped Mama make them!" Megan jumped up from the floor, leaving Olivia to practice with her top.

"It's been a while since we made cookies." Jessalyn tried to shrug, but the gesture came off more stiff and jerky than intended. "I figured—"

"It was the first time ever, and it was fun!" Megan bounced up and down on the balls of her feet.

"It wasn't the first time ever, it's just been…" Four years? Five? *Too long.*

How quickly the girls had grown while she'd been elbow deep in a pile of mending. This year she'd even been too busy to take off all of Thanksgiving Day to spend with them.

And even today, without a stitch of mending to tend, their time together was ending. The scent of sugar and flour called her back to the oven, as did the simmering soup on the stove. Did time with her daughters always have to pass so quickly? No more than the curl of smoke from a chimney before it disappeared into the winter air.

She pushed to her feet and headed into the kitchen, then reached for her potholders and pulled the tray of cookies out.

"Pa, can all of us go outside and build a snow family after dinner?" Claire wrapped her arms around his neck and rested her head on his shoulder. "The fire melted our old one."

"Hmmmm. That depends how long it takes to make dinner. I have to work tonight, and it looks to me like someone's tired." Thomas chucked Claire under the chin.

Work? As Isaac's deputy again? A chill traveled up her spine. Hopefully he and Isaac would do nothing more than sit in the sheriff's office.

"Can you make dinner fast, Ma?" Claire stifled a yawn against her father's neck. "I want to play before bed."

"Dinner's already made." Jessalyn pulled a tray of biscuits from the oven. "That is, unless you want something different than soup and biscuits."

Thomas set Claire down and came up behind her in the small kitchen, looking over her shoulder into the pot of soup. "Jess…"

A hand landed on her waist, and she jolted, her muscles tensing for an instant before relaxing against the familiar feel of her husband's hand. He settled it in the same spot he'd always placed it after they were married and when she was pregnant with Olivia. He'd come up behind her to ask what was for dinner, if she wanted help doing dishes, if her back was bothering her, or any other number of things.

She pressed her eyes shut against the decade-old memories.

"When I left you here earlier, I didn't intend for you to play maid and work all afternoon." His voice was low and deep.

"I didn't exactly have sewing to do." The words tasted bitter, even if they were true. What was she to do without her shop?

His hand tightened at her side, holding her in place. *Today I woke up next to my wife for the first time in five years. I wish your dress shop never would have burned, but I can't go back and change that. I can, however, change today. How I act toward you, how I smile at you, how I show my love for you.* He may as well be whispering his words from this morning in her ear given how they echoed through her mind.

This was what she'd wanted, wasn't it? She'd watched Tressa meet and fall in love with Mac, Victoria with Elijah, Lindy with Dr. Harrington. Not all marriages ended up broken and full of heartache. And here she was, getting a second chance she'd not dared dream of.

"You could have taken a nap, angel." That he did whisper in her ear, bringing back another rush of memories that involved his breath brushing her cheek, her neck, her ear.

Should she give Thomas another chance? Her hand tightened around the soup spoon. He'd broken her heart when he left, leaving her to cry herself to sleep in an empty bed every night for months.

She'd been too sick to eat at first, too sick to go to church, too sick to do anything. And she'd not known where their next meal was coming from or whether they'd have money for rent. But somehow she'd gotten out of bed day after day, even if the only thing pushing her forward was her daughters. Then she'd started mending, and her days slowly turned from a hopeless trial into a steady, dependable way to provide for her family. She had a system and she had security. It had all been enough—until Thomas returned.

If she allowed herself to love him now, would he crush her again?

Or would they be stronger together than they were apart? Would they love each other and make sacrifices for each other and live a full, happy life, like Mac and Tressa?

She stared down into the pot and stirred the soup, but that didn't stop a single tear from rolling down her face and splattering onto her apron.

"Olivia, it's my turn." Claire's voice floated through the kitchen.

"I want one more time," Olivia answered.

"You promised I could have it next."

Jessalyn looked over her shoulder. Her two eldest girls argued, yes, but there was a comfortable sort of ease to it, just like there was a comfortable ease to Thomas standing behind her, his hand on her waist while she tended dinner. Had Thomas never left, would things have been like this? Would she have spent afternoons and evenings with their daughters rather than digging through endless piles of mending? Would she take comfort in knowing she didn't need to provide for the entire family on her own, but had a reliable husband who saw to that?

Except the Lord build the house, they labour in vain that build it.

She had to give God a chance to rebuild her house with Thomas, even if it meant Thomas broke her heart all over again.

"I accept," she whispered into the pot.

"What was that?" Thomas leaned closer, his breath fanning against her neck this time.

"I said I accept. The truce, that is."

"You accept? Truly?" He spun her around to face him, and the smile that spread across his face was so large she felt her own lips tilt up in response.

"Truly." She tried to press her lips into a firm, straight line, but couldn't quite manage it, which was just as well since Thomas was laughing, his eyes almost as bright as the day soon after they'd been married when she'd told him she was pregnant with Olivia.

"That's wonderful." He hefted her into his arms.

She squealed, and he raised her even higher, then twirled them both around in the small space between the stove and the table.

"Thomas, put me down!" All she'd done was agree to a trial. A marriage trial to the man she was already married to. It hardly deserved a big celebration.

But Thomas didn't seem to think so. His eyes danced as he spun her around a second time, still laughing, still with that big, silly grin spread across his face.

And then he set her down, but not the same way he picked her up, oh no. He slid her down him, her body held tight against the strong, muscular form that had so fascinated her when they'd first met. And when her feet finally touched the floor, he leaned in, his breath brushing her chin for an instant, and then his lips were soft against hers.

She stilled, not quite able to pull away, and not quite able to move her mouth against his. A tear slipped down her cheek, then another. Too soon. This was too soon. She might be ready to let him back into her life, but not for the intimacy they'd once shared.

"What are they doing?" Claire's voice again.

"They're kissing, silly, like Mr. and Mrs. Oakton do." Olivia that time.

"I've never seen Mr. Oakton kiss Mrs. Oakton like that."

"I think it's nice."

"Then why is Ma crying?"

Thomas moved his mouth to travel from her cheek to her jaw, his kisses impossibly tender against her skin.

"Mama, I'm hungry." Something tugged at her skirt, then a small body wedged its way between her and Thomas's legs.

Thomas's hold slipped away a moment later, then he frowned and took his thumb to swipe at the tear trickling down her cheek. "You're crying. I didn't mean to upset you, angel." He dropped his hands to her shoulders. "Are you all right?"

"I…" Was she? She didn't feel like she'd been all right since he'd returned.

"I never agreed to kissing," she whispered through her swollen throat. Kisses would muddle her senses until she couldn't think clearly. Already she wanted his arms back around her, his warm lips against hers.

"No kissing?" The frown crept back onto his face. "I don't recall you saying that was out of bounds before agreeing to the truce."

She pulled away from him. "Maybe not, but you never said it was part of the truce either."

"What if I want to kiss you?"

She wrapped her arms around herself, a poor replacement for her husband's arms that had held her so solidly a few minutes ago. "Kissing will only confuse things between us, and we hardly need more of that."

"Confuse things, huh?" His frown turned into a smile, and then he winked at her. Actually winked! As though she were some trollop to be flirted with rather than a woman who'd been married for a decade. "It'll be fun seeing who wins this argument, won't it?"

Then he leaned down and kissed her again, except this time when their lips met, she couldn't quite manage not to kiss him back a little.

Chapter Eighteen

Something shifted beside Thomas's face, and he rolled over to find a warm body lying beside him in bed. Jessalyn. He sighed and nestled closer.

"Thomas!" She sat upright. "You're back. You're all right."

Hands ran over him then. Familiar hands. Long and slim and… caring.

"Jess." He groaned. She couldn't keep touching him like that, not unless she intended to act like his wife in other ways too.

Her hands stilled on his chest, and her head rested there a moment later. "I probably shouldn't worry about you working for Isaac, but I do."

He raised his hand to stroke her shoulder, a warm sensation sweeping through him. "It wasn't dangerous work last night. We just did some patrolling."

"Patrolling for what?"

If only he knew. "Anything out of place or suspicious." Of course, if they'd found something while patrolling, the job would have taken a quick path into dangerous territory.

"Do you still think my shop fire was arson?"

"Unfortunately. Reed Herod's brothel was burglarized down to its last nickel during the fire, so it seems likely the fire was a distraction."

"Oh… I didn't know. I'm… I'm glad we got out then."

He hugged her close. "Me too."

Commotion sounded from outside the door, Megan's girlish voice followed by one of Claire's giggles.

"We should probably get up." Jessalyn covered a yawn with her hand.

Thomas groaned again, his shoulder aching. "I want to pray first."

"Pray?"

"As husband and wife, for our relationship, for our daughters, for God to direct our steps." He rolled out of bed and knelt on the floor, never mind the popping in his knees. "I messed up the first time around with you. I don't intend to make the same mistakes again."

Silence lingered between them for a long moment, then Jessalyn slowly scooted over the bed toward him and knelt. "No. I don't suppose you do."

The question was, were they both too set in their ways to change things ten years into their marriage? Or was there time left to start anew?

~ ~ ~ ~ ~

Nothing. They had absolutely nothing.

Isaac blew out a breath, long and hard, as he trudged over the packed snow on Center Street.

How did a person—or group of persons—steal so much from a brothel without anyone seeing a thing and without leaving tracks back to where they'd taken their loot? It had to be the work of several men, but where could they store so many things? With the harbor frozen, they could hardly move a brass chandelier or a gold-plated mirror out of Copper Country, which meant the stolen goods had to be stashed somewhere nearby.

But where? He looked up to survey the wooded hills surrounding the town. So many trees. Without a trail to follow or a witness who spotted something in the forest, it would be impossible to find where the goods were hidden. He and Thomas could spend from dawn until dusk snowshoeing every day, and they still wouldn't cover half the places someone could have set up a makeshift warehouse.

He huffed out a breath, which turned instantly white in the dry winter air, then passed the front door of the bakery and rounded the side of the building, heading to the back. He knocked on the door that led into the kitchen from the alley.

Ellie Spritzer, the oldest of Ruby Spritzer's eight children, opened the door a second later, her carrot-colored hair contrasting with the white clapboard wall. "Sheriff Cummings. We're just closed for the day, but if you want to look over some of the goods that didn't sell while we clean, I'm sure I could—"

"Actually, I'm here to visit Miss Brogan." Which was why he'd timed his visit for after the bakery closed.

"Miss Brogan?" Ellie's hand stilled on the door handle for a moment, then she looked over her shoulder into the kitchen. "I'm not sure that she wants any callers."

"It's sheriff's business." At least in part. And if there was another part of him that wanted to see her again? Some unofficial part that ached to glimpse the flaming color of her hair, or watch a smile inch across her lips rather than a frown?

He cleared his throat. "Definitely sheriff's business."

"Come in, then." Ellie motioned him inside. "Aileen, the sheriff is here for you."

"For me?" Miss Brogan looked over her shoulder from where she stood by the counter, her hands buried in a big bowl of dough.

"Miss Brogan." He took off his hat. "Might I have a word with you?"

"You can go into the bakery while I finish up in here." Ellie nodded her head toward the swinging half doors that led from the kitchen to the storefront, then trotted to the sink full of sudsy pans.

"I'm sorry. I assumed you'd both be done working by now. I can come back later if that would suit better."

"No." Miss Brogan's voice was nearly panicked as she spoke the single word.

Then again, he should have expected as much. The woman had almost suffered a fit of nerves last time he'd tried talking to her alone. Why hadn't he thought of that sooner?

"That is, I've just finished mixing up the sourdough." Her jaw was hard despite the tremble in her voice. "Let me wash my hands and I'll be done."

"Instead of going into the other room, perhaps you could go for a walk with me?" Maybe she'd feel less threatened if they were out in the open.

Indeed, a bit of the tension eased from her movements as she washed her hands. "Aye, a walk sounds better than sitting in the stuffy storefront."

She headed over to the coats hanging by the door and pulled one on that had been patched in three places. It looked thicker than Ellie's, but that wasn't saying much since the Spritzers were the poorest family in town. If the rumor about Ellie's mother being pregnant again was true, then things were about to get more worrisome for the family.

"I won't keep you long." Isaac moved to the door and held it open, allowing Miss Brogan to precede him into the cloudy afternoon.

As soon as she stepped outside, she sucked in a breath of winter air. "I must admit, Sheriff Cummings, I didn't give much thought to what winters would be like when yer sister offered to bring me to Eagle Harbor."

"Colder than Chicago, huh?" He offered his arm, then led her around the building to Center Street.

"And Ireland."

Did they even get snow in Ireland? Isaac scratched his head and eyed the clouds to the west, dark and heavy enough they'd probably drop a foot of snow or better overnight.

"What did ye want to speak with me about?"

Your accent. Your family. Your fiery hair. Whether there's snow where you come from in Ireland. "Has Virgil O'Byrne bothered you at all since Thanksgiving?"

She stopped walking, right in the middle of the street, and turned to look at him. "That's why ye stopped by? To make sure that brute's leaving me alone?"

"Is there another reason I should have stopped?" Like perhaps she wanted to see him? Talk with him? Take a walk?

Her throat worked. "No. I just... thank ye. For checking. I appreciate it."

"You don't need to thank me for doing my job." But he'd hardly complain if she wanted him to stop by and take her on another walk when they didn't have anything official to discuss.

She started walking again, her hand still tucked in his arm. "Not all lawmen take their job as seriously as you."

That was probably supposed to be a compliment, but he couldn't quite take it as one. "What do you mean? Did Sheriff Jenkins ignore other problems you had while here?"

She raised her head to the harbor, letting the wind toy with the loose tendrils of her hair, and he could almost see her standing on Ireland's emerald slopes, her face raised to the sea while the sun brushed her skin. "I don't want to talk about it."

Was she this unapproachable with everyone, or just him? She seemed to get along with Victoria, Tressa, and Ellie well enough. And she and Lindy had lived together for several months before Lindy married Dr. Harrington. Surely she wasn't so standoffish with them. "Whatever happened to you, Miss Brogan, just tell me it didn't happen here. That you weren't hurt because Sheriff Jenkins was remiss in his duties and that there aren't scoundrels in town I need to be watching for."

"Not here, no." She drew in a deep, shuddering breath. "But I thought I saw a shadow last night."

"A shadow?"

"When I came home from the Oaktons', though it was gone too quickly for me to be sure."

"A shadow of what?" They turned from Center Street down Front Street, where the wind off the harbor whipped at their coats.

"A man, maybe two. Like I said, it was just a glimpse when I rounded the corner of the bakery, then it was gone."

His muscles tensed beneath where her hand lay on his arm. "You ought not be going about town unescorted right now, especially after dark."

"It wasn't quite dark, but I probably stayed out later than I should have." A shudder traveled through her. "I'll make sure to get home earlier from now on."

They turned down South Street, already heading back to the bakery. "If you need an escort, don't hesitate to ask. I'm happy to assist you in any way."

"Thank you."

They continued quietly for several minutes, heading down Front Street and then turning onto 3rd Street. The soft patter of their footsteps filled the silence between them, and snow sparkled around them, with yesterday's dusting of several inches still laying pristine over the town. Her hair truly did flame against the whiteness, a single, unmistakable splash of color so vibrant he nearly reached out and fingered one of the flyaway strands hanging by her ear.

They rounded the corner of 3rd Street, bringing the bakery back into view. "Miss Brogan, might I stop by and see you tomorrow? Take you on another walk, perhaps?"

Her brow furrowed. "To make sure Mr. O'Byrne hasn't called? Or that I didn't see anything more in the shadows?"

"Ah…" He cleared his throat. "I was more thinking I'd visit you as a man interested in a young lady than as a sheriff doing his job."

She jerked her hand off his arm, and a haunting pain etched tiny lines around her eyes and mouth. "I don't think… or rather, it's probably best… that ye don't. Come by, I mean. Unless it's on official business." She wrapped her arms around her middle. "It's nothing against ye, but what I'm trying to say is—"

"You don't need to say anything more, Miss Brogan." He took a small step away from her. He'd been a fool to ask, especially considering how eagerly she'd escaped his presence on Thanksgiving. "I thank you for your time today. I'll make sure to keep a watch out at your building for anything suspicious."

She nodded, but no relief swept her face. If anything, her gaze only grew heavier and the lines on her brow deepened. "If such a thing as a good man exists, Sheriff Cummings, then I'm sure ye're one of them. But me, I'm just not the type to make a good wife. I don't think I'll ever be, at least not anymore. Ellie Spritzer though, she's nice. A hard worker, too. And not too hard to look at with all that bright hair she's got. Bet she'd love it if ye stopped by the bakery tomorrow and asked her for a walk."

Ellie Spritzer? He coughed. Did Miss Brogan think any woman would suit? As though he'd drilled a hole for an axel in a toy wagon, and one rod would fill the space just as well as the next?

And here he was being foolish again. He barely knew Aileen Brogan. He shouldn't be upset if she refused a walk with him.

But still, there was a part of him that ached to wipe that sorrowful look off her face and put a smile there instead. What was so wrong with that?

Everything, since she isn't interested in me.

But whether interested in his suit or not, she had one thing wrong. He wasn't a good man—because a good man didn't watch his father drown without attempting to save him.

Chapter Nineteen

"Yes, this came in last night." Mrs. Runkle handed a slip of paper across the telegraph office counter.

Jessalyn glanced down at the missive, which was longer than most telegrams. But then, if a person had an unlimited amount of money to spend on wedding finery, a person probably had an unlimited amount of money to spend on telegrams.

New seamstress procured. Sorry unable to do wedding. Will see you once you come to Chicago. Hope you can still do dress for me.

The edge of the telegram crinkled in her grasp. She'd not anticipated Dorothy Hanover would have any trouble finding another seamstress. But the woman was still willing to work with her after she moved to Chicago? Despite the hundred dollars in green satin she'd lost during the fire?

"Would you like to send a reply?"

"Sure." Jessalyn looked back up at Mrs. Runkle, her gray hair frizzy in the afternoon light. What should her reply to Mrs. Hanover say?

It was a simple answer, really. *I'd love the business and I'm still planning to be moved by May.*

But moved to where? Chicago? What if she could be happy with Thomas in Deadwood?

"Oh, I nearly forgot. I have a telegraph here for your husband too." Mrs. Runkle handed her the slip of paper. "Came all the way from South Dakota, that one did."

"Thank you." Jessalyn slid it into her pocket.

"He gets them every week, but then, I'm sure you knew that."

She hadn't, no, but it wasn't as though she'd asked Thomas for details about his hotel either.

"Aren't you going to read it?" The widow raised an eyebrow.

"I'm sure it doesn't pertain to me."

The widow humphed. "You ask me, a wife should know her husband's business just as well as he knows hers."

How lovely. Except she hadn't asked Mrs. Runkle's opinion.

"So does this mean you're not moving to Chicago anymore? You want me to put that in a telegram back to the rich lady?"

"I don't wish to reply at present, but thank you for your time." Jessalyn turned and darted out the door before the widow could come up with any more questions. Or worse, invent a story to share with Betty Ranulfson. Was it uncharitable to hope Mrs. Runkle would decide the telegraph office was too much work given her age, and somebody else got hired to replace her? Somebody slightly more discrete?

Jessalyn sighed and headed across 4th Street and into the mercantile.

She needed to pick up some flour if she was going to make another batch of cookies with the girls, and maybe a few ribbons to gift the girls for Christmas. Though ribbons seemed a small thing to give considering the dresses she'd been making for them before the fire.

She settled the flour into her basket, then headed to the aisle with the ribbons. Yellow for Olivia, purple for Claire, and pink for Megan. That would do nicely.

But what was she going to give Thomas? A new razor for shaving in the morning? Perhaps a new hat? She moved toward the shelf filled with haberdashery supplies. She could make a vest to go with one of the pairs of pants she'd made him, but without her sewing machine, she'd have to stitch it entirely by hand.

Yet none of her ideas felt quite right. What did a woman give a man who seemed to have everything he needed? A razor, a belt, a hat. None of them were a good fit for the man who had once owned her heart, then abandoned it, and was now trying to wriggle his way back inside.

"Mrs. Dowrick." Ruby Spritzer headed toward her, a threadbare shawl pulled tightly across her shoulders while her growing stomach protruded from her thin frame. "I was sorry to learn about your fire."

"Thank you, Mrs. Spritzer." *Ruby.* But the one time she'd called the other woman Ruby, Mrs. Spritzer had blinked, then gone right on calling her Mrs. Dowrick.

"I suppose that means you won't have no more mending for me?" The woman's jaw trembled the slightest bit as she spoke.

A quick glance at the fraying basket she carried told Jessalyn there was only enough food inside to feed the Spritzer brood for a few days. "No work. I'm sorry."

There had been no shortage of people stopping by the apartment since the fire, but most of them were men wondering if their coat or shirt or trousers had been spared. Thomas had started leaving her with a stack of dollar bills to give the men for each garment lost so they could go to the mercantile and purchase another.

"I don't think I'll be taking on any more sewing between now and when I leave in the spring. But if anyone stops by with something to be mended by hand, I'll send them your way." She'd been planning to hand over her sewing clients to Mrs. Spritzer come spring anyway. After all, Ruby Spritzer needed steady work more than any other woman in town. But would she be able to keep up with both a new baby and the town's sewing demands?

"Thank you for your time." Mrs. Spritzer gave a brief nod. "And Merry Christmas."

"Merry Christmas." Except she didn't feel very merry as the mother of eight—soon to be nine—walked to the back counter with only a handful of things in her basket.

Jessalyn blinked at the shelf in front of her, shoe polish blurring with the razors and mirrors and belts. A Christmas present for Thomas. That's what she'd been thinking about before Mrs. Spritzer approached.

She reached for one of the pairs of black stockings sitting on the bottom shelf. Stockings were a nice gift for a man. Always useful, but not too personal.

After all, she was already sharing an apartment with her husband and sleeping beside him every night. They hardly needed to become more personal than that.

And praying with him every morning. And helping him clean up dinner every night, making him oatmeal in the morning before he left to walk their daughters to school.

Oh, who was she kidding? She was already far too personal with her husband for a woman who was planning to move to a different state without him in a few more months.

And if she didn't move to Chicago in the spring, how many other women like Ruby Spritzer would go unhelped?

And here she was breaking a truce that was only two weeks old. She'd promised not to think about what would happen in the spring, and so she wouldn't.

She headed to the back counter where she paid for the flour, stockings, and ribbons. Then she pushed through the door of the mercantile and into a light dusting of snow falling from the sky.

And there he was, pulling the girls down North Street on a sled, their delighted giggles filling the air while a handful of other children trailed after them, all clamoring for a turn.

He paused, laughing as he ousted Olivia from the sled and let Alice O'Byrne and Jane Oakton climb on. They loved him. Not just their own children, but half the children in town flocked to him.

How could she not fall in love with a man like that?

She tilted her head to the side and rubbed her brow. Why hadn't she seen what would happen once she declared that truce? Once she let the walls she'd carefully built around her heart crumble?

But then, how could she hold herself back from the man who had fathered her daughters? Who wrapped his strong arms around her every night when they slept, yet had never once asked she give him anything in return?

Who called her angel?

He may have been gone for five years, but now he was part of their lives again, in a permanent sort of way that couldn't be removed without causing pain and suffering.

She looked down at the stockings laying in the top of her sack. What was she going to do?

~ ~ ~ ~ ~

Thomas shucked off his tan trousers and reached for the dark blue ones hanging on the peg in his room. He was late to meet Isaac—again. What was he going to say when he found the sheriff? That he'd spent too long playing checkers with Olivia? That Olivia had beaten him twice?

He glanced at the perfectly made bed in the corner. When he'd first volunteered to be a deputy, he hadn't been living with Jess and the girls. Now he was giving up evenings with his daughters and unable to fall asleep next to his wife, and all so he could spend half the night wandering around in the cold for free.

He must be going daft.

"Thomas?" The door to their room opened, and Jessalyn stepped inside. "The girls are in bed and I was… oh."

She swept her gaze briefly down his union-suit clad chest. "Are you going out on patrol again?"

He reached for the dark blue shirt that went with his trousers and plunged his arms through the sleeves. "What gave it away? Surely not clothes the color of night."

She bit the side of her lip and took a hesitant step closer. "I was hoping you wouldn't have to go tonight."

"Were you now?" His hand stilled on the top button of his shirt. "And why is that?"

She swallowed but kept her gaze pinned to his in the dim lantern light. "I… I don't know. I'm being foolish, I suppose."

"I don't think it's foolish," he rasped through a throat that had grown suddenly tight. Did she truly want him to stay? Just him, Thomas Dowrick, her husband? Not someone taller than her who could clean the top of the cupboards or stronger than her who could carry a crate up the stairs? Him alone? "I'd rather stay too."

"You would?"

"Is that so hard to believe?"

She looked down, then back up at him. She'd been awfully quiet this evening. She'd handed him a telegram from Deadwood but had barely spoken to either him or the girls, and he hadn't had a chance to ask if something was wrong.

"Why?" Her voice was barely more than a whisper.

"Why what? Stay and spend time with you? Maybe because you're my wife. Because I…" *Love you.* He'd already told her after the fire, yet at times she was still so hesitant, so uncertain of him. Would saying the three words burning in his heart for a second time send her scurrying away again?

His hand fumbled with the button at the top of his shirt once more. Whose idea was it to give a shirt as big as this such small buttons anyway?

"Here, let me." She closed the space between him and reached for the button. "Are you late again?"

Her hands brushed his chest, and an ache filled him. Did she feel it too, the energy that hummed between them when they touched? Probably not, if the brisk, efficient way she slipped the buttons into the small holes was any indication.

"It was that second game of checkers with Olivia," he croaked. "I shouldn't have played it."

"Oh, I don't know about that. She was pretty happy when she beat you." Her nimble fingers continued down the row of buttons.

"Which was precisely why I shouldn't have played it. Between Olivia's smiles and my large hands, I'm out the door late every night."

Jessalyn's fingers slipped on the last button, and she looked up at him. "I don't think your hands are too large."

He held them up. "Come on, Jess. They're the size of bear paws."

She tilted her head to the side and giggled. Actually giggled. As though she were as carefree and full of life as Claire or Megan. "I always liked how big they were. You can fit my whole face between them." She reached for one of his hands, then brought it up to cup her face.

"And that's a good thing?" He swallowed, her skin soft beneath his work-roughened palm, then brought his other hand up to hold her face in both hands.

The air grew still around them while the breath from her lips brushed his face. A simple dip of his head, and their lips would touch.

His own breathing grew shallow. Should he kiss her? He'd not attempted to since she'd agreed to their truce, and she'd hardly been eager for his kisses then.

God, how do I know when to kiss her? When to tell her I love her? When to show her I love her with nothing separating us?

Standing in their bedroom with only lamplight surrounding them, most men would lean down and kiss their wives without thought, then carry them to the bed. Yet he couldn't, and he had no one to blame but himself. He'd been the one to gamble away their savings. He'd been the one to leave and assume she was fine for five years.

He didn't deserve another chance, yet she'd given him one anyway—or was trying to. But she was still so fragile, like a butterfly emerging from a cocoon to open its wings for the first time. If he pushed too hard or too fast, she might fly off without him.

"Your hands always made me feel small, but in a good way." Her voice broke through the stillness surrounding them, then she reached up and laid one of her own hands atop his, and turned her face slightly into that palm. "Delicate, like I was one of those pretty china dolls in Henry's warehouse, and you were my protector."

Protector. Right. Except he hadn't been her protector for five long years.

He dropped his hands and took a step back, the guilt nearly choking him. "Well, I suppose the best way to protect you now is by finding the arsonist who burned down your shop."

"That wasn't what I—"

"I have to go." He took another step back, then left without so much as a glance over his shoulder.

Because one more look at his wife standing by their bed, and he just might not make it out the door.

Chapter Twenty

"I c-can't even have them for Christmas." A tear rolled off Victoria's cheek and plunked onto the table. "Why couldn't he have found a place to stay after Christmas?"

"I'm sorry," were the only words Jessalyn could muster. They echoed quietly through the lighthouse kitchen, inane and trite as they were. But what did one tell a woman who'd adopted orphans into her heart, only to turn around and give them back to their birth father? And on Christmas Eve, no less?

"We'll be over tomorrow for Christmas dinner." Tressa set a platter of cookies on the table. "Your place will be full of children, I promise."

Tears welled in Victoria's eyes anew. "It's j-just not the s-s-same as having the O'Byrnes there."

"Is there anything we can do for you?" Jessalyn reached over and rested a hand atop Victoria's limp one. When Tressa had invited them over to visit on Christmas Eve afternoon, none of them had anticipated Victoria and Elijah giving the O'Byrne children back to their father right beforehand. "I can't imagine how hard it would be to lose them."

Victoria sniffled and wiped a tear from her cheek. "Why can't Elijah and I be blessed with a b-baby of our own? Maybe then losing the O'Byrnes wouldn't be so hard."

Again, another question to which there was no good answer.

Tressa set a pitcher of milk on the table, then wrapped her arms around Victoria's shoulders from behind. "I'm praying for you, dear."

"Thank you. I need all the prayers I can get this Christmas." Victoria wrung her hands. "How long do you think I should wait until I visit them? Elijah said to let the children spend Christmas undisturbed with their father. Do you think I could see them the d-day after?"

"I think the day after will be just fine," Jessalyn spoke over the lump rising in her own throat. If Victoria was this heartbroken over losing children who had only been with her a few weeks, what must Thomas have felt like when he'd returned to town only to have her ask him to keep his distance?

But he'd never complained. Never accused her of being unfair or needlessly hurtful.

Then again, he hadn't exactly kept his distance either.

The door to outside flung open, and a rush of cold swept the room. Elijah ducked inside, allowing enough space so little Jane Oakton could enter on his shoulders without bumping her head. He stilled as soon as he saw his wife, causing children to pile up behind him.

He swung Jane off his shoulders and headed straight toward Victoria, never mind the snow he tromped through the kitchen. "Aw, Vic, don't cry again. I told you everything will be all right."

"I know, but it just d-d-d-doesn't seem all right at the moment." A fresh mound of tears welled in her eyes, and she pushed her chair back from the table and went into Elijah's arms.

The lump returned to Jessalyn's throat, and she looked away. Thomas held her every morning when she woke up next to him, true, but how long since she'd gone willingly into his arms? How long since she'd approached him with a problem and trusted that, no matter what was happening around them, they could face things together and be stronger for it in the end?

"Ma, will you come outside and play with us?" Megan rushed up to her. "Pa has to go."

"He does?" She glanced behind her to see Thomas standing in the entrance to the kitchen with Claire on his shoulders, the snow on his boots quickly melting into a puddle. "Where are you going?"

"Isaac's in the yard with Mac. He wants to take another look around town before we go to the candlelight service. Says I might actually get tonight off if all stays quiet." He gave her a lopsided grin, but when Claire wriggled on his shoulders, his grin turned into a grimace, and he sucked in a sharp breath. "You can't move like that, princess. It hurts me."

Jessalyn stood. "I wondered if something was wrong with your shoulder. When did you hurt yourself?"

"A while back." Thomas used his left arm to swing Claire to the ground, a grimace still on his face. Then he stretched his arm out and rolled his shoulder, which only caused another wince to cross his features.

"You got into a fight while you were on patrols with Isaac, didn't you?" A chill swept through her, and she tamped down the worry that climbed into her chest. "Thomas, I really think your job is too dangerous for a man with a family."

"No, Ma, it's Pa's bad shoulder." Olivia shrugged, then reached for a cookie on the table. "Sometimes it pains him."

"Bad shoulder?" She looked between her daughter and her husband. "Since when do you have a bad shoulder?"

And why hadn't he told her about it? Or more to the point, why had he told the girls but kept it from her?

"I injured it last spring." He turned and started down the trio of steps that led to the outside door. "Anyway, Isaac and Mac are waiting, but the girls didn't want to come in yet. I said maybe you could play with them."

"But what about your shoulder?" She followed him to the top of the steps. "If you didn't injure it working for Isaac, then when—?"

"Later, angel." He climbed back up the steps and pecked her on the lips, just a quick brush, but it was enough to set her cheeks burning.

Then he left her there, right in the middle of the kitchen doorway.

Silence filled the room behind her, and a fresh burst of fire swept her face. She turned to find everyone's gaze exactly where she'd expected—on her.

It wasn't fair. No one had ogled Elijah when he'd hugged Victoria, and that had lasted longer than the brief brush of her and Thomas's lips.

Because everyone expects it from Elijah and Victoria, but not from me and the husband who left me for five years.

"Ah… I'm going to go with the men, see if I can be of help. Maybe Isaac and Thomas will get a quiet Christmas." Elijah bent down and pressed his lips to the top of Victoria's head, then rubbed her arm. "You don't mind, do you?"

Victoria sniffled and wiped at a tear on her cheek. "Go ahead. No sense in staying here. I'd just be a watering pot with you around."

"I love you." Elijah brushed a strand of hair out of Victoria's face, then bent and gave her another kiss, on the lips this time, and he wasn't in any hurry to finish it.

Heat climbed back onto Jessalyn's face, and she forced her gaze to the window. Frozen rocks and an icy harbor greeted her, but she'd take that over watching a man kiss his wife in a way she'd insisted Thomas not kiss her.

"Ma." Little Megan came up and tugged on her skirt. "How come you and Pa don't kiss like that?"

"Sorry." Elijah pulled away from Victoria, his voice low and rough. "Forgot about the young'uns."

"That's quite all right." Jessalyn pressed a hand to her cheek. Surely the heat in her face had something to do with the warmth of the kitchen at this point. It was impossible to blush for five straight minutes, wasn't it?

"Can I have a cookie?" Claire asked from where she stood at the table.

"Me too." Megan ran to the table and peered at the plate.

Elijah's bootsteps echoed through the kitchen behind her, the door to the lighthouse opening and closing a moment later.

Jessalyn headed over to the table. "I thought you wanted to play outside."

"After we eat some cookies." Olivia tugged at her ear before reaching for a second cookie off the platter.

Jessalyn handed her two younger daughters cookies, then sank into her chair and took a cookie for herself. "Girls, do you know what happened to your pa's shoulder?"

"The mine collapsed on him." Claire's shoulders rose and fell in a shrug. "May I please have some milk, Mrs. Oakton?"

"The mine collapsed?" Jessalyn's bite of cookie turned to sawdust in her mouth. Why hadn't he told her he'd been hurt? And here she was worried about his lawman job being too dangerous, but in truth, walking around town with a gun strapped to his hip probably wasn't half as dangerous as going underground.

"It's why he came back." Olivia tugged at her ear again. "He wanted to see us and make sure we were all right. Didn't he tell you?"

She shook her head, her throat suddenly too tight to speak. What if he'd died in that mineshaft? Would she have ever learned what happened to him? About his hotel in Deadwood? That he'd made his fortune?

But hadn't Thomas owned his hotel for four years or better? If so, then he shouldn't have been in a mine before he came back to Eagle Harbor.

"Why would Pa tell us and not you?" Claire scrunched up her nose.

Probably because she'd never thought to ask why he'd suddenly returned. She'd been too busy fuming that he'd arrived at all, let alone expected them to walk away from their lives in Eagle Harbor and go to Deadwood.

"How did the mine collapse on him?" she asked it absently. Carelessly. Forcing a lightness into her voice she didn't feel. Never mind that it was a silly question. There wasn't exactly a "how" behind a mine collapse. Gravity was the how, and it happened to workers all the time. Anything from a small smattering of pebbles to large chunks of rock to an entire tunnel cave in.

"Olivia." She looked at her oldest daughter, now busy dunking her cookie into her milk. "Tell me what happened to your pa."

Olivia finished the bite of cookie in her mouth before speaking. "He saved a girl like me. She went into an old mine even though her ma told her not to, and she got lost. Pa and some other men were looking for her, but then some rocks fell on Pa. He was stuck there a whole day before the helpers could get him out, and his shoulder got hurt."

"And the doctor made him lay in bed for a long time, but when he got better, he decided to come home and see us." Claire shoved her final bite of cookie in her mouth.

"And make sure we obey you so we don't go into any old mine shafts." Olivia's cookie plunked into her milk, but she didn't bother to fish it out, just tugged on her ear instead.

"'Cept the mine's all the way in Central, not here." Megan wrinkled her nose. "Isn't it silly Pa thinks we'll go into one?"

"Silly, yes." She croaked through a throat that felt as though it had been filled with crushed mine rock. He'd not been lying when he said he'd come back for them, that he still cared about them even though he'd left.

She raised her gaze from her daughter's face and met Tressa's eyes.

Her friend drew in a deep breath, then let it out. "I told you there was a reason, Jessalyn. I told you he'd changed."

Yes, yet despite the time he lavished on the girls and the hundreds of small ways he'd tried to help her, she'd been so focused on herself, on how he'd hurt her in the past, that she hadn't been willing to look beyond herself and see how fully he'd changed.

Or maybe that had been the problem with their marriage from the beginning. Maybe she'd always been too concerned about herself and what Thomas could do for her. He could take her away from the slums she'd grown up in. He could promise her affection—at least more affection than Henry's pick of Walter Shunk for her husband.

She had a whole list of things Thomas could do for her, but had she ever asked what she could do for him? Up until the day he'd left, everything had been about her and how they needed to set aside money so *she* didn't end up back in the slums where *she'd* grown up.

Except the Lord build the house, they labour in vain that build it. But she hadn't been letting the Lord build anything at all. Instead, she'd been standing in the way, insisting everything go exactly how she desired or she didn't want any house at all.

She dropped her head into her hands and drew in a deep, shuddering breath. Oh, what a fool she'd been.

~ ~ ~ ~ ~

"The town is too still. Too ready for something to happen." The packed snow on the road crunched beneath Thomas's boots as he swept his gaze over the houses and shops lining Front Street.

"Maybe I should stay on patrols with you tonight." Elijah turned to Isaac, who was walking beside Mac. "Don't suppose I can get one of those tin stars you gave Thomas?"

"Go home to your wife." Thomas headed toward the Fletcher's warehouse. Not that another visit would yield any more clues given the six inches of snow that had been dumped on them last night, but he had to do something other than stand around and wait for the next burglary or arson. "This is a horrible day to give the O'Byrne children to Virgil."

"I asked him to wait until after Christmas." A sharp edge cut through Elijah's voice. "But he wouldn't be swayed."

"I'm sorry, Elijah." Mac rested a hand on Elijah's shoulder, pulling his brother to a stop in the road.

"I keep asking myself if I was wrong for volunteering to watch them. I thought it would be good for Victoria, give her some young'uns to spend time with and whatnot. Guess I didn't think it through hard enough. She was attached to those young'uns the day after we brought them home. So I thought we needed to look harder to find their pa so she didn't get even more attached, but I assumed their pa was the honorable type. The kind that would do right by his children, not..." Elijah shook his head.

The hair on the back of Thomas's neck rose, and he looked around. Was someone watching them? Nothing seemed out of place. On the contrary, really. Everything seemed too easily in its place.

"I'm sure it's not as hopeless as it seems." Isaac gave Elijah a couple thumps on the back.

Thomas turned back to Elijah, keeping the shipping office across the street just visible from the corner of his eye. "Does Victoria know that you tried to wait until after Christmas to give the children back? Or that you worked so hard to find their father?"

Another shake of Elijah's head.

"I think you should go home and tell Victoria everything you're telling us. Be honest with her. There are a lot of things you seem to want for your future, but one thing you don't want is to start keeping things from the woman you married." If there was anything he could go back in time and redo, it wouldn't be staying in Eagle Harbor, but rather being honest instead of letting little grievances go unspoken. Maybe then he wouldn't have gambled their savings, or hid the truth from Jessalyn, or felt that he needed to leave before he got himself into more trouble.

"Just be honest," he muttered more to himself than the others.

"I'm probably worse at that than you might think." Elijah wiped at his nose with his sleeve.

"All the more reason to be honest with her then." Mac surveyed the buildings surrounding them.

Did he feel it too? The sense that someone was watching? The inkling that things were unnaturally calm?

"All right, enough about me. Aren't we trying to catch some thieves?" Elijah started down the road.

"And arsonists," Thomas growled, watching the shipping office for another moment before following the others.

"Maybe between the arson and the thefts, the town council can push that tax increase through and hire a couple deputies." Elijah picked up his pace. "Actually pay Thomas here, not that he needs it."

"It's being fought a little too hard if you ask me." Isaac started down the path to the warehouse, where no new footprints lay in the snow.

"What do you mean?" Thomas checked the door. Locked up tight, but the hair on the back of his neck still stood on end.

Isaac surveyed the perimeter of the clapboard building, even walking to the far side and checking the wall that faced the water. "We've raised taxes before without everyone on the town council getting voted out of office. I think someone doesn't want the law in town to change. Someone with money and influence. Someone who has an interest in keeping the lawmen preoccupied with bar fights and arsonists we might never find. Then there's less time to look into the thefts."

"Never thought about it that way." Elijah rubbed the stubble on his chin.

Isaac let out a deep, long sigh, his shoulders slumping. "After patrolling the streets for nearly a month and always being called away for a bar fight just when we're about to check something, I can't help but think—"

"Sheriff Cummings. Sheriff Cummings!" An unmistakable Irish accent announced the speaker even though the side of the warehouse shielded her from view.

"You see what I mean." Isaac headed out toward the street.

"He has a point." Thomas started after Isaac. There'd been a whole heap of bar fights over the past month, and he certainly had his share of bruises from breaking them up. "Sheriffing isn't a job Isaac should be handling alone."

He stepped onto Front Street to find Isaac standing with a pale-faced Aileen Brogan.

"I th-think someone wants to kill me." Her frantic words echoed down the street.

Thomas hurried his steps. Was her life truly in danger? And if so, was the same person threatening Miss Brogan also responsible for the fire at his wife's building?

The crimes that had hit Eagle Harbor had to stop before someone died. But what if he and Isaac couldn't catch the criminals before the unthinkable happened?

Chapter Twenty-One

"You're sure the hairbrush is the only thing that was taken?"

Aileen wrapped her arms around her middle and huddled against the wall, almost as though if she got close enough, she could disappear into the lath and plaster. "I think so. But they moved so many things around, it's hard to tell."

Isaac glanced at her bed, where her white shift had been laid out along with Betty Ranulfson's missing necklace and one of the knives from the bakery downstairs. The only thing missing from the eerie ensemble was animal blood splashed on the white gown.

"And you were only gone for two hours?" He'd already asked her once, but there was no harm in repeating the story, not when someone had broken into her apartment and left such a disturbing sign, yet not bothered to steal anything besides an antique silver hairbrush.

"Not even that. I had a few Christmas gifts I made for the Spritzer family. All I did was drop them off and have a cup of tea with Ellie and Mrs. Spritzer." Aileen shivered and wrapped her arms even tighter around herself.

He picked up the necklace and held it to the light from the window. It was almost as though the thieves were taunting him. Why else leave a stolen necklace here that he'd been searching for since October?

"Th-thank ye for coming. For believing me."

He frowned and turned back to Aileen. "Why wouldn't I believe you?"

She glanced at his badge and then away. "Not all policemen are willing to believe a woman like me, ye see."

No he didn't see, but it made him want to have a little chat with whatever policeman she'd dealt with before—the kind of chat that involved fists rather than words.

"Let's put this away." He nodded toward the shift on the bed while slipping the necklace into his pocket. Betty Ranulfson would be happy to have one piece of her jewelry returned before Christmas, but he'd almost rather the necklace stay lost if getting it back meant Aileen received chilling threats.

"What do ye want me to do with the other shift?" Aileen left her place against the wall and began folding the white fabric with brisk, efficient movements.

"What other shift?"

She gestured toward the traveling trunk that sat in the corner, which she probably used as a dresser. "The one they put in there."

"They put a shift in your things?"

Redness burst onto her pale cheeks, and she swallowed. "It's… not mine."

"Let me see it."

"Um…" Her cheeks grew so red they nearly matched the color of her hair. She opened the trunk and clenched a silky white garment in her hand, then thrust it at him and looked away.

One glance at the material told him this wasn't the shift of a normal, working class lady. He held up soft fabric, revealing a garment that was nearly all lace, a plunging neckline, and slits that would travel clear up to a woman's hips.

"It, ah… probably belongs to one of the girls at the Penny that was robbed a few weeks ago." Except all of the prostitutes had claimed they were locked in their rooms that night and hadn't seen a thing. How would a burglar get a garment like this without going into one of the girls' rooms?

"It's not mine," she whispered. "I don't wear... that is, I wouldn't... I can't afford..." She turned away and sniffled. "Can you take it away?"

He balled the garment up and shoved it under his arm. "Certainly, but Miss Brogan, Aileen..." He reached for her, though what, precisely, he should do with a woman fighting back tears, he didn't know.

And it didn't much matter since she took a step away from him and huddled in on herself.

A knock sounded on the open door, and Thomas stepped in from the hallway. "We found a set of footprints in the alley behind the building, but that's it. They were impossible to follow once they got out to Center Street. Mac's replacing the locks on the doors, and Elijah went to rent a horse and wagon from the livery. He figured Miss Brogan might want to stay with them until the vandals are caught."

A horse and wagon. Why hadn't he thought of that? She absolutely couldn't be left here alone. He turned to Aileen. "Are you willing to stay with my brother and his wife, or do we need to make some other kind of arrangements for you?"

"Yes, please, I'll stay with Victoria or... anywhere." Her hands fluttered nervously about her midsection. "Just don't leave me here by myself. What if they come back at night when I'm sleeping and...?" She pressed a hand to her throat.

He met Aileen's frightened gaze with his own, then waited for her to calm. "We'll catch them, I promise." And it was a promise he fully intended to keep.

The only trouble was, he'd been trying to catch the thieves for two months already, and he didn't seem any closer to finding the culprits now than the first day he'd pinned a badge to his chest.

~ ~ ~ ~ ~

So much for going to the candlelight service with his family, or even getting home at a sane time of night. Thomas rubbed his bleary eyes as he climbed the dark stairs to his apartment. He'd watched the bakery for hours, hoping whoever had broken in earlier hadn't realized Aileen was staying with the Cummingses. Yet he'd seen nothing—just like all the other nights he'd been on patrol with Isaac. They'd split up tonight, with Isaac patrolling The Pretty Penny and The Rusty Wagon, but Isaac hadn't seen anything suspicious either.

Thomas huffed out a breath. There were criminals either in town or somewhere close enough to easily visit, so why were he and Isaac having such trouble finding them? It had been five weeks since the arson, and they didn't have so much as a suspect. He unlocked the door at the top of the stairs and opened it, then blinked at the soft light. His wife lay curled on the couch, a dressing gown tied about her waist.

Why was she there? Had she been trying to wait up for him? He hung his coat on the peg and moved toward the couch, where he lifted her into his arms. He sucked in a sharp breath and winced at the pain that shot down his shoulder and into his fingers, but it was worth it to hold—

"What are you doing?" She jolted awake.

"Taking you to bed." He pushed the door to their room open with his foot, only to find a dim lantern burning on the dresser.

"Thomas, your shoulder." She trailed her fingertips over the wounded muscle, her touch so light he couldn't feel it beneath his flannel shirt and union suit. "You can't carry me."

"Sure I can." He set her gently on the bed, but she scrambled off the mattress to face him.

She laid her hand over where his arm met his shoulder, her touch still too tender to cause pain. "But it hurts you."

"Sometimes." Did she realize how close she stood to him? That her breath brushed his chin when she spoke? That her hair shone like a waterfall of spun gold in the lamplight? He reached out to finger a strand.

"You should have told me about the accident in the mine."

He offered a lopsided smile. "I assume the girls let you in on my not-so-secret secret?"

"It should have never been a secret."

"I didn't intend for it to be, which is why I told the girls. They asked why I'd come back the day we built the snowman."

A smile tilted the corners of her mouth, carefree and beautiful like the smiles she'd given him when they'd first met a decade ago. "You've built three dozen snowmen. That hardly narrows things down."

"Not three dozen." Possibly two dozen though. "I'm just glad they're willing to spend time with me considering how much of their lives I've missed. I thought of telling you a couple times, but the timing never seemed right."

The smile left her face, and her gaze fell to where her hand still rested on his shoulder. "Is there a wound?"

"More like a scar. It's healed now, or as healed as it will get. The doc in Deadwood said there'd be no changing the damage on the inside, though some days I think it's getting worse."

She wet her lips. "I want to see it."

He took a step back, letting her hand slip from his shoulder. "It looks like I spent seventeen hours trapped beneath a rock fall. Beyond that, there's not much to see."

And yet there was so very much to see. How imperfect he was, how close he'd come to not returning to his wife and daughters. How his body bore the flawed, painful marks of five years of his life gone wrong.

"I want to see it anyway."

And since she was his wife, she had every right to see it.

She didn't help with his buttons this time, but stood back and watched as his thick, fumbling fingers pushed the wood circles through their small holes. Once he removed his shirt, he undid the top half of his union suit, then paused. The scarred skin already peeked out from the opening around his neck, nothing like the tight skin and hard muscle that covered the rest of his torso.

What would she say when she saw all of it? That it was hideous? That she wanted nothing to do with him?

No, she'd never say something like that, not years ago when they'd first met, and certainly not now. She'd always been the person who saw him as more than the son of the town drunk or replaceable immigrant riffraff.

So why couldn't he make himself take his arm out of his undergarment? If he wanted to build a new life with her, then he needed to show her his scars—and not just the ones that puckered his skin, but the ones that marred the fabric of their tattered relationship as well.

He slowly pulled his arm from the flannel, wincing at the movement in his shoulder.

A thick silence crept into the room, and he raised his gaze to his wife's. She stood in the shadowy flicker of the lantern, stillness surrounding her as she pressed a hand to her mouth.

"You almost died, didn't you?" Tears glittered in her eyes. "I almost lost you for good."

"You'd already lost me, Jess." His voice was low and gravelly in the small room. Once his hotel was up and running, he hadn't been able to walk away from the money it brought in, not even for his family.

"God had to work harder than He should have to bring me back."

She reached out and touched the mangled skin. He rooted his feet to the ground and looked away. Did she know she was the first person to see the scar apart from a doctor? The first person to touch it besides himself and a physician, and not even he liked touching it? He gritted his teeth while her fingers ran over the angry, ridged skin that had hardened into something the doctor in Deadwood called scar tissue.

"I'm so thankful you survived." Jessalyn's quiet words floated into the dimness.

"It doesn't make you loathe me?"

She blinked up at him, questions in her eyes, but once again, he couldn't hold her gaze.

"I'm not a whole man anymore, Jess. I'm broken, scarred. I'll never be able to work underground again." As much as he'd grown up hating the dank, dark tunnels that yielded coal in Cornwall, he'd always had a way to provide for himself and his family. He'd always been able to put in an honest day's work. Perhaps it was chopping away at rock with a pickax or hauling crates around Henry's warehouse, but now he'd never be much besides a hotelier. "Even the deputy job wears on this shoulder."

"The scar just makes me all the more grateful to have you back."

She was grateful for him? He swallowed and brought his gaze back to meet hers. When had she changed from the woman who didn't want to speak two words to him into one that was glad to have him around?

She pressed her palm against the injury, her fingers splaying against his shoulder. "Like Christ's scars on his hands, this is a testament of what you've endured, not a reason to despise you."

"I'm not a full man anymore. If anything happens to my hotel, I'll never be able to earn a living underground again."

"You're whole, Thomas, just not perfect. But I'm hardly perfect either, and neither are the girls." She kept her hand over the angry, puckered skin, preventing him from covering it with his union suit. "But I'm still so very sorry for everything you went through."

He shook his head. "There's nothing to apologize for. You were hardly responsible for that rock fall, or for the girl who went down into the shaft after she had a fight with her mother."

"But I was the reason you were in Deadwood."

Yes. No. Maybe.

"I suppose." If not for her insistence that he find a better paying job, he'd probably still be swinging a pickax underground at Central every day—provided a rock fall there hadn't killed him by now.

He smoothed a strand of gold silk behind her ear, then let his fingers linger there, in the soft place where her jaw and ear and neck met. The longer she touched him, the warmer his mangled skin turned beneath her hand, until he couldn't stop the tingles of warmth that traveled from his shoulder to his heart.

"I'm the one in the wrong here. From the very beginning of our marriage, I've been wrong." Her gaze dipped away before coming back to meet his again. "I should have tried harder with you. I should have taken time to count my blessings. I should have rejoiced in the little, good things we had together instead of always being so focused on money and not ending up back in those tenements."

He shook his head. She made it sound as though so much of their troubles were her fault, when the blame should be laid at his feet first. "You weren't the one to gamble away our savings. You weren't the one to walk away and not return for five years."

"No, but I was so focused on the size of our savings that I lost sight of the man I fell in love with—and the reasons I love him."

The breath stilled in his lungs. *Love him?* Today? Not loved ten years ago or eight years ago or five years ago, but right now, this very moment?

"'Except the Lord build the house, they labour in vain that build it.' Tressa told me that verse just after you returned, but I wasn't interested in letting the Lord build our house then, just as I wasn't interested in letting the Lord build anything before you left. I was only ever interested in what you could give me and do for me and bring me."

She still kept her hand over his injury, half over his heart, which thudded against his ribs in jerky, sporadic bursts. "Marriage should be full of sacrifice, a picture of Christ and the church. Two people love each other enough to sacrifice their own wants and desires for the other, just like Christ sacrificed his life for believers. And yet I could never look beyond myself to make any sacrifices for you. Even now, standing here, I can't think of a single thing I've done for you."

"My trousers." He glanced down at the pants she'd sewn for him in less than a day. "You made my trousers."

Tears glittered in her eyes anew. "Those hardly count, not when I've been so scared to love you again, to let you love me, to open myself up lest you hurt me another time. But that's all selfishness. Who comes at the front of every one of those thoughts? Me. Not the girls or you or even God. It's all me and all about how I can protect myself from getting hurt again. But if our example of marriage is Christ and the sacrifice He made for us, then I ought not be asking how I can protect myself from those who want to love me, but what I can sacrifice for those I love."

Her voice trembled, and she reached up to dash a tear from her cheek. "When I think of things like that, it's a miracle you came back to find me at all, because I certainly don't deserve your love."

"Oh, Jess." His own voice shook as he gathered her close and leaned down until their foreheads touched. "If you don't deserve my love, then I don't deserve yours either."

"Mine's barely worth having, as selfish as it is."

"I'm not nearly so ready to say your love doesn't matter. You were the only person who ever looked at me and saw potential, a future, what I could be instead of where I'd come from. To everyone else, I was the son of the town drunk or a piece of immigrant trash. But not to you, never to you."

"No, instead you were a workhorse I whipped when you didn't bring home enough money." Another tear slipped down her cheek, but rather than wipe it away, she left it to glitter in the lantern light.

He pressed his lips to her skin, absorbing the little bead of moisture. "It wasn't quite that bad. Even now, you see my scars as a testimony rather than a scourge."

"Maybe. But there's so much else I should have done differently."

"We both did wrong. We both need to forgive."

"I forgive you, Thomas, for all of it. I just hope you'll forgive me too."

"Everything's already forgiven, angel." He drew her head down to his chest, cradling it against the very scar he'd hesitated to show her. This must be what forgiveness did, not take away a person's scars so much as overlook them, make them not matter anymore.

She sighed and wrapped her arms around him, and he held her there, in the middle of the room beneath the flicker of lantern light early on a Christmas morning.

He'd have stood there with her until dawn arrived in a handful of hours, but she shifted eventually, turning in his arms until her lips brushed the mangled skin of his shoulder.

He stilled, the gesture somehow more intimate than all the kisses they'd shared before, even the ones that had led to their three daughters. Then her lips traveled higher on his shoulder, then to his neck. The underside of his jaw.

"Jess," he groaned. "What are you doing?"

"Loving you. The way a wife is supposed to love her husband."

She was standing on her tiptoes now, but still not quite able to reach his cheek.

He leaned down and let her soft lips brush the side of his face. "Let me love you back. Tonight, in our bed. Like a husband is supposed to love his wife."

She broke her kisses and looked up, her eyes large and luminous. "That seems like the best Christmas present you could give me."

Chapter Twenty-Two

"Stockings?" Claire wrinkled her nose at the gift in her father's hand. "Ma got you stockings?"

Heat crept up the back of Jessalyn's neck. It had seemed like a good present the other week at the mercantile. But after what she and Thomas had shared last night...

She glanced over her shoulder at the bedroom door. The gift didn't seem like nearly enough for the man who'd spent last night loving her. Nor did the gift seem like enough for the man who'd come back to protect her and their daughters after nearly dying in an abandoned mine shaft.

Her second present wasn't going to seem like enough either. And what would he say about her third present—she reached into her pocket and fingered the rough object resting inside—if she even had the courage to give it to him?

"I suppose she did get me stockings." Thomas turned the black hosiery over in his hand before looking up at her.

Jessalyn swallowed. It didn't matter that she stood near the sofa while he was on the other side of the room by the window. He may as well have added ten logs to the fire with the way his gaze made her skin burn.

"Don't worry though." A slow smile tilted his lips, and he winked.

Actually winked. As though they were school children and he'd just offered to share his lunch with her. "That's not the only present she gave me."

Oh dear heavens. Her neck flamed. Did the girls know what their father was talking about? She glanced at Olivia, laying on the couch with a hand pressed to her ear, probably in too much pain to even remember what her father had said. Claire and Megan were on the floor by Thomas's feet, playing with the ribbons they'd opened a few minutes ago.

Olivia repositioned her hand over her ear and let out a small groan.

"Have another sip of tea, dear." Jessalyn bent and held the mug of bitter willow bark tea to her oldest daughter's mouth. The poor girl had gone over a month without an earache, only to wake up on Christmas morning with one so severe she had trouble walking.

"I got a ribbon, see?" Megan held up the strip of shiny pink fabric, then looked around, a frown creeping onto her face. "Where's my new dress to match the ribbon?"

"I don't have a dress for you this year. Remember how the shop burned?" She'd already explained they'd be short on presents, but evidently Megan hadn't understood what she'd been saying.

Indeed, the five-year-old looked around, then poked out her lip. "A ribbon is all I get?"

"What about me? Do I get a dress?" This from Claire.

"Honey, I told all of you, I couldn't make dresses this year, not with losing the shop."

"But Sally Holcomb will have the prettiest dress at school now, and we always have prettier dresses than Sally." Claire poked out her bottom lip to match Megan's.

"That's enough, girls." Thomas's voice cut through the room. "God saved you from a fire. You should be thankful to have your lives, not be grumbling about dresses."

Claire turned to her father. "But you don't understand, Sally—"

"Plus he gave you your father." Jessalyn glanced at Thomas. "Don't you enjoy having him back?"

Megan looked at Thomas, then nodded and popped her thumb in her mouth, her ribbon clutched tightly to her chest.

"Thanks for the toboggan, Pa." Olivia's words slurred with pain, but her gaze fell to the tall sled standing against the wall in the corner. "Can't wait to use it."

Thomas's eyes followed Olivia's to the sled. "I was hoping we'd be able to go sledding today. I'm sorry you're so sick."

Olivia sighed. "I'll get better eventually."

"I have another package for you, Thomas." Jessalyn set the mug of tea on the floor beside the couch, then crossed the room and handed the paper-covered gift to him.

"More than just stockings, eh?" He winked at her again, and another flush traveled down her body.

She twisted her hands together as he unwrapped the package, then held the shirt out in front of him. Would he like it? It wasn't especially fancy. She'd just used the mackinaw fabric from the mercantile to make it.

"You gave me big buttons." He traced his finger over one of the unusually large buttons, then smiled. "Thank you, though I wasn't exactly complaining about my other method of getting my shirts buttoned."

Now her fingertips seemed to burn. Though he had a point, since she wouldn't exactly complain about standing close enough to Thomas that his warmth seeped into her while she helped him with his buttons.

"How come you can make Pa a shirt but you can't make me a dress?" Claire's jaw trembled with an angry frown.

"I don't know." Jessalyn crossed her arms. "Maybe because your pa is grateful for what I give him?"

"Did you make this by hand?" Thomas examined the stitching.

"Lindy Harrington has a sewing machine. I used that a couple afternoons while the girls were in school, but I did the rest by hand, yes."

"It's not fair." Claire pushed herself up and stomped her foot on the ground. "If pa can have a shirt, then I should have a dress."

Jessalyn blew out a breath. Did their middle daughter always have to be so pushy? Couldn't she at least take a break on Christmas, of all days?

"Not fair, is it?" Thomas stood, his knees popping with the movement. "I agree with your mother. If you can't be grateful for your ribbon, then you don't need to come downstairs and see what I got your ma."

"You got me something more?" Jessalyn couldn't quite keep the curiosity from blooming inside her.

"Of course."

"Really, Thomas." She cleared her throat and forced calmness into her voice. "The reticule was enough." Especially since she'd lost her last one in the fire and had been keeping her money in her pockets ever since.

Thomas merely sent her another wink. "Come on, Megan, put your coat on. Do you want to see it?"

"I want to come too." Claire scampered to the peg with her coat and stuck her bottom lip out at her father. "Please."

"Will you stop complaining about your presents and be respectful to your mother?"

She nodded, her eyes wide.

"All right then. Get your coat." Thomas helped Megan into hers. "We'll have to go outside and around the front of the building to the telegraph office."

Jessalyn grabbed her own coat off the peg. "Since when do you have keys to the telegraph office?"

He smiled. "Since Mrs. Runkle decided to be kind and let me store your present downstairs."

Olivia stayed on the couch while the rest of them headed outside. Snow had fallen all night long and still cascaded from the sky in flakes of fluffy white, though the beauty of the morning didn't stop the frigid air from working its icy fingers around her calves. She trudged around the side of the building to North Street and the entrance to the telegraph office. A moment later Thomas pulled the keys out of his pocket and unlocked the door.

Even in the shadows of the dark office, she could make out the silhouette of the large, familiar object sitting in the middle of the floor.

"How did you manage this?" She rushed toward the sewing machine while Thomas fumbled with a lamp.

"I, uh, paid to have it brought up from Calumet by sleigh." The lantern flared to life, casting its orange glow over the room.

"Now Ma can make me a dress." Claire ran her hand over the smooth table that extended from the machine.

"It's prettier than the other one." Megan touched the shiny metal that formed the head.

"You paid for it to be brought all the way up from Calumet through the snow?" She looked over her shoulder at him. "That must have cost a fortune."

He wrapped an arm around her waist and leaned down to her ear. "A fortune well worth it to see the smile on your face."

"I don't suppose you ordered some green satin from Calumet so I can finish those dresses for the Hanover wedding?"

"No, but I did bring some pink." He released her and headed around the counter toward where the telegraph machine sat. A bolt of pale pink fabric landed on the counter a moment later.

"Yeah!" Claire clapped, a smile lighting her face. "I can get my dress now, right Ma?"

"And I got some of that dark red color so you can make yourself a new coat." He set a length of wool on the counter beside the pink cloth.

The rich fabric instantly drew her, and she tilted her head to the side. "You're telling me you like my cranberry-colored coat? Mrs. Ranulfson says it's too bright for a respectable woman to wear."

"Cranberry, is it? Who knew colors could have such fancy names." He came around the counter toward her. "But yes, the color looks nice on you."

"Look. It's Jane and Gracie." Claire flew toward the door, Megan scampering behind her. "I wonder what they got for Christmas."

"You can say hello, but stay..." *In sight of the building.* The girls were out the door before she could finish her sentence. She watched through the window as they raced across the empty street toward the Oakton family, then turned back to Thomas.

He'd had a sewing machine brought up from Calumet through the snow. How could she not give him her final present after that? She reached down and clasped the item inside her pocket.

"I... I have something more for you. You'll probably think it's silly, but... well, here." She pulled out the chunk of stone wrapped in a small bit of linen, then held it out for him.

He opened it and frowned. "Charred rock?"

Her cheeks heated, and this time it had nothing to do with the warmth of the fire upstairs. "It's foundation, from my building next door. Tressa said I needed to clear away the ashes of our relationship and see if there was any foundation left to build a new life with you. When I first looked, all I saw was burned wood. But after a little shoveling, I found stone too."

She lifted her shoulders and let them fall, the familiar gesture suddenly tense and awkward. "I chipped a bit of stone off with an ax. I've been carrying it around in my pocket ever since, telling myself that the two of us have a foundation, and we can build a life on it, and…"

Her throat squeezed shut, and tears burned behind her eyes. "Oh, I told you it was silly."

She reached to take the rock back, but he caught her hand with his empty one instead.

"It's not silly, Jess. It's…" His hand closed into a fist around the chunk of stone, and he tugged on her arm, bringing them chest to chest. "…The best present you could give me."

I want to go to Deadwood with you.

Was it too soon to tell him? Her jaw trembled as she stared into his handsome, work-roughened face. It was time she made a sacrifice for their marriage. She sucked in a breath of air, then let the words out in a rush. "I want to go to Deadwood in the spring."

"You…" His Adam's apple bobbed, and he gripped her shoulders. "Say it again."

"It's my turn to give something toward our marriage. If you've built a life for us in Deadwood, then I can lay aside my plans to move to Chicago and go to South Dakota instead."

It wasn't that she had no more desire to sew or could even stop new dress patterns from springing into her head. But if Chicago was what she needed to give up to have a good marriage, then she'd find a way to be happy there.

Thomas swung her up into his arms and twirled her around, a laugh lighting his face. And then his lips descended on hers.

His mouth was firm against hers, his lips confident, as was the way he held her in his arms, pressing his hands into her back and tilting her so she had no choice but to relinquish her balance and rely on him to keep her from falling.

She sighed and let her eyes slide shut, surrounded by her husband's strength and heat. If last night's kisses had been about tenderness and forgiveness, about healing the broken places in their relationship, then this morning's was about the future. Bright and full of hope, with promises of life and love and laughter, of future secrets waiting to be shared and adventures ready to be explored.

A burst of cold hit her back, followed by the sound of the door closing.

"Look, it's just like Mr. and Mrs. Cummings," Megan's voice rang out.

"Are you always going to be kissing now that Pa's back?" That from Claire, of course.

Jessalyn grinned against Thomas's lips, but couldn't force herself away from him. Instead, she wrapped her arms around his neck and clung tighter.

His lips left hers, but only for a moment. "I told you kisses were a necessary part of the truce."

He had indeed, and she'd been so very wrong to have resisted. What other things had she been wrong about?

She couldn't wait to find out.

~ ~ ~ ~ ~

Isaac blinked through the dimness, his eyes narrowed on Virgil O'Byrne's shadowy form across the table. The man's jaw was clamped as tight as a sprung bear trap, his eyes flickering with belligerence.

"Answer the sheriff's question," Thomas spoke from where he sat in the chair beside Isaac. "What do you know about the items stolen from Aileen Brogan the day before last?"

"Well, it sure wasn't me. You can ask Jack here. We spent the day unpacking." Virgil's gaze flickered to where Jack and Alice stood mixing some sort of batter near the stove.

When the O'Byrnes had been staying with his brother, Elijah's home had been filled with constant chatter and giggles, and an endless mess of paper and paint and toys had always been strewn about. But with their father, Jack and Alice were far from the exuberant, happy children he'd seen just three days ago.

Isaac rubbed the back of his neck and eyed the scruffy man seated across the table. "Did you see anything unusual or suspicious?"

The lumberman shook his head. "Nothing. Ain't that right, Jack?"

"Yes, sir. That's true." Jack came to the table inside the small, two-room cabin that was so newly built it still smelled of pine. Rather than go to his father, the boy stopped by Isaac. "We were here all day on Christmas Eve. Pa wouldn't even let us go to church for the candles and singing."

Isaac placed his palms on the table and leaned closer to O'Byrne. "That seems to be the trouble with you and your friends, O'Byrne. Nobody ever sees anything, which is mighty suspicious considering all the things that have been happening lately. I have prostitutes and respectable women alike claiming to see strange shadows, business owners and Cousin Jacks all saying they've heard strange noises and footsteps. Yet you and your friends never see or hear anything out of place. That tells me straight off you're lying, and it makes me wonder if you know a whole lot more than you're letting on."

"Now see here, Sheriff." O'Byrne slammed the side of his fist onto the table, which wasn't nearly as new as the cabin. The worn wood bent under his hand. "You can't prove nothing."

"He's not asking what he can prove." Jack's lip turned into a snarl. "He wants to know if you helped scare Miss Brogan, the lady with the nice voice who buys us cookies whenever we visit the bakery."

Something tugged on Isaac's sleeve, and he looked down to find little Alice standing beside him, her lip caught between her teeth.

She raised onto her tiptoes and leaned close to his ear. "If Pa goes to jail, can we go back and live with Mr. Elijah and Miss Victoria? Please?"

Isaac settled a hand on her shoulder. Though she'd filled out some during the time she'd been in Eagle Harbor, her frame was still alarmingly slight beneath her faded dress. "Mr. Elijah and Miss Victoria wouldn't want things any other way."

She smiled. "Can you take me to visit them when you leave? I miss them."

"What's that you're talking about, girl?" O'Byrne's fist hit the table again.

Alice turned to her father, her jaw trembling, and ducked her head to the side.

Isaac patted her back. "She wanted to know if I'd take your children to visit my brother and sister-in-law when we leave."

"I keep telling you, girl, you're my young'uns, not theirs. Now didn't I tell you to make biscuits?"

Tears filled her eyes. "I tried but they don't look right."

"It's flour, water, and lard. How hard can it be?"

"You forgot the salt." Jack's voice was dry. "And if making them is so simple, why don't you do it?"

Silence snapped through the cabin, crackling the air for a full half minute before O'Byrne broke the stillness and leaned forward.

"Cuz I'm the pa, which means I'm in charge around here." The logger's voice was calm, controlled, and chillingly soft. His gaze latched onto his son and stayed, so sharp and intense that Isaac felt himself swallow.

Thomas shifted, causing his rickety wooden chair to squeak, but kept his mouth shut. Though if the look on Thomas's face was any indication, there were a host of thoughts running through his deputy's head.

Isaac cleared his throat and sat back in his chair, his pose deliberately relaxed. "Perhaps my brother and sister-in-law can watch the children for you when you're at work?"

"I don't need no help watching my young'uns. 'Sides, Jack here's old enough to tend the little ones while I'm gone." The man's gaze still didn't leave his eldest son.

Jack's shoulders finally slumped, and he ducked his head. "Yes, sir."

"You watch yourself, boy, or I'll find you a job at the mine in Central."

"No, don't make Jack go there!" Alice buried her face in her hands.

"Come here." Thomas gathered the girl up and pulled her onto his lap. "Where's Toby?"

Alice huddled against Thomas's chest. "Sleeping in the room."

"Pa gets upset if he makes too much noise." Jack's hands tightened into fists at his sides, but he kept his shoulders slumped, his gaze averted.

Isaac shifted again. So maybe he wasn't the only one in this cabin purposely acting relaxed. "I'm interested in seeing where you work, Mr. O'Byrne. Where did you say this logging camp you manage is?"

O'Byrne straightened. "It ain't none of your business. I tell you where the camp is, and the next day I'll have other shanty boys moving in on our wood."

In the backwoods, felling a tree with an ax didn't mean ownership, but possession did. Still, it was rare for a group of loggers to move in on a track of land their lumber company didn't own. "I'm not a logger, Mr. O'Byrne. I'm a sheriff. And I resent the implication that I'd use any information you give me dishonestly."

"Maybe you would, and maybe you wouldn't. But I don't hav'ta tell you if I don't want to." The man pushed back in his chair, his protruding stomach bumping the table as he stood. "Now if you'll excuse me, I need to get out to camp and make sure the others are back to work. I gave them Christmas off, you see, but they had strict orders to start working at dawn today."

"Are you sure I can't go visit Miss Victoria while you're gone?" Alice raised her head from Thomas's chest, hope lighting her eyes, even in the dimness of the cabin.

"No!" O'Byrne's shout echoed through the room, only to leave vast silence in its wake.

Isaac gripped the edge of the table so tightly his knuckles turned white. It was wrong, the children living here, with a shifty father who shouted and shook his fist at them—and hopefully that was all he did with his fist.

Yet what could he do? Virgil O'Byrne was their birth father, as unsavory as the thought might be. He needed a valid, legal reason to remove the children from this home, and though he had suspicions aplenty about O'Byrne and his unscrupulous friends, not a one would hold up in a court of law. Yet.

He stood, his chair scraping against the rough floorboards. O'Byrne had said the children couldn't visit Elijah and Victoria, but he hadn't said anything about Elijah and Victoria visiting the children. Somehow, he didn't think Jack would turn them away should they arrive a half hour or so after O'Byrne left.

Isaac reached out and patted Jack's shoulder, then leaned down near the boy's ear. "You're doing a good job. Don't let your pa discourage you."

Jack blew out a shuddering breath, causing his father's eyes to narrow on the two of them. Then the boy straightened, a tough mask settling over his face.

"Goodbye, Alice. I'll see you later." Isaac dipped his head toward the girl scrambling off Thomas's lap. "And tell Toby I said hello when he wakes from his nap."

"Bye, Mr. Isaac."

He pulled on his coat and left the cabin, the brightness of the snowy outdoors surrounding him the second he stepped outside. He blinked against the sun reflecting off the snow. Had a shadow just moved in the trees? Was someone watching them?

Thomas followed him out a moment later and blinked at the brightness. "For a man who just built a cabin, you'd think he'd bother to put more than one small window in that place."

"Maybe he didn't have the money for more than one." Isaac stared at the spot where the shadow had moved. Who would be watching them come to the O'Byrnes? Had someone followed them out here?

A gust of wind blew in off the harbor, causing the skeleton-like tree limbs to sway and moving the shadows spread against the forest floor.

Isaac blinked again. As soon as the wind died, all seemed calm. The movement had probably been the wind jostling the trees, but it was still worth checking on.

He hunkered into his coat and turned to walk along the tree-lined path back to town. He and Thomas could double back once they reached the sheriff's office. Maybe if someone was watching, they'd head back in the direction they'd come, and he and Thomas could return and follow the tracks.

"I have a feeling that single window is because O'Byrne doesn't want anyone seeing what goes on in there." Thomas rubbed a hand over his chin. "But windows or not, I don't trust him."

"Neither do I." Isaac shook his head to clear it of images of shadows and thieves, only to have new images spring up. Alice curled onto Thomas's lap, and Jack setting his jaw and staring down his father. "But am I crazy for being just as concerned about those children as anything O'Byrne knows?"

"No. It's hard seeing them there, especially when they were doing so well with your brother and sister-in-law."

"The first mistake he makes, the first sign of him not caring for those children, and I'll see to it he never gets them back."

Thomas's hand landed on his shoulder. "Can you do that? Legally, I mean?"

Isaac's throat closed. "I don't know. Sometimes legally right isn't the same as morally right, but that doesn't mean a person should turn their back on the moral part of things."

Especially a person like him. He hadn't been able to save his pa, but maybe, just maybe he could help save the O'Byrnes. And Miss Brogan.

Or maybe he'd be as big a failure at saving them as he'd been with his father.

"Are we headed to your office?"

"What?" Isaac looked up to find himself headed down North Street and almost across from the telegraph office. "Oh. Yes."

At least for a few minutes.

"Mr. Dowrick. Mr. Dowrick!" The door to the telegraph office flew open, and Mrs. Runkle came running outside, never mind her lack of coat in the bitter winter air. She waved a missive in her hand and headed straight for Thomas. "This just came for you."

Thomas reached for the paper and scanned it, his face turning dark. Then he shoved the note at Isaac.

Land dispute over hotel. Man claims never sold property to bank after fire. Has deed. Come quickly. Court date set for Jan. 14. —Bernard

"Looks like you'll have to finish up this sheriff business on your own." Thomas's jaw was hard as he spoke. "I'm needed in Deadwood."

Chapter Twenty-Three

Thomas yanked open the drawer to his dresser, scooped up his clothes in one giant heap, and plopped them into the carpetbag on the bed. Did he need anything else, or was that it?

"You're leaving so soon?"

He glanced over to find Jessalyn leaning against the doorway, the telegraph clutched in her hand. "Where are the girls? I want to say goodbye before I head out."

"Olivia's sleeping in her room. She still has a fever from the earache, but Claire and Megan are sledding with the Oaktons and O'Byrnes."

"I'll stop by the hill on my way out of town." He turned back to the dresser, where he grabbed his shaving supplies and tooth powder.

"Or you could wait until tomorrow to leave." Hope threaded Jessalyn's voice.

"Want to see how far I can get before dark." If the telegram had come first thing that morning, he could already be part way to Calumet.

"I don't like it." Jessalyn came to the end of the bed, crumpling the edge of the telegram where her fingers curled around the paper.

He heaved out a breath, took Jessalyn by the shoulders, and rested his forehead against hers. His hotel or his family. He was finally supposed to have the two of them together, yet a day after he'd won his wife back, he'd turned around to find himself in danger of losing his hotel. "I don't like leaving you either, but…"

Wait. He didn't have to leave her behind. He dropped his hands from her shoulders and headed to where her extra dress hung on a peg.

Jessalyn narrowed her gaze at him. "What are you doing?"

He stuffed the dress into the carpetbag. "Packing."

"My dress?"

"If you come with me, then we don't have to be apart." He turned and pulled open the dresser drawer where she kept her underthings.

"Thomas." Her hand landed on his arm, stilling him before he could scoop up what lay inside. "That wasn't what I meant when I said I didn't like this. I just… something's not right."

"Of course something's not right. I'm about to lose a hotel I purchased legally and have the deed to. I wouldn't call that right." He grabbed her clothes from the drawer.

"If you have the deed, proving ownership shouldn't be that difficult. Can't you—"

"I've been gone for four months." Was she really going to stand there and argue? And now of all times? Couldn't she find an extra pair of shoes or something to pack? "I have no idea what'll be waiting for me when I return. Could be Bernard proves just as dishonest as Henry and sold my hotel out from under me, then took all the profits, and fled to Canada. I don't know."

Did she need anything else? Rosewater? More stockings? He reached for her toothbrush on top of the dresser.

"I can't go with you." She stayed beside the chest of drawers, her arms crossed even though her shoulders slumped. "The road to Calumet will be nearly impassable. Megan's too small for such a trip, and Olivia has another ear infection. They wouldn't survive the journey."

"I wasn't planning on taking them." He put the toothbrush in the bag and surveyed the room for anything he'd missed. Would the single pair of shoes Jessalyn wore now be enough? "I'm sure Elijah and Victoria will watch the girls, and if not them, then Mac and Tressa."

Her face turned white as the snow blanketing the ground outside. "You can't mean for me to leave our daughters."

He sank down onto the bed beside the carpetbag and rubbed his head. "I just got you back, Jess. I'm not ready to lose you so quickly."

She came forward and wrapped her arms around him. "We're not losing each other again. It's different this time."

In some ways, yes, but in other ways it felt like five years ago all over again—him leaving his family behind. For how long this time? A month at the minimum, but what if it was more? What if it took several months? Or years? What if—

"Like I said earlier, maybe you shouldn't rush off right away." Jessalyn's arms tightened around him. "It'll be dark in a few more hours. Why don't you stay until morning? Pray with me?"

"I can't." He unwound her arms from him and stood. "Each minute I stay here puts my hotel at risk."

"I just want you to tarry for a few more hours, not risk your hotel." Her eyes turned suddenly moist. "I understand how hard you've worked for it."

"Then you understand that it's our means of living, of paying for food and housing and clothes—however fancy or plain they might be. And providing for Olivia's ear surgery." Never again would he be able to go into the mines and earn a living through sweat and labor, not with his shoulder. Office work was his only means of caring for his family. "We have to leave tonight. We have to make sure all is well with my hotel."

"Don't make me chose between you and our girls." Her raw,

fervent plea filled the space between them. "If we both go and something happens to us, they'd be orphaned."

"People travel all the time." He reached for the carpet bag and closed the latch. "Nothing will happen."

She threw up her hands and paced in the small area between the bed and the window. "You're talking about a thousand-mile trip during winter. You can't promise nothing will happen. Besides, the weather has barely cleared. What if we get more snow, and we're caught out there? No one would find our bodies until spring."

She stopped pacing and met his gaze, wrapping her arms around herself. "At least let me stay here and care for the girls. I'll pray for you every day. And when you return, we'll pick up where we left off. You, me, this apartment, the girls. Or if this business takes months to clear up, we can come to you in the spring."

The words were right. Sincere and true and hopeful. But coldness traveled through him. Their relationship was too new, too tenuous. What if it didn't survive such a long separation?

"You promised, Jess." His words were deathly quiet, yet they filled the room like a thousand shouts. "Just yesterday, you told me you loved me, and you promised to come to Deadwood."

"I never said I'd leave the girls behind." She pressed a hand to her mouth, her brow knit with confusion and worry and a dozen other emotions he couldn't quite name. "You were fine with me not going when I walked into the room."

"I hadn't thought of you coming along then." If she was only now discovering what she felt about him, only now deciding how committed she was to him, what would another separation do to their relationship?

"Then I wish the thought had stayed out of your brain." She started pacing again, shaking her head all the while. "I love you, Thomas, but I won't put our girls needlessly at risk."

What about their relationship? Was she willing to risk that? Evidently, if she insisted on staying with the girls rather than coming with him. "Did you mean it? Yesterday when I gave you that sewing machine, and you said you'd come to Deadwood, did you…?" His throat closed, and a hollow pain filled his chest.

Her breathing hitched. "Of course I meant it. How can you ask such a thing?"

He blew out a shaky breath, then opened the carpetbag and started piling her clothes onto the bed. "If you're that opposed to coming with me, then I won't force you."

They sounded so very much like the words he'd spoken five years ago. *If you don't want to come west, then fine. I'll go ahead without you.*

But things were different, this time… weren't they? He knew where Jessalyn lived, and she knew where he was headed. There was no reason they'd be separated for another five years.

So why did his leaving feel the same?

He closed the carpetbag and stood, clenching the handle so hard his nails bit into the flesh of his palm. "Tell Olivia I didn't want to wake her to say goodbye."

"Thomas…" Jessalyn threw herself into his arms and clung to him so fiercely he dropped the carpetbag to the floor. "I don't like this, not any of it."

"You know I'll come back, right?" He smoothed a strand of hair from her forehead, then drew in her scent. Surely God wouldn't give him his family back only to tear them apart permanently.

"I know you'll try." She looked up into his face, her eyes glassy with tears. "But neither of us can know for sure. And, well, this is just… it's going to be hard for me."

He crushed her to his chest and wrapped both arms around her. "It's going to be hard for me too."

Because as much as he wanted to tell himself he'd return, that he'd look into his wife's angel blue eyes and take her into his arms again, he couldn't quite quench the flames of fear burning in his belly.

~ ~ ~ ~ ~

"I came as soon as Mac would let me out of the lighthouse this morning."

Jessalyn looked up from her oatmeal to find Tressa standing in the doorway of the apartment, her hair pulled up into a sloppy bun with straying wisps pointing out every which way.

Jessalyn heaped oatmeal onto her spoon only to tip it over and watch the tan-colored blob plop back into her bowl—just like the twenty blobs before it. "You look as though you just rolled out of bed and spent all of two minutes putting yourself together."

"Not true. I fed the children before I left too." Tressa unbuttoned her coat and draped it over the back of a chair, then sat down across the table. "Isaac stopped by last night and said Thomas left. I'm so sorry he had to go."

"He didn't even wait until morning, just packed as soon as he got the telegram." She slanted a glance at the closed bedroom door where her girls slept, then shoveled another bite of oatmeal onto her spoon before letting it drop back into her bowl.

"Oatmeal?" She nodded to the pot on the table. Making it had given her something to do, but she'd expected the girls to be awake by now. Then again, considering how late they'd stayed up crying over their pa leaving town, she shouldn't be surprised they were still in bed.

"No, I don't want oatmeal." Tressa reached across the table and gripped her hand before she could plop another spoonful of oatmeal back into her bowl. "I want to know how you are."

Sad, worried, missing Thomas. Wishing he didn't have to be gone.

"He needed to go, you realize. There wasn't much choice about it."

"That doesn't tell me how you are."

She looked down and stirred the oatmeal around in her bowl. "He asked me to go with him."

"So why didn't you?" Tressa's words were soft in an apartment already filled with too much silence.

"The girls." Her spoon clinked against the bowl as she kept a constant circular motion through the thick sludge. "Megan's too little to make the trip, and Olivia's too ill."

Tressa reached for her hand again, but Jessalyn pulled it away and slumped over her oatmeal.

Tears stung her eyes, but rather than stem them, she let them streak her face and mix with her silent prayers. *God, please save his hotel. God, please keep him safe. God, please keep us strong.*

Tressa pushed her chair back and rounded the table, then wrapped her arms around Jessalyn's shoulders. "What can I do?"

She shook her head. Nothing, there was absolutely nothing Tressa could do, because none of this was her fault. Oh, why hadn't she taken Thomas back sooner? Why hadn't she trusted him from the very moment he'd arrived in Eagle Harbor? Then they could have had even more time together before he had to leave. Instead, she'd pushed him away so many times, told him she didn't need him or want him around, when all along she should have been showing him how much she still loved him.

And now she might never see him again. She trusted he'd try his hardest to return to them, yes. But some things were simply out of his control, and she'd worry about him until she felt the strength of his arms wrapped around her and the thud of his heartbeat beneath her cheek.

Another sob welled in her chest, and she buried her face in her hands.

"Oh, honey." Tressa sank into the chair beside her, somehow still managing to give her a sideways hug. "Don't cry. Traveling to Deadwood is dangerous this time of year. It's wise not to risk your daughters going."

"And yet Thomas is taking the trip alone. Isn't that somehow worse than taking it with another person?"

Tressa rubbed soothing circles on her back. "You did the same as I would have done."

She looked over at her friend. "Abandoned your husband?"

"You didn't abandon him."

"Well, he's in one place, and I'm in another, so it sure feels like one of us abandoned the other." She shook her head and wiped her cheek with her palm. "I thought I was doing what the Bible said. I thought I was letting God build our house. But how can God build anything with Thomas gone? Somehow we're back to building our own separate houses instead of a single house together."

She closed her eyes and drew in a long, deep breath. But frustration and a sense of loss rose up to choke her anew. How could she hope for a restored relationship when her husband was headed halfway across the country without her? And how could she blame anyone but herself for the state of their relationship when she'd held him at arm's length for so long?

Chapter Twenty-Four

The horse's hooves pounded against the packed snow, each clomp taking Thomas farther from the family he loved.

His hand tightened on the reins of the horse he'd rented from the livery, and he forced himself to stare at the scenery drifting past. A cluster of pines laden with snow so heavy their boughs sagged beneath the weight, a stand of maples with their bare, spindly branches twisting up toward the sky, a thicket where a rabbit emerged for a moment, only to catch sight of the horse and dash back to safety.

It all seemed startlingly perfect, even the brightness of the afternoon sun which caused the snow to sparkle like the crystal goblets at his hotel in Deadwood.

But his heart was anything but perfect.

Except the Lord build the house; they labour in vain that build it. That's what he was trying to do, let God build his house this time around. If he and Jess tried building it themselves, they'd only fail again.

But how could God build their house if he and his wife were in two separate states?

Temporarily. It wasn't as though he'd left her forever.

But it felt like forever. How long would this business with his hotel take? He wanted to be back in Deadwood overseeing things, true, but not more than he wanted to be with his family.

His ownership of the property shouldn't even be contestable. He had the deed sitting in his safety deposit box in Deadwood. If proof of ownership was the only thing needed to clear up this dispute, then couldn't he just wire Bernard and tell him where to find the deed?

Unless Bernard was up to something unsavory and creating some sort of ruse so he could get the deed. Thomas huffed out a breath, which puffed white against the air. He'd been focused on Jessalyn and the girls for so long, he didn't even have an inkling what was happening with his hotel.

He supposed he could wire Sheriff Haynes and see if he'd heard anything about a land dispute. If something was going on, surely Deadwood's sheriff would know. Which he probably would have thought of before he'd left Eagle Harbor, if he hadn't been in such a rush to start his trip yesterday. He rubbed a hand over his chin. Looked like there'd been something to Jessalyn's idea about staying the night and leaving today.

Just like there'd been something to her fear over leaving their daughters. True, he'd seen nothing but blue skies and sparkling snow thus far, but that could change in a blink. He rubbed his forehead and glanced out over the layers of white. Was he making the right choice in taking this trip?

He had to be. They couldn't afford to lose his hotel in Deadwood, especially not with Jessalyn's seamstress shop gone.

But then why did his heart feel so heavy? Why could he only scowl at the passing scenery rather than smile? He'd worked so hard to gain Jessalyn's trust again, but this trip was already straining their relationship.

Even if he did lose his hotel, wasn't Jessalyn worth the sacrifice? Wasn't his family more important than a building?

A building that earned him five hundred dollars a month in revenue.

He drew in a breath of air so frigid it stung his lungs before dissipating. His family was more valuable, yes, but going to Deadwood didn't mean he was placing his hotel above them. He'd left Jessalyn with a place to live and money aplenty for any needs she or the girls would have in his absence. It wasn't as though he'd just up and abandoned them.

So why did each clomp of the horse's hooves against the snow make him feel like a traitor?

~ ~ ~ ~ ~

Jessalyn ducked her head against the wind and hurried down the dirt path toward North Street. Behind her the lighthouse tower was dark, its lantern unlit during the winter months when the harbor iced over. But lights shone brightly through the kitchen and parlor windows, where her daughters were playing with the Oakton children.

The girls had been planning to spend the night at the Oaktons since before Christmas, and she couldn't tell them no. Never mind she hadn't known Thomas would leave two days ago.

As if facing her second night without Thomas wasn't hard enough, she would now be alone once she got back to the apartment. But first she had to drop off dinner for Isaac. With her own belly full of Tressa's pasties, cornbread, and pie, she could hardly begrudge the stop. Hopefully he wouldn't ask her how she was doing—she'd had a hard enough time keeping a smile on her face for the girls through dinner. She tucked the blanket tighter around the basket on her arm and quickened her pace. If she didn't hurry, Isaac's dinner would be cold before she reached the sheriff's office.

Her feet left the little path and found the snow-packed road of North Street, and a chill travelled down her spine. But not from the wind, no. She looked over her shoulder. Was someone watching her? Someone following?

How silly. Who would follow her? But the sense of foreboding persisted. What if Thomas was in trouble? Was he sick somewhere, or hurt? Had he gotten caught in a blizzard on the road to Calumet?

She gripped the handle of the basket tighter. Maybe he needed her help, but what could she possibly do without knowing for certain something was wrong? It would be ten sides of foolish to rush after Thomas, alone and in the cold, all because of a feeling.

The sacrifices of God are a broken spirit: a broken and a contrite heart, O God, thou wilt not despise.

She'd found that verse at some point yesterday after Tressa left her apartment. She'd already decided to make sacrifices for her husband, but it seemed that God wanted a different type of sacrifice from her, one that involved being broken, because she certainly felt broken with Thomas gone. Maybe she needed this time alone for God to grow her personally before God could grow her and Thomas together.

Maybe. Or maybe she was grasping at straws, because everything simply seemed wrong without her husband.

The sheriff's office looked dark as she approached, the curtains drawn. Maybe she could drop the basket off, provided he'd left the door unlocked. But wait, no, there was a dim light shining from beneath the curtains after all. She climbed the steps to the porch.

"Isaac? I brought dinner from Tressa." She knocked on the door once. The knob turned easily in her hand, so she slipped inside. "A pasty and... Ah!"

Large hands grabbed her and slammed her against the wall. The wind left her lungs and her head throbbed from the impact. She opened her mouth to scream, but a meaty palm covered her mouth.

"Quiet there, princess." A hulking bear of a man loomed over her, his massive build and features familiar, but there was nothing familiar about the cold, emotionless look he wore.

267

She sucked a reedy breath in through her nose, and would have opened her mouth to gulp air, but his hand still covered it.

He held her there for a minute, her body pressed so hard against the wall her joints ached. His eyes raked over her, his jaw firm, muscles taut, but he kept his thoughts shuttered behind his cold, hard eyes.

"You scream and I'll crack your head open." His hand left her mouth, but she barely had time for a breath of air before he jerked her forward, his hold on her upper arm so tight she winced. "Should have known it'd be you. Always meddling. Always in the way."

She gripped the basket tighter despite her trembling hands, as though she didn't know quite what else to do with it. Could she use it as a weapon? Panic clawed into her chest. What good would a Cornish meat pie do against such a large man?

"You don't even remember me, do ya?" He dragged her toward one of the chairs sitting opposite Isaac's desk.

"I remember. You showed up during the blizzard asking for your coat back. I'd barely had a chance to replace your buttons."

"Sit down." He threw her into the chair so hard the simple piece of furniture would have toppled backward had the man not grabbed it.

She dropped the basket to the floor and tried to scramble up, but once again he was faster, his big hands landing on her shoulders and shoving her down with enough force to leave bruises.

"I don't understand." She tried to stand again, but this time a length of rope wrapped around her middle. "No!"

Her cry echoed through the empty room. With his brute size and strength, he had her tied to the chair in a matter of seconds, her hands bound behind her back while her middle was strapped to the wooden frame behind her.

Then he hunkered down and leaned in close, his breath brushing her cheek. "You scream like that again, and I'll break your jaw so hard you'll never scream again."

Her heart thundered in her chest and blood rushed in her ears. This man was large, probably bigger than Thomas, and just as strong. He'd have little trouble shattering her jaw. "Let me go. The sheriff will be here any minute, and when he finds you, he'll—"

A deep, jeering laugh resonated from the man's belly. "The sheriff's a mite too preoccupied breaking up a fight down at the Penny to bother with his office just yet."

"My husband, then. He's a deputy, and he'll return soon." A lie, but she'd tell it again if it frightened this man into letting her go. "And if he—"

"Your husband ain't coming back." The man ambled to the door and slid the deadbolt, then headed over to Isaac's desk, where he'd set his dim, narrow-beamed lamp, the only light in the room. "He ran off two days ago, thinking he needs to go save that hotel of his."

Her chest deflated on a giant rush of air. How stupid of her to try bluffing. If this man spent any time in Eagle Harbor, of course he'd have heard about the deputy leaving.

"Traveling's hard this time of year, you know. Good chance your husband won't reach that fancy hotel of his. And even if he does, he'll have a nice little surprise waiting for him." He picked up a stack of papers from the desk and began shuffling through them.

"What do you mean?"

"Getting rid of him was a mite too easy." He looked up at her and sneered. "How's it feel to know he left you for it because of a simple telegram?"

Too easy? A surprise when Thomas got to Deadwood? Her hands dampened with sweat and perspiration beaded on her forehead. "Did you send the telegram? Did you want him gone and—"

"I don't owe you any answers." The man set the stack of papers back down where he'd found them, with the top one slightly askew, then bent and sorted through a desk drawer. "Now quiet."

She clamped her teeth together, her jaw already throbbing as though he'd struck it—just not hard enough to break it yet.

The scents of pasty and cornbread from the spilled basket rose up around her, churning her stomach rather than causing her mouth to water. She expected him to riffle through things, make a mess of the papers on the desk, but instead, he was meticulous about his searching, slow and methodical. He put everything back just how he found it, or close enough that Isaac would never realize someone had been through his office.

Her gut churned again. What about those times she'd struggled to find things in her shop? The basket of buttons moved from where she usually kept it by the other buttons and shoe laces. The way she'd not quite been able to find the sketch of her bridesmaid dress.

"You've done this before. You've been through my shop." The words slipped out before she could stop them.

He merely grunted and continued working, no threat about breaking her jaw. He pulled pieces of paper out here and there, folded them precisely into quarters, and stuffed them into his pockets. But he must not have found whatever he looked for, because he still kept searching.

She twisted her hands against her bindings. With him on the other side of the desk, nothing blocked her path to the door. If she could just get free, then she could run for Isaac. Hadn't the man said he was down at The Pretty Penny? But the more she struggled, the tighter the ropes seemed to get.

He shoved a stack of papers down onto the desk and looked up at her, eyes narrowed. "Where's the map?"

She blinked. "What map?"

"The one from my coat pocket."

Another blink, this one accompanied by a swallow. "The coat you dropped off at my shop?"

His gaze turned dark. "That'd be the one. Now what did you do with the map?"

She shook her head. "I don't remember any map being in your pocket." But even if she'd found one, did he know how many coats she fixed? How many papers and trinkets and coins ended up on her floor? She always stuffed things right back into whatever pocket they fell out of and went on mending.

"Don't play stupid with me. The sheriff and your husband are searching the woods, asking too many people too many questions."

She shook her head and moved her wrists slowly against the bindings. At least with her hands tied in back of her, he couldn't see her work at the ropes.

"Who'd you give it to, your husband? Is that why I can't find it?" He rummaged through the papers again, but it was more erratic this time. He crinkled the top two papers of the stack he grabbed, then left another lying in the center of the desk.

"I never gave Thomas a map. I just told you, I never even found a map. People leave things stuffed in their coat pockets all the time. If something fell while I was replacing the buttons on your coat, I would have put it right back."

"The sheriff then. Where's the map you gave him?"

"I never gave anyone a map. I never found any map at all." Frustration edged into her voice. Was he truly going to keep her tied up here, interrogating her over a piece of paper she'd never seen?

"Well, the map wasn't in my pocket when you gave me back my coat, so either you're lying, or you're a fool and stuffed it in someone else's coat." He stopped his searching and stared at her, his jaw moving back and forth. "Suppose I don't got no choice either way. Probably didn't have much choice after you strolled in."

271

The dull, matter-of-fact tone to his voice caused her heart to hammer and a chill to skitter down her spine. "No choice for what? What are you talking about?"

He took the unlit lamp from the shelf behind Isaac's desk, then came around the desk toward her.

"No choice about this." He threw it at the bottom of her chair. The glass crashed, splintering over her feet and the wooden legs.

She squealed and jerked her legs up, but she could only move so far with being tied to the chair.

"I told ya no screaming. Not unless you want me to break that pretty jaw of yours before I kill you."

Kill you. The words sent a wave of fear crashing through her. He'd probably been intending it all along, probably was right about not having a choice now that she knew he'd been in Isaac's office looking for a map.

"Please, no," she rasped through a shaky voice. "I promise I won't say anything, ever, to anyone. Not about seeing you here or about any map or about anything at all. Just let me go. You'll be safe, I swear."

He grabbed the lamp hanging by the door and threw it at her feet.

She didn't dare make a peep, not even when a shard of glass bit into her shin.

The man reached for another lamp. "Just in case the sheriff gets all picky about where the fire starts again."

"Fire? Again?" She twisted her sweaty hands against the bindings. What did he mean by *again*? Unless...

All Thomas's talk about arson flooded back to her. She'd barely paid attention to him, not when she'd been so upset over losing her shop, so sure the fire had been due to her own negligence.

"You started the last fire." Her voice wobbled as she spoke. "Why?"

He shattered a lamp against the wall by the door, causing the scent of kerosene to overpower the aroma from Tressa's ruined dinner. "I don't owe you any answers."

First, he searched her shop, then he set fire to it, then he sent Thomas away. Just how much had this man she'd met only twice affected their lives over the past months? And all because he'd left a piece of paper in his coat?

More blood rushed in her ears, and she sucked in thin, shaky breaths, but they were as big as her constricting chest would allow. "You'll never get away with this. Isaac will start an investigation, and Thomas will come back at some point. They'll find out what happened. They already know the last fire was an arson. They're already looking for you."

He took another lamp, shattering this one against Isaac's desk, soaking the papers atop it with oil. "Precisely why this office needs to be torched—along with a pretty little woman who knows more than she should."

He walked behind her, disappearing from view, but another crash sounded a second later.

She wriggled against her bindings once more, and the rope gave just a bit. If she kept the man talking, could she get free before he set the place on fire?

Footsteps sounded behind her, and the stench of kerosene grew even stronger. Then the man appeared in front of her. His hand dipped into his shirt pocket for a moment, and he pulled out a flask.

"Why?" Her breath hitched, and more sweat slicked her forehead. She pulled at her ropes, but more out of instinct than a belief she'd free herself while he stood a foot away. "If you're going to kill me, at least give me an explanation."

He unscrewed the top of the flask, but instead of spirits wafting into the air, the odor of more kerosene filled the room. He splashed some at her feet near the spilled oil from the lamp. Then he hunkered close, his wheezy breath brushing her face in another rush of sour air. "It's like I said, I don't got no choice but to take care of things before anyone else learns too much."

Her breathing hitched, and her heart pounded against her ribcage.

He reached out with a thick finger, damp from the spilled lamp oil, and trailed it down her face.

She tried to lurch away from his touch, but her bindings prevented her from moving more than a few inches.

A feral grin crept across his lips. "Aren't as keen on my touches as you are on your husband's, I see. Maybe if I had more time, iffen we were at your apartment instead of this office, we could have had some fun."

Bile rose in her stomach, and she pulled at her bindings again. "Let me go."

His laughter filled the air between them with his rancid breath. "It's too late for that."

"It's not too late for anything!"

He stood and pulled a box of matches from his pocket, then tipped the bottle of kerosene, creating a trail of fuel as he walked backward toward the door.

"Wait, no! I promise not to breathe a word of anything about you, not even to Thomas. If you would just…"

His deep chuckle choked out her words. "Sure, princess. Anything you say."

An icy sensation filled her. He was going to start the fire from the door, where the flames would head straight toward her. It wouldn't take more than thirty seconds before her dress caught fire.

She screamed, loud and long. What difference would a shattered jaw make if he was already going to kill her?

"Ah, deciding to scream anyway, are you?" The man laughed again, bold and cruel. "Reckon it's not worth the time it'd take to break your jaw, not when you'll be dead in a few more minutes."

"No," she gasped. "Don't kill me. Please don't." She couldn't lose her life over a piece of paper. Of all the foolish, ridiculous reasons to die.

But oh, the things she would have done differently had she known. She'd have welcomed Thomas with open arms when he'd first arrived in Eagle Harbor. She'd have spent more time with her daughters. She'd have put more effort into the things that truly mattered—the things that would outlast her own short life—rather than earning money.

The man slid the deadbolt behind him, then opened the door. A rush of bitter winter air filled the shop, warring scent of kerosene. Then he opened the matchbox and withdrew a single match.

"Don't do this," she choked through the panic climbing from her chest into her throat. Her eyes grew damp, her breathing more erratic as she struggled against the ropes a final time.

He struck the match, and a tiny flame appeared at its tip.

Chapter Twenty-Five

Jessalyn sucked in a breath, what would assuredly be one of her last, as a tiny flame flickered at the end of the match.

The man grinned again, the look both wild and disturbing. "You best say your final—"

A second person lunged through the door, tackling the man from behind, the rush of movement taking out the flame from the match. The match in the man's hand hit the floor along with him a moment later, but only a faint curl of smoke rose from it.

"Isaac," she gasped. But no, the second man was too big for Isaac it had to be…

"Thomas!" What was he doing here?

Her attacker twisted beneath Thomas on the floor and let his fist fly.

Crack! Thomas's head snapped back.

"Thomas, please. Knock him out. He wants to burn the building down. He covered my feet in kerosene, and half the room too." She was babbling now, yanking furiously at the ropes that prevented her from escaping. If she could just loosen the rope a bit more, then she might be able to wriggle her hand out. She gave a yank so hard the legs of her chair wobbled, but her wrists still didn't break free. She tried again, but her second effort proved just as futile as the first.

On the floor, Thomas locked his hands around the other man's neck and pressed his thumbs to the man's throat. The man tried to buck him off, but Thomas somehow managed to jam his knee into the other man's stomach.

Dear God, give Thomas strength. Let him defeat this man.

The man lurched upward, trying to knock Thomas's hands from about his neck. Then his eyes rolled back in his head, and he slumped to the floor with a thud.

Jessalyn let out a small cry. "Is he... dead?"

Thomas scrambled up and rushed toward her. "Unconscious. Are you all right?"

"I'm not hurt, just..." Terrified. Her heart still thrummed against her ribcage like a pickax pounding against mine rock, and her breathing refused to slow. "Hurry and cut me out of this."

Thomas touched her shoulder, but only for an instant before he went around to her back. "My shoulder's too weak to drag him into a cell by myself. I'll need this rope to tie his feet."

"All right." She sucked in another frantic breath. Calm. She needed to calm herself. There was no reason to still be upset, not now that she was safe, not now that Thomas was back.

He worked at the knot, causing his fingers to brush against her wrists, and she winced at the contact.

"You rubbed your skin raw trying to get free." His voice was so gentle moisture welled in her eyes.

It was foolish of her. Why did she want to cry? The time for tears had been earlier, when she was pleading for her life. The ropes finally fell from her arms, and she turned to Thomas, but he'd moved behind the desk, where he grabbed a pair of handcuffs before heading across the room toward the man on the floor.

"How are you here?" She slumped into the chair, her legs trembling too badly to stand. "Shouldn't you be in Calumet?"

Thomas rolled the man over with a painful grunt—likely do to his shoulder—and snapped the handcuffs into place with two clicks. "I turned around."

"Why? What about... No, wait, your hotel isn't in danger." She'd nearly forgotten as she'd watched her assailant douse the office in kerosene.

Thomas looked up and met her eyes. "Why do you say that?"

"He said something about needing you gone. Said you were sniffing too close, asking too many questions." She glanced around the kerosene-soaked room and another urge to cry welled inside her.

Thomas tied the man's feet together, his legs bent at the knees so the rope attached to the chain that linked his handcuffs as well. "Whatever the reason I got that telegram, I came back because it's not as important as you or our daughters. You were right about me leaving too quickly, and I should have seen it sooner. I'll wire Deadwood first thing in the morning and ask the sheriff to look into anything if he needs to." He checked the bindings, then stood and looked down at the man. "This is one of the loggers that runs with O'Byrne. What was he doing here? And with you? What did he want?"

She started trembling all over again. "He... he..."

Thomas stepped over the man and came toward her. A moment later she was folded in his arms, his hold strong and steady. "Shhh. When you're ready, angel. Tell me when you're ready."

"He was going to... going to..." The flood of tears she'd been holding back hit her then, and there was no stemming them. She buried her head against Thomas's shoulder and shuddered in his arms. "He was looking for a map. He dropped off mending before Thanksgiving and said he left the map in his pocket. He thought I'd seen it, that I'd given it to you and you were searching the woods for him. But I don't remember anything from his pockets."

"Did he say what the map was to?"

"Only that he had to k-k-kill me since I knew about it." Another bout of tears surged.

He stroked hair back from her face, then settled his arm around her again, pulling her close. "Shhh. It's all right. You're safe now. I've got you, and I'm not going anywhere."

"I'm so sorry," she mumbled over her tears.

He held her tighter. "For what? You did nothing wrong."

"I should have trusted you sooner. I should have welcomed you back with open arms when you first returned." She sniffled, trying to blink back the tears, but her eyes were two endless watering pots. "I held myself back from you, and all because I was afraid of getting hurt. But when you left and I was here alone, I realized—"

"I never should have left. I was wrong for putting my hotel before you and the girls. But I'm just so scared to lose it, especially with my shoulder. I can't even keep you safe without hurting it."

She pressed a hand to it, and he hissed out a breath. "Did my attacker hurt it?"

"Everything hurts it. Don't you see? I'm confined to desk work for the rest of my life. I can barely manage to keep you safe when your life is at risk, and even now, I can't get that criminal into a cell without help." He shook his head, his gaze dropping down to his feet.

"No, Thomas, I told you. Your shoulder is like the scars on Christ's hands."

"Except Christ could still use his hands, but my shoulder..."

"I love you anyway. I don't need you to haul crates or chip away at mine rock, Thomas. If you can love me with all my flaws, then I can love you with yours. And what I see right now, standing before me, is a husband who kept me safe even though doing so caused you great pain."

279

"You don't…" He brought his gaze up to hers, then dropped it once more. "You don't see me as less of a man because of my shoulder?"

"Oh, Thomas." She wrapped her arms around him and hugged him so tight he hissed again. "Never. You just saved my life. And when you left for Deadwood two days ago, I saw a man who wanted to provide for his family the best way he could. I should've respected your desire to provide for us more, should have respected that all along. I wish I'd never told you I wouldn't go to South Dakota with you, not even when you first came back. I should have up and left for Deadwood that day and trusted God would work everything out."

He rubbed his hand up and down her back in long, soothing motions. "There was a snowstorm. You couldn't have left even if you wanted to."

She sniffled and grinned up at him. "You understand what I mean."

"I'm just glad you're safe." He stopped stroking her and crushed her against his chest.

She breathed in the scent of him, crisp winter air and man. "I love you, Thomas, even with your flaws. And I'm so very sorry for losing sight of that."

"I love you too. Now let's go find Isaac and get this brute dragged into a cell where he belongs."

~ ~ ~ ~ ~

"O'Byrne," Elijah called across the snowy street.

The man didn't acknowledge him as he climbed the steps to the mercantile.

"O'Bryne," he tried again, then bent his head against the pelting snow and hastened toward the mercantile. What had started out as a mild winter was quickly turning into a beast. They'd had sun for two days since Christmas, and every other day had pummeled them with snow.

Virgil O'Byrne pulled open the door to the mercantile, not bothering to hold it open behind him.

Elijah shouldered through a moment later and stomped his snowy boots on the rug. "O'Byrne. Can I have a word with you?"

The man muttered something and disappeared down the dry goods aisle.

"It won't take long." Elijah followed him to where he stood in front of the flour, the snow from his boots creating a small puddle on the floor.

"If this is about Frank, I already told the sheriff. I don't know nothin' 'bout him trying to kill that woman. And I don't know nothin' 'bout whatever papers he did or didn't have in his pocket neither."

Elijah held up his hands. "This isn't about Frank Ebberhard. I wanted to ask about your children."

It was the wrong thing to say. The man's posture grew stiffer, and he muttered something under his breath before speaking. "I keep telling everyone, they're my young'uns. Not no one else's. Don't know why everyone's suddenly got their dander up about a man being a pa to his young'uns."

Elijah held up his hands again, the least threatening gesture he could think of. "I don't have any problem with a man being a pa to his children. Heaven knows I'm grateful for how good of a pa I had growing up."

The muscles at the side of O'Byrnes mouth twitched.

"Thing of it was, my ma was always around to help him. He was a fisherman, and if he'd had to put in a full day's work on top of caring for us young'uns, well, let's just say I don't think I'd have as fond of memories of my pa as I do."

The words hung in the air between them, and Elijah ran his eyes over O'Byrne. He'd been praying about what to do ever since he and Victoria had taken the children to their father. He couldn't go on not seeing them when they lived in the same town. Couldn't go on getting sparse reports from his brother about how the children were faring and sneaking out to the cabin when their father was gone.

He took his hat off his head and twisted it in his hands. "So I was wondering if Victoria and I might help with that a bit. Must be hard, not having Jenny around anymore, and before that, the children had their mother, didn't they?"

O'Byrne gave him a brisk nod.

"We'd like to invite you over for dinner after church every Sunday, both you and the children. Even if you don't go to church, you're welcome to come to dinner. And then Victoria and I were thinking we could pick another day of the week and watch them for you. A man who works as hard as yourself needs a break every so often. Maybe we could even watch them on Fridays or Saturdays so the children could spend the night." Elijah twisted his hat again. If the man said no, he'd pound the gates of heaven with his prayers until he had some kind of agreement worked out with the logging boss.

O'Byrne scratched his beard. "Ya really don't mind having a bunch of young'uns underfoot?"

Mind the young'uns? Elijah swallowed some of the thickness in his throat. Had Alice ever curled herself onto her father's lap the way she'd curled up on his? "Not in the least. You got yourself some mighty special children."

The man shrugged. "Don't see no harm in you watching them some. Maybe ya could come get them tonight? I've a hankering for a drink or two."

A smile spread across Elijah's lips, probably the biggest smile since he'd learned the other man was in town. He'd take O'Byrne's offer. And he'd thank God for it. And he'd keep trusting that God knew what was best for him and Victoria, all the while praying God would see fit to give him and Victoria the desire of their hearts—in the form of a child or two.

One day at a time, one visit at a time, one prayer at a time. If God could help him through the death of his father, then that same God could help him and Victoria through their childlessness.

Chapter Twenty-Six

Thomas pushed open the door to the telegraph office, his shoulder giving a slight twinge as he left the blustery road and headed inside. It had been a week since he'd taken Frank Ebberhard down on the floor of the sheriff's office, and his shoulder still pained him.

Was it ever going to get better? How could he provide for his family when he could barely open a door without hissing in pain?

No, Thomas, I told you. Your shoulder is like the scars on Christ's hands. Jessalyn's words from that night inside the sheriff's office floated back to him. *I don't need you to haul crates or chip away at mine rock. If you can love me with all my flaws, then I can love you with yours.*

He sighed. He needed to start thinking of himself as a whole man instead of always grumbling about his shoulder. Wasn't there a verse about being made strong through weakness somewhere in the Bible?

But if given a choice, he still wanted his good shoulder back.

Except it looked like God wasn't going to give him a choice—at least not in this area. Which meant he better accept his ailing body for what it was—frail and finite—and move on. Besides, he was blessed with other things that were more important than his shoulder anyway.

"Mr. Dowrick, why didn't you ring the bell?" Mrs. Runkle

bustled out from the back room and gestured to the little bell sitting on the counter. "I didn't hear you come in."

"I was just getting ready to, ma'am." He tipped his hat at the grandmotherly widow.

"It's a good thing you stopped. I have a telegram that you'll be hankering to see." She headed to the counter, her gait slow and stiff, which was probably to be expected considering her age. "Now where did I put it?" Her brow furrowed, and she looked down at the counter, then began rummaging through a small stack of papers.

He took a step closer. He hadn't actually expected a message to be waiting for him. Was the quick reply time a good thing, or a bad?

Probably bad. It couldn't possible to…

"Ah, yes. Here it is." Mrs. Runkle straightened and held the piece of paper up, then handed it to him.

Thomas stared down at it, the words blurring together for a moment as he tried to make sense of them. Too soon? That proved how much he knew.

"Are you unwell, Mr. Dowrick?" Mrs. Runkle shifted on the other side of the counter. "I was under the impression you'd look forward to the news, what with all the other telegrams you've had me send over the past few days."

He looked up, then smiled and glanced at the telegram one more time before slipping it into his pocket. Yes, he really had just read those words. Yes, they were true. His smile widened into an all-out grin. "Couldn't be better. It's good news, indeed."

The woman's eyes lit. "Does anyone else know?"

"No." He patted his pocket. "And I need it to stay that way until I tell my wife."

She gave a firm nod, her lips almost trembling with the news.

Which meant he had all of five minutes to tell Jessalyn before the other woman started spreading the story. "I'd best be on my way, then."

He squashed his hat low on his head to combat the driving wind outside, then pulled open the door.

"Thomas." Isaac hastened across the street toward him. "Figured you'd be in your apartment."

"What can I say? I enjoy being home with my wife and daughters." Every night. And every morning. And every afternoon. And all the times in between. After saving Jessalyn from Frank Ebberhard's attempted murder, he hadn't been able to tear himself away from her.

"I have this for you." Isaac turned his shoulders away from the wind and handed him a paper. "The judge will be in town next week for Ebberhard's trial. You'll need to testify about the kerosene and finding Jessalyn restrained. It wouldn't hurt if she could give a few words of testimony too, but if she's not up to facing Ebberhard, we should be able to get a guilty sentence just on what you have to say."

"Next week." Thomas tightened his grip on the paper lest the wind carry it off. It brought an odd sort of comfort, the crinkle of the paper in his gloves, the undeniable black words that stated a man would go to trial for attempting to kill his wife. He drew in a breath, then handed the paper back. "I thought I just got good news from Mrs. Runkle, but yours might be better."

"He's going to be put away for a good, long time." Isaac took the paper and folded it before slipping it back into his pocket. "Don't suppose this means you'll come back to work now?"

"Maybe after the trial." Thomas stared up at the porch rafters. Jessalyn was somewhere above them, inside the apartment, happily sewing a shirt or sketching a dress design, maybe even cooking. "I don't like the thought of that villain being only a street away from Jess, even if he's behind bars. I want him behind bars *and* at least three states away if I'm going to leave Jess and the girls alone at night."

"Not sure I can get him three states away, but southern Michigan is about six hundred miles from here. Have to admit, I'll be glad when this is settled next week. I'm ready to put this business behind us, though probably not as eager as you." Isaac blew out a breath so long and hard it rivaled the wind gusting over Lake Superior. "Wanted to let you know Elijah and I searched Ebberhard's house yesterday."

Thomas turned at that. "I don't even know where he was staying."

"In the woods about a half mile out with one of the other loggers. I found the rest of Betty Ranulfson's jewelry there and Miss Brogan's hair brush, all of which Ebberhard's roommate claims Ebberhard took on his own."

"Anything to tie him to the thefts at the brothel and warehouse?"

Isaac shook his head. "If not for Ebberhard confessing the first fire to Jessalyn, I wouldn't even be able to tie him to that."

He'd have thought sure Jess's shop fire and the brothel burglary were connected, seeing how they both happened on the same night. Thomas scratched the back of his neck. Truth be told, he'd hoped investigating Ebberhard would lead to the arrest of whoever was behind all the burglaries in town. But maybe Ebberhard's burglaries were truly separate from the others.

So did they still have another burglar or two to catch? Or had the thieves moved on to another town? Outside of Ebberhard's actions, things had been quiet for over a month. "What about the map? Did you ever find it, or at least find out what it was to?"

Isaac shook his head, his face grim. "The man won't say a word to me. I figured once he sat behind bars for a few days, he'd start talking. But he's given me nothing. I'll have the burglary charges added to Ebberhard's case when the judge comes through."

"Jessalyn still swears she never saw a map."

"It likely burned in the fire, is why he torched her building in the first place. He only thought she saved it after we started searching the woods."

"Except we didn't search the woods because of any map, but because it's the only place that makes sense to hide the warehouse and brothel goods." His gaze drifted next door, to where two feet of snow now blanketed the rubble heap of Jessalyn's building.

Isaac rubbed a hand over his jaw. "Ebberhard didn't know that though, and so when we were searching, he figured Jessalyn had given us his map."

Thomas looked out over the street. "Have to admit, I'd like a few more answers, but if what we have now means he'll not be able to hurt Jessalyn again—or anyone else, for that matter—then I'll take it."

"I agree. With a man as obstinate as Ebberhard, I doubt we'll ever know the full story, but he'll be locked up for a good, long time." Isaac stomped his boots on the porch, probably to get some feeling back in his toes if he'd been outside for any length of time. "Even if you don't come back to work when this is over, thank you for your help."

Thomas clasped a hand on Isaac's shoulder. He'd not come to Eagle Harbor looking for a friend, but it seemed he'd gotten one anyway. "I'll be back in another week, if you can tolerate a deputy with an ailing shoulder, that is. It seems the least I can do for you after you looked out for Jess and the girls the years I was away."

Isaac offered a small smile. "She's happier now than she ever was when you were gone. Don't let her tell you otherwise."

Thomas's gaze drifted up to the porch rafters once more, and he smiled. "I don't plan to, Sheriff. But speaking of my wife, I need to go see her." And quickly. Mrs. Runkle's five minutes of silence were bound to be up.

He stepped off the porch and headed around the side of the

building to the second-floor entrance and stairs, a whistle on his lips. And if his hand just happened to slip into his pocket and feel the paper of the telegram, well, he could hardly help touching it, or the smile that spread across his face as he did so.

He bounded up the stairs. The scent of cookies reached his nose before he opened the door, and his grin widened. "Smells good in here."

Jessalyn turned from where she stood near the stove, a smudge of flour on her cheek. "I know they're not as good as the bakery's, but I needed to make biscuits for dinner, so I figured I'd do up some cookies too."

"Whoever said they're not as good as the bakery's lied." He snagged a cookie off the cooling rack and let the warm, sweet taste fill his mouth.

Jessalyn rolled her eyes. "More like whoever said they were better than the bakery's is the one lying."

"I don't think so." He caught her around the waist then pressed a kiss to her cheek, his mouth still full of cookie.

She pushed away from him and swiped at the crumbs clinging to her skin from the sloppy kiss. "I need to get these biscuits mixed if you want them in time for dinner."

"I have something for you first." He reached into his pocket and held out the note.

She looked up, her eyes suddenly worried. "Not another telegram. I barely survived the last time you got one of those." But she took it anyway, her brow knitting as she glanced at the words. Then her head jerked up. "Somebody wants to buy your hotel?"

"They don't just want to. They are. I already sent a message back accepting the offer."

"But I… we… this…" The paper trembled in her hand. "It's twenty-five thousand dollars. Is your hotel worth that much? And even if it is, how do you know this isn't another ruse?"

"I was hoping for more along the lines of twenty-two thousand, so I won't complain about twenty-five." He hooked a thumb in his belt loop and rolled back on his heels.

"But... it's your hotel." She shoved the message back at him, her hands still trembling. "You can't sell it. It's the only means we have of providing for the family. Don't you want to keep it? It's the reason you left when you got that telegram after Christmas, you had to save your hotel."

He slipped the paper back into his pocket, then stepped closer and covered her hands with his own. "I thought I wanted to keep it too, until I realized I was treating the hotel like it was more important than you or the girls."

Tears brimmed in her eyes. "You never did that."

"Didn't I? I left you alone so I could try to save it, when you were the one in danger, not my hotel."

"You thought your hotel was at risk. It's perfectly understandable."

"Perhaps, but on the road to Calumet, I realized that I'd spent five years of my life pursuing money and success before you. I turned around the moment I understood what I'd done. That's why I came back in time to save you from Ebberhard, and I don't want to walk down the path of making other things more important than you again."

She shook her head, her jaw trembling now along with her hands. "You didn't put those things before us, you were working on the hotel because of us, remember? When you first came back, you even said—"

He leaned forward and covered her lips with his own, her hands still clasped in his. He lingered there only a moment, just long enough to silence her and taste the sweetness of her breath. "But I put the hotel between us when I came back too. If I'd told you I'd follow you to Chicago, here, wherever, whenever, whatever you wanted, I'd have had your heart back in a week's time."

She tugged one of her hands from his and pressed her fingers to her mouth, as though trying to savor his kiss even though he'd gladly give her another anytime she wished. "I don't know if it would have happened quite that quickly, but… I would have been more willing to hear you out, less afraid of what was going to happen with you back in our lives."

He squeezed the hand still left in his. "The truth is, I could have left Deadwood numerous times to come and ask your forgiveness during those five years I was gone. I didn't because I'd convinced myself that earning money, building a grand hotel, was somehow just as important as having you and the girls in my life."

"Are you sure you want to sell? Because I'll go with you to Deadwood, Thomas. I promise I will. There's nothing left for us in Eagle Harbor now anyway, and I don't even know why I was so stubborn about—"

He pressed a finger to her lips. "Yes, I'm sure. I wired Bernard and Sheriff Haynes in Deadwood the morning after I returned to find Frank Ebberhard trying to kill you."

She blinked. "But that was a week ago."

"I didn't want to say anything until I had a buyer. Could be the hotel was for sale for months and we still went to Deadwood come spring."

She pulled away from him and paced a few steps one direction before pivoting and turning back the other way, shaking her head all the while. "I was supposed to be the one working on being less selfish, yet you're giving up things for me instead."

He caught her hand as she tromped by. One swift jerk, and she was pressed up against his chest—right where she belonged. He tilted her head back and stared down into pale blue eyes the color of the harbor ice, but so much warmer than when he'd stood before her two months ago. "There'll be plenty of time for you to be the selfless one, because I'm not leaving your side again."

"But are you sure about selling the hotel?" Each word sent a puff of warm breath against his chin.

"I am."

She wrapped her arms around him, her gaze not leaving his. "What do you plan to do then? Where do you want to go? I'll follow you anywhere. Even to a mining town in California."

"I don't want to go to California."

"No?" Her brow drew down. "Back to Cornwall with your family?"

"I was thinking more along the lines of a big city on the southern shore of Lake Michigan. One that's in need of a ladies' fashion designer and a dress factory."

She sucked in a breath, quick and sharp. But he laid a finger over her lips before she opened her mouth.

"Selling my hotel will give us the money we need to start a factory right away instead of just a small dress shop. I want you to have your dream, Jess. And truth be told, I like the idea of providing jobs to women who need solid work over selling people a place to sleep for a night." He leaned down to plant a kiss on her forehead. "The more I think of it, if we're serious about letting God rebuild things between us, then we both need a fresh start. No Deadwood for me and no Eagle Harbor for you. We need to go somewhere we have memories of being together instead of apart." He moved his lips to her temple and kissed her there.

Tears glittered in her eyes. "I love you, Thomas."

He didn't deserve her love, not with the mistakes he'd made, not with the way he'd put money and success before his family. "I love you too."

292

She closed her eyes, leaned her head against his chest, and drew in a long, deep breath. "This is better than I dreamed."

He rested his chin on the top of her head. "No, it's exactly what you dreamed, and I count it a blessing that I can give it to you."

She shook her head against him. "You're wrong, when I had those dreams and put my plans together for the dress factory, I never dreamed I'd have you to help me."

This from the woman who'd once kicked him out of their daughter's medical examination and slammed the back door to her dress shop in his face. From the woman who'd said she'd never be able to trust him again.

He gathered his wife more fully into his arms, holding her so close that not even air separated them. If anyone was undeserving of the life laid out in front of them, it was him. Nine months ago he'd been confined to a sickbed, a man with a ravaged shoulder and a forgotten family. But God had taken him in his ruin—in the dark, hopeless winter of his life—and led him into a future bright with dreams.

It might still be winter outside the window, but his heart felt like a warm spring day, green and fresh and filled with sunlight, with new possibilities for the future springing up everywhere he looked.

Epilogue

Five Years Later; Chicago, Illinois

"Mrs. Dowrick should be back any moment, but I really don't see the situation changing. I'm so very sorry." Thomas met the clear green gaze of the widow standing across the counter from him. If only he could offer more help.

Her red hair was slipping from its updo and the thin cloak she wore didn't seem remotely thick enough to keep her warm from the brutal winter wind outside. He could send her on her way with a bit of money, but that would hardly fix her troubles.

"Are ye sure? I was told to speak with Mrs. Dowrick directly, ye see." The woman shoved a bit of hair behind her ear, her voice thick with the sound of Ireland. "I'll take anything ye have. I don't care whether it be sewin' or cleanin' or even runnin' messages for ye."

In the corner, three children in rags just as thin as the ones their mother wore played with Olivia. Olivia had produced two dolls from the bin of playthings behind the counter as soon as she'd seen the children enter beside their mother. His oldest daughter was becoming more and more indispensable around the factory office, never mind she was only fifteen and worked but a few hours after school each afternoon.

"I'll take your name down in case we have an opening." He bent to search for the clipboard beneath the counter, the one with a list that had grown entirely too familiar over the past year. Where had Marcy set it? Their secretary had run back onto the factory floor with Jessalyn a few minutes ago, and while he knew where things were in his own office, he didn't know where Marcy kept half her papers and files.

"Are there any others ahead of me?" The widow leaned forward over the counter.

He pulled the list out from beneath a stack of dress sketches and nearly winced. "Um, a few."

Seventeen, to be exact. He swallowed the sigh that rose in his chest. There were so many needy women in Chicago. So many people ready and willing to work... if they could find a job that paid them enough to live on. But most factories paid women half of what they paid men, even if the women did the same work. For the women who didn't have the support of a husband, the pennies they earned per day would never be enough to care for a family.

How had Jessalyn managed to support herself and their daughters during the years he'd been away? He'd known sixteen years ago today, when his wife had walked down the aisle to him in a fashionable, yet affordable blue gown, that he was marrying someone special. But he'd not realized just how special until they opened the doors of her dress factory four and a half years ago and poured through the flood of women applicants hoping to make a decent wage for the first time in their lives.

The bell above the door jingled, and he nearly groaned when he glimpsed a woman cloaked in fur, with diamonds dangling from her ears.

He slipped the widow a blank piece of paper and a pencil. "Write down your name and address, and I'll transfer it to the list later."

Which would be better than letting her write the information on the list directly and see how many names were before hers.

The rich woman strode up to the counter, her chin tilted in that arrogant angle that spoke of extreme wealth. She barely glanced at the bare brick walls of the office and the dust and grime that always seemed to coat the place—regardless of who he hired to clean it. He'd learned after only a few weeks that a factory office was never as neat and clean as a hotel one.

The woman set her reticule on the counter, the handbag laced with nearly as many jewels as the ones winking from her hair. "I need to speak with Jessalyn Dowrick, please."

Yes, well, so did he. Thomas eyed the clock and then the door where his wife had disappeared into the factory with their secretary, muttering something about how she just needed to show Marcy the new dress pattern and then they could go to dinner early. Somehow fifteen minutes had slipped by. "I'm afraid she's unavailable. May I take a message?"

"No. I'll wait. I need to make changes to a dress I ordered, and I can't risk miscommunication." The woman turned and glanced around the small office at the front of the factory.

Thomas could almost hear her thoughts. *But where shall I sit? Certainly not on that bench in the corner. Why, it's dusty, and there isn't any padding.*

The widow slid farther down the counter until she stood wedged against the wall before she started writing on her paper.

Thomas clenched his teeth together. Why couldn't the fancy woman have left a message for Jessalyn at the shop where she'd ordered her dress? "We have more comfortable accommodations in our shop off Prairie Street. You're always welcome to go there to discuss orders."

The woman gave a stout nod. "Yes, but I'll wait here, if you please."

Olivia looked at the door that led to the factory floor, then rose, leaving the children to play with the dolls by themselves, and came around the counter. "How long ago did you place your order?"

"Yesterday, but I'm afraid it's a rushed job. I need the gown for the wedding I'm to attend at the end of the week." The woman fretted with her necklace.

"Ah, yes. I believe Mother was working on the sketch earlier." Olivia headed straight to the shelf with the sketch and then approached the counter. "Does this look right?"

"Oh." The woman took the sketch in her hand. "She added lace around the sleeves, did she?"

"Yes, ma'am."

Thomas held his tongue as Olivia peered over the counter to look at the sketch with the woman. Jessalyn hadn't added anything, Olivia had. They needed to find a way to credit Olivia for her own work, rather than having the girl always pretend it was her mother's.

"That's what I was stopping to discuss with her. I saw Mildred Covington's dress today, and she has four-inch lace around the sleeves. And I simply can't be shown up by Millie, you understand."

Olivia nodded sweetly, as though she understood completely, when she probably didn't care in the least, as long as she got to design dresses for her mother. She'd grown so much during the five years they'd been in Chicago. She'd once been the girl who'd spent half of her days before her surgery sick with constant ear infections, yet now she was a sweet, healthy young lady starting to garner attention from a few too many of the boys her age.

"Here be the things yer needin'." The Irishwoman scooted her paper toward him, then tightened her coat about her and turned to gather her children.

Thomas headed around the counter just as the door to the factory opened, letting the noisy sound of busy sewing machines into the room. Marcy slipped inside and shut the door behind her.

Thomas paused picking up the dolls the children had been playing with and raised an eyebrow in silent question.

Marcy raised her hands only to let them fall again. "She was behind me just a minute ago, but then she stopped to talk to Sally. She should be here soon though."

Thomas glanced at the wealthy woman at the counter, still discussing her dress with Olivia in low tones. Maybe it was better Jessalyn hadn't come into the office, or they might be stuck here another half hour. "I'll go find her in a minute. I'm just going to see these folks…"

He frowned and looked around the office, which was now empty of the children and widow. Had they slipped outside while he was talking to Marcy? He set the dolls on the bench, then grabbed his coat off the hook by the door and rushed outside.

The family hadn't even reached the curb yet, the brutal Chicago wind whipping their thin coats so hard it was difficult for the littlest one to walk.

"Let me catch you a cab." He hurried up behind them.

The widow turned and looked over her shoulder, clutching her own thin coat to her neck with her gloveless hand. "Thank ye, but we'll take the street car."

"A cab will be simpler, and don't worry about the fare." He spotted one farther down the road beside the glass factory and raised his hand as it approached.

The woman bent and hefted her youngest child, balancing him on her hip while he burrowed closer—probably seeking warmth. The boy looked only a year or so younger than Violet, the daughter God had blessed him and Jessalyn with three years ago.

The daughter at home with her nanny and sisters right now, who had more winter coats than she could ever use. Surely she had a dark blue or brown one that would suffice for a boy, and since he already had their address, he could see that the coat was delivered first thing tomorrow.

The woman glanced at the approaching cab, then turned back to him. "Why are ye so kind to me?"

There wasn't enough time to explain that his wife had once been in a similar situation, and a good part of it had been his fault. "The cab fare isn't any trouble, I promise. My wife and I have funds set aside to help people in difficult situations."

A couple months after they'd moved to Chicago, the police traced a second bank account back to Jessalyn's cousin-in-law, and that one hadn't been nearly as empty as the first. They'd gotten back every last penny of the nearly six thousand dollars he'd sent Jessalyn while they were separated. He'd wanted to put it toward the factory, but his wife had other plans, and he hadn't been able to argue against their using the money to help poor women.

The clomp of horse's hooves drew near and the cab slowed to a stop. Thomas opened the door for the woman, who ushered her children in first.

When she moved to climb inside behind the little ones, Thomas took her hand and pressed a bundle of bills into it. "To buy some food, and maybe pay a month or two's rent. I'm sure you need it."

Moisture glinted in the woman's eyes. "I still don't understand why ye're so kind to me, but thank ye."

She shouldn't be thanking him, not when he'd turned her away. But Thomas swallowed his response and closed the door behind her, standing on the street an extra moment while the cab lurched forward. Across the street, an elaborate carriage that could only belong to the woman inside the office stood parked behind his own. His coachman gave him a glance, but Thomas opened his hands and shrugged. He couldn't exactly leave to celebrate his anniversary without his wife, but if they waited much longer, the shift would be over and the factory closed for the day, which meant he and Jessalyn would leave the same time they usually did. He turned back toward the long building that housed the dress factory. Instead of returning to the office, he headed inside the factory entrance.

The clatter of seventy constantly working sewing machines echoed off the brick walls of the building, filling his ears with a noise he'd grown all too used to. He scanned the long, cavernous factory floor with row after row of sewing machines, each with a woman seated in front of it, working on any one of the five dress patterns Jessalyn currently had in production. Next month she'd switch to five different dress patterns, and she'd switch again the month after that, occasionally bringing back popular patterns that sold out quickly in the Chicago stores.

"Have you seen Mrs. Dowrick?" He bent near the closest woman, Annie, if he wasn't mistaken. She didn't have a family of her own yet, but helped support her mother and younger siblings by working at the factory.

The young woman looked up, then shook her head. "I saw her pass by maybe a half hour ago with Miss Stevens, but haven't seen her since."

"Thank you, and the dress is coming along nicely, by the way." He jutted his chin toward the deep red and cream colored creation draped over her sewing machine. "You're getting faster at your sewing too."

She beamed at him, her blush nearly so bright it drowned out her freckles. "You're welcome."

He straightened and scanned the large room for Gwendolyn Stevens. She'd been Jessalyn's first hire when they'd opened shop, and the woman had proved more faithful than a sister to Jessalyn. If he ever wanted to whisk Jessalyn away from Chicago for a few weeks, he could leave everything in Gwen's hands and know it'd be well taken care of.

He spotted Gwen at the far end of the factory, near the industrial-sized bolts of cloth they stored at the back of the building and started her direction, but something purple flashed two aisles over. He stopped and narrowed his eyes. Hadn't Jessalyn worn purple that morning? He rounded the end of the long, narrow workbench that held a string of ten sewing machines and stalked toward the wriggling mound of purple satin huddled under one of the sewing machines positioned against the factory's brick wall.

Sally Bartle stood beside her stool, looking down where Jessalyn had crawled beneath her machine. "I'm really sorry, Mrs. Dowrick. I wasn't pushing too hard on the treadle. I swear I wasn't. I was just…" Sally glanced up to see him approach, and her face paled. "Um, Mrs. Dowrick, I think you should—"

"Just a minute. I've almost fixed it." Jessalyn called from beneath the workbench.

He leaned a hand on the bench and bent to see into the little nook where his wife had crawled. "And here I thought I'd married a dressmaker sixteen years ago, when it turns out I actually married a repairman."

"Thomas!" Her head came up so quickly it banged on the bottom of the bench.

He winced and held out a hand to her. "What are you doing? We have people we can call on to fix this."

She rubbed the spot where she'd bumped her head. "This one treadle is always sticking. I think we should replace it."

He kept his hand extended, though she seemed happier to sit under the bench in a puddle of satin rather than crawl out of the tiny space she'd wedged herself into. "And you needed to fix this now? We're almost a half hour late for dinner."

"Dinner. Is it really that late?" She did take his hand then and scrambled up. "I'm so sorry. I lost track of time and then I—"

"Decided to make a mess of yourself." He brushed at the blotch of dust smeared across her shoulder, never mind the streak of it starting just below her waist and stretching almost the entire length of her skirt. He ran his gaze down her and then back up, stopping at the gentle bulge in her stomach most of the workers hadn't yet noticed. "Are you all right?"

He nearly reached out a hand to rest it on the growing lump, but that would give more away than Jessalyn wanted revealed quite yet.

Her own gaze dipped to her stomach, and her cheeks brightened. "Yes, I'm fine. And I'm sorry. I guess I wasn't thinking about... that."

Did she realize how beautiful she was, looking up at him so earnestly, a touch of embarrassment flickering in her light blue eyes? She might have a few more lines around her eyes and mouth than she'd had sixteen years ago, might have gained a few pounds over the years too, but she was still so very lovely to him. He extended his arm for her. "Let's get you out of here before you find another sewing machine to climb beneath."

"Sure. Just let me get my coat, and then we can—"

"No." He tugged her down the aisle toward the factory entrance and away from the office. "If you go in there, it'll be another half hour or better before I get you out." Especially if the wealthy client was still in there.

"You said this morning we were supposed to get snow." She walked along beside him, not resisting his pull though she glanced over her shoulder toward the office a few times.

He slipped his arms out of his own coat and draped it over her shoulders. "I believe you have an extra in the carriage, but if not, you can use mine."

"You'll freeze."

"Worth it, if it means I won't lose any more time with you." He tugged her outside and into the snow that had indeed started falling while he was in the factory. The coachman pulled the carriage up to the side of the street, then hopped down from his perch and opened the door for them. Thomas handed his wife up, and a few minutes later they were snuggled inside the heated carriage and lurching forward.

Her extra coat indeed hung on a hook at the front of the carriage, but rather than offer it to her, he wrapped her in his arms. "Are you warm enough?"

"Yes. Thank you." She snuggled into his chest.

He dropped his lips onto hers for one sweet second, then pulled back and sighed. Why hadn't he thought to give that extra coat to the Irishwoman?

"What's wrong?" Jessalyn laid a hand on his arm, her angel blue eyes full of questions.

He fingered the thick wool fabric of the coat Jessalyn was wrapped in. "I added another woman to the list of people to hire this afternoon. A widow with three children. I think her husband died on the docks."

Jessalyn leaned back against the seat and fiddled with one of the large buttons on his coat. "I always hate turning them away."

"Did you know there's eighteen women on the wait list now?"

"Yes, but I was hoping—"

"We need to open another factory."

She jerked her head up, her brow furrowed. "Another...?"

"And we'll need to promote Gwendolyn to manager of our current one." It wasn't quite what he'd planned to discuss with his wife for their anniversary celebration, but he still couldn't banish the image of the Irish widow and her three children from his mind.

The corners of Jessalyn's mouth tipped up in a soft smile, one that said she knew something he didn't. "I don't want another factory, Thomas."

"What do you mean? This is your dream… our dream." And it was. Somehow over the past five years, Jessalyn's dream of a dress factory had turned into his dream too. A very busy dream that involved him overseeing the daily operations of the factory while his wife spent her time designing new dresses to be produced. But he wouldn't trade it for anything, not even for a certain hotel in Deadwood. The women they helped by paying the same wage as the glass factory down the street paid men, the popularity of Jessalyn's designs, and his business experience from his years of owning a hotel all fit together like pieces of a tightly-crafted puzzle.

"Dreams can change." She shifted closer and laid a hand on his chest, that knowing smile still on her lips.

"Are you saying you don't want to own a dress factory anymore? Because if you're thinking of selling, I really—"

"I don't want to sell our factory." She arched her neck and planted a kiss on his jaw. "I love it."

"Yes, so much so you crawl around on its floor when we're supposed to be celebrating." He settled a hand over the growing mound in her stomach and kept it in place. What wasn't she telling him?

"I'm content to keep the factory just how it is."

"Let me look into this a little more. If I can find the right manager for a second factory and get a good group of people over there to help, you won't even notice we have a second factory. If anything, it just means you get to design more dresses. Besides, don't you want to create more jobs for those eighteen women on our list? Expanding distribution won't be hard. We have more orders than we can reasonably fill even now."

She settled her hand over his on her stomach, interlocking their fingers. "I do want to help those women, but not by starting another factory."

"How then?"

She peeked up at him, then ran her lip through her teeth before softly speaking. "It's what I was going to talk to you about tonight. I want us to buy a hotel."

"You want to…?" The air stilled around him. Had she just said what he thought? They'd decided years ago, when they'd moved back to Chicago, that they were going to pursue Jessalyn's dress factory instead of a hotel.

But a hotel. It had been years since he'd taken a customer up to an immaculate, polished room, or dug a crib out of storage so that new parents had somewhere to rest their little one while they got a decent night's sleep. Since he offered a room at half-price to a man who'd lost a family member and came to town for a funeral, or given a large family with children a spare room in the hotel at no extra charge—just so the parents could have a bit of privacy for an evening.

Hotels had a constant stream of people, someone new to meet every day, with their own unique past and story that somehow had driven Thomas's life to intersect with theirs for a short time.

But he didn't need new people to keep him happy or give him something to do, not like he once had. He gazed down at his wife, soft and serene and angelically beautiful as the snow floated down outside the carriage. "I don't need a hotel to keep me happy. I have you and our daughters."

Four of them now, since they'd added little Violet to their family three years ago. He narrowed his eyes at her stomach and gave the bundle inside her a little pat.

"But this one had better be a boy." If he was going to be surrounded by women both at work and at home, asking for a single boy surely wasn't expecting too much of their Heavenly Father. "We should just expand the factory. It will be simpler in the end."

"Not really. That team of people you want to hire to run a second factory? I think you should hire them to run the factory we have now, and you can turn your attention to a hotel, at least until it's on its feet like the factory is. Besides, I do look at the financial reports you leave for me, you know."

He raised his eyebrows. "You do?"

"Well of course, you put them on top of my dress designs, so I at least have to move them if I want to get back to my dresses."

"I should have guessed," he muttered, but couldn't resist tugging on a strand of her white-blond hair.

"Well, it doesn't take more than a glance to see how large our profit margins have grown, but I also know that you loved being a hotelier." She shifted against him, straightening to better see his eyes, though she still kept their fingers laced over their child. "Don't try to deny it. I see the way you notice the details of hotel rooms whenever we travel, and how you can't help but examine everything about a restaurant when we eat at a fancy hotel. You've given me five years to chase my dreams, and we've succeeded, more than I ever could have hoped. Now it's time to think about your dreams."

A lump rose in his throat, and his eyes misted. If they truly did buy a hotel, his family could be a part of everything this time. His children would grow up constantly meeting new people and learning the value of hospitality, the support and comfort a simple room could offer others. Maybe they could even live in a suite of rooms on the top floor, just like the rooms he'd once had built for his family in Deadwood. "You mean it, don't you? You've been thinking about this for a while."

"Of course. We can hire those eighteen women to work at your hotel just as quickly as we could hire them to work at my factory. I asked the bookkeeper to come up with cost estimates and business projections for a hotel, but Lucinda didn't know what kind of expenses to factor in for a hotel."

"You...?" His tongue was too thick and sluggish to work. "You realize hotels are rarely for sale. Most people who own a profitable hotel aren't of a mind to sell it."

"There's an old apartment building I saw advertised in the paper just before Christmas, but it hasn't sold yet. I clipped the article out and was going to bring it tonight—until someone refused to let me get my coat. Even so, I think the location will prove—"

"You want to restore an old building into a modern hotel?"

She glanced down, then peeked back up at him from beneath her lashes and offered him a shy smile. "I figured it would be a little like us. We used to be broken and forgotten, and look at us now."

Yes, look at them now. He pulled her close. Did she realize how blessed he was to have her in his life? Things hadn't always been so easy between them. Yet God had found them in their brokenness and had restored their relationship into something better and richer than he'd ever dreamed.

Except the Lord build a house, they labour in vain that build it.

He reckoned that was true for hotels too, because it was certainly true for marriages.

～ ～ ～ ～ ～

Want to read more Eagle Harbor novels?
Don't miss Isaac Cummings and Aileen Brogan's story in
Love's Bright Tomorrow.
Keep reading for a sneak peek on the next page...

Love's Bright Tomorrow
Chapter One

Eagle Harbor, MI; June, 1884

The dream came in waves, soft and gentle at first, the crackle of the fire in the hearth, the sound of her da's voice, the hunched form of her brother seated at the table with her da, studying the checker board.

The sun from a hundred different afternoons, beating down until her skin darkened with freckles while she worked the land.

"Look out the window, Aileen."

Aileen leaned closer inside the hot, stuffy cottage, straining to hear her father's frail voice where he lay in bed. "What was that, Pa?"

Sweat beaded on his forehead, and his face held the gray color of death. "The window. Look out the window."

Not the window. Not again. She sat back in her chair. "Later, Da. I'm too busy tending you right now. How about I get another cloth for your forehead instead?"

"I told ye, look out the window." The faint words nearly disappeared before they reached her, but his eyes held a glassy sort of determination.

She swallowed her sigh and rose, heading over to the closest of the cottage's two windows. She knew what she'd see, had been staring it since she was four and old enough to push a chair to the window and peek outside.

The rolling landscape of Ireland filled her vision, a vast expanse of emerald fields sloping softly down toward the ocean.

"Everything the sun touches, it'll be ours one day." Somehow Pa's voice floated across the room to her, as though knowing she'd gone to the window had given him a sudden burst of strength. "One day I'll buy those fields for meself. One day the land we work will be ours."

She stared out the window, and a sheen of tears glazed her eyes. The land wasn't ever going to be theirs, not when they couldn't even afford the rent. Her brother Conan was in town at this very moment, trying to talk the land agent into giving them a bit more time to come up with the money.

Money they weren't going to have this year, not with Da so ill, not with the falling crop prices, not with the surge of rain they'd gotten over the summer. Half their potatoes, turnips, and carrots were rotting from the moisture in the soil.

"Da, we're not…" She turned back to face her father, the strong man who had caught some kind of fever over the winter that he didn't seem likely to recover from. Despite his glazed eyes and wheezing breaths, his gaze held such hope. She swallowed her words of truth and forced new ones out instead. "Yes, Da, the land will be ours one day, and you'll be the best farmer in all of Ireland."

And then she was no longer eighteen, but six, standing in the field with her father, her apron full of seeds for planting while the rich scent of freshly plowed soil filled the air.

"Close yer eyes and lift yer face up to the sky." Her father's booming voice rumbled from his chest, strong and hearty.

She did as he asked, letting the faint breeze off the ocean ruffle her hair, and drawing in a breath that tasted of both fresh soil and salty sea.

"Do ye feel the sun on it?"

She nodded, the spring rays of the sun kissing her face with their warmth.

"Now open yer eyes and look out over the fields."

She did so, staring out over the gentle knolls of rich brown earth dotted with patches of green that gave way to blue ocean in the distance.

"Everything the sun touches, it'll be ours one day."

Tears streaked her face, and she took a step back from him, then another, until the land behind him blurred, until the towering form of her father disappeared into a swirl of brown and green and blue. *It won't be ours, Da. It won't. Don't tell me lies. Don't fill my head with nonsense. Don't make me hope for things that will never be.*

But he'd filled her head with it anyway, and Conan's too. Every time they worked the fields, every time they took a wagon full of vegetables to the land agent to pay their rent, every time they set up a booth at the market to sell their goods. It didn't matter where they were, what they were doing, or the time of the year, there was one thing Da never stopped talking about—one day they'd own the land.

Crash!

Aileen woke with a jolt, the fields of her homeland slipping away as she sat up on the narrow bed and pressed a hand to her heart. It stampeded against her palm like sheep running down a hillside.

"What did you do?"

A man's voice. She froze at the sound. Where was it coming from?

"I didn't do nothing. It fell all on its own." Another man's voice, this one a little deeper.

Were the men downstairs in the bakery? Despite the darkness, her gaze found the door to her room, and she stared at the handle. The fear in her chest rose into her throat, so thick and suffocating she nearly choked.

"Clean this up, and be quick about it."

No, the voice wasn't coming from the hall, but from the alley. She moved her gaze to the window, and her stampeding heart slowed a wee bit. That was normal enough, wasn't it? Nothing to be alarmed about. People could use the alley at any time of day or night.

But in nearly a year of renting rooms above the bakery, this was the first time she'd been awakened by people behind the building.

She blew out a shaky breath. Should she go to the window and look? Probably not. It was best they not see her.

But what if they were trying to break in?

Her heart started pounding anew, and she twisted her sweaty hands in the tangled sheets.

The notion was ridiculous, or rather, it should have been ridiculous. There was a time, back in Ireland, that the idea of strange men forcing their way into her room at night seemed unfathomable.

But someone had broken into the bakery just this past winter, leaving one of her shifts laid out with some stolen jewelry and a knife from the bakery downstairs on her bed. A chill traveled through her at the memory, but the perpetrator had been caught, so what did she have to fear?

More talking sounded from the window, where the gauzy curtains fluttered in the nighttime breeze. The voices were lower now, more secretive, more... suspicious.

Probably because they were trying not to wake half the town. Yes, that was the reason the men outside were being quiet, not because there was something sinister going on right outside her window.

"Hurry before someone sees us."

Or maybe not. She yawned. There'd be no sleep for her if she stayed in bed knowing strange men were outside. She could at least try to figure out what they were doing. Drawing in a shaky breath, she shoved her covers down with her feet and swung her legs over the side of the bed.

Muggy air, unusual for so early in the summer, surrounded her, and the thrum of blood in her ears was so loud it nearly drowned out the voices as she crept toward the window. She paused by the wall, her back pressed to the white plaster, then drew in a steadying breath before she peeked out the window.

The silver moon slanted a shaft of light between the buildings and into the alley, where a group of men clustered just beneath her window. There were more than two. But how many? Four? Five? It was hard to tell given the way thick shadows cloaked most of the alley.

The men appeared to have a large crate that had somehow split open. Two of them picked up objects shrouded in shadow and set them into a second crate, which appeared to be loaded onto a dolly of some sort.

What were they doing? It almost looked like they were dockworkers taking cargo to the warehouse. Except dockworkers didn't work at night, and the pier and warehouse were several blocks from the bakery. There'd be no need to haul cargo this far from the beach. She attempted to swallow the lump stuck in her throat, but it lodged there, unmovable.

Two more men approached from the direction of the harbor, pushing their own dolly. "Ye still haven't got that cleaned up?"

Irish. Aileen sucked in a breath. One of the voices was unmistakably Irish.

"Ye take much longer and someone'll spot ye."

It was too late for that. She twisted the fabric of her nightdress in her hands. Oh, she'd have to report this to the sheriff come morning. But would the men figure out who'd seen them? In a town as small as Eagle Harbor, news that she'd seen something unscrupulous outside her window would be all over town by lunch. What if the men came back for her?

"We're hurrying the best we can." One of the men below moved to pile things in the open crate. "Just be careful of that there rock so your crate doesn't topple as well."

A group of two more men with a dolly approached from the opposite direction. "Only one more load left. We'll see you at the wagon."

The wagon? What were these men doing that needed a wagon? And why use the alley and not the road that ran along the front of the building? Aileen leaned a bit closer

Two of the men passed the ones working to clean up the spill, then hurried down the alley toward the harbor. Through the patchy moonlight, she could just make out the shadowed forms heading to...

Not the harbor.

Had they stopped at the back of the bank?

She gripped the molding beside the window. Surely she wasn't watching the bank being robbed.

She glanced down at the objects littering the alley that the men scrambled to clean up. Could it be money? It seemed too heavy, but maybe the bills were bundled together.

She shifted closer to the window. If she could find a spot where the moonlight reached the ground, maybe then she could see if—

One of the men jerked his head up her direction.

She stilled. Had he seen her? It should be too dark to see inside the second story window from the street... or so she hoped.

Her heart thundered against her ribs, its beating so loud the workers below likely heard it, even if they couldn't see her.

The man stayed where he was, his head still angled up her

direction. She shifted back just a bit, then stilled.

The man below didn't move, but neither did he call out to her.

She shifted another little bit, paused, and moved again, until the wall blocked most of him from view.

"We need to be done. Now. Get a move on it." The voice from below floated up to her, and she shifted even farther away from the window.

A few minutes later, footsteps thudded on the packed earth of the alley, but if the dolly moved, its wheels gave nary a creak.

She stayed perfectly still, her back pressed to the wall, her chest heaving with frightened breaths she didn't dare let all the way out. She stood there for a full five minutes before peeking out the window once more. The night that greeted her was as still and dark as the burial shroud that had covered her father back in Ireland.

Oh, what was she going to do? She wasn't about to step foot outside the building now. Not when someone could easily be waiting for her. Not when one of the men might have seen her. But morning would be here soon enough, and she'd have to go to the sheriff.

Which meant everyone in town would know who'd seen the bank get robbed—perhaps even the robbers.

~ ~ ~ ~ ~

Ding-a-ling. Ding-a-ling.

Isaac Cummings twisted on his bed and groaned. What had possessed him to hang a bell pull outside the door of the sheriff's office below his apartment?

Ding-a-ling. Ding-a-ling.

He cracked an eyelid to glance out the second-floor window where the bell hung.

Morning. Kind of. He yawned and rubbed his eyes. Though after a night like the one he'd just been through, the faint pink hue spreading across the sky shouldn't count as morning.

Ding-a-ling. Ding-a-ling.

He groaned again. Putting a bell up had seemed like a good idea when he'd done it. He'd even given a speech at one of the town council meetings, his words infused with noble claptrap about wanting the residents of Eagle Harbor to reach him whenever they had a need.

Claptrap indeed. The bell had lost its appeal on the third morning after it had been installed, when Mrs. Kainer had woken him at four-thirty to help search for her missing cat.

Ding-a-ling. Ding-a-ling.

He sighed and forced himself out of bed, then reached for the shirt hanging over his bedpost.

"Sheriff Cummings, are ye in there?"

That voice. He'd recognize it anywhere, lilting and soft and unmistakably Irish. A voice he'd like to hear more than just at church on Sunday or when they happened to see each other around town. He shoved his arms through his shirtsleeves, then thudded across the floor while he started on his buttons.

"Miss Brogan." He stuck his head out the window, revealing only the top of his shirt as he worked to button the bottom half.

She looked up at him, her rich red hair shoved hastily into an updo that looked as though it might come falling down any second. Even in the early morning light, her face and hands were the color of fresh cream.

"What's wrong? Did someone break into the bakery again?" A chill swept through him at the thought. The criminals better not have touched her.

"No." She glanced around the empty street, then twisted her skirt in her hands. "Let me in. We need to talk, and it shouldn't be out here."

"I'll be there in just a minute." He turned and grabbed his trousers hanging on the bed post, then pulled them on along with his boots.

What was so wrong that Aileen couldn't tell him through the window? This past fall there'd been a rash of robberies, and the bakery where Aileen Brogan lived had even been broken into, an eerie sort of message left for her.

But the man responsible, Frank Ebberhard, had been caught just after Christmas and was now sitting in a jail cell for the rest of his life. Outside of the weekly drunken brawls at one of the town's two bars, Eagle Harbor had been quiet ever since.

He strapped on his gun and holster and headed downstairs into the sheriff's office below. A quick glance at the door that separated the jail cells from the rest of his office told him no noise sounded from behind it—at least not yet.

He hurried across the floor and slid back the deadbolt before pulling open the door.

She stood there in a white shirtwaist and plain blue skirt, her face so pale it nearly blanched the smattering of freckles spread across her nose and upper cheeks. She gripped her hands together, twisting them once more, and looked around the empty street before stepping closer, her eyes filled with worry.

"Miss Brogan, what is it?" He nearly reached out to grip her hands, to see if he could stay the trembling, but stopped himself. Last time he'd tried reaching for her when she was upset, she'd jumped away from him so quickly she'd sent both herself and a chair crashing to the floor.

"I... th-think someone robbed the bank."

He nearly choked. A bank robbery? In Eagle Harbor? He glanced around the street that suddenly seemed too still and too peaceful. He stepped out onto the porch, pulling the door shut behind him. "Let's go wake up Ian. You can tell me what you know on the way."

He started down North Street toward where one of his deputies lived a block off the main road. He'd leave Miss Brogan with him to be questioned and then escorted home while he and his other deputy roused the bank owner and investigated the robbery. A sick feeling twisting his stomach as he turned off North Street. He had his own savings in that bank, as did his brother Elijah, and Mr. Foley, the mercantile owner, Mrs. Kainer, the boardinghouse proprietress, and just about everyone else in town.

He raised his gaze to scan the hills that rimmed the town. The thick forest covering them offered too many places for criminals to hide. If someone truly had robbed the bank, the townsfolk probably wouldn't ever get a lick of their money back.

~ ~ ~ ~ ~

She was a fool. An utter and complete fool.

Aileen stood with her back to the wall of the bank while the bank owner, Mr. Ranulfson, talked with Sheriff Cummings. Behind them, the safe door was open, and two bank workers and both of the sheriff's deputies stood counting the money in the safe—for the second time.

Yet nothing seemed to be missing. Here everyone had been woken up and called to the bank two hours early, and all for nothing.

Those men last night hadn't been doing what she'd thought. It would be impossible to move so many crates of money out of the bank and not have anyone notice by now. And here she'd left Ellie to start work at the bakery by herself this morning without even bothering to leave her a note. Instead she'd rushed off to find the sheriff as soon as the sky turned light.

Aileen took a step toward the door. Ian Fletcher, one of the sheriff's deputies, had already questioned her at the sheriff's office, but rather than let her go to work, he'd brought her to the bank, saying something about the sheriff probably having more questions and wanting to look at the alley with her. But the sheriff was still busy with Mr. Ranulfson, and she really couldn't afford to stay here any longer. Besides her biggest question was already answered—no, the bank hadn't been robbed.

No one seemed to notice the first step she'd taken toward the door. The deputy who'd questioned her was just as busy counting money as the other deputy, and the clerks also counting hadn't so much as glanced at her. Sheriff Cummings and Mr. Ranulfson had their backs to her as they studied the alley's entrance to the bank. She took another step away from the men, then another. Maybe she'd come back during her lunch break and apologize for disrupting everyone's morning. Or better yet, bake an extra batch of cookies and deliver them when she apologized.

One more step took her out of the offices at the back of the building and into the empty lobby. The room was lovely, with rich dark walls and fancy rose-colored carpet that must have cost a fortune to ship to Eagle Harbor. Why, the room almost looked elaborate enough to be inside one of the two mansions in town. It certainly looked fancy enough to belong in the Sinclair family mansion she'd worked at in Chicago.

But nothing inside this lavish, showy room was for her. She'd never once had enough money set by to bother saving it in a bank, and she probably never would. Why bother with a fancy bank account when she could just stash her extra money beneath one of the old floorboards in her room?

Aileen quickened her pace before anyone noticed she'd left. Surely if she got to the bakery, the sheriff wouldn't come drag her away from work, not when she needed to save money so badly.

She pushed out the front door, and the mugginess of the air outside hit her like a wall. It was going to be another hot day, yet the view of the harbor was lovely. It stretched out before her with its calm green-blue waters, and beyond lay Lake Superior, an endless expanse of wavy blue, large enough to rival an ocean. The golden morning sky painted the sand and street and town pier with a yellow brush, and the gulls above called out against the sound of gently lapping waves.

She might not have had a choice about leaving the emerald slopes and sparkling sea of County Mayo, but she could hardly complain about replacing the view from her childhood home with the one from Eagle Harbor.

She hurried along Front Street, then turned away from the harbor and started down Center Street, where the bakery lay three blocks ahead. Hopefully Ellie wasn't too far behind with the morning's baking, and maybe if she talked to the bakery owners, she could find a way to make up the work she'd missed this morning.

"Aileen Brogan, stop right there."

Aileen paused and turned toward the female voice, only to find herself staring at the large Sinclair family mansion that towered a story over the rest of the town. Who had—?

"I'll be down in a flash." The voice called again. A flurry of auburn hair and yellow dress disappeared from one of the second story windows.

Aileen couldn't stop her smile. Looked like Rebekah Cummings— or rather, Rebekah Sinclair—had returned. If the woman would have stayed in the window longer, she'd have told Rebekah to meet her at the bakery. But Rebekah had never been good at standing still for more than two seconds.

Aileen looked down the road toward the bakery, then back at the elaborate gray mansion with fancy gables and trim. She didn't have time to wait. Should she just go to the bakery and hope Rebekah found her?

The front door opened, and out stepped Gilbert Sinclair. Despite the early hour, his three-piece suit was immaculate—she'd never seen it any other way—and his blond hair was slicked down and perfectly pomaded until it was almost glossy beneath the morning sun.

"Miss Brogan, is my wife shouting you down in the middle of the road?" A gentle smile tilted the corner of his mouth, and his angel blue eyes danced. He reached for her hand, then bent and pressed his lips to it. "I fear she lost all semblance of manners the second we disembarked from the ship last night."

Aileen grinned, even if she tugged her hand back a little quicker than was proper. Had Gilbert really been successful in teaching Rebekah manners? She could only imagine what those lessons had been like. Though Rebekah must have learned some. She couldn't exactly envision Rebekah hosting fancy dinners for Gilbert in old fishing trousers and a flannel shirt. "I didn't know ye were back yet, so I don't mind her calling out to me, except that I'm late for the bakery. Can ye tell Rebekah to—?"

"Aileen Brogan." The slam of the mansion's door reverberated through the still morning, and Rebekah strode straight toward them. "Good to see you."

Aileen blinked. It was rather odd seeing a woman who'd had trouble wearing the simple serving uniform the Sinclairs had required in Chicago now dressed in a fancy yellow dress made of fine, smooth fabric. Though it did lack the puffed sleeves and ruffles and flounces that adorned most rich women's dresses. Yet Rebekah's deep auburn hair was pulled back into a thick braid that looked like something a woman in a plain gingham dress would wear.

Rebekah marched straight toward them, then drew her into a hug so hard she could barely breathe. True, they'd not seen each other since Rebekah had gotten married almost a year ago, but that didn't mean the woman had to crush the breath from her.

Then, as quickly as the hug started, it was finished, and Rebekah was leaning back studying her, eyes narrowed as they ran from the top of her head down to her hem and back up again. "You look too thin. Have you been eating enough?"

Had she? Aileen glance down at herself. "I… don't know."

Though her dress did seem a little loose, now that she thought about it.

Concern knit Rebekah's brow. "Your letters made it seem like you were faring well enough."

"I'm fine," she answered a bit too quickly. Or at least she was trying to be, though the news she'd gotten from Ireland this past week certainly wasn't going to help things. Aileen looked back at her friend—or at least the closest thing she had to a friend since coming to America. "And how have ye been yerself?"

"Away too long." Rebekah scanned the street, then peered down the road toward the harbor. "I suppose Elijah's left for the day already? I wanted to go out with him this morning, but someone here forgot to wake me up before dawn." Rebekah jabbed her elbow into Gilbert's side.

"Yes, I completely forgot, darling. Maybe I'll do a better job of remembering some morning when you have more than four hours of sleep." He dropped a quick kiss onto his wife's forehead, then grinned. "But you do look lovely this morning, even with this." He tugged on her braid.

Judging by the glare Rebekah gave him, the tug hadn't been all that gentle. "I needed to come see Aileen, and the maid was taking too long with my hair."

"You've not been in Eagle Harbor a full day, and already you're turning into a hooligan." Gilbert's voice was dry.

"That's because hooligans have more fun, isn't that right, Aileen?" Rebekah winked in her direction.

"I… ah…" Aileen twisted her hands. Being a hooligan hadn't turned out all that well for her brother Conan, but then, she doubted Rebekah had ever been a true hooligan.

Rebekah narrowed her eyes at something down the street. Then a smile broke across her face, as wide and brilliant as the sun at noonday. "There's Isaac. I'll be right back."

Rebekah strode toward where Sheriff Cummings headed in their direction, making no effort to take dainty steps the way most women of her station would. A few seconds later, she threw herself into her twin brother's arms, pushed up onto her toes to place a kiss on her brother's cheek, then wrapped her arms around him for a long, comfortable hug.

Gilbert sighed and rubbed at his temple. "Maybe one day I can convince her not to clobber people on the street for all the world to see."

Aileen coughed. "Good luck there. At least ye got her in a dress."

"Yes, now if only I could get her to make use of her lady's maid and stop braiding her hair." His voice was dry, but his eyes were riveted to his wife, a faint smile turning his lips.

Aileen tilted her head to the side. "Methinks she looks nice with a braid."

"She always looks nice, even in trousers and a flannel shirt, with her hair wild and free and tangled, and her cheeks sunburned from a day of sailing."

Aileen smiled. "Ye love her."

"Unequivocally."

Leave it to Gilbert Sinclair to use a fancy word like that to describe his love for his wife. But though he might grumble about Rebekah's uncouth ways, he didn't mind them, not really. If anything, Gilbert probably loved Rebekah more because of them.

Gilbert turned his eyes on her then, and gone was the tender look he had for his wife. In its place was an assessing gaze that belonged to the inventor-turned-businessman whose wealthy family she'd once worked for. "Have you been well, Aileen? Truly? I heard what you told Rebekah, but I doubt that's the whole of it."

How was she supposed to answer that? She looked away, but that didn't stop the flood of memories from last summer from rising up, pain and fear and uncertainty all bombarding her until she could hardly draw a lungful of the thick air surrounding them.

"Aileen?" Gilbert took a step closer, concern etched across his face.

She shifted away, then pushed the air from her lungs and clamped her teeth down on her tongue. The sharp bite of pain cleared her mind. She was being ridiculous. Gilbert Sinclair, of all people, wasn't going to hurt her.

"Yes." She forced the word out, because it seemed the right thing to say, even if so many other things in her life were wrong. "Yes, I've been…" She hugged herself, and a strange coldness invaded her despite the muggy heat. "Better."

She couldn't quite claim she'd been well, but she was certainly better today than she'd been at this time last summer.

That counted for something, didn't it? "I'm late for work."

It was true, never mind that she'd tell a blatant lie if that's what it took to get her away from this conversation. She moved to step around Gilbert.

"Aileen!" Rebekah's voice echoed down the street. "Wait a minute. Isaac needs to talk to you."

She pressed her eyes shut. Couldn't she at least get a couple hours of work in first? Besides, she'd already told him everything once, then sat through Deputy Fletcher's list of questions. Though she did need to tell the sheriff she was sorry for waking him so early and causing a commotion about nothing. But she'd have been better off telling him that after she'd baked him a batch of cookies.

She turned back around to face the set of twins, their auburn hair, hazel eyes, and fair skin declaring their blood relation to all the world.

The official look in the sheriff's eyes told her just what kind of questions to expect, but at least these questions would be better than the one he'd asked this winter. Except ever since she refused his request to court her, he'd taken to looking at her in that soft way he had, the way that showed too many of his thoughts, the way that held too much concern.

The way that made her feel like a lout for refusing him.

But she wasn't being a lout, she was being smart and sensible. So why did she feel like wrapping her arms around her middle and huddling into herself?

Sheriff Cummings pulled out his notepad and pencil, but the unruly tuft of auburn hair near his forehead made her want to reach out and smooth it. "Miss Brogan, tell me again what you saw last night."

"What did you see?" Rebekah gripped her arm, the other woman's gaze moving between both her and the sheriff.

"Nothin'." Aileen tugged her sleeve away from her friend. "I'm sure it was nothin'. I'm really sorry to disturb ye and Mr. Ranulfson so early in the morn though, especially since it was all for naught."

"But you did see something, correct?" The sheriff raised his head and gazed between the buildings toward the alley where the men had been last night. "Something in this alley right back here? You told me a noise woke you."

At least he was keeping things official rather than asking her on another walk, now if only she could manage to ignore that curly bit of hair sticking up. "Aye. It's as I told ye on the way to the bank. Nothin' changed. I saw men moving crates on dollies." She twisted her skirt in her hands. "I thought they were going to and from the bank, but I was wrong, and 'tis sorry, I am, for wakin' ye."

"You said one of the crates broke? Where did it break?" The sheriff stopped his writing and moved his clear hazel gaze to her.

Did he realize how pretty his eyes were? How they swirled brown and green together into a color that looked like the rich plowed fields of Ireland mixed with the greenest pasture? She looked away. "Just behind me window. Ye might find even a few boards from the broken crate left in the alley. I didn't look before I went for ye."

"And what time did you see the men?" He started writing again, his gaze no longer seeking her out.

Good. At least it was supposed to be good, wasn't it? "Three, maybe four. I thought of coming to get ye sooner, but last time ye said to wait until I thought things were safe." It had seemed like an eternity as she waited for the sky to lighten.

"Last time?" Rebekah crossed her arms over her chest. "What happened last time?"

Aileen swallowed, yet another thing she didn't want to dredge up, but knowing Rebekah, the woman wouldn't let her leave until she'd told her every last detail. "We found some—"

"What time did your ship dock last night?" The sheriff was looking at Gilbert now, a shrewd gleam in his eyes.

"Nearly eleven," Gilbert didn't pause before he answered.

Sheriff Cummings scrawled something more on his pad. "Why so late?"

Gilbert shook his head. "It's not my ship, if that's what you're after. Rebekah was anxious to get here, so we took the first ship from Chicago bound for Eagle Harbor."

"Who owns the ship?"

"My brother Warren. I agree that it docked abnormally late though."

Aileen looked between the two men. They seemed to be speaking of something more than just the ship, but she couldn't quite grasp what. Why would the sheriff be so interested in the ship in the first place? And what did that have to do with the men she'd seen in the alley?

"Did it make any unusual stops?" The sheriff went back to writing in his notepad again, the breeze from the harbor ruffling his hair to make it even more unruly.

Gilbert moved closer to the sheriff, peering over his shoulder to see the notes. "It stopped in Marquette yesterday afternoon, and it took so long to load and unload the cargo, I assumed we'd dock there overnight, but the captain called the crew back around dinner time, and we left for Eagle Harbor."

Chatter sounded from the direction of the harbor, and a group of sailors turned from Front Street onto Center Street, likely coming from the same ship the sheriff and Gilbert spoke of. One of the sailors shoved another as they rounded the turn. Then the second sailor shoved the first sailor back, which prompted a larger man to get between the two men and bark something about behaving.

Aileen narrowed her gaze at the sailor on the far side of the group. There was something familiar about him, about the way he moved. Was he one of the men from last night? With his hat pulled down and his face half hidden behind the other sailors, she couldn't tell.

And what did it matter if he was one of the men? She didn't have any evidence of a crime being committed.

The group passed them without even a nod in their direction, likely on their way to the bakery.

The bakery. The ship in the harbor. Oh, what had she been thinking? Or maybe the better question was what *hadn't* she been thinking? The morning after a ship docked, they usually had a rush of sailors wanting breakfast, and Ellie hadn't had so much as a lick of help from her.

"I'm sorry, but I have to get to work now before the Oaktons up and fire me." She dashed off without giving either the sheriff or Rebekah a chance to bid her farewell.

~ ~ ~ ~ ~

"Miss Brogan, please wait." Isaac glanced up from his notepad where he'd been scrawling Gilbert's information about the ship docking in Marquette. "I want you to…" *Show me the alley.*

But she was already halfway to the bakery.

Rebekah scowled up at him. "You need to be nicer to her. Don't you know her brother died last year, and a cousin is the only relation she has over here? And I doubt she's seen him since she left Chicago."

Isaac raised his hands, his paper pad included. "Be nicer? All I did was ask what she saw last night, and I was perfectly nice while doing it."

Rebekah's chin tilted up in defiance—evidently not something her fancy husband had been able to cure her of, even if the man should be commended for getting her in a dress. "Then why does Aileen seem so anxious to get away from you?"

Probably for the same reason she was always anxious to get away from him, not that he had a clue what it was. He glanced over to see Miss Brogan rushing down the street, her plain blue skirt swishing about her ankles.

"I didn't do anything to her, I promise." Unless asking Miss Brogan if he could court her this winter counted against him. But when she said no, he'd left her alone, as simple as that.

Except it really wasn't simple. Not in a town the size of Eagle Harbor, where he saw her at church every Sunday and where she was always invited to his family's gatherings on holidays. Not when she was the last thing he thought of most nights before he drifted off to sleep, and the first thing he thought of in the morning.

And the main thing he thought of at lunch.

And walking down the road.

And—

"Then why are you staring after her like that?"

He blinked and forced his gaze away from Miss Brogan pulling open the door to the bakery just ahead of a group of mariners and looked at his twin sister. "Like what?"

She planted her hands on her hips. "Don't treat me like I'm an imbecile, Isaac. You know exactly what I'm talking about."

"Rebekah," Gilbert's voice held a warning note, but rather than look at her husband, Rebekah kept her gaze pinned to him, eyes narrowed accusingly.

Sisters. He'd been thinking he missed his, but he'd clearly forgotten how eager his twin was to needle him. "I haven't done anything other than try to be kind and helpful, or question Miss Brogan as any sheriff would when troubles come up. That's it."

Rebekah glanced down the street toward where Miss Brogan had disappeared into the bakery and furrowed her brow. "Is she really just that frightened of you?"

He shifted and tucked his notepad into his shirt pocket—since his sister didn't seem apt to let him get back to work anytime soon. "I wouldn't call her frightened, but she's never been comfortable with me, no."

"Is she that way with everyone?"

"Ah…" He scratched the side of his head. "She's a mite better with Elijah than she is with most men, but beside him…"

Rebekah bit the side of her lip, her gaze still latched on the bakery. "But I don't understand. Things were supposed to be better for her here." When she looked back at him, her eyes shimmered with moisture. "Coming to Eagle Harbor was supposed to help."

He sighed. How was it his sister could be as tough as an anchor rope one minute and as soft as pie filling the next? "Help what?"

"And I think it has helped, darling." Gilbert reached for his wife and pulled her to his side. "But not everything can be fixed overnight."

Rebekah's shoulders rose and fell on a sigh. "It's not overnight. It's been almost a year. I guess I was hoping…"

"To find her married with a child on the way?" Gilbert rubbed the side of her arm and looked down at her, the gaze in his eyes so tender Isaac nearly turned his back to give the couple a bit of privacy. "You knew better than to expect either of those things from her letters."

"Maybe not married with children, but I wanted her to be happy." Rebekah looked up at her husband. "Did she seem happy to you?"

"I…" Gilbert shook his head and sighed. "Not really, no, but we only saw her for a few minutes, and it seems like she had a difficult morning."

Rebekah turned back to Isaac, her shoulders sagging. "You've seen her more than we have. Does she seem happy in Eagle Harbor?"

Isaac coughed. "I… ah, don't really know her well enough to say."

Though that had been her choice, not his.

Her words from last winter drifted back to him. *If such a thing as a good man exists, Sheriff Cummings, then I'm sure ye're one of them. But me, I'm just not the type to make a good wife. I don't think I'll ever be, at least not anymore.* The snow had sparkled around them, the previous day's dusting of several inches still laying pristine over the town. Her hair had flamed against the whiteness, a single, unmistakable splash of color so vibrant he nearly reached out and fingered one of the flyaway strands hanging by her ear. Even now, in the dead of a humid summer, he could almost taste the crisp winter air on his tongue, almost smell the wood smoke curling up from nearby chimneys.

"What aren't you telling me?" Rebekah asked softly. She took a step closer to him, myriad thoughts churning behind hazel eyes the same shade as her own. "Has being in Eagle Harbor helped her or not?"

He shook his head. "Stop needling me. I already said I don't know." His sister might have been gone from Eagle Harbor for almost a year, might be fancied up in an expensive dress Gilbert had bought her, but despite all the changes, she was still the same old Rebekah. "I don't even know what being in Eagle Harbor is supposed to help Miss Brogan with."

Rebekah and Gilbert shared a look, but neither spoke.

He raised his hands helplessly, only to let them fall back to his side. What was it about Miss Brogan no one wanted to tell him? "At least tell me what happened to her in Chicago."

There wasn't any question in his mind that she'd been hurt in some way, not since the very day she'd arrived last summer with Rebekah. She'd been too skittish to even say hello to him, had just climbed the stairs to the loft where she was going to sleep and stayed there until after he'd left.

Rebekah's shoulders rose and fell on a sigh. "If it were up to me, I'd tell you. But it's her story, and she probably doesn't want you knowing."

"Yet both of you know it." The words tasted bitter on his tongue.

Rebekah looked up at Gilbert, but Gilbert just pressed his lips together.

Fine. If that was all the information he was going to get, then he had work to do. Both of his deputies were supposed to head this way after they were done questioning those who lived near the bank about whether they'd seen anything suspicious last night, and he'd told them he'd start searching the alley.

He rubbed a hand over his face. He didn't have evidence of a crime being committed quite yet, but he wasn't a fool either. A ship docking abnormally late and men running boxes away from the harbor in the dead of night pointed to one thing.

Smugglers on his doorstep.

Order your copy of Love's Bright Tomorrow *today.*

Thank You

Thank you for reading *Love's Christmas Hope*. I sincerely hope you enjoyed Thomas and Jessalyn's story. The next full length novel in the Eagle Harbor Series is Isaac and Aileen's story, *Love's Bright Tomorrow*. Click here to purchase.

Want to be notified when the next Eagle Harbor Novel is releasing? Sign up for my author newsletter. Subscribers also get a free copy of *Love's Violet Sunrise*, a prequel novella to the Eagle Harbor Series. Sign Up Here.

Be sure to add naomi@naomirawlings.com to your safe email list so that the emails go through. I keep all subscriber information confidential.

Also, if you enjoyed reading *Love's Christmas Hope*, please take a moment to tell others about the novel. You can do this by posting an honest review on Amazon or GoodReads. Please note that to leave a review on Amazon, you need to go directly to Amazon's website. Your e-reader may ask you to rank stars at the end of this novel. The star ranking that you give does not show up on Amazon as a review. I read every one of my reviews, and reviews help readers like yourself decide whether to purchase a novel. You could also consider mentioning *Love's Christmas Hope* to your friends on Facebook, Twitter, or Pinterest.

Author's Note

Thanks for sharing Jessalyn and Thomas's story with me. This novel was a bit different for me, because I've never written a story about an already married couple before. I've personally been married for over a decade, and I love my husband so very much. He's an honorable, Godly, loving, supportive man—most of the time. But every marriage has its moments, mine included. The trouble comes when those bad moments start to outnumber the good, when the hurt and resentment piles up until it's easier to focus on bitterness and pain instead of love and forgiveness.

Except the Lord build the house, they labour in vain that build it. The words of Psalm 127:1 are as true for homes today as they were when the verse was originally penned thousands of years ago. Praise the Lord that God has given couples and marriages a path to hope and redemption and new beginnings. Praise the Lord for taking the broken parts of our lives and restoring them into something beautiful, even if it isn't perfect.

I hope and pray this book is an encouragement to you. And on that note, shortly after I finished this novel, my husband and I attended a Weekend to Remember seminar. It was good and encouraging, and perfect for all types of married couples, whether you're struggling in your marriage or you're convinced you've married the world's only perfect man. You can learn more about Family Life and the Weekend to Remember seminars here if you're interested.

I hope you're enjoying the Eagle Harbor Series. It's been my favorite series of novels to write, though I admit to being a little biased since I live in a little town on Lake Superior myself, only a couple hours from the real-life Eagle Harbor. I look forward to writing many more books in this series. Isaac Cummings and Aileen Brogan's story is next in *Love's Bright Tomorrow* releasing in the winter of 2018.

Other Novels by Naomi Rawlings

Eagle Harbor Series

Book 1—*Love's Unfading Light* (Mac and Tressa)

Book 2—*Love's Every Whisper* (Elijah and Victoria)

Book 3—*Love's Sure Dawn* (Gilbert and Rebekah)

Book 4—*Love's Eternal Breath* (Seth and Lindy)

Book 5—*Love's Christmas Hope* (Thomas and Jessalyn)

Book 6—*Love's Bright Tomorrow* (Isaac and Aileen)

Short Story—*Love's Beginning*

Prequel Novella—*Love's Violet Sunrise* (Hiram and Mabel)

Belanger Family Saga

Book 1—*Sanctuary for a Lady*

Book 2—*The Soldier's Secrets*

Book 3—*Falling for the Enemy*

Stand Alone Novels

The Wyoming Heir

Acknowledgments

Thank you first and foremost to my Lord and Savior, Jesus Christ, for giving me both the ability and opportunity to write novels for His glory.

As with any novel, the author might come up with a story idea and sit at her computer to type the initial words, but it takes an army of people to bring you the book you have today. I'd especially like to thank Melissa Jagears, my critique partner for *Love's Christmas Hope*. I'd also like to thank my family for working with my writing schedule and giving me a chance to do two things I love: be a mommy and a writer. Also thank you to Roseanna White and Lynnette Bonner for assisting with the editing and providing early feedback. And finally, a special thanks to my former agent Natasha Kern for encouraging me to keep working on the Eagle Harbor Series.

About the Author

Naomi Rawlings is the author of numerous historical Christian novels, including the Amazon bestselling Eagle Harbor Series. While she'd love to claim she spends her days huddled in front of her computer vigorously typing, in reality she spends her time mothering, chauffeuring,, cleaning, picking up, and pretending like her house isn't in a constant state of chaos. She lives with her husband and three children in Michigan's rugged Upper Peninsula, along the southern shore of Lake Superior where they get 200 inches of snow every year, and where people still grow their own vegetables and cut down their own firewood—just like in the historical novels she writes.

For more information about Naomi, please her at www.naomirawlings.com or find her on Facebook at www.facebook.com/author.naomirawlings. If you'd like a free Eagle Harbor novella (Mabel and Hiram's story), sign up for her author newsletter.

Made in the USA
Middletown, DE
23 July 2022